FOX DEN
BOOKS
Oregon

FURY

Disclaimer

This book contains dark themes, and content that is graphic, descriptive, may be distressing to others and may involve the following subject matter: Abuse, sexual assault, child abuse, violence, kidnapping and abduction, death and dying, blood, mental illness, sexism, and misogyny.

FURY

A fantasy by

Miranda Mayer

FURY

Miranda Mayer

www.mirandamayer.com

Editing:

Helen Gallaway

Cover Art

Feffie's Cottage

Dedications

To every soul who's been there;
find your fury.

To Helly;
building closeness with you
has been transcendent.

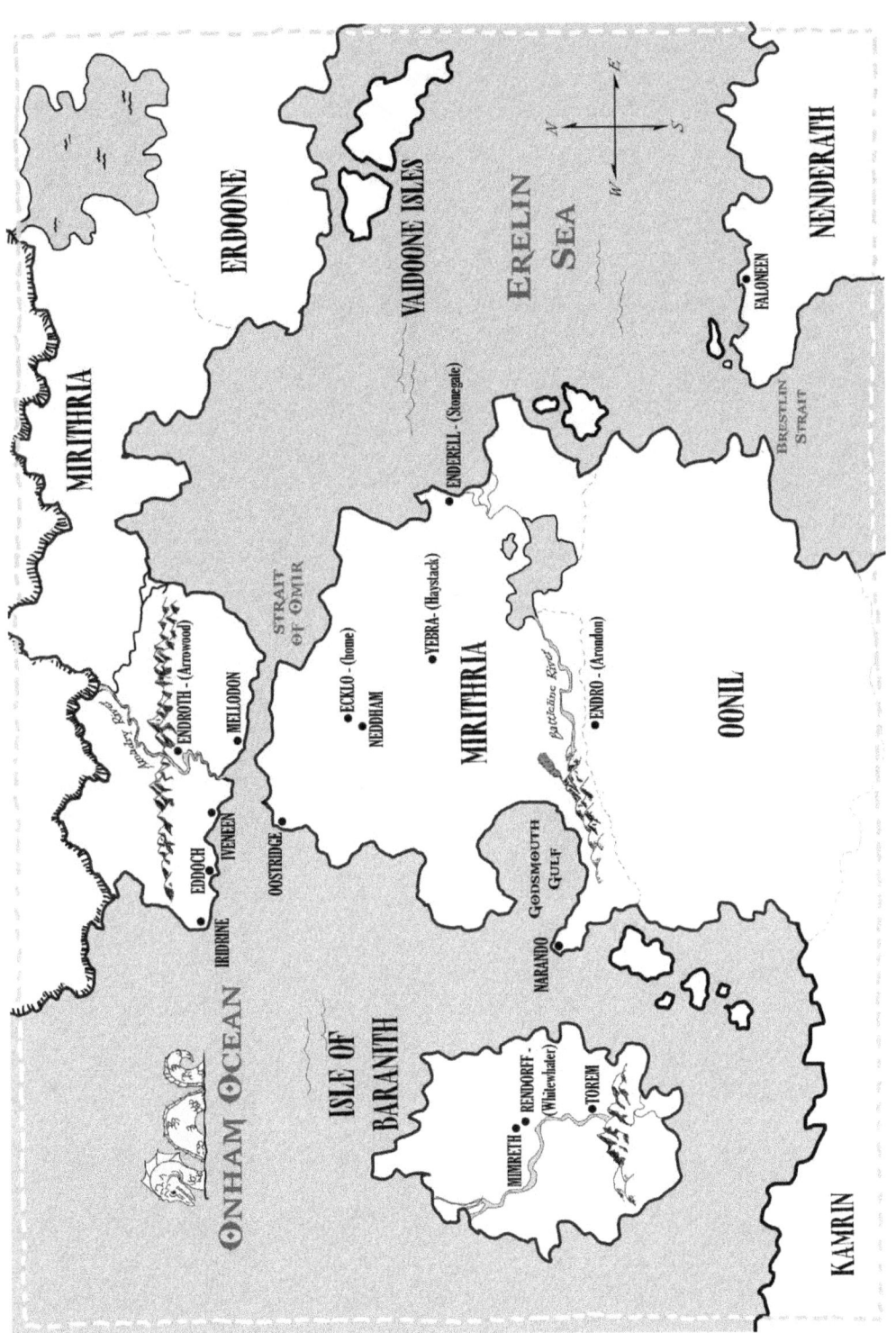

CHAPTER 1

Love is not always founded upon beauty, adoration and romance. Love can also be built upon a foundation of pain—and the bond of such a love can be more powerful and fixed than love of any other kind.

For certain souls, this might be the only way love can be achieved; for their hurt and brokenness define the very essence of who they are as people and finding unfettered acceptance of such deep and tender scars invites a tie that few can sever. This requires the right circumstances, the right timing and serendipity.

Forrest thought himself incapable of love. He lived a youth of indifference towards others—in many cases, contempt, and disdain. He believed he was not in possession of the feelings of love and attachment, of affection and trust, not even truly feeling attraction to anyone—even through the ostensibly passionate years of the teens. He believed there was something intrinsically wrong with the very essence of his character. Such was the heaviness of self-loathing and blame that gripped his heart. He saw himself as a ruination, of something slightly below human. He had never felt the appeal and desires that his peers experienced in their lives. He was quite certain of this, until in his fourth year of higher university, he was blindsided; struck with a heap of bricks, when the bell on the top of the door pealed, and *she* walked in.

He first beheld her as she entered the academy bookshop. She caught his eye as she did everyone else's—for her exquisite, nearly preternatural beauty—a loveliness of a caliber so rare, she was almost ethereal. Never before had he felt drawn in from a glimpse—captivated by the simple appearance of a person. He sat up and leaned forward, peering through the balusters of the mezzanine railing to see her better.

She had a pale, heart-shaped face with a sharp widow's peak, and skin like pale snowy silk. Her eyes glassy blue, piercingly so, like the cutting clear hue of a crisp morning sky—ringed in dense, long raven lashes, her small mouth a rose blossom. Her pearly upper teeth were barely visible as she momentarily licked shine upon her lips before she mouthed a title to the clerk, whose eyes could not be torn from her face.

Her form was petite, but elegant, all graceful lines, from the sweep of her delicate neck, her perfect jaw line, to the flawless flow of her profile. Her body, neither too voluptuous nor too lithe, each curve drawn against the drape of her academy uniform, was the ideal. Her movements were feline; imbued with grace and ease, yet a coiled tension thrummed underneath. Her poise was impeccable.

Her hair was jet—a mane of large waves cascading loosely and informally onto her back from a simple milkmaid plait that encircled the crown of her head. School had yet to begin, and she had not coiffed it off her shoulders. Although she wore the navy and burgundy of the uniform as required on campus, she was still at liberty to let her locks tumble free for the time being.

She was, in Forrest's immediate estimation, the most exquisite person he had ever witnessed, the first whose beauty had enraptured him. But it wasn't simply this external loveliness, which fixed him so directly upon her. Unbeknownst to all, Forrest possessed a rare ability to tap into the emotions and feelings of those around him, if he wished to. It was why he was here, at Whitewater Academy, to hone his magical skill. It had taken him many years to learn to quiet the din of the collective around him. He rarely reached out; rarely found reason or motivation to do so, as few people piqued his interest.

With this skill, his mind stretched out to hers almost before he could will it to so. His thoughts funneled across the space between them, and once locked into the strange, controlled sound of her inner being, he listened and searched. There, as he had correctly suspected, he found a great deal more to be perceived than what one could glean from her exquisite face value. He spied a great deal in her physical demeanor, but he could see what only a keen eye—a knowing and capable mind could identify. What he felt in the very core of his magical brain was quite intriguing: hints of something graver and telling, something more profound. It was only a suggestion of it. There were no rounded thoughts or memories that spoke of what he sensed. She had built up a barrier that let only hints escape.

This girl's feelings were shut off, gated; a wall of defense not against him, but against herself. The gate was absolute, buzzing, and strong, powered by unfathomable pain and fear. He could feel it—even taste it. He pushed, a little, not too much, but got only a feeling of static shock in his head. This girl had secrets. She had an ache that surprisingly pressed upon his own heart.

He was one of the few that understood what kind of determination and strength one had to accrue to hide so much behind a façade; to withhold it even to oneself. No matter what lay behind that door of feelings, it was not trifling. She had fortitude few possessed, to keep it there, to keep it hidden, governed, and controlled so perfectly that someone even with Forrest's incredible magic, could not access it without invasive methods.

In this brief failed intrusion, he understood a great deal about her—and by the cast of her gaze, the silent language of her movements, and the defensive barrier around her emotions, she spoke to him. The overt signs, these were all a familiar dance to Forrest. The way the sweep of her gaze connected with no one, dismissive—almost indifferent and affected. She emitted an icy air that belied her divine loveliness. All of this was what made her even more beautiful to him. He knew he could relate to her. Behind her graceful and fair mask, there was darkness, artfully hidden under the surface. Temptation pressed upon him, to pry more against her emotional defenses but understood the disrespect it would represent to invasively continue. He did not want to violate this perfect creature's sanctity. He would respect her desire to keep people out, and hope that she would instead, somehow, invite him in. He withdrew.

He watched her in silence from the plush leather chair on the shop's mezzanine. Suddenly, she looked up, and her sharp, unforgiving gaze slashed across his and held for an uncomfortably long moment before releasing. Two more flashing glimpses they shared, and then she seemed to shake off some thoughts, took her books and left, a final flourish of the hem of her skirts and redingote flaring gracefully behind her as the wind blustered through the open door.

It was only after she left that he noticed that every eye in the shop was fixed upon her until she disappeared into the cloisters.

Reluctantly, Forrest returned his attention to his steaming cup of tea, and the copy of *Herrid's Complete Anatomy of the Magical Body, Ninth Edition – Revision 11 by the 30th Council of Physicians, Anno 756*. The book was fresh off the press with a fine blue leather cover and shining gold letters and elegant scrolling borders and cartouches impressed in the spine. He loved new books. He lifted the gold-edged pages to his nose and took a deep breath of the woody scent of the paper blended with the slightly astringent aroma of the ink tannins, returning him to equanimity, but his moment of tome worship was rudely interrupted by a regrettably familiar and irritating voice.

"I saw you staring at her!" Teneen was also a lovely creature, but only on the surface—a little meretricious irritation in Forrest's life. She had no underlying darkness or complexity that made her intriguing. She only had a headful of selfish narcissism, and a bloated sense of entitlement. She was the daughter of one of his late father's peers, and he had known her for as long as he could remember. He had countless memories of her riding up the drive of Chestnut Hill Hall on her grey dapple pony, whenever she pleased, demanding he come out to play.

She now stood at the side of his chair, her hands gripped onto her hips, her face dour and angry. He looked at her impassively for a moment.

Although there was never any such agreement or assumption on the part of the adults on the matter, Teneen had it in her mind that she would marry Forrest someday and become lady of Chestnut Hill Hall and the Countess Outvallen. Forrest hated her. He did not hate much in his world, but he hated her. She was repulsive and vile. The very sense of her emotional deficit was painful for him to be around.

"Take your leave, Teneen," he snapped. "I'll only ask once."

She pushed back a hanging tendril of her deep red hair that fell into her pretty face, and her lip curled, and she stormed down the stairs of the mezzanine to join her homely friend Miss Maere.

There was almost immediately another intrusion. *Was there to be no peace to be found today?* He supposed he oughtn't expect it at the bookshop at the beginning of an academic year. He emitted a sigh.

"Gods on the Mount, there is a new northern girl to rival all girls to ever grace these hallowed halls of Whitewater since the dawn of time," Meddin Ansmore exclaimed before he was even fully seated in the chair next to Forrest. He was one of the only friends Forrest tolerated for more than a few moments. Mostly because Meddin was rather simple of mind; not stupid, but rather feckless without any introspection to speak of. Meddin was the kind of person who stumbled through life happily ensconced in the present, and made no effort to dwell on memories, or hold onto them, or worry about the future. Everything was now for Meddin. These were traits only a mind-reader could sufficiently appreciate.

He arrived in a swish of school robes and a gust of air that reeked slightly of old beer. "I heard rumor, and was skeptical of the claims, but I just saw her myself, and she was beyond any expectation after hearing of her. Ferine help me..." he intoned. "Have *you* seen her? "

"Yes," Forrest replied in his velvety baritone voice. He emitted an air of detachment.

"You may let it be known that the northern girl is off limits. No man's land. Anyone, especially any fellow, who dares to approach her will suffer at my hand." He said this with casual boredom, in the midst of leafing through the pages of his new textbook.

Meddin Ansmore's face blanched, his ease left him, and his carriage stiffened. "Of course..." he replied stoically. "Consider it done." Forrest could feel Meddin's puzzlement. Nobody knew better than this hapless, clueless friend, that Forrest never took that much interest in anyone, especially a young lady. But Meddin knew to inquire would be fruitless, and instead, he capitulated and would obey his friend.

Iselle was scarcely astonished by the attention she drew. It was for a long time, her truest bane. She wished she had the privilege and character of a girl that would thrive upon such a thing, but instead she desired only anonymity. She longed for normality, to laugh and preen like other girls, but would give everything to just fade into the background and become invisible. That would be enough. She could not, however, aspire to ordinary things. No amount of wishing could change that. It had been a problem enough to warrant transfers to new schools and universities, an affliction that took her from one place to the next, uprooting her, rendering her without constancy.

This affliction typically surrounded her instead with vapid people who cared only to connect with her for her appearance and the quality of what she wore—people content to call her friend without true friendship. Shallow, meaningless connections were her staid companions. It was exhausting. And more so when the attention was imbued with envy and pettiness. She still could not decide which was worse. The fervent attentions of attracted boys, or that of spiteful girls.

She resolved that at this new academy she would not allow it to dominate every aspect of her scholastic experience. She hoped this move would free her of her worry, of her past, perhaps even give her a fresh start. *I might be far enough this time,* she mused. This first day did not bode too well. Young men lingered outside the door of the ladies' dormitory, Oak Hall, to spy her already as rumor of her presence spread. They followed her around the campus. They rushed around her to stand in front of her and try to engage her without invitation. They fought amongst themselves and squared up over her attention, and used any affected, insincere gesture they could as opportunities to introduce themselves.

She was asked all manner of personal questions, received several undesired requests and flirtations, and suffered many unwanted attempts to draw her into conversation or company. It became increasingly difficult to hide her annoyance, her desire to be rude, and roll her eyes and say something untoward to them. But that would excite other situations she was not willing to partake in—escalations of interactions she already had no stomach for.

One day shortly before the curriculum began, all those tiresome encounters abruptly ceased.

There was a marked, puzzling halt to all masculine interest in her. The young men even skirted a respectable circumference around her when she passed through the populated spaces. It was inexplicable. She made no complaints, in spite of being bewildered by the whole matter. It felt like a bit of a dream to be this free. She could scarce recall a day when some activity or another was not intruded upon by an unwelcome disturbance or another by yet additional enamored, grinning, effusive and simpering young man, which invariably set her nerves on edge.

By day three of this peaceful, extraordinary development, she was openly taking delight in the week before classes began, free to do what she liked. She could not help but be suspicious of it all, and her conditioning made her wary of it. But the freedom of it, the peace, was intoxicating.

She divided her time settling into her small room, becoming familiar with the campus and the nearby town of Rendorff, browsing the many shops catering to the student population for necessities, feigning that for that moment, she had not the slightest worry in the world; pantomiming what normal would be. Her wariness, her vigilance never truly went away. Even when not a soul bothered her—not even the men of the town proper. She convinced herself that there was perhaps some magic at work, to cause such a phenomenon. Cast by whom remained to be seen. She was truly unsure as to whether she should be grateful or afraid.

The ladies on the other hand were not *all* so kind as to offer her whole peace. The anticipated vitriol from her own gender still occurred. The cold sneers. The whispers. The backhanded remarks in nearby conversations, uttered *just* loudly enough for her to hear. She was used to it. Girls could be so cruel to one another. She was hardened to it. As bleak as it could be, she had built herself a defense against it long ago. She was used to being friendless.

"Hullo there, coal-head," she heard a girl mutter at her at the end of her blissful third day. "Psst, coal-head."

The girl was a golden-haired beauty of the common type, nothing remarkable about her. There were at least ten more like her, sitting about the cavernous ladies' common room amongst the various groups of idling lady-students—all in the same uniform; plain sleeveless navy gowns, crisp white muslin chemisettes underneath, with long sleeves and flared cuffs that brushed their knuckles. A ruched ribbon of scarlet silk tied around the high waist, knotted without flair, or bow just below the shoulder blades, the ends hanging down onto the dense pleats of the back of the skirts. She was standing by the wall by a sideboard that offered plum wine in a decanter a few strides from Iselle.

Iselle was putting a small stack of parcels onto a table. These were her spoils from the market square, which she planned to unwrap at this little isolated table in the light of the tall lancet window beside it, and sort into her pencil box and leather bag. She drew up a chair and removed her plain wine-colored redingote with the escutcheon of the Academy embroidered upon the left breast. She draped it over the chair and sat down.

As she did, the girl called her again. "Don't ignore me, coal-head."

Iselle glanced at her, nonplused. She made as if she only just now noticed the appellations.

"Oh, you mean to address me?" Her brows rose. "That oh-so-clever phrase seems to be in drearily common use by those of the Tradelands. Am I supposed to be offended by it?" She paused, looking at the duo of girls that stood nearby, peering at her with half-sneers on their faces.

They offered no reply. "Is it merely a descriptor? As often as I've heard it, it appears I might have to consult the dictionary to see if it's become lexicon to describe anyone north of Ernine." She then reached into her bag and withdrew her embroidered pencil pouch, and placed it upon the table, with an expression like she had not the slightest care in the world.

The girl who had been the one speaking, chuffed and glanced at her companion, a mousy thing with shaggy brown hair styled sloppily into a frizzy hedgehog. They traded a look and smirked knowingly at one another.

"Word is, the academy's infamous tyrant has put out word that no man is to approach you," Hedgehog declared. Iselle's attention was now focused upon them.

"Indeed?" The puzzlement in her tone was genuine. "Huh. That explains that, then. How fortuitous," Iselle exclaimed with affected cheerfulness. She then shrugged and picked up a packet, untying the twine that bound it. She would stack the paper wrappings from her purchases and then put them in the fireplace on her way out, she decided.

"Good luck finding a suitable match now," the wheaten-haired girl giggled. "Not a single man will look at you."

Iselle pursed her lips and shrugged lightly. "Then it is most advantageous that I did not come to Whitewater to seek romantic prospects, isn't it?" Iselle murmured flippantly. She extracted a little bundle of pencils. These were of the sort Iselle liked, with the bark still on the twigs that were used to make them. She put them on the table and picked up another packet wrapped in brown paper. She paused, a quizzical look crossing her features.

"Tell me... does this tyrant fellow truly have so much power that a word from him would command all obeisance?" she asked.

"Nobody dares to defy Forrest Outvallen. He is *Earl* of Outvallen and holds *profound influence*," Hedgehog exclaimed as if these were not only accomplishments, but that they were her own. But Iselle knew this was all nonsense.

"If he's still matriculating, he is simply a mister," Iselle retorted admonishingly. "It won't be until he is inducted into full peerage that he can be called an Earl and formally addressed as one. His having any major influence outside of this campus is doubtful. His inherited title is meaningless until he rises to claim it as an adult."

The girls stared at her stupidly for a moment.

"He's an infamous ruffian. A black-hearted evil soul. He can flatten the best fighters. Everyone is afraid of him."

"Excellent then. Perhaps you would be kind and courageous enough to request that he expand the embargo to all, so I will be delightfully spared of listening to vapid prattle from the likes of you as well." Iselle placed two jars of ink down on the worn, waxed surface, and reached for a third packet. As she grasped the thin, long, flat parcel, the two girls, in a flurry of skirts click-clacked away on the wooden floor whispering feverishly at one another.

She put down the packet of new quills, and leaned back into her chair, her forget-me-not gaze sweeping out onto the student common. The fingertips of her right hand tapped on her thumb, each finger in turn, as she sank into thought. *Tap, tap, tap, tap. Tap, tap, tap, tap.*

It was the first time in all her school-aged years that Iselle was at peace to put all of her resources to learning. It was so much of an advantage to have fewer distractions impeding the process of matriculation. She already had enough worries to manage. This lightened her burden so greatly; she was thankful to this ostensible tyrant. At least tentatively so.

Now her disruptions, apart from the worries that existed in perpetuity in her mind, were paltry ones. The activity of starlings on the trees outside the window, the shepherd managing the herd that kept the lawns trimmed, the sound of the yellowing ivy leaves scraping against the window frame in the wind. These she could manage. She bent her head over her notes and quietly sketched whatever came to mind while the professor droned on. At the moment it was a little sparrow.

"Miss…" history Professor Margate, paused to consult his student list, "Moon. Miss Iselle Moon, perhaps you would care to answer the question?" Margate's tone was wry and mocking. Seeing the young lady with her head leaning on her fist, and her pencil engaged in what was very clearly not notetaking, irked him as it had many instructors over the years.

Without looking up, nor setting down her pencil, she replied in a bland voice: "It would be the Ramshead campaign of 692, Professor. When Mandos Grey, a mere Brigadier, ended the Canal War," she said.

There was an awkward beat or two of silence as the Professor took stock of his failure to humiliate her. It befuddled him. "Ah. Very well. That is correct," he said haltingly. Then he got back to the job of lecturing until the bell tolled.

"Miss Moon, may I have a word with you please," the Professor called as the class was dismissed. She made her way to his lectern as the students filed down the wide steps of the auditorium. She took notice of the perfect light in the room, washing over the dark wood rows of desks and chairs, the paneled walls, and the worn flagstone floor. How she liked this place, she thought.

When the room was empty of everyone, the professor frowned at her, adjusting his pince-nez spectacles on his nose and gaping at her. "I much prefer *engaged* students Miss Moon."

"I fail to see how you think I might not be one of those," Iselle retorted with a puzzled face.

"I prefer you don't doodle during my lectures Miss Moon. It is disrespectful. You should be looking at *me*. At the board. Paying attention to the lecture."

"This is *how* I pay attention. Looking up, I will see things that will take my mind from the words. Someone tapping their pencil. The pendulum of the clock. The way that tree moves in the wind. Looking down at a simple task keeps my distraction centered upon one thing, and I can let my active mind fix on what I'm hearing." She blinked her eyes at him, her lashes fluttered. *He* became distracted and for a moment, was unable to reply.

"Best ignore me during class," she surmised. "Let my examination scores demonstrate how well I heard your teachings, don't you think?" She offered him the same smile she had offered to many other teachers that had been confused by her ostensible detachment from the world. "My marks have always been exemplary, I assure you, Sir. Might I beg for your trust?" And true to form, he dismissed her, a little flustered by how pretty she was.

As she slid out the door into the bustling hall, she was accosted by another pair of girls, one that was remarkably lovely with green eyes and wefts of lustrous deep red hair piled upon her head over a small hair rat. Its felted tangle was slightly visible underneath the smooth, shining natural hair on the girl's head. The coiffe itself was rather lovely, with two stacked side curls on each side, and a large, coiled queue dangling down her back.

"That's her," the second girl exclaimed, pointing at Iselle. The companion to the redhead was not pretty in the slightest. She had a disproportionately large chin that was covered in large, enflamed spots and an enormous, hooked nose. She had teeth so large she could not close her mouth naturally over them and worse, they were arranged higgledy piggledy, one pushing up in front of or behind another, several were a strange yellowy green in color, while others looked like old parchment. Her eyes were a deep brown, and her hair was blonde, a rather lovely shade, and quite voluminous and well-styled. But that could accomplish little in compensation for her unfortunate appearance.

The pretty one swept her gaze from Iselle's face down to her toes, and curled her lip in a way that immediately rendered her prettiness into ugliness.

"What makes *you* so special?" she hissed.

"Maybe it's because she's a foreigner," the unattractive companion offered.

Iselle wondered if they all came in twos like this, these little harpies. They often did. But not always. One was always prettier than the other. She wanted to understand this dynamic but also didn't.

"Stay away from him and know your place," the pretty redhead snapped.

"I would ask you who, but I honestly could not care any less if I tried," Iselle articulated in her breezy, melodious voice. She then smiled at both of the girls with a carefree air and walked away before either of these two could speak again.

She had yet to encounter her mysterious benefactor—this tyrant of the Academy. She didn't want to; lest she discover the intent behind it to be what she dreaded most. She didn't want to know the motive. It never was altruism when it came to matters like these. Why would a tyrant and bully that everyone feared do such a thing otherwise?

Every place she'd ever schooled had one or two tyrants, but none with this level of influence. Even the all-girls school she'd attended for her sixth year had the notorious bully, Andra. That one, surprisingly had been worse than any of the male bullies that followed. There was calculated, vindictive emotionality in her acts compared to the simple violence and spite of her male counterparts.

The bullying was so common, it was predictable. First, amongst the girls, there would be many who would first attempt to ingratiate themselves with her, but once they encountered what they would interpret to be her cold demeanor, would take it personally and hate her thereafter. Others simply hated her on sight.

Iselle brushed her hair smoothly, the waves from her day's braids still shaping her locks. She wrapped her hair up onto her crown, using a wooden hairpin to fix it into a neat bun on the back of her head. She stared in the mirror at her face. She couldn't see what they all did. She only saw a pale visage peering back at her, with wide, lost, desperately lonely eyes.

She often watched in silent envy, the students that had bonded in truly close friendship. She wasn't sure why she couldn't figure out the trick that made a person a desirable friend. She couldn't find someone who could understand her, either. She would sometimes find someone odd; someone on the fringes she could make a connection with. But never like the friendships the others had. Rarely so.

She had only once found a devoted friend. It felt fleeting, but it had been wonderful. It was at the last school; the one she'd attended the longest. Redlan was his name. He was a wildly extravagant boy who loved the world—who saw *her* when he looked at her. He was not interested in girls, so his attention was simply and blissfully platonic. He liked how strange and remote she was. Effusive people unnerved him, in spite of himself being quite outgoing and confident.

Redlan made no demands as a friend. He had no expectations of her. He combed her hair and styled it for her sometimes. He chose their leisure ensembles for free days they spent together. She sometimes imagined that Redlan thought she was his porcelain doll to play with. She didn't mind it a tittle. He wrote romances and read them to her. He would lay his head upon her lap and sing to her while she tatted lace. He was a companion almost tailored for her.

But he is dead now.

It had started to rain outside her window. The sounds of the girls in the dormitory had quieted down, as it was only a quarter hour until the lights-out bell. Iselle listened to the drops pelting the panes.

I miss Redlan. Her eyes glossed over, and she shook off her grief.

She allowed herself to simply and quietly exist for a few ticks of the clock, sinking into the single narrow wingback chair by the tiny fireplace.

She had asked her uncle for this; the private room. It was an added expense, but he did not complain. He understood and sympathized with her circumstances and indulged her. Although detached and busy, he was not uncaring—and like her, he was a stiff, hard, cold character with a pleasant face. He expressed his affection with complaisance to her wishes, and unspoken empathy.

He had raised her with guarded, veiled affection. But even with this closeness in its limited state, she longed for it; as she spent the lion's share of her young years drifting from one intern school to the next and away from him, against all of their desires. She was now over nine hundred miles from home, hoping with all her might that she would not be found, even though every day, she felt so very, very lost.

Iselle's mother had died bearing her. Her father sailed away for trade two years after that, and the ship never returned, leaving Iselle orphaned. All she had left was her patient, reserved, staunch bachelor Uncle Ude. He dwelled quietly in his tiny chateau in the middle of the lake, when he wasn't at his law office or donning his perruque and gown for court.

I miss him too.

She rose with a sigh and stood in front of the mirror by the window. The person staring back at her looked hollow. She studied her reflection for a moment. Her hands slid to the bow of the drawstring at her neckline, and she pulled it apart. She began to strip away the layers of her uniform. The jumper gown, the chemisette. Her petticoat followed. With a groan of relief, she loosened her tiny stays constricted around her bosom, lifting it to its best advantage, and pulled them over her head. Lastly, she drew off her shift, rendering her nude. She clucked her tongue, noticing tiny flecks of blood on the back of the white muslin garment. She turned her back to the mirror and scowled when she looked over her shoulder.

There was still scabbing and swelling around the carvings in her skin.

In the light of the fire and the candle, the scars looked like embossing. They were crisscrossing lines scrawled across the entirety of her back.

They spelled out *YOU ARE MINE*.

With a deep, tremulous sigh, she reached for her nightgown on the edge of her bed and drew it over her body. Two months, and it had not healed yet. Two months, and the scars would forever remain.

Forrest was rarely perplexed. He was the sort of person who knew his mind. His decisiveness and boldness were off-putting to the people around him. He inspired fear with his strong will and determination. He was also tall, looming and thus intimidating. His features were handsome but unconventionally so. His body was toned and wrapped in the lean muscles of a martial fighter.

He had learned the art of hand-to-hand combat due to his late father, a grizzled fighter in his own right, who had served in the Baranith Royal Army and had risen to the rank of Field Marshal. He was peerage, but he had been anything but pampered or soft. He was a hard, determined man with a black temper, ropey muscles, and a sharp discipline. And he had expected of and imposed the same upon his son.

Forrest shuddered a little and frowned, deepening his concentration. His body was a walking memory of his father. The physical shape of it, from the endless hours of repeated motion and training, but also, in the permanent marks left by a man who hated his son. The small round holes made by the pointed iron thumb of the fireplace poker; the burn of it when it was glowing orange with heat; the slash on his calves, even across each one, from the edge of his father's saber.

That was when he was but a boy. As a young man, his father challenged him as if to test him. He grew increasingly brutal, the more skilled Forrest became. Forrest had thought that his father trained him with the specific goal that one day his son would finally become good enough to best him and put him out of his misery.

He got what he wished for.

Forrest's brow darkened and his jaw rippled. His hands, positioned flat, with precision, pressed out from his chest, extended his arms forward, and slid his weight from one foot to the other with the graceful precision of a predator; his muscles sliding liquidly below his scarred and storied skin.

The late Earl had demanded that combat art methods be taught to Forrest from an early age, and he often practiced alongside him and sections of his men in specialized training. This became as much a habit to Forrest as breathing, and walking. Even now, with his father gone, it was a daily exercise, even if it came with the inevitable feelings of animosity connected to it through his father. This routine was a double-edged sword for Forrest. Although it offered him a means to hone his discipline, his focus, to calm and quiet his mind, to teach his brain to compartmentalize his physical state and center his magic to keep the noise of the many out or seek a singular voice, it was inevitably a hard reminder of his father. Undeniable benefits, garnished with feelings of bottomless resentment.

Forrest would rise early every morning before breakfast and seek out the empty sporting atrium. There he would train, and practice all the fighting movements in turn, in a silent agile dance, undisturbed, cast in the cool predawn light of autumn.

His excellence at fighting was in turn unmatched. Few squared up to him. Those that did served as the examples that prevented others from challenging him again.

Forrest's face rested in a permanent expression of disdain and indifference. While the rest of the young men of his class amused themselves by mucking about, laughing, mock fighting, chasing young ladies, Forrest would brood nearby, watching, or decamp somewhere to spend quiet time on his own. He read a great deal. He listened to the orchestral class play, walked or rode his horse in the park alone. He preferred his solitude. For their normality, primarily, he envied them. But he resented them too, for the breadth and weight of their emotions. They assailed him with feelings he could not understand or relate to most of the time. They were things he knew he would likely never experience himself.

Freedom. Guilelessness. The unburdened joy of ignorance and privilege. The feelings that came with growing up happy. This made him even dourer.

He effortlessly dropped his body down into a crouch, simultaneously stretching out one leg, his muscles flowing as he punched his left arm straight out, twisting his palm up, while the right was held close, fist against his chest.

The fear of Forrest extended to everyone in the school. He was brooding and grim and spoke rarely to anyone except to disparage, insult, command them to go away, or to shut up. There were few people who dared breach his dark demeanor. His friend Meddin somehow managed it, but it was still a friendship at arm's length, with a great deal of carefully chosen words and kid gloves on the part of Meddin. The boy used humor and easy airs to appease Forrest. Although Forrest did not respond with the like, he accepted it from his friend. There was a balance, a lightness to Forrest's darkness. A few others had managed to ingratiate him or obtain his tolerance. But they were exceedingly rare, and only Meddin was tolerated in Forrest's company for more than a few moments.

Now, as Forrest washed his skin from the basin in the currently unoccupied baths adjacent to the atrium, and wiped down his rugged body with a towel, little skeins of his wet hair falling into his eyes and shedding droplets, he found himself dwelling on a conundrum—a deviation to his normality. This had never happened before. This irregularity shook his norm.

It was that girl, Iselle.

He found himself seeking her out at any chance he could. He eavesdropped when cohorts reported the gossip they gleaned of her between classes, which was spare at best. He normally despised such mutterings, but they were all fascinated with her, and when she was the subject, he listened.

She was refreshingly uncontroversial in all truth; the gossipmongers had little to criticize except her disinterest in everyone else. The rumors and gossip usually centered around the people who deliberately provoked her instead.

He saw at least that his edict had been obeyed. They left her alone. It was simple to recognize just upon his first encounter with her, how uneasy she was by the attention of the young men in the book shop. From then, he observed when he could. Her body language showed a slight recoil when one came near—the mask of indifference tinged with anxiousness when they engaged her. Even the girls around her made her uncomfortable and prickly, even if she tried to appear unphased.

She did not extend trust to anyone. Like him, she had underlying fear inside her disguised as misanthropy. A fear of what remained to be seen.

"Teneen sought her out today. Moradel told me," Meddin declared over dinner. They'd chosen to take a meal in town. Forrest wanted beef. A nicely seared steak basted in butter, with just the perfect sprinkle of salt.

He sat in front of Meddin and was busily sawing chunks off and eating them in turn. He paused in his chewing and looked up at Meddin. His gaze was even more sullen now.

"Bloody Teneen," he murmured while he chewed. He took a swig of his port and then sighed angrily.

"She won't respect your word like others do, I'm afraid." Meddin drank too and sliced off a piece of rare meat and shoved it in his mouth. He used bread to sop up some of the pink drippings from the plate and ate it. "She's threatened by your protection of the new girl." Meddin paused. "You like this new girl?"

"Shut up, Meddin," Forrest growled.

"Seems like it'll be a hard road with a girl like that. She's a frosty one," he added. Forrest shot him a glare across the table.

But Meddin, like usual, was right. He had a habit of saying things off hand, which were often dismissed and scoffed at, that ended up being true. He was wildly observant. He claimed it was a magical gift, but he still managed to be wrong about many other things. And his magical abilities were not of the kind to make him intuitive in that nature.

He was right about this matter. A challenge Forrest had been puzzling over for days—and that was discovering a way to gain Iselle's trust for himself without provoking her anxiety.

Forrest's friendships were mostly shallow and based on his status and ability more than on who he was a person. But at least he *had* friends. Iselle lacked any companionship at all. She was bristly and even rude to people. But in her defense, he mused, the girls were downright intolerable and cruel to her for being a northerner, and more beautiful than the lot of them, by leaps and bounds—although it hardly bothered her that *they* treated her ill, he was bothered on her behalf. And he felt partly responsible for that because of Teneen. The girl had believed him to be hers from when they were but children, and continued to act as such, in spite of his utter dearth of interest in her.

Now there was Iselle. He could see the darkness in her and he was intensely intrigued by it. He wanted to know her story. He had never cared to know anyone's story. But he did hers. He had no idea if she was approachable at all, and he was self-aware enough to know how unapproachable *he* was, and how fearful she seemed of men.

The only time she even looked in his direction was in the bookshop that very first day. No matter how many times he made himself present in her vicinity, her gaze was perpetually disassociated with the people around her. Always daydreaming, rapt in thought, eyes disengaged with reality about her, as if all the people were faceless and meaningless figures blurred into the background as she made her way about the campus. At least this was what it all outwardly appeared to be. She passed her eyes over people like they were but a background because she put all of her focus into watching for someone in particular; to be observant of the shadows lurking between the irrelevant bodies. He felt this when he could reach the surface of her thoughts. She lived in vigilance; while always looking like she was as remote as a lone island.

He resolved that he would seek the means to somehow find her alone—and suss out a way to interact with her without driving her away. And he had one more thing to see to, and that was Teneen.

CHAPTER 2

"Miss Moon! Stop running at once!"

The sound of her name barked in the shrill voice of her governess, Mrs. Hallwell, was eerily similar to the shriek of a distressed goat, Iselle concluded with a smirk. But she did not stop. She continued running until her pale gown and pinafore were obscured by the brush and the wild blackberries that snagged at her hem. The path that wound between them was narrow; barely suitable for a twelve-year-old child, but wholly so for a scarecrow of a widow. She was out of sight, and soon out of earshot. Iselle continued to run for as long as her legs and her breath could propel her, but she soon became winded and she stopped to bend herself in half, and lean on her knees, panting, and also laughing from exhilaration. There was much excitement to be found in the act of escape.

She examined herself when she had caught her breath, and straightened, patting down the disheveled skirts and her flyaway hair. "Count this frock as a loss," she murmured, picking up the torn hem of her thin hyacinth-blue voile pinafore. Blue was one of her favorite colors; and she preferred the lighter shades of it.

An empty chestnut burr had caught in the lace of her petticoat. She shook it off and peered forward into the coppice. It had been left to grow wild for the past few decades, transforming from a timber farm to her uncle's hunting grounds. It was here where he found solace in fowling, dispatching myriad game birds for dinner. He would often be found at the beginning of autumn, stalking the fringe of the woodland with his firelock rifle against his shoulder with a brace of birds hanging from the barrel, his most trusted black flusher dog Grimm gleefully at his side carrying a pheasant, grouse, or a duck clamped in his teeth.

It was not autumn, however. It was the earliest of spring. The snow had gone, but the ground was still frozen. The puddles of day melt had a crust of ice over them that cracked when Iselle's leather ankle boots stamped in them. Her sodden stockings would be irreparably stained by the leather dye, and the dirty water that seeped in at the seams. She did not notice the cold. Her body was steaming from her run, and her breath made clouds as she walked. The biting air smelled sharp.

Iselle made a habit of escaping Hallwell at every opportunity. She'd spent the better part of her morning practicing her penmanship, and scrawling out the calculations of word problems asking how many pounds of pork would cost divided by this many ounces, and all such nonsense. It was nauseatingly boring.

Hallwell was walking her to the conservatory where they would take lunch and enjoy the late winter sun for a spell. The glass and iron building wasn't too far from the main house on the lake shore. They hadn't bothered with cloaks or redingotes for the quick jaunt, and once outside, Iselle had other ideas and sprinted away.

Now, gleefully free of her warden, she turned west towards the trade road. She would walk all 'round the coppice, and find the main road to the drive, and the bridge that led to the chateau on the water. She was most familiar with this wood, and its myriad paths and trails amid the trees.

Hallwell would likely not have followed and would have retired to her room in frustration by the time Iselle got home, she assured herself. She ventured forth, free and happy.

When she finally found the smoothened riding path leading to the trade road, fragrant from its even coat of brown pine needles, still hard from the frost, she took a deep breath and began to skip along, her skirts flouncing. She picked up a stick and batted it at the dormant growth, flushing out a rabbit at one point.

A little, ittle pinprick and the sparest drop of blood,
The river beast would taste this even in a flood,
Slither through the water, like trout against the flow,
And gobble gobble gobble, down its throat you go.

She sang as she skipped to the tempo of her song. She fell quiet when she heard the cadence of hoofbeats at a brisk trot nearing her. She peered over her shoulder and saw the figure of a man on a horse approaching. She stepped aside, and stopped, waiting for him to pass.

The horse was a half-draft of some sort, bulky and marble grey, still velvety with its dense winter coat. It had thick fetlocks and a wild forelock and mane. The tack was shining chocolate. The man in the saddle was tall and lanky, with the dark hair of a northerner, and a hard angled face with sharp lines and hooded eyes. Iselle couldn't quite determine his age. But she thought he was perhaps five and twenty from her nearest guess. He peered at her as he came closer and slowed his horse to a walk. When he came abreast of her, he drew his reins and leaned back in the saddle. His horse halted with a snort.

He was a well-to-do man, judging by his riding attire; fine fawn leather breeches, navy wool greatcoat with two layered capelets and silver buttons, a beaver topper and shiny topboots. Iselle had been told that she ought to run away if the person wore rags, but this man looked respectable enough.

"What are you doing wandering about the horse path, young lady?" he asked in a grave, languid manner. His horse, impatient to keep moving, lifted its foreleg and struck the ground loudly two times with its hoof.

The man's eyes had a peculiar quality to them—so pale a blue, they seemed white. They were searching and curious, examining her with great fascination.

"I'm playing catch-me with my governess," she told him guilelessly. "She's going to find me if I wait about too long," she gave him an impish grin. What had prompted her to say this was unknown to her. She had no certainty that Hallwell had followed her at all. But she had told him so. Perhaps by some instinct she was not entirely aware of, she felt the need to lie. Rags or polished wool alike, she instinctively wanted to run away from him.

The man's eyes smiled too. He stared at her for a long, awkward moment. There was something uneasy about the intensity of the gaze.

"You're quite the perfect beauty, aren't you?" he murmured, intensifying his scrutiny of her face, tilting his head just slightly. It reminded her of a raptor, spotting scurrying things from its roost. She squirmed a little. She hated it when people pointed out her supposed beauty. From the moment she could remember, they would say it.

"She's so pretty! What a striking little girl, what a stunning child, she will devastate the hearts of men, Ude, you will be burdened for the beauty of this child." She heard it all. It came from the society that surrounded her uncle—from the countless women who hovered about him and pretended to adore her for the sake of her uncle's approval. It came from the men he gamed with, and who came out at the end of summer to hunt birds.

None of them had looked at her with this kind of avarice, though. She felt an icy sensation in her belly.

Be polite. That is what Uncle Ude, and the governess told her. "If you are complimented, be polite. Say thank you. You are receiving a kindness, and kindnesses should be returned."

Iselle did not want to be polite.

"Your garments are ruined, young lady, it isn't ladylike to tramp about like this," the man observed.

"You are without cloak or coat, young Miss. And you are cold." He mistook her anxious shiver for a chill. "Give me your hand. I will take you home. You can ride in front of me here." He patted the smooth pommel of his saddle sitting over the wide withers of his mount. He reached out his gloved hand to her. Goosebumps washed over her skin.

"I can't. But thank you. I must go," she blurted. "The governess will be right furious at me for running." She backed away several steps. The man pushed his horse to sidle towards her, his hand still reaching for her. The way the light caught the sharp angles of his face, the glint of his eye made the hair stand up on the back of her neck.

"I assure you, sir, I'm fine," she insisted, putting her hands behind her back and stepping away.

He remained wordless. His expression was something unrecognizable to the twelve-year-old girl. And before she could react, his hand snaked out and snatched her by the upper arm, pulling her towards him, trying to lift her onto the horse. Her terror was so overpowering, she could not even scream. "Let go of me, please, sir," she implored. "My governess is looking for me…" she exclaimed shrilly, struggling to get away.

He pulled her up so hard, it hurt her arm. She whimpered.

"*What are you doing!?*" the explosive power of this voice cut through the chill like a jagged knife. Never once had Mrs. Hallwell emitted such a sound. It shivered the limbs and branches and set volleys of birds into the sky.

And Iselle was never in her life, happier to hear it.

She was immediately released, and she stumbled onto her backside. The stranger startled in his saddle and his horse shied from the piercing rebuke. He dropped his hand and took up his rein. Iselle scrabbled to her feet.

Mrs. Hallwell was sweaty and disheveled, her hems muddied, her boots sodden. She looked apoplectic. The air throbbed around her.

For the first time in her life, Iselle ran toward Mrs. Hallwell. She reached out her hand and tightly grasped onto the governess's. Mrs. Hallwell, for all her faults, did not fail to read the situation, and she clutched her hand just as tightly.

"I wasn't going to let you get away this time, child. What are you doing talking to this stranger? Have you learned *nothing*?" She scolded Iselle but it didn't feel sincere. It was anger from worry. She then directed her ire towards the stranger. "And you sir, ought not be hanging about a child like that. Putting your hands upon her? Have you no manners, no propriety? Be off with you!" she cawed.

The ground shivered, and the air grew prickly. The horse whinnied and began to dance, eyes rolling. Iselle saw leaves and pine needles rise up from the ground to float above it for a fraction of a moment.

The widow was nearing sixty, but she already looked like a cantankerous old crone with hair gone a stormy, wiry grey, and a lifetime of frowns etched in lines on her dour face. She never came out of her mourning attire and was forever sporting her widow's weeds. She was a tall woman. A frightening woman. But something more radiated from her being that day. Something dark and powerful.

The man noticed it too. He drew his horse back a few steps and studied the governess for a moment. He then made a choice to retreat, his face showing anger and wariness as he wheeled his horse.

"I was merely concerned to see her on the path without governance, ma'am…" He tipped his topper at the pair and gathered his reins, urging his horse into a jaunty canter towards the main road. They waited until he was well out of sight.

"We'll go back the way we came. Can't have him following us home," she hissed, glaring back where he had been. Still holding Iselle's hand, she led the child back through the trees and bramble. Mrs. Hallwell said nothing more to Iselle. She never let go of her. They were silent but for the breaths of their effort.

The sky was pink and gold with underlit clouds, when they arrived on the lawn of the estate park. The lake, mirroring the sky like watercolor, the tiny castle and its bridge silhouetted against it, beaconed to them. They crossed the bridge home, safely, their skirts tattered, but themselves, intact and unharmed.

Iselle was not chided or rebuked for her actions. Hallwell seemingly did not tell Uncle Ude about it, for she heard nothing of it that night at supper. Relieved, the young girl gained a new appreciation for her governess.

Iselle's innocence prevented her from understanding exactly what she escaped.

But that day changed everything.

CHAPTER 3

Nobody truly stood out to Iselle. It was a rare thing. But Dorya was hard to miss. She was tiny. Like a child of nine or ten. The first time she came out from the veil of her disengagement that morning, she spied the girl, with her hems clumsily pinned up, leaving the Oak Hall dormitory. The girl walked straight up to Iselle and asked:

"You stay in this hall, I venture? Please, please, *please* tell me you have a sewing box… these uniforms aren't made in child size," she implored. "The drawstring makes it fit well enough up here, but these skirts will not do." She made no backhanded or pointed comments to Iselle. She just wanted needle and thread. "I do not want to walk about looking like this, all the way to the proctor's if I do not have to."

"I have a sewing box," Iselle replied matter-of-factly. "Follow me." She brushed past the girl back to Oak Hall. "Did the house proctor not bring in a fitter for you?" Iselle queried. Dorya followed in a half-run.

"No time. I was sent here post haste. I arrived only this morning. I was just starting at Oridden University. I was forced by my family to leave. They did not like who I was associating with," she murmured with a tinge of spite in her explanation.

"I see," Iselle murmured. "This way," she turned up the left stairway after they entered the main door and climbed up two floors.

"The faculty secretary left the uniforms and a box of pins on the bed for me. I was going to the proctor's residence to see if she could help beyond a stack of pins." Dorya said this between gasps of air as they ascended the stairs.

Iselle responded with silence. She led Dorya to her room, after Dorya caught her breath, she introduced herself and finally asked Iselle's name.

"Oh, you are from a rich family, with a room such as this of your own…" The wee girl exclaimed untactfully as they entered the space. Iselle closed the door behind them and glanced at Dorya.

"My uncle is a lawyer and sometimes a judge for a neighboring borough and is a knight bachelor. He is well off enough on his own. My grandfather had a plantation that grew Mandoli. He distilled doli wine. He made his fortune as such, and my uncle now owns the distillery and farm. We live in a little chateau formerly owned by a bankrupt baron. So," she concluded, "I'm not *peerage* rich. Not obscenely rich. Just rich enough for my uncle to afford me a humble private room. Certainly not the luxurious apartments of the privileged."

She was unsure why the accusation of being rich always made her feel defensive. She didn't like that other students held that against her as well. It was always the foundation of the first impression they drew from her. Money first. Then it was appearances. Dorya seemed to take it in without judgement, only a passing envy for the space.

Iselle realized that this was the most she said to anyone that wasn't a sharp retort to insults, since Redlan. She turned her face away to hide her sudden rush of emotion towards the bedside table, where she stooped, and opened the little cabinet below the drawer. She occupied herself by removing the books from on top of the small wooden sewing box she kept. Everything she kept was spare or small. Designed for quick removal, as necessary.

"It's cozy and pleasant in here," Dorya observed. "I share a room with one other. I have yet to meet her."

Iselle turned and handed her the box. She then set to restoring the books to her cabinet.

Dorya took it absentmindedly, her eyes still roving about the space and its contents.

"Oh, that's lovely," Dorya said. She was staring at the single bonnet that Iselle owned. It was a lovely, timeless piece of a soft pale green silk, with magenta and pink embellishments and feathers. It sat on a hat stand on the wall shelf over her desk.

"It's my favorite garment," Iselle replied softly. Dorya then pivoted both her body and the subject matter.

"Should I cut the skirts? Or simply turn the hem up inside? That might make it heavy, I imagine. Do we return these garments when we graduate?" she rambled.

"They grow shabby from use by the end of the year. You are not obliged to return them. Cut the hem," Iselle murmured passingly. She had straightened herself and was standing by the bedside cabinet, her hands clutched against her stomach.

Outside, a bell rang, and students began to populate the pathways in droves, their voices rising up to the dorm windows. Girls began to return to the building.

"You know, you're not as scary as you look," Dorya observed in a non-sequitur, which she seemed to be partial to.

"I beg your pardon?" Iselle uttered.

"You're intimidating upon first sight. Downright terrifying. Like you're not real. But you have a kind air once you speak." She stood and unbuttoned the gown, wriggling out of it before Iselle could say another word. Dorya recognized that she was being forward and paused.

"I can't leave here looking like this again," she said, indicating with a jab of her chin in the direction of the door, the noise of girls filling the dorm halls. "I'll be quick. I'll do the others in my own room. I don't want to hear any nonsense for being small and wearing an ill-fitting uniform. I've had enough nonsense today." She then stepped out of her gown. Standing in her petticoat and underpinnings, she shook out the dress and draped it over the rug. She used the pins that were already in it to mark the cut.

Iselle watched her with one of her brows arched. "Do I really look menacing?" she asked. She went to her desk and poured water from a decanter into the unused mug and put it on the floor next to Dorya. The smaller girl took a long drink from it and came up for air. Iselle spectated as she took out the scissors from the box and cut carefully along the bottom of the line of pins.

"Yes. Well… you *were*. But as I said, you're actually kind. But at first glance you are rather hard looking. Unapproachable, if you will. If I weren't so desperate not to look like an idiot on my first day here—one must get ahead of these things early on, do we not?—I might have avoided you like a plague."

This made a snort of laughter bubble up out of Iselle's nose. She lifted her hand to cover her lower face in shock. The girl's casual, wry humor was rather fun, she decided. There was an innate fascination with the idea of Dorya. She was what Iselle imagined a lively friend to be. She had seen so many like her through her schooling—laughing, bright, merry, girls giggling together, whispering together of silly secrets. Dorya represented a kind of friendship Iselle had never had. Something light. Something diverting. Something *normal*.

Dorya was blissfully unaware of all this introspection and veiled mirth from Iselle. She threw aside the trimmed broad circle of fabric and then slid gracefully into a cross-legged position from her kneel. She reached for the sewing box.

As if reading Iselle's thoughts, Dorya exclaimed: "I suppose I'm now obliged to be your friend." She grasped a spool of black thread and drew out a length. She said this with a belabored breath. "It's that or I will be indebted to you. I'd rather not owe you anything. So, friends it is." She cut the length of thread from the spool with her teeth. She didn't pay much heed to Iselle, who looked on, interested, almost fascinated. Was it this easy to find such companionship? All this time, did she miss opportunities to make friends for lack of knowing?

"What is your field of study then?" Dorya asked.

"Villainy," Iselle replied airily, "with a minor in the terrifying." She then walked to the window to widen the heavy brocade curtains and let in more light.

"Can't say it doesn't suit you." She exclaimed brightly, as she gingerly threaded the needle an inch from her eyes.

"In all seriousness, it's law. Specifically Mystical Law. But I lack abilities myself." She sat down on the side of the bed, looking down at this strange little creature sitting on her floor, needle and thread dangling from her mouth as she turned the gown inside out and folded in the trimmed hem and pinned a length of the edge.

Dorya plucked the thread from her mouth, which was at present set in a bit of a sneer at the mention of law degrees.

"You ought never put needles in your mouth. One of our chambermaids inhaled one by accident, and had it not been threaded, which allowed for quick removal, she might have died, for it lodged itself in her throat."

"That's quite grim," Dorya muttered. "I suppose I'll take better care then." She paused and then continued. "Do they actually *need* legal protection? The magic bearers? Why can't they just magic themselves out of legal conundrums?"

Another unnoticed smirk and another chuff.

Dorya meanwhile drew the gown onto her lap and began blind stitching the hem in place. She was quite deft at it, her delicate hand moving with precision.

"What about you?" Iselle queried.

"I considered philosophy. But then I realized I wanted to eat food and buy things to live if I am not fortunate enough to marry a rich man. So, I decided upon architecture. But I'm tragically inept at it. I can't draw a straight line. Even with a rule."

This time the laughter escaped in a giggle. The tiny brunette was stolid, focused on her task, all while being playful. Iselle was, in terms of the idea of having a normal, typical girls' friendship, besotted.

"I shall be a barrister with nobody to represent. And you will design perilous, crooked, and ugly buildings," Iselle surmised.

"We do our best," Dorya sighed as her needle picked up the sparest bit of the fabric and drew the thread through it before catching the edge of the fold again. "Even if we *are* useless. We are *women* after all. Far be it from us to aspire to even mediocrity in a man's world. We can be destitute together. Ah... no... I can be destitute as your companion, as *you* are rich."

"Not peerage rich."

"Good enough," Dorya retorted. "As long as you spare me a sewing kit now and again to repair my rags and fit into enormous gowns."

Iselle watched her finish her hemming, rethreading the needle a few times as she toiled along.

She studied the petite girl comfortably occupying her floor in her underthings. She envied her for her easiness and humor. Dorya was an oddity to Iselle. She might not be so for girls who were not in Iselle's predicament, for girls who did not grow up mostly isolated from others her age, for girls who were not existing in a constant, unceasing state of fight or flight.

Dorya was quite lovely, Iselle concluded. She had a carefree kind of prettiness, with long chestnut hair she had styled up onto a voluminous arrangement on her crown, with a wavy rag-curled weft hanging on her right shoulder. Although the academy regulations forbad hair on the shoulders, many girls ignored it for the fashionable masculine queue.

Dorya had hazel eyes bright with humor and goodness, and a smattering of freckles washed across her nose and under her eyes. She looked a bit too thin, and her eyes looked swollen. But she did not project any of the discomfort or troubles she had clearly experienced. To start at a new school two weeks into the year was not usual. Iselle didn't want not pry. But taking her cue from Dorya's behavior, she did.

"Why did you have to come here upon such short notice?"

"I fell in love," Dorya sighed. "I've been weeping for days. They sent me away and he was sent away. I am heartbroken." Her hands continued to stitch along.

"I'm sorry for you, Miss Dorya." Iselle pursed her lips, her brow knitting. She wondered what that was like, to fall in love. Dorya offered a shrug.

"Tragic, unrequited love... isn't that what we are all supposed to endure at this age? All broken hearts and impassioned tears? Until I am of age, and no longer dependent upon my family, I will be subject to their desires. I feel that my love was not true enough for me to defy them, leave of my own volition, and elope with him. And neither did he. Broken heart or no, it was likely not true love."

"I've heard my uncle describe infatuation as a deceptive imposter for true love. He warned that I should recognize it for what it was and not be fooled into an unhappy marriage by naïve and alluring romantic feelings. He told me to evaluate the man objectively, and that *true* love is acceptance of everything he is, plain and simple, and the reverse. If I would want anything changed about the man I profess to love, that he is not the person for me."

"Your uncle is a sensible man. Tenedros is a fine fellow, but thinking upon it, there were myriad qualities I wished were different about him. Perhaps this was all for the best, then," Dorya concluded. "Maybe I can stop crying now," she laughed ironically.

The new friend used her teeth again to cut the last thread after knotting it.

"I intend to liberate your sewing box. You'll very likely never get it back. Hopefully, it's not special to you." She put everything back into it before tucking it under her arm.

"Well…" Iselle exhaled laboriously. "If we are indeed obliged to be friends, why don't you come with me. Let's go and have some lunch. Then I'll show you about the place before afternoon classes begin. Best put your gown on first, though," she said with a rare smile.

"Oh, you don't know? Everyone knows *that*. I'm the premier expert at notetaking. Truly the greatest expert. In fact, people call me *Her Highness the Master Notetaker of All the Land's Notetakers* back in Anniluth," Dorya never seemed to stop talking. If she wasn't going on about class, or people, she was making meaningless prattle or her idea of humorous pointless noise, like she was just now.

It wasn't as much an annoyance to Iselle as it was a hindrance. It stood in the way of her focus. As she endured the disruption and distraction of the girl, she wondered if it was always like this; these types of friendships. Such idle talk and silliness. She found amusement in it sometimes—as she assumed this was the attraction of such a connection with other girls. Mirth and bubbliness, easy empty chatter, and gossip. She was still undecided as to its value to her. She liked Dorya. Far better than other girls in the school, mostly because Dorya wasn't afraid of her or jealous of her—she was blind to the qualities that repelled other young ladies from Iselle. She accepted Iselle. So, Iselle accepted her in turn, for all her prattle and vivaciousness that Iselle could not mirror.

Iselle ignored Dorya's babble and continued working as she had been trying for the past hour. They had settled in Iselle's favorite table in the library, far at the back by the window, closer to one of the smallest of the fireplaces, and away from where most everyone else congregated. It was nestled in a little glade of sorts, in the forest of shelf stacks, between Ancient History and Geographical texts.

Outside, there was a class of Biological Magic students out on the lawn holding osmium-glass divining implements. They looked quite ridiculous, arms outstretched, the instrument held aloft, with its mirrored indicators pivoting about like the hands of a clock, their shining surfaces catching the light. The group eventually congregated over a patch of lawn, where they began to collect samples of the weeds and the browned grass growing there. Iselle wondered if she ought to have pursued something other than the Multi-Interdisciplinary Magic track. Something earthly. Like Dorya, who sought to build ordinary buildings. Magic could be so changing and difficult to pin down—even for the best practitioners of it, and she had no magical skill at all. To understand it well enough to defend its users wouldn't be easy. *Should I change to something less complicated?* She would ask Dorya her opinion, but she knew Dorya would not have one of substance. This discouraged Iselle a little. Redlan would have offered her good advice.

She exhaled audibly, downcast and confused. She turned the page of the library book: *Case Studies in Research Methodologies of Mystical Law.*

"You think I'm entertaining. I can sense it. But you don't laugh." Dorya sounded crestfallen and disappointed.

"I've never been the fulsome type," Iselle muttered. "You best get used to it. I am unlikely to change. If you insist on being my friend, then you must accept this about me." They both paused in their scribbling. Dorya studied her for a long spell.

"I am trying so ridiculously hard to imagine you throwing back your head in unrestricted mirth. I can't do it. I might even think it's an impossible thing for you."

"You may be assured that I am laughing heartily inside my mind," she replied. She dipped her quill and lifted it to the end of the faded script that preceded it.

"Hm." Dorya didn't resume her work. She crossed her arms instead and leaned deeply into the soft back of the library chair. She sat on a cushion given to her by the library's docent, to reach the proper height to make proper use of the tabletop.

"What about other feelings and emotions? Do you do all that inside your mind too? Or do you not feel them at all?"

"Such as?" She did not stop writing. Her quill scratched along the paper. She scarcely hid the annoyance in her voice. This remark had hurt a little. She was not *unfeeling*. She hated that Dorya thought so.

"Hatred. Love. Sorrow. I know you must feel these things…"

"I don't. I'm a block of wood." She said this with a bite of bitterness. She tried to hide it, but it came out regardless. She hoped Dorya would not be shaken by it. Her right hand reached to refill her ink. Her left turned the page of the book that she was making notations from.

".. and humor as well." Dorya added. Iselle frowned for a moment and then looked up. Her eyes were dark.

"I *am* human. I *feel* things." She was defensive yet again. *Redlan never put me on the spot like this.* She did not like it.

"Do you? Like what? Have you ever been in love?"

She hesitated, and her demeanor darkened further. She glowered. "No."

Dorya leaned forward now, laying her arms on the table.

"Never *once*?" She was incredulous. She said this loudly. Too loudly for a library.

"No." Iselle jabbed her quill into the pot and gave Dorya her full, prickly attention. "I have never felt anything like that for anyone. I've never understood the attraction to be honest."

"You desire no companion? No mate? No children?"

"This has nothing to do with what I desire. I adore children. I hope to be a mother someday. I would *like* to be a loving wife to an adulating husband. The prospect of being alone, to be excluded from the joyfulness others may experience, but I cannot... it is as shattering to me as it would be to anyone else.

"I am overcome with envy for those who have the easy capacity for it. But I would rather live alone than live a lie with someone I feel nothing for. But do not think that I do not desire what everyone else does. The affection. The true, and ardent, wholly accepting, *mutual* love. The romance. But I have seen how these gestures and that initial devotion are all so fleeting. If I could have that, I want it to be like that forever, with someone who is dedicated and faithful only to me, and I want to feel devoted only to him as well. But I've never felt anything like that. Not even the infatuation we're all supposed to feel when we are younger. So, I would be without, than settle for someone I am not drawn to, who will make a half-effort to woo me, and then cease the moment he succeeds. I want the romance of perpetual tender love from both, like in fanciful novels, or nothing at all." She slashed her hand with finality.

Dorya's lips turned into a tight line, and her eyes averted to the fire. "Now I feel depressed. You make it all sound so bleak. A whirlwind of passion, turned into being taken for granted."

"Hm." Iselle grunted and picked up her quill again. *Good*, she thought. *A little taste of reality couldn't harm someone so naïve.*

"You're young. It's not as if someone can't sweep you off your feet tomorrow."

Iselle's hand froze. Her eyes rolled up to fix on Dorya's pretty face. "There isn't a man I can trust. They're all animals. I don't want to be wooed.

I want them all to leave me alone and keep their distance." Iselle's fiery words and expression startled Dorya.

The girl gazed at Iselle, her eyes searching. Her face grew serious.

"What happened to you, Iselle? To make you this way?" Dorya said this and set off a prolonged pall of heavy silence. Her usual warm and bright face looked worried.

Iselle remained tight-lipped. Her eyes dropped to her work. Her anger dissipated and there was a chilly air that settled around them. She regretted her tone, and that she'd revealed her simmering hostility. She felt that if she spoke another word, she would succumb to weeping. She did not want to do that. Not with Dorya. She suspected the girl would not let it go if she did—and Iselle distrusted Dorya's capacity for truly relating to it or understanding and turning Iselle's anguish into something about herself.

Dorya mulled quietly for a brief moment, at least accepting without protest, that she was not going to receive an answer. She studied Iselle for a spell and then sighed.

"At least on one end, *that* wish has been granted. The men *are* leaving you alone," Dorya finally observed. Iselle nodded.

"Yes. The faceless tyrant of Whitewater is ostensibly the one I should thank for that. But chances are he is an animal just like the rest of them."

"Has he made any demands in return for his favor?" Dorya reached for the decanter and goblets and poured them each water. She slid one across the table to Iselle. She almost had to climb onto the table to reach Iselle's side.

"No. I've never seen his face. I don't even know who he is. I was told a name early on by some vapid girls, but I forgot it." Iselle took the faceted, stemmed glass and sipped. Her eyes were cast to the side, as if contemplating.

"Everyone knows who he is. Anyone would tell you. I'm new here and I already do."

Iselle pursed her lips and let out a quiet snort. "You talk to people. I don't."

"Ah, yes. There is that..." her companion concluded. She sat gripping her goblet with both hands over her mostly empty paper. "He is leaving you alone. I suppose that's a sign he's not like the rest."

"It might be nothing more than the most dominant dog marking me as his territory. It wouldn't be the first time." Iselle's usual poise frayed for a moment and an edge of anger slipped out with the exclamation.

"Well, if I see him when we're together, I'll point him out to you. You will at least know who it is you are trying to avoid, or who it is you should thank. His name is Forrest something, that much I know. I've seen him in town. He likes the bookshop and the public house. He's a frightening character to behold. All loft, darkness and strappy muscle."

Iselle put the goblet of water down and with a look of warning, she went back to studying. Dorya, reluctantly, followed suit, returning to her book on ancient design.

Forrest leaned against the bookshelf and pondered what he had just heard. *Perpetual devotion.* He felt, however, that perhaps it was not the kind of devotion that was closer to infatuation. To desire. To obsession. He sensed in his core that this was all Iselle had ever experienced. What she wanted was often thought to be idealistic and unrealistic. Fictional even.

With such ethereal beauty, it was of course that the majority of thoughtless, unimaginative, simplistic, lust-driven, selfish, and stupid men she encountered elucidated her early on of that reality. It was no wonder she saw men as animals.

In truth, he realized that Iselle was very much like him. Seeking the impossible perfect match, one of mutual understanding, or willing to give up on all of it if never found. He was sure from the bookshop when he first beheld her, that she was that one for him. She evoked feelings he was not aware he was capable of. Not just her profound beauty, but the story he detected in her movements, her zealously guarded feelings, and her eyes. There was so much more to her than her physical being. So much more to who she was.

He wanted to know who she truly was.

How would he be able to catch her eye or her heart, he mused, when his first gesture towards her amounted to nothing more to her than a dog lifting its leg on a tree?

He groaned quietly in irritation at his impulsiveness.

He was careful not to reveal his presence so near to them as he moved stealthily away, back towards the main hall, before turning back, taking a more direct route, making himself obvious. With resolve he straightened and adjusted his collar and cravat and determinedly stalked forward.

He pondered about what affect he could adopt that would work to draw her interest. But he paused at the thought. Would she even be interested in him if he were pretending to be someone he wasn't? *I cannot offer pretense or try to manipulate her. I am who I am*, he thought. Abrasive, cold, distant. *And there's that other thing too…*

He paused and reflected upon the secrets he kept himself. *Would she hate me if she truly knew me?*

Either she would come to see his appealing qualities, whatever those were, or she wouldn't. He could only just be. *Just be,* in her orbit. *I am obliged to be the unlikable cur that I am. She can accept me for that, or not. I can only control what I can control. But I can try. I'll never know unless I try.*

He ran his fingers through his tousled hair and strode from the canyon of the stacks toward the table where Iselle and Dorya sat, snatching a book from the humanities shelf in passing. He was overcome with nerves, and it rattled and irritated him. He was struck by the duality of his feelings. He simply forged forward, determined to be the person he was, come what may.

Iselle felt the advance of the figure almost at once. As if the presence of this young man had some kind of mystical magnetism that forced her eye away from her work to the looming shape that approached. He strode towards the table and stopped with an expression of annoyance. She recognized him from somewhere. She remembered spotting him from a distance, and thinking he was rather good-looking—something she could rarely attribute to anyone she met. She simply never lent any importance to those things because she did not pay heed to people in general. His handsomeness, however, was overshadowed the moment he opened his mouth.

"This is where I sit," he snapped. "Go sit elsewhere." Dorya jumped a little at the suddenness of it all. They both gaped at him for a moment. Then Iselle replied.

"No. There's no assigned seating. Go someplace else yourself." She then turned her attention back to the notes before her. But her notes looked like nonsense scribbling to her all of a sudden. Her heart was pounding like a marching drum. Her cheeks were hot, and her mind aflutter. *Is this what it is like?* Why was she being so rude and responding so adversely? Is it because he was so abrasive from the outset? She wasn't sure. It made her angry.

"I forbid you to return to this place. I will be magnanimous today, because you clearly don't know how things work around here yet, and I will allow you both to remain. But I won't tolerate your presence here again."

Iselle's cheeks grew hotter. She turned to glare at him. She tried to ignore the way she felt when she saw him. His dark chocolate brooding eyes large, and tucked inside the folds of his lids, his hair, raven like hers, so rare in a southerner, cut long on top so the smooth, silky skeins fell into his eyes.

She wondered if this hooligan was called coal-head by his peers too. She doubted it. His raven locks were trimmed close to his head on the sides, his long sideburns clipped to perfection. He had chiseled features, a strong jawline, and a slightly aquiline nose. He did not meet the standard of traditional good looks. But it was good looks nonetheless—in her estimation, the handsomest man she could recall—with his tall, imposing form with broad shoulders, his triangular upper body sculpted and lithe, visible even in the tailored school uniform and robe. He had lean legs and hips, arms that were clearly hewn and strong, elegant wrists, and large, masculine hands.

All these good looks somehow fueled her anger at him, in spite of it addling her brain and making her ears and cheeks red. "I don't know who you think you are," she began.

"It's him… the possessive dog," Dorya hissed through her teeth. Iselle glanced at her with wide eyes, and then her expression darkened. But her poise never left her. She spoke with grace and elegance, in spite of the seething anger building up inside her.

"I don't care a jot about your magnanimousness or your commands. You are not an authority. You're a brute and a bully to saunter up to strange ladies and speak to them in such an infamous manner. I will sit where I please, and there's nothing you can do about it," she said genteelly, carefully enunciating every word.

"I can pick you up and carry you out, if I desire," he retorted. "Both of you. You're naught but a slip of nothing, I'll wager. Easier to carry than a bale of straw. You would require even less effort to toss onto the steps of the library." He said this with an air of irony, not threat.

"You so much as lay the tip of a finger on me, I'll break it," Iselle retorted haughtily.

He didn't say anything for a moment. They glared at one another for the duration.

"Your defiance makes me want to match it. If you refuse to leave, then you will have to endure the space *with* me," he said. "And I'm neither quiet nor considerate."

"I'm shocked," Iselle murmured drily. She turned her attention back to her page of meaningless words and tried to focus on them again. But her awareness was absorbed upon this unnecessarily attractive thug. He pulled out a chair at the end of the table and sat down. He slammed his book loudly on the table and threw it open. He began to hum as he read, flipping the pages with as much disturbance as he could muster.

The next two hours were a silent rivalry of who was the most stubborn—of who would give in first. They worked without words. Dorya looked as if she were about to sprint away at any given moment, but she stayed out of loyalty to Iselle. In spite of the man making his noise, and being a nuisance, Iselle was able to push back her strange reaction to him— the discomfort that made her heart race but fueled her panic about it. How could she react like this to him, of all people? It was absurd.

Despite his obvious attempt to disrupt her, and her discomforting feelings, she was able to do some work. The presence of the brute also made Dorya silent, which was a surprising, pleasant benefit. And when she was done and dinnertime loomed, she started gathering up her things. Stacking her notebook and research books, tucking her quill after wiping it, and pencils into the little pouch she kept them in. As soon as she began this process, so did Dorya and Forrest. Nobody wanted to be the first or last, so they all stood at once. Iselle and Dorya pulled on their redingotes and fastened them closed on the breast, both staring impassively at him as they did. He simply idled, leaning back in his chair, and watched with a rather self-assured look on his face. Iselle gathered her things in her arms, elegantly defiant with every move.

She then pushed her chair back in. He moved quickly to his feet to block her way, and she stopped in front of him, her chin lifted. She looked him in the eye, feeling her cheeks and ears burning. She swallowed her reaction and her fear.

"Best choose another table from now on, this is my spot," he insisted, glaring down at her. With that, he started to turn away with his book under his arm.

"I act upon my own will and always have" she retorted acidly. He stopped, pivoted, and glowered at her. She went around him, sailing past his looming figure, and joining up with Dorya to exit the place and leave him behind. But he followed, just at their heels. His irritation was so palpable she could feel it emanating from him.

"This is no way to treat the person who *thoughtfully* commanded everyone to leave you in peace. My concern for your clear discomfort around people is rewarded with such rude defiance," he sneered. "I should revoke my command and let them all hound you to exhaustion."

Iselle halted so abruptly that he nearly ran into her back. She spun to face him, and her baleful glare cut up towards him like twin blades.

"You go right ahead. It's not as if I haven't lived like that my *entire* life," she choked. Her throat unexpectedly tightened, and her eyes began to burn with the onset of tears. This was so humiliating. She knew he could see the moisture collecting in the brim of her eyes. She lowered her gaze and looked at something nebulous near his leg. "I didn't ask for your consideration. I question your motives, and it's not going to make me like you…"

"I don't need you to like me," he interrupted. "Have I given you any indication that I wanted you to like me? I would think I have only shown the opposite…"

"So, you're a liar too… Why would you do anything for *me* otherwise? A person with not the remotest connection to you?" she snapped, her misty eyes finding him again.

"Because when I saw you, I thought you looked like you were in desperate need of peace, security and solitude in *spite* of your being irrevocably alone, and nobody understands that need more than *I* do." The hardness of his voice cracked.

His compassionate and empathetic reply was jarring and unexpected. She was so confused. She suspected that he was too. She suspected it because she recognized the shadow of pain that crossed his eyes when he said the words. Nobody had ever done that. Not once.

She clapped her mouth shut for a moment, befuddled. She stood there in astonishment for a few seconds and then shook herself back to awareness. A tear fell onto her cheek. She wiped it away ruefully, shamefully. Her heart hurt, and she felt withered and defeated all of a sudden. In embarrassment, she spun on her heel.

"Dorya. Let's go," she blurted with a bit of a gasping sob, and they both escaped as quickly as their legs could carry them.

CHAPTER 4

He had a name. And he was where he was least wanted.

Iselle was met with a wave of prickly intuition that made the fine hair on her neck and arms rise up. It happened the moment she passed from the kitchens through the main hall.

He was here. Sitting in the parlor, waiting for Uncle Ude.

His face brightened when he saw her pass the open doorway and glimpse him. He was smiling in recognition. Her face drained of color to see him there. It had been two days since she'd met him on the path. But here he was, more composed in his appearance. His hair styled to sweep towards his face, wearing black linen fall-fronts instead of suede breeches—black slippers instead of top boots—red stockings with white clocking. He wore two layered waistcoats, one with coral and red stripes, and the other solid rose-colored silk. His frock coat was deep burgundy; the less recent cutaway style, with a collar so high, it brushed the middle of his ears. He had taken great care in his appearance. If Iselle had not already experienced the kind of person he could be, she might have imagined him handsome. But there was that glimmer in his eye, that look of greed, that dark shade of desire that she was too young to understand. It seemed only monstrous to her; and her instincts were all but screaming at her. He frightened her. She stiffened.

He rose from his seat and approached her in the doorway. She backed up a step or two.

"Well, if it isn't my little runaway." He bent forward, reached out his arm and placed his hand upon her head. A pang of discomfort flashed in her brain; followed by a wash of dread. She writhed out from under his hand, and her eyes rolled up at him. He shook the hand as he withdrew it and then examined the palm.

"This is where you live, it seems. I am happy to find you again by chance. Your governess… she is a bit of a harridan. Scared me right off that day," he joked casually. "I am glad of the opportunity to offer my regrets for startling you. I meant no ill."

He straightened and peered down at her for a pause. He then pivoted on his heel and returned to his seat. There, he sank down again into the upholstery, crossing one leg over the other. She stood in front of the open doorway, bewildered as to why this man had any reason to be sitting in her parlor drinking tea and eating little cakes brought by Mrs. Wends.

"I have literature to study," she muttered, her voice hoarse. She began to walk away.

"What's your name?" he called after her as she disappeared. "I'm delighted to have run into you again," he added, his voice receding. She did not reply. She pretended not to hear him.

She went to Mrs. Hallwell's room and rapped upon the door with her little knuckles.

"Come," the governess's voice replied. Iselle found her by her small fire in her low, squashy old olivey-brown colored velvet chair, drinking tea.

Her silvery hair was done up neatly today with a white cap on it as diaphanous as a morning mist with a dense ruffle around her face. Today, she wore the bib-front with the tone-on-tone black fabric and inky lace edging the hem. Her false sleeves of sheer, pale grey voile brushed her knuckles, and there were some pale ink-stains on the cuff of her right hand. Her teacup was stained and chipped, but she drank almost religiously from it. It was a pale, muted lilac blue, with white cameo-like figures running in a strip around the cup. Iselle liked it because when she held it to the light, she could see the figures through the fine ceramic, silhouettes seen from the inside of the cup, like shadow puppets.

She stepped inside the room, her face drawn, and a look of worry upon her features. Mrs. Hallwell's attention was immediately set upon her.

"What is it, girl? Aren't you supposed to be reading?" Mrs. Hallwell valued her private time. The child was already an ever-present fixture in her life. She took great pains to ensure that she had a few moments of each day where she could be free of the mischief and of the demands of a lonely little girl. Living in the home with the family meant she was not at liberty to govern her own time whenever she pleased. The child was largely alone during the day, and in turn, Mrs. Hallwell was the only person besides the house staff that Iselle had to go to. Even when she ran away from Mrs. Hallwell, she inevitably returned and sought her attention.

Iselle intruded upon the governess's private room fairly regularly, looking for something to do, or attention of some kind or other, she wasn't fussy about which kind. She might rebel often against her teacher and guardian, but she was also deeply attached to the widow. And Mrs. Hallwell could not help but admit that she was deeply attached to Iselle as well. In spite of her cool nature, she always felt warmth around the bright-eyed child.

By the stricken look on the girl's face as she entered the room, Mrs. Hallwell didn't require any further information to know something was amiss. She could tell the girl was extremely anxious. "What is it, child?" she repeated, peering down at the child's wan face. Her irritation had melted from her voice, and she offered the girl a look of apprehension.

"That man is here," Iselle replied.

Mrs. Hallwell's face grew red with anger. She leapt to her feet, gripped her elbows, and paced in front of the fire. Iselle sat in the chair and watched her governess. Iselle was glad that her own fears were mirrored and not irrational. How could it be unreasonable if Mrs. Hallwell showed the same concern? She was a child, and did not know what to do or what to feel. She knew what her instincts were telling her. She was happy that she had an ally.

Mrs. Hallwell did not shoo her away as she often did when Iselle trespassed into her personal apartments. She allowed her to remain and gave her a little ball of brown yarn and a small ivory crochet hook and Mrs. Hallwell showed her the simplest stitch and set Iselle forth to create something. It kept the girl occupied and quiet, sitting on the floor by the fire on the rug, cross-legged in her little dress, fixed silently upon her little project.

It was only two hours later, *he* was sitting across from her at the table, gazing at her over a forkful of braised pork and part of a new potato. Her uncle had divulged her name to him, unknowing. She sat listlessly, staring at her food, and trying to avoid his gaze. "Twelve years old," he exclaimed with wonder. "You are excessively pretty for such a youthful thing," he declared. Uncle Ude merely shoveled another spoonful of white soup into his mouth and used the tablecloth to daub his chin where some had dripped.

"Mr. Lacklow, I am still perplexed as to why you would require my assistance. I cannot see the advantage of it for either of us." Uncle Ude reached for his glass of port and took a graceless gulp of it. Iselle was glad of his interruption, as it diverted Mr. Lacklow's attention away from her. She picked at her food, pushing a few drab green peas around her plate, counting down the minutes to where it would be appropriate to excuse herself. Normally, she loved these squashy peas. They were sweet. She would be scooping them up and gobbling up every one of them. Now her meal sat mostly untouched.

"Your reputation is the reason I came to you this evening, Sir. Your expertise in admiralty law is renowned. My investment in this small fleet of commercial vessels will come with all manner of legal matters when it comes to international shipping, types of cargo, docking permits, tariffs and transport. I do not wish to step into this new venture unprepared. I was informed that *you* were most eminently qualified with your extensive experience representing greater shippers. I would very much like to retain you for your counsel. I will be out of town tomorrow and the week to follow, so I did not have the time to wait to meet you at your office. Again, I apologize for the intrusion, and I thank you kindly for inviting me to stay to dine," he added.

"My work with shippers pertains mostly to damaged vessels, suits against the shipper for one mishap or another: lost cargo, lost crew, lost passengers... Although I have a great deal of background on the business end of the legal matters, I rarely provide this kind of advice and counsel. There are far better lawyers than I to meet your needs." Uncle Ude had become slightly irritated.

"You came highly recommended, Sir. Highly recommended," the unwanted guest insisted. His eyes kept wandering back to Iselle, who could not help but notice it. Mr. Lacklow continued to go on and on about all the remarkable things he'd heard about Ude.

Iselle knew her uncle better than anyone. He didn't like to be coddled and cajoled. Extensive flattery, and affected respect were things he could scarcely abide. He liked honest people, straightforward and ingenuous people. And Mr. Lacklow was anything but that. He was caressing Uncle Ude's ego. Or trying to, and he wasn't subtle about it. Iselle, even at her youthful age, could appreciate how insulting it could be to her uncle that this man thought he was stupid enough to believe any of his simpering words. Uncle's hackles were rising with each passing compliment. Iselle's practiced eye recognized it in her uncle's familiar demeanor.

"Uncle, if I may be excused... I do not feel well." Iselle used her large pale eyes and fluttering lashes to her advantage and peered at her guardian plaintively. He was absorbed in his prickliness, and he grunted at her with a nod. She got up and with a listless, halfhearted curtsy, she fled the room.

"Goodnight, Miss Iselle!" the intruder called after her.

She slid the dining room pocket door open to almost collide with Mrs. Hallwell, who was heading up from the kitchens. Her governess glimpsed inside the dining room, and Iselle heard her small gasp at the sight of the man. Iselle shut the door and ran upstairs, leaving behind Mrs. Hallwell, who stood by the dining room, wringing her hands.

Upstairs, Iselle bided her time by leafing mindlessly through a picture book, and waited to hear him leave. He had come in a coach, and he left in one shortly after she had fled. She peered out the window at him. She had snuffed out her candles in her chambers, she did not wish to be seen, or for him to know where she roomed in the house. But when he vaulted down the steps onto the cobbles of the yard, towards the waiting coach, he spun around and peered up at the windows. He seemed to be staring right at her. He tipped his hat at her and smiled broadly before he disappeared into the bowels of his garish coach.

She shrank into the shadows away from the glass and shivered. She did not exhale until his coach was well out of sight through the old portcullis and over the bridge.

The following morning at breakfast, she slid into her chair at the table in the small, informal morning room that overlooked the water of the lake, and beyond that, the faceted glass of the hothouse. It was a foggy morning, the grass was dusted in silver dew, and the low planes of mist hovered just above the backs of the sheep that trimmed the lawn. The light was infused with a powdery pink from a sunrise neither could see due to the fog.

"Good morning, Buttercup." Ude greeted her as he always did. Half-warm, half distracted.

Iselle stared at the tabletop while Mrs. Wends put down a plate with several rashers of bacon upon it, as well as a trio of plump pork sausages. There were soft-boiled eggs in little ceramic cups, and toasted bread soldiers to dip in them, a pot of mixed berry jam that Iselle had helped to make, a lump of freshly churned butter, some sweet buns, and some expensive oranges.

Mrs. Wends threw Iselle a sweet smile. Iselle liked her round, ruddy red cheeks and glistening green eyes. She always had a loving expression for the girl. She and Mrs. Reed, who oversaw everything in the kitchens were her favorite friends in the house. Mrs. Hallwell was a disciplinarian, and these two other motherly figures were more indulgent and forgiving of Iselle. They were far pleasanter company, and they often set Iselle to work doing little tasks to be helpful about the house.

The housekeeper gave the table one last look before retreating in a swish of black polished cotton and her starched muslin apron, her silver chatelaine jingling lightly.

Her uncle had already tucked in and was devouring the food when Iselle's eyes returned to the table. She gazed at him for a moment and then spoke.

"Uncle..." she began. He froze; his blue eyes fixed upon her.

"I don't... I don't like that man."

It took her uncle a moment to collect his thoughts. He straightened in his chair, and scratched his wiry, thick side-whiskers. He gave a nod of acknowledgment. He bit into a piece of bacon and chewed loudly. His eyes were like hers, pale and bright. Uncle Ude had been, and still was, a handsome gentleman—a committed bachelor, who had many lady friends. His hair was rakish and elegant, shining and with streaks of silvery white coming in at his temples. His locks were brushed stylishly forward onto his brow. He was a lean, healthy man who took long walks almost every day, with a patrician air from his excellent education and background. With Iselle, he was always comfortable in his own skin, and he cast off the niceties of social engagement. He was himself.

He then bent over his plate and took a few more bites of his food. He was a man who ate unthinkingly, as if it were one more function like breathing, or passing gas, a necessity rather than a joy.

"I didn't like him much either, my little buttercup," he finally agreed darkly.

"You won't do business with him, I hope," she ventured.

"Oh, don't worry your little head about that. As if I would involve myself in any capacity with a simpering flatterer. They never have good intentions, those types. They are neither honest nor trustworthy. However, I must commend you, my little buttercup, for recognizing these things about him. You're so bright and sharp. I'm proud of you," he said gregariously. These soft moments were rare. But they happened.

He reached out and patted her left hand that was resting on the table. "Now eat some breakfast, you look pale and listless." He was not often this full of praise for Iselle, but she knew he felt this way about her. He had always called her his little buttercup, because the moment she came to him when she was two years old, he said her face was so bright and warm, and she was so tiny and fragile all at once.

Clearly, he was concerned about her, or something about her, to be this warm and thoughtful. She wondered if he had an inkling that something had happened between her and the stranger named Mr. Lacklow.

"*Anyone* would be pale and listless if they were consigned to a *whole day* of schooling under Mrs. Hallwell," she grumbled with the sparest shade of a smirk.

"Well then... Let's consider this," he suggested in his usual impassive expression. "I'll trade with you. I'll go and take penmanship lessons with Hallwell, and you can plead a disastrous case of chancery law before the tribunal," he suggested. "The judges are especially bellicose and cantankerous at midweeks," he added with a forbidding, gravelly warning.

She offered him another emotive smirk, which like him, was more demonstrative than usual. He stared at her for a moment, after he drained his dark, fragrant cup of coffee.

"I know he unsettled you," he suddenly said.

She nodded.

"You haven't been yourself since you saw him here," he observed.

"I feel unease when he is nearby," she admitted.

"Yes. I have reason to believe that his visit was contrived," her uncle murmured thoughtfully. "It has already worried me."

"I feel anxious," Iselle intoned. Her uncle stared at her contemplatively for but a moment or two.

"Rest assured, my buttercup, he will not darken our door again. I feel I no longer have need to ask you not to go wandering about."

She nodded, bowing her head shamefully. If she had not done so, there would not be such a situation.

Uncle Ude paused and contemplated something. He then leaned his elbows on the table and peered at Iselle. "Hallwell made it a point to come into my office last night and told me that Lacklow had encountered you on a walk. She said that he had been too forward with you. Is that what makes you fearful?"

He could tell she was hiding something. "Was the governess not party to the whole truth?"

Iselle's chin touched her chest.

"Tell me," he insisted.

Iselle reached over with her right hand and grasped the cuff of her left sleeve, and she pushed the pale gold printed fabric up until her bare arm, and the yellowing bruise of Prentiss Lacklow's handprint came into full view. "I didn't show Mrs. Hallwell this," she said. The brims of her eyes filled with moisture.

Uncle Ude's face turned scarlet with fury, and he straightened. She could tell he was biting back a rebuke for keeping this from him. But he measured his words, and took a deep, purifying breath.

"Superintendent Ederswinn is to join us for our weekly dinner this evening. I'll have a word with him about the fellow, make sure he doesn't linger about town; have the constables keep an eye out for him. Don't worry yourself on the matter." His words did not match his air. There was rage crackling around him. His teeth were clenched behind his words. He tempered his rage for Iselle. His azure eyes observed her attentively as she struggled to hold back her tears.

"Thank you, Uncle."

He reached out and softly patted her cheek. "Don't trouble your head about it, little buttercup. I only ask you to be more thoughtful about what you do. Men can be dangerous, and the more you grow, the more I worry about the attention you will receive from them. No more running from the governess, as intolerable as she might seem to you."

"Yes, Uncle." She pulled her sleeve back down to her knuckles and folded her hands in her lap. She thought about how she initiated the whole situation with her thoughtless mischief. But she felt differently about Mrs. Hallwell now. She had felt a lot of things being in her care all these years. But since that day, feeling safe in her presence was a new consolation for the child.

"Good girl." His voice cracked a little. He made a show of eating a few more bits of food, and then got up, bidding her good day and stalking out of the room.

Uncle Ude was gone until the fifth toll of the old clock and came in just as the Superintendent arrived. Mr. Ederswinn was a merry man, heavy-set with gin blossoms on his cheeks, and spidery veins on his bulbous nose. He had a ring of silver hair and a naked pate, and muttonchops that bristled from the side of his face like a goat.

He was the father of one of Iselle's only friends of similar age; Ylly, who was at present at a finishing school because as her father had described it; her manners were barbaric and the expensive frocks she wore barely disguised her descent into heathenry. Iselle couldn't really say that she missed Ylly all that much if she was honest. The girl was indeed a little torment and beset upon Iselle all manner of blame for things Ylly did.

"That's a pretty little gown you're wearing, Iselle," the man declared merrily. He patted her head, knocking her silk ribbon diadem out of place. She fixed it with a bit of a scowl as he strode by. She wasn't wearing a pretty gown. It was a simple, rather tatty cotton muslin day-gown made from fabric cut from one of her grandmother's many garish old-fashioned dresses. There was enough fabric pleated into the broad skirts of one of those old gowns alone to make three round gowns for Iselle, without any piecing necessary. These were used for days when Iselle wanted to knock about the house and garden and not worry about stained, scorched or torn hems, ink, or dropped food. She wore them most often when she was painting watercolors or dawdling about in the kitchens hoping Mrs. Reed would invite her to knead dough or top off pork pies with jelly after they came out of the oven.

The men vanished into the smoking room. The earthy scent of pipe smoke seeped into the corridor where Iselle stood only a few moments later. She was often like this; without direction or attention, lurking about the house while everyone went about their business. If she was not in lessons with her governess, she was nowhere. Just existing.

As she lingered, her eyes rolled up as they often did, to fix upon the portrait of her mother on the wall over the rise of the stairs. She studied it as if it were the first time, every time. Mrs. Arrylis Moon was a devastating beauty. There wasn't a trait that she possessed that her daughter did not. The same pale skin, the same widow's peak, the same hauntingly light eyes, the same flushed rosebud lips.

Those who did not know Arrylis often assumed this representation was not a real subject, but a painting of an ideal, a distortion of reality, a figment of the artist's imagination. No woman could be so lovely. But she was indeed as beautiful as the painting. Uncle Ude told Iselle this often. She would stand next to him, and listen to him wax nostalgic, about his brother, but mostly about his ethereal wife. His eyes would glisten when he spoke of Iselle's mother. His words were slightly strangled when he spoke of her. It was such an anomaly for the girl, to see such an emotive moment from a man who was generally cool-headed.

"She would have loved you so," he said to Iselle. "You are the image of her, and I imagine you will look even more like her, the older you get." His look upon his niece was one of abject adoration. "It is such a shame she cannot watch you grow. But she and my brother have instead bestowed that honor upon me."

The woman gazed out at Iselle from her prison of oil paint, the tresses of her hair, styled beautifully over her head, with hanging ringlets that rested against her blushed cheeks, almost invisible against the depths of the mottled background; lifted out from the darkness with the finest highlighted lines of paint. Little streaks of ivory white, individual hairs, the hint of a plait crossing her crown, the shadow of a curl. Her pale shoulders, with their graceful curve from her doe-like neck stood out against the gloomy reddish black behind her. The pearly white bodice and sleeves of her gown suited her milky skin. The folds of fabric detailed so neatly, the narrow lace tucker that edged her neckline, the heavy sapphire in its white gold setting on her decolletage. Earrings to match hung from her lobes, a bracelet on the wrist just barely visible at the bottom of the canvas, the ring glistening on her finger. These jewels, along with myriad other sets, parures, were all Iselle's now. Tucked away for her coming out.

Each time, that portrait took Iselle's breath away. Was her mother truly such a divine creature? It had never occurred to her why it hung in the stairwell of her uncle's little castle. There was no portrait of her father here, only in the gallery above-floors. She only knew that having it here felt as if her mother was watching over her, because few people were doing so otherwise.

Iselle tore her eyes from her mother's lingering, direct gaze, contemplating what she could do besides falling into lamenting thoughts.

She made her way back towards the informal parlor to find something to draw. As she did, there was the peal of the doorbell followed by a few hasty knocks upon the door. Mr. Hoops, the new butler, who was holding an empty crystal decanter, loped across the atrium on his bandy legs that were wrapped in sage-green stockings, to answer the door. As he pulled the door open, a rather handsome young windblown relay-rider in a wide-brimmed rain hat and an oiled-leather greatcoat bowed and proffered a package wrapped in brown paper. Outside, it was growing dark.

"For a Miss Iselle Moon," the fellow declared.

"Of course, sir. Thank you, sir," the butler said, claiming the package and closing the door. There was the sound of hoofs retreating almost immediately after—even before the butler closed the front door and started walking again.

This butler was still a stranger to Iselle. Old Mr. Forde had been a fixture in the house for ages—since before she had come to live here; however, he had reached an age when he could scarcely totter to the door, or shuffle up the stairs, or be of use to anyone, truly. He'd also become hard of hearing, and Uncle Ude grew weary of roaring at the top of his lungs because Forde couldn't hear the bell. It was inevitable that Uncle Ude would send him to retire to the gatehouse with a servant of his own. He then employed the rather stiff and taciturn Mr. Hoops in his place.

The new butler spotted Iselle, who was like a little shadow, standing in the archway just off the atrium, gaping at him. He started towards her.

She'd never gotten her own package before. She stepped out of the archway. Mr. Hoops put the package on the round table in the center of the circular foyer and gestured to her to take it. He then scuttled away to replenish the decanter of brandy for the smoking room, his dark green tails swaying behind him. She peered after him for a spell before she moved to the table and inspected the bundle. Her uncle was snug inside the smoking room; she was left alone with it.

She reached out and untied the twine that held the wrapping fast against whatever was inside. She peeled the stiff paper aside. Inside was a costly porcelain doll. It was imported, no doubt, by the subtle style differences in its dress. It was of the highest quality, was about a foot tall, and was wigged in human hair, styled under a delicate organdy and lace cap. She wore an emerald-green silk printed day gown with real mother-of-pearl buttons as tiny as mouse-eyes fastening the stomacher. She had over that, a hooded navy cloak made of the thinnest wool Iselle had ever seen. She even had tiny leather boots with filament laces. She frowned in puzzlement. As pretty and adorably detailed as it was, she was too grown for dolls. Who would send her a doll?

As she peered quizzically at it, the doll's little eyes blinked and it climbed to its feet and stood up on the table. Iselle suddenly felt a sharp pain in her skull, and a wash of nausea which caused her to stagger back. The doll blinked at her as the sensation waned and it tilted its head.

Iselle shrieked and drew back another step, eyes wide and wild. Her alarm brought the two men rushing out of the smoking room to her side. As they arrived the doll curtsied gracefully and began to sing:

Dearest Iselle,
He's under your spell,
Your blue eyes have captured his soul.
By your side he'll soon be,
And he will say "Marry Me."
A girl so divine,
He will soon call her mine.
No other girl can aspire,
To be so admired,
To be as lovely as his beautiful belle.
He will suffer the days,
That he is woefully away,
From his lovely, perfect Iselle.

Before she realized it, she stepped forward, snatched the doll off the table and flung it violently against the marble floor, shattering it into bits. They scattered out across the smooth, matte tiles.

"He's mage," Uncle Ude muttered, his face growing stricken. "There's no end to the things an animal such as he can accomplish with powers..."

"This is the man?" the Superintendent asked. "The one you just..."

"Yes. It's clear now that my concerns were warranted," Uncle Ude interrupted.

The Superintendent looked upon them both with alarm.

"She's only a child," The visitor mumbled, incredulous. "Who makes *this* kind of gesture to a *child*? This is deeply concerning, Ude. He is forward and shameless, to send such a thing to this house. This is not normal. This is dangerous," he continued.

"She will forever be unsafe if he can enchant things like this," Uncle Ude growled. "This is not to be borne." The man shared a furious glare with his friend. They held the look for a prolonged moment, while Iselle, who stood between them, hiccupped and sniffed, wiping her eyes with her sleeve.

"I have someone in mind who might be of help," the Superintendent suggested.

"Come with us," Uncle Ude blurted. His hand wrapped around hers, and they moved to the library in a clatter of heels, Iselle stumbling behind, three steps for their every one.

Two days later, Iselle was in a coach with her uncle's man accompanying her, bound for Yebra, to begin at her first intern school—the Institute at Haystack Hill. It had been decided to send her away until the danger could be mitigated by her uncle and the Superintendent. Until they knew who this man truly was, where he came from and what he was capable of, Ude was unwilling to risk any harm to his niece.

He lifted her into the coach, and put his hand upon her cheek, which was still damp and cool from her tears. "Don't fear, my little buttercup. We will do what we can. For now, you are safe." He patted her reticule. "Hold that little bauble close to you at all times," he told her.

Inside the little drawstring purse, which she clutched tightly against her belly, there was a small talisman figure of an ancient spider spirit, hewn from bloodstone and imbued with power by a sibyl of the old order of witches.

Her uncle had invited the old woman with the crooked back inside the house to sweep it of the remnants of the uninvited magic. She was a wisp of a creature, with a drawn face and sunken eyes. She looked like she was two hundred years old, Iselle thought. She wore a gown as black as soot, with a little bum-roll tucked under her skirts, just at the bottom of her bodice. It lifted her skirts just enough to make her appear even more hunched and bent. She had wild, steely silver hair, and a gaze cast through two cloudy eyes, which was terrifying to the little girl.

Iselle looked on trepidatiously, clutching Mrs. Hallwell's hand tightly, as the witch gathered up the broken bits of doll and the little dress, cloak and cap and constructed a pyre out of rowan wood in the garden. She sprinkled the doll parts upon it and set it afire. She danced and swayed and chanted and wailed for half the night around the blaze, until the fire had died down to embers.

There was as much fuss and pomp over the bloodstone spider, if not more. Humming and moaning and speaking in tongues, her hands waving over it, sometimes with bundles of sticks and feathers. This continued for so long, that Iselle had been obliged to leave the viewing of this madness and go to bed. Come morning, the old woman was gone, and all that was left behind was the spider talisman and a smoldering black hole in the lawn.

Iselle was then gathered up by the staff, and swathed in travel clothes, her belongings placed in a trunk and was sent away as soon as the team was harnessed to the carriage. She was not even able to bid her uncle a proper goodbye before it rolled away. She twisted in the seat and waved. He lifted his hand in reply, his shoulders slumped in defeat.

Thus began Iselle's lonely life away from Uncle Ude, and the home she loved.

CHAPTER 5

Dorya and Iselle exited their respective classrooms after the bell, joined together down the hall, and wove their way through the throng of students. It was time for lunch and they both expressed their peckishness. As they had walked toward the refectory, the high and mighty redhead and her homely companion brushed past them, and the girl deliberately bumped her shoulder into Iselle. Iselle was quick to react and stepped on the redhead's train as she brushed past. The little harpy stumbled as her progress was abruptly halted and there was a nearly inaudible sound of a seam tearing. The girl glowered at Iselle when she turned to yank her hem from under Iselle's foot, which only made more sounds of threads snapping.

"Look out, you black-headed tramp!"

"Mind yourself, carrot, you can't even walk a straight line," Iselle replied airily. Dorya snickered and the two then ventured on, leaving the fuming duo behind them.

"Must one become a bully to defeat a bully?" Dorya ventured.

Iselle emitted an exhausted sigh. "It isn't defeat that will change them," she replied starkly.

They made their way to the refectory to where they sat habitually during mealtimes. It was at the far end of the room as always. Iselle always felt most comfortable closest to corners, or walls. It seemed strange to others, but she liked it when nobody was behind her or outside of her line of sight.

On the table, there was a tureen of potage soup of some kind, one of many in a tidy line down the center of the long table. Alongside that, a plate of pork chops, a bowl of boiled potatoes, a boat of gravy, and a platter of steamed candied carrots. Desserts were arranged prettily stacked on the plain stoneware tiered platters that were often used for teatime foods as well.

The girls scooted their chairs in and settled at the table before they served themselves of the soup.

He came just then. The grumpy Forrest. He sank down beside Iselle without invitation. He took no time in taking the ladle to spoon his bowl full. He made no greetings, no snide remarks. He simply set himself to slurping up the thick soup from his spoon and dunking some rustic bread into it now and again.

"Leek," he said with an approving nod, and he filled his spoon anew.

Iselle was confused as to why he had chosen to sit with them, especially after their first bizarre and confusing interaction. Yet here he was, unbidden and unfitting, planted in their midst as if he belonged there. When one of his acquaintances turned up seeking him out, himself looking confused by Forrest being there, he was told abruptly to go away by the taciturn character. The young man promptly did as he was told, with a look of puzzlement on his face.

Forrest's presence had a positive effect, however. There was a padding of two vacant seats on each long side of the table, between their group and everyone else. All because he had chosen to sit there. The rest of the table bustled with movement, and the sound of silverware on stoneware rattled, and conversation filled the air. Their end of the table was relatively quiet. Iselle wasn't sure what to make of having Forrest there beside her, or why he was there to begin with. Yes, he'd been abrupt and rude. Yes, they'd sparred. But he'd also said something that was remarkably kind to her. Kind and observant. She was perplexed by his conduct.

Forrest brusquely asked Dorya to pass the potatoes. That was the sum of the conversation that involved him at all. Instead, Dorya, who was clearly discomfited by his presence, prattled nervously about little nothings. They dined quietly in his company, enjoying the benefit of his presence repelling others.

Iselle somehow succumbed to a tacit acceptance of his presence. She wasn't quite certain as to why she found it acceptable. He was not intrusive, perhaps a bit gruff and rude, but no threat. She was not afraid of him, even though everyone else was. There was little doubt he was interested in her, if not intrigued. There would be no other reason for him to linger about like this. But she got the sense that he somehow understood and respected that she was shut off to such things, and he might be trusted to leave her be on that end. As long as he was respectful of her.

Toward the end of the meal, a young man approached the table, ignoring Forrest's black glare. Iselle at first thought it was another one of Forrest's friends. But he was not. He came in search of her.

"Excuse me, Iselle?" he asked. "I am surely not mistaken," he added.

"It's Miss Moon, you graceless idiot," Forrest snapped.

She turned to take in this person with a look of bewilderment; that this stranger would know her name. The person was a handsome fellow with deep brown hair, and bright hazel eyes that caught the light from the window. He had an elegance to his features—possessing of a narrower, finer-featured face than Forrest's, more androgynous in appearance--gentler in his air. A tapered chin, slightly tilted eyes, a sharp, perfect nose. But his pleasing appearance and polite manner didn't prevent Iselle from glaring at him, pointedly silent, irritated at the familiar address, and worse, interruption from enjoying her small piece of rustic apple cake. Not even Forrest, who sat quietly by, had gotten between her and her enjoyment of her cake.

Her eyes could not tear away from the young man's face, however. There was something familiar about him she could not place. *Where have I seen him before?* she wondered.

As if reading her mind, he exclaimed: "I'm Ryle. Ryle Kloze. I'm unsure if you remember me. We schooled together before. I never imagined I'd see anyone from Arondon here, so distant from where we were." He smiled and sank down in one of the empty seats next to her. She wasn't comfortable with his proximity and drew away a bit. Ryle clearly was not observant like Forrest. He soldiered on undeterred by the shrinking of Iselle's little form.

"I also understand your field of choice is Mystical Law. I cannot say I am surprised given your history. But this is the very reason I have sought you out. I do recall you reading a great deal on the subject of magical ability. They were the books you most often chose from the library. Do you remember me now? I sat at the desk in the library at Arondon often, to help Mr. Davin. You were never the type to engage in idle chatter, but I remember you quite well. You are unchanged, I dare say."

She scrutinized his face, and she finally began to see it. His features were plumper and rounder then, speckled with enflamed spots and blemishes on his skin. He had been awkward and graceless. His spectacles were nicer now. The old ones had a heavy wooden owl-like frame that fell off his nose more often than not. These were elegantly crafted glasses, bound in two thin silvery bands connected to the pince-nez, which rested lightly on his now good-looking face. He, unlike her, was very much changed.

When he first mentioned Arondon, her heart went cold. An immediate sense of alarm made her stomach clench. However, the anxiety faded when she recognized the earnest look upon the fellow's face. It was clearly a coincidence that they were schooled here together again.

"I think I do remember you," she uttered, politely but curtly.

"I thought you would," he grinned, effusive and warm.

"You look quite altered from seventh year," she muttered distantly. He further beamed in response to her observation.

"Why are you bothering everyone?" Forrest suddenly interjected. "Finish what you have to say and move along," he growled.

Ryle did not acknowledge Forrest's outburst and merely continued. "I've been at the Modrinu annex studying the physics of conjuring with the renowned Mage Telli, and we have transitioned back to the main campus now. I was shocked to see you crossing the quad yesterday, but it occurred to me that you could be of significant help to me the moment I recognized you.

"I wonder if you would be so kind as to indulge me but a moment, with a chat. I know you have more than a little knowledge of mythology surrounding the practice of magic and the old gods, and you are studying inside the same track as me. I have a paper I must complete before the end of the second quarter, and it pertains a great deal to the mythologies that describe types of magic that are no longer in use," he blathered.

Iselle recognized the hidden motivation in his regard. But she brushed aside the flush of his cheeks and his hopeful smile. Instead, she answered him.

"Those magics you describe may never have been in use to begin with." She had come to this conclusion herself, after many years of desperate research.

"Perhaps. But we know there are certain old magics still in use today."

Iselle thought of the pendant hanging around her neck. "It's quite possible that magic has never changed. It's likely that the modern magics can likely achieve the same ends as the old kind. The practices have changed remarkably over the past century. The old mage are often disparaging towards the arts of the newer mage. It could be that the newer mage simply aren't as apt as the older generations."

A flash of defensive irritation washed over Ryle's face, but he did not take the bait. He took further pains to contain his reaction when Forrest, brooding and ever sinister, followed Miss Iselle's assertion with an ironic snort.

He continued, instead: "These are things you can help me with. You spent a goodly time at the library at Arondon reading everything you could find on the subject. I recollect your frequent borrowings of these books quite well. Do you not recall the reading lists I compiled for you from the stacks? I could use your expertise."

His insistence and deference for what amounted to a hobby were distasteful to Iselle. He reminded her of Mr. Lacklow, sitting at her father's left at the dining table, lavishing him with praise.

"I would hardly call it such," she said flatly. She delicately took a bite of her apple cake. Forrest emitted a withering sigh, and drank water from the goblet, his eyes resting languidly and disdainfully upon Ryle.

Iselle first looked at Dorya, whose bright features and wide eyes drew her attention. She nodded almost imperceptibly at Iselle, with an encouraging smirk just slightly expressed on her mouth. Iselle frowned at the girl and shook her head oh-so subtly. The girl returned a scowl at her. She'd expressed her disinterest in romance with any young men at the school more than once to Dorya. But Dorya was a romantic, and she saw potential in any handsome young man. Iselle saw only the boy who'd been helpful to her previously, now attempting to capture her attention with a possibly fabricated need for her knowledge, for a project that would ultimately be useless.

She then glanced at Forrest, whose expression was at the moment detached, but dark, nonetheless. His intrusion in her business still irked her. It was already enough that he'd unilaterally assumed a place in her sphere. She could accept that. But his passive reactions to things that had no bearing on him were annoying. She had to guard herself and establish that she was the one who decided what she ought to do or not do. Not Forrest with his chuffs and subtle impatient sighs.

Ryle's words drew her back, and she sank into a moment of contemplation over his requests. Although it had been fruitless, her research had been all-consuming, and it had gotten her through the stretches of solitude and emptiness she experienced being so alone and isolated from her home and her uncle and Mrs. Hallwell. It had also given her at least the smallest hope to hold onto, that she could take back some power over her life.

The research had been a source of comfort; something to focus on when everything felt so very much out of her hands. She concluded that it couldn't hurt or would provide some diversion to explore her previous fixations again. Harmless study with Ryle wasn't a threat to her or him. He was just another student. And besides, she ventured, her vain and wasted hopes of acquiring magical skills had never *wholly* been abandoned. She still longed for this fairy tale to come true. *What harm could come of it?*

"I can assist you to the best of what I know," she said. Dorya smiled broadly, and Forrest glowered.

"Excellent. Where and when would be convenient for you?" the bright young man exclaimed, his winsome face glowing.

"I can meet you at the worktables in the main library after dinner," she said. She then turned her attention cooly back to her cake and ate what remained in two bites before rising to go to the afternoon classes.

To her dismay, she found Forrest at her favorite table in the library when she arrived after dinner.

"Why are you here?" she muttered angrily.

"It's my table, if you haven't forgotten," he reminded her in a muffled voice, with an air of detachment. He went back to writing down something on the top sheet of a stack of papers he had before him.

"I'm meeting Ryle here. You best move," she said, sitting down across from him. She was too stubborn to give in to Forrest. To let him have his table and his way. She glared at him.

He had situated himself in the seat opposite where she had been that first day they met, where Dorya had placed her cushion. He had moved it to the seat next to him.

Dorya, who was not invited, arrived only a moment or two later, looking bright and inquisitive. Iselle was about to ask her why she had come, when Dorya started to complain about her shifted cushion.

"Why did you move my seat. That's where I sit!" she hissed at Forrest.

"Will you cease your noise? Cry to the Gods, you're the most irritating person I've ever met. Always in a state of commotion. Just sit or go away," he snorted, and continued to scratch his quill across the page.

Ryle arrived before Iselle could contribute to the bickering, and he sat beside her, taking a moment to eye the intruders sitting across from them, one, scribing notes and staring at his work, the other climbing onto the chair and shifting about affectedly to demonstrate her displeasure. Forrest didn't even look up or greet him.

"I brought some notes that I've made, summaries of individual legends I've found. Also, some references to stories I've heard that we can see if we can find the sources for. I'm focusing mainly on divine magic. I'm going to try to demonstrate some evidence that these are the types of magic that are the foundation of our elemental and biological magics and the like, that we use today," he said enthusiastically.

Iselle was on the least glamourous end of the track of magical studies. She dealt with none of the practical aspects of magic. She studied its methods superficially, in the way that magic's use had consequences and effects that would apply to legal strategies and litigation. How evidence can be gathered from its use, how its use could be traced and identified and how that could be applied to the courtroom. It was mind-numbing and extremely dry if she thought about it honestly.

She chose law because that is what Uncle Ude practiced. She chose magical law because of the fixation on the practice of magic she'd developed from the time she left home. She wasn't particularly certain she wanted to do these things. She had not given herself the luxury of thinking about the future. It was simply an occupation to keep her engaged and busy.

She enjoyed learning. But she did not look to the end and see some kind of accomplishment from it.

If she had a future at all, she had no idea what she hoped to do with it. Would she sail about a law office in the robes of an attorney? Sit as a judge? Would she give it all up, marry and do idle things and care for a tiny horde of little children, like so many girls did after graduating from school? So few that she knew of pursued careers. It was too new for women to have the freedom to do such things. She hadn't given it much thought. She had never had the luxury nor the freedom to.

She had secretly harbored the dream of somehow becoming proficient in magic, in having gifts she was not born with; on dreams of finding some secret way to gain them—unrealistic and deluded; she told herself. One day, the truth of it came to her, and she had to acknowledge it. It had taken a heroic effort on her part to accept the reality that this desire would remain unfulfilled. Her wish to have the power to defend herself was a formidable one. Her uncle and his friends, unable to pin down the man who brought her so much strife, she was mired in this unending pursuit. Accepting the pragmatic truth, that she was consigned to this existence as it was, until something happened, it was difficult. But accept it, she did.

She wished only to have a defense against the gifted—so she could exist safely, and go home, and never have to rely on someone else or an undependable bauble to protect her. She craved the luxury of planning a future, having dreams, and fulfilling a purpose. She desired the freedom to discover what she wanted to do, what she loved, and not what desperation forced her to do. She didn't want to tread water. She wanted to swim.

She was envious of Ryle, and of his lark of a project which would highly likely end in offering nothing particularly novel or valuable. It seemed strange to frame it around subjects that were likely nothing more than myth and speculation. But in doing it, he could gain something from it. She couldn't. Simply because she could not lift her hands and make magic happen.

She glanced at the young man's wholesome, warm expression, but could not mirror it. She could scarcely hide the envy and disappointment from her eyes, and she dropped her gaze to his page lined with neat sentences, each one bulleted with a dot of ink. How he could think she would be of any real use was not easily apparent to her. But at least she had some scholarly knowledge of old fairy tales and ancient, mostly forgotten gods.

"How do you justify that our present forms of practical magic originated from a type of magic that we've never seen any empirical evidence of ever existing?" she exclaimed. "I've read extensively on the subject of the origins of our modern magical practices, and I've seen the connections drawn between types of magic and the gods they think they originated from, but there simply is no evidence to support a connection. And again, you can't even prove that the gods themselves ever existed. It's presupposing two conclusions from the start."

"Ah, now this is what I want to argue. That there *were* gods; or what we would *interpret to be* gods in our earliest civilizations; for how would we explain things we don't understand otherwise? And I want to explore the roots of the god beliefs, understand the figures themselves, and where their myths might comport with our modern reality," he argued. Iselle was dubious. But that irrational part of her wanted someone else to validate what she wished to be true. The idea of such was compelling and tempting to her. This brought to bear those old wishes—this overrode the decision she made to move on from those dreams.

"You cannot turn your incredulity into a sound argument for something that has no evidence," she replied. "Mark my words, I've explored all these ideas and hypotheses. I've studied the ancient gods *and* their abilities ad nauseam, and found no credible evidence either existed, except only as myth and statuary. It's an enjoyable subject to examine, but for personal indulgence only. I cannot imagine this paper of yours will explore anything that hasn't already been explored or deemed unprovable."

"I think I can approach it from another perspective if I can find some alternative sources for information. I think you would be of immense help pointing me in the right direction."

"You are ambitious or perhaps, dare I say it, delusional to think you will be able to do all this research before the end of the second quarter, and shine light upon things that have been previously undiscovered," she articulated dismissively.

"Yes. It is ambitious. But I think I can do it. I will be even more confident if you help me."

She exhaled laboriously and frowned. "I have my own studies to attend to, you know. And I don't get credit for the work I do for you."

"You will. I will credit you on my report, I vow." He lifted his hand solemnly. "There's a chance you can receive some academic credit for the work as well, I can speak to the head of the department."

"Leave her alone. You chose the ridiculous subject, you bear the burden of its work," Forrest mumbled with frigid annoyance. Iselle's hackles immediately rose.

Who is Forrest to speak on my behalf? Her cheeks reddened and she grew indignant.

"Well then. Let's start with the Myth of the Mountain God," she exclaimed sharply.

Two and a half hours, Iselle dedicated to the work with Ryle that evening. She had disappeared into the stacks and emerged with books. She sat shoulder to shoulder with Ryle. It was uncomfortable and nerve-wracking. But somehow, the fact that Forrest was across from her both irritated her but also settled her mind a little. She wasn't alone with Ryle. And Forrest seemed more... *useful* than Dorya if something untoward would happen.

She glanced at Dorya. The girl was slumped, leaning far back into the chair and had a book, resting open on her chest. Her head was tilted back and her eyes closed.

How dare you sleep! She thought sharply. *Why did she even come, then?*

Ryle asked a question and grasped a book, leafing through the pages in search of something. She turned her attention back to their work. The books, as they so often did, renewed her interest in the subject. Ryle's enthusiasm for her perspective was also gratifying, even a little flattering. Perhaps his compliments and deference were working. *Would Uncle Ude be disappointed in me?*

To be regarded with respect for her knowledge on magic, when *he* was the one who possessed it. And his speculations, like hers had been, were even a bit convincing, even if it was all merely coinciding with her long-held wishful thoughts.

She gazed at the delicate, colorful woodcut images of gods and mythical creatures on the pages of the large tome she had open on the table. They reminded her of the frescos she'd seen when her eighth-year class visited a sacred order temple. She pondered this, running her fingers over the layered colors and lines.

"In Torem... I've heard of an old village with a temple complex nearby. ... oh, I forget its name," she paused, trying to recall.

"Ideyon," Forrest blurted, turning over one of his sheets of paper, and resuming scratching his quill, and dipping its saturated tip into the ink bottle.

"Yes, that's it, Ideyon," Iselle repeated. "There is the old temple complex, mostly ruins now from what I understand, but there are statues and representations, friezes, that sort of thing, studiously maintained and restored by the sacred order. There might be things to see there, to supplement this paper," she suggested. "You can make wax rubbings of the wall glyphs and carvings."

Ryle contemplated this for a moment. "We should go!" he exclaimed so loudly that Dorya jumped, and her book slid off her and fell onto the floor with a crack. Woken abruptly, she sat up in her chair, disoriented, but immediately intrigued.

"*This* endweek. We can leave after classes, get there the next day, and come back in the evening, if not the morning after. It is visited frequently, I'm sure. We can secure rooms at the inn at Ideyon," Ryle said brightly.

"You cannot go alone." Forrest interjected, "That would be inappropriate," Forrest straightened from his writing and clasped his hands, laying them on his paper. "A chaperone will have to accompany you. I will volunteer as I've wished to visit the place anyway. And I'm quite sure this little lady that follows Miss Moon about like a shadow will want to go as well."

"I do!" Dorya nearly squealed, "but you best not accuse me of what you are doing as well," she snapped at Forrest. "Shadow, my foot!"

From someplace in the stacks, someone hissed a loud *SShhshhh!*

Iselle peered at Forrest, who peered at Ryle impassively, and then looked back at the young man. "Yes. We can do that. That would be proper." She would rather have Forrest, the burden she was acquainted with, rather than some other stranger or unpleasant person along that she didn't know, to lurk over them. At least, until this point, Forrest had proved himself a safe companion. A passive one, who lurked but did little else. She folded her hands on her open book and nodded. "We can conclude for today then. I am tired."

CHAPTER 6

Haystack was a jarring transition for a coddled child with only two rarely seen friends near her age. To be thrown into a girl's intern school, into a group dormitory, where a child with her own room and her own governess, was now exposed in a roomful of strangers—watched vigilantly by the dorm proctor, every action scrutinized, and interrogated for so much as rising to use the chamber pot—it was a great deal to swallow. It caused her distress, and for the first month, she was listless and inconsolable.

She was never away from home for more than a few days. If she traveled at all, it was with Uncle Ude. Here, she had no grounding. No roots. Nothing familiar. She was surrounded by girls her age, in such numbers and groupings, such intricate social hierarchies she knew nothing about. She could not find her footing.

There were the girls who could discern the quality of her shoes, her refined manners, her polished language, who recognized her unusual beauty, and they tried to forge friendships based on those things alone. Then they found that this girl was standoffish and remote. She did not respond to their attention and flattery and so they turned their back on her.

She was alone in a sea of young ladies like her, but nothing like her all the same.

Once she recovered from the shock and newness, she immersed herself in her learning as a way to pass the time. She learned things she might not have at home. She had for some time fixated upon the enchanted doll, which prompted her present predicament. It was her first experience with applied magic. Here, there was a library a hundred times larger than the one she had at home, and with countless more titles than the circulating library to which her Uncle Ude had secured her a subscription. She used that to learn more about the art applied by Mr. Lacklow.

Upon studying the fundamentals of magic, she found it to be oddly satisfying. It taught her things she had never even the tiniest inkling of. She discovered by chance that Mrs. Hallwell's unusual birthmark at the nape of her throat indicated she descended from an ancient line of mage. This was a surprise, to realize that there was magic in her own home all this time. Was magic use not as rare as she had been told it was?

With the knowledge she was absorbing, she deduced that the day Mr. Lacklow had tried to take Iselle, that it was her governess and not Mr. Lacklow that had made the leaves and needles float, and she remembered that her voice had indeed been otherworldly and had shaken the ground and trees. Mr. Lacklow used enchantment type magic according to the books she read, and the forces at use that day were not typical of enchantment magic. Therefore, the power Mrs. Hallwell likely possessed was something more akin to natural magic, or elemental magic.

Mr. Lacklow's magic was considered parlor magic. To animate things; to endow animation upon inanimate things. It was not on the most part considered a powerful skill amongst the mage. But natural magic, elementals, these were more dominant. A natural mage could draw from the power of the elements themselves, and use air, fire, and water and the like to manipulate the world. Natural mages used to accompany armies to use the world's natural elements to aide in battles.

Perhaps, thought Iselle, Mrs. Hallwell had never trained for her skill—that the magic was incited by her acute emotions that day. Perhaps it was her choice to ignore her legacy, or perhaps she was raised never knowing that the little whisp of rosy skin meant something. Iselle had read something of the like in a book called: *The Wild Bearers*—a book written about mage that did not know they were mage. It told of how they discovered their power by accident alone; but unknowingly releasing devastating magic. Iselle wished ardently that she too had such a lineage, that she too had undiscovered power that would manifest itself in terrible situations. She ardently desired such an advantage to protect herself from *that* man.

She would be able to go home if she had her own arts—to learn from, or even *with* Mrs. Hallwell again. How greatly she had taken her governess for granted. She felt terrible now and missed her keenly still.

The harder lessons Iselle learned at Haystack were the ones about social structures, exclusion, and bullies. Particularly a girl named Andra, who, along with four other girls, dedicated every spare moment to deride and speak ill of Iselle. Laughing at her. Mocking her—all while knowing nothing at all about her to begin with. Nobody bothered to get to know Iselle, as she was awkward, lonely, and homesick.

Haystack was the loneliest of the schools. It was too new. Too raw.

The frosty reception and spurning from the others consigned her to the comfort of the library, where there, she pinned her hopes and dreams upon stories of people with no magical abilities, who were able to acquire them. These were fairy tales and myths. But she read as many as she could in her brief time at Haystack. That was her consolation—her retreat from the harsh reality of her new life.

Iselle would have had little chance to truly acclimate to the school. She was forced to leave for another institution after only five months.

One misty morning, secretary sought Iselle out on the yard where she was sitting on the stone wall by the small lake, by herself as usual, eating a flaky pastry, and watching the blue-winged ducks and their chicks glide atop the mirrored water. Her eyes were puffy from crying, and she was wearing a gown two sizes too big, and it sagged terribly around her. She wore no school robe over it. Only the burnt orange under gown the girls wore beneath their school trappings, and a pair of worn slippers that were not hers.

That morning, after the girls had just risen, Iselle found all her clothing to be absent from her trunk at the foot of her bed. Her uniforms, her own garments, all gone, even the shoes. She was forced to go to the proctor in but her night shift, as even her little dressing gown had disappeared from its hook by the window.

She missed breakfast, dressing in borrowed garments, accompanying one of the school's caretakers about the campus in search of her belongings. Her garments were discovered in the lake. The caretaker took his net and pole and fished what he could out. He would search for her shoes later on that afternoon, wading in with his apprentice to collect what remained.

She was given something to eat and was excused from classes for the day. She carried it out to be alone. It was already a deeply unpleasant day, and it wasn't even lunchtime. She still had hiccups from the bouts of weeping. She was already so tired of being treated like this by someone who knew nothing about her.

Now, the secretary appeared, walking down from the upper gardens, clutching a package. "This was sent for you, young Miss Moon," the tall woman intoned. She reached out and proffered it to her. "You should follow me to the office, for your uncle instructed that if you were to receive any parcels, we were to oversee the opening."

Iselle complied and trudged behind the secretary. It seemed all too ridiculous to do this. It was likely something from her uncle, or Ylly, who had already sent her four letters. Surely Mr. Lacklow would not find her here. It irritated her that such a trivial matter warranted a special delivery and trip to the office, and she had yet to see anyone find the culprit who'd thrown her clothes into the lake.

When in the office, the secretary, the provost herself, and the professor of ciphers stood by and watched Iselle unwrap the packet. Iselle wondered why they weren't overseeing Andra's punishment instead. She drew aside the paper. Inside was a simple silver bracelet. It sat atop a letter.

As Iselle reached for the letter, the bracelet twitched and then twisted. It rose up like a serpent and then snaked up her hand and encircled her wrist in a smooth undulating slither. The alarm of its movement was enough to set her into a panic. The doll had already overturned her entire world. To have another object doing such a thing was simply too much.

She shrieked and frantically attempted to yank it off to no avail. It would constrict every time she tugged at it and relaxed when she did not. In her terror, she pulled and pulled, and it squeezed and squeezed. Tears streaked down her face, and she hyperventilated as the equally horrified faculty tried to pull it off too.

Only when Iselle had calmed down to a state where she could hear reason, and sat hiccupping yet again, her face blotchy and red, eyes bloodshot and swollen, her hands resting on her lap with the bright silver circlet about her wrist, did they rationally begin to contemplate what to do.

As they dispatched the secretary to find the advanced Mystical Arts professor, and the provost went herself to find the jeweler specializing in magical items from the town, Iselle reached shakily for the letter, which had been forgotten on the table on top of the brown paper wrapping. She opened it, and her eyes fell upon elegant script, her sobs resuming as she did.

My dearest, dearest Iselle,

How I've missed you. I hope you cherish my last gift to you. It came all the way from Jadras. Imagine that!

Your uncle has been most inconsiderate of our bond and has taken you away from me. Although my sight of you was fixed, there has been a wall between us that has come and gone over the weeks. It has taken great patience and power to find you at last. I suspect now, we will never be parted.

Although you are still very young, I will not press you to become my bride until you are of age. I think sixteen will be a suitable age for us to marry. I will let you continue your matriculation, as an accomplished wife is a good wife. But I cannot allow any more walls to get between us. I ask that whatever means your uncle has taken to shield you from my sight, that you seek to remove it at once. I know your love for me will compel you to do this. For you surely do not desire us to be parted. It is most off-putting and irritating to me that such people will intervene. In the meantime, I have gifted you this betrothal bracelet, to remind you that you belong to me, and that no other man might set his sights upon the perfect wife chosen for me.

I believe, from the moment I set eyes upon your perfection and beauty, that we were destined to be together. I think of nothing else but of your eyes and your guileless expression... how much I wish to make you mine this very moment. You must

appreciate my generosity, to not claim you as a man from a hundred years ago would and make you my child-bride. I esteem you enough to permit you a childhood.
I will soon see you now that I've found you. I will always be near you.
With the most ardent love,
Your devoted affianced, Prentiss Lacklow.

With the help and cooperation of both the professor of Mystical Arts, and the jeweler, they were able to suppress the animation enchantment long enough to use a severance spell to cut the cuff from her wrist. They performed it twice to sever it into two parts, for even with the opening on the band, it proved to be unbendable. The jeweler took the parts with him when he was done, overtly fascinated by the thing.

Iselle sat, rubbing her wrist, where a deep reddish-blue bruise formed. A letter was sent to her uncle with the express relay, and she was directed to stay in the divining room for the duration, where the cold iron-infused bricks would keep her safe from any malevolent magic.

It was gloomy, and windowless, and far from the bustle of the dorms and the halls. Some of her things from her table and cabinet were brought into the rounded space, and a cot was set up for her, a desk, and a candelabra for the dark room. The clothes had yet to return from the laundry. She had no idea where her shoes were.

She sat on the bed and stared at the pinnace symbol inlaid into the worn floor. The masted boat with the lanterns on its crosstree might represent such powerful ideas as transformation and enlightenment in the mystical arts, she neither felt enlightened nor transformed. She felt lost.

The professor knocked lightly when he followed the porters in. They brought her trunk at last, replenished of its contents, along with all its sundries within. "Miss Moon," Professor Han said. "You *have* protection, but you must have it on your body day and night. Why have you not applied it?" he inquired with worry.

"I don't understand," she murmured.

"There's something here, I can sense it. Whatever happens from here, wherever you may go, you must always have it on your body. I don't know what it is, but I feel its magic inside this trunk. What is the item?"

She remembered her bloodstone token. The black widow curled up and delicately carved into the smoothened stone. She opened her trunk and found it among her sparse jewelry and hair accessories. She handed it to the professor. It was a dark lump, like a smoothened pebble, small but perfectly honed into its shape.

"As long as you remain in this room, you will be safe. I will take this and see that it is made into a pendant you can wear about your neck. That way, you will be protected at all times. It is likely he has cast a seeing spell, a descrying enchantment upon your body or something of the like. He could be able to see through your eyes if you do not have this on you.

"If it's some kind of attached location spell he's put on you, this could block his ability to find you. I do not know what spell it is; I do not have the capacity to see such things. None of the Mystical Arts faculty do. So, we cannot dispel arts we cannot identify. You *must* rely upon this little talisman until you can find someone who can. This way, this person cannot follow you wherever you go. You can no longer remain here now that he knows your location. That is what your uncle specified. That if at any time you were in danger, we were to alert him, and you would leave here."

Iselle's heart sank. She melted into sobs when the professor left her alone in the suffocating room. She didn't understand how enchantment magic could conjure all these spells the professor had spoken of. He was a parlor magician, nothing more. Was she not already far enough away from him? Where would she go next? Would she ever be able to go home? She missed Uncle Ude terribly. She even missed Mrs. Hallwell and her shrill voice. She promised herself that if she could go home today, she would never, ever run away from her again.

The next day, in the late afternoon when the relay had come and gone, she was told she would be leaving Haystack. As much as she disliked the place, she was inconsolable. For more distance meant a slimmer chance of going home.

She left the next morning. Upon the calendar in the office, she saw that it was her 13th birthday. The day uncelebrated, alone, sitting next to a tradesman on his drey from the local inn, where the provost had brought her, she huddled under a cloak and hood, the black widow hanging from her neck on a thick ugly chain. She would go four days away, to a place called Arondon, another school, where she would finish her sixth year and transition into her seventh, alone.

CHAPTER 7

Forrest hung back but remained near enough to hear and respond to conversation if the opportunity to do so arose. He and Dorya tagged behind Iselle and Ryle. He quietly ruminated upon his actions of the prior evening. He had pulled Teneen aside after supper, and laid upon her a threat even she would cow to. Her sense of familiarity with him had presented a challenge, for out of all students in the school, she feared him the least. She did not know the dark history that hung over him, only the times she bossed him about as a child. She was insolent the moment he glowered at her, jutting her chin up and setting her lips into a thin line.

He threatened her reputation. For if there was any advantage of being saddled with this unwanted creature for so long, he had at least been present to witness things she could be shamed for. And he'd seen her canoodling in the hedge maze with her family's thirty-year-old land manager when she was only fourteen. He would tell her family, he warned her. And she knew, with the unbending snobbery of her relatives, that such a thing would cause her ruination, and the man's as well, as he was still employed with the household.

He thought he ought to have done that much sooner, and derived a devilish glee from watching her defiance transform into blubbering supplication when his words sank in. She would no longer torment Iselle. She promised she would not come near her at all.

He mulled over his thoughts on the matter as he followed the others along the damp road towards the temple.

They were a suitable foursome of young, unattached people—students upon a scholarly pursuit of enlightenment. There was nothing scandalous or improper to be seen. They remained in their uniforms to further legitimize the purpose of their excursion.

The public stagecoach ride had been irksome and exhausting, with little conversation as the four of them were knotty and uncomfortable wedged inside the conveyance with three other passengers, subjected to the brash and loud rooftop travelers. They overnighted with the coach and horses at a shabby little inn at a way station, ate a simple, unfulfilling breakfast of dry bread with a leathery crust, some smoked sausage and hard cheese. They were grateful to be underway. A passenger disembarked at the first stop, freeing up a little space, and making it a little more breathable.

Iselle was wedged up against Dorya on one side, and Forrest had taken her right side. Ryle sat across from her next to a remarkably old man and his grandson—or likely his great-grandson. The boy was no more than seven or so years. They both had the exact same upturned nose and deep green eyes. The child stared unreservedly at Iselle, his legs swinging as he did.

"I'm still astonished by the breadth of knowledge you possess on the subject matter of my paper, Miss Moon," Ryle blurted. "It's rare that someone who isn't mage would take such a deep scholarly interest in magical subjects. I imagine it would be mostly fruitless if you cannot apply it practically to your arts."

Iselle swallowed a biting response, and instead Dorya's pretty brow wrinkled.

"That's a bit harsh," she interjected. "The acquisition of knowledge is never fruitless. You can know about building houses without being able to lift a hammer or use a saw."

Forrest's eyes turned upon Dorya, and his face exhibited a fleeting look of warmth.

Iselle felt reluctant to pursue the path of this question, but she also felt trapped in this coach with the expectant gaze of the young man she hardly remembered resting weightily upon her. She exhaled, resigned.

"I have wished for many years, that I was gifted with magic," she explained.

"Don't we all," Dorya murmured. The staring boy nodded solemnly in agreement.

It was Iselle's pall, the heaviness of her silence that drew the next question.

"Is there a particular reason you would want to possess magical skills? A particular kind of magic that drew you?" Ryle continued. "I've always wished to ask you this, since our library days."

Iselle sighed shallowly and wriggled in her seat, Forrest's arm pressing against hers; Dorya's elbow inadvertently jabbing her on the other side as she shifted about restlessly.

"I'm interested in learning about magics that are stronger than object enchantment and glamours, something that can overcome discernment or descrying." She then clapped her mouth shut, realizing how specific she had been.

Forrest's chin turned slightly in her direction, but he did not look at her.

"It was because a childhood friend could do those things when we played, and I always had a dream of beating her at her own game," she added a little too quickly. "I've never known anyone to have much more than menial magical skills. To know there are some more powerful, who can do much more profound magic; people who can speak to the dead, people who can see into the future, people who can manipulate the lives of others—who can summon wind, and fire. It's remarkable—and fascinating." She capped her gaffe with credible, earnest thoughts. It did fascinate her. It filled her with envy. *To possess the capacity to direct your own fate, with no regard to anyone else interfering with or controlling it.*

"Your fascination was evident. It was all you could do to read every book you could get your hands on at Arondon," Ryle remarked "She was in the library nearly every day, taking one or other book back to her room. I must admit, it was her obsession with the subject matter that inspired my own," he added warmly. "I am pleased to have the opportunity to experience the myths of the ancient gods together. I feel like it is a continuation of the journey we began in seventh year. Your search for knowledge is inspiring."

Forrest's arm stiffened a little against Iselle's side.

"Iselle is naturally studious," Dorya declared. Then her stomach rumbled so loudly, everyone in the coach looked at her.

"Seems like someone ought to feed the little nubbin," the old man suddenly exclaimed in a gravelly voice, chuckling twice, dryly.

"Sir, it is unkind to speak of our friend in such a manner," Iselle snapped.

"You young people have such thin skin. Only *you* give words power." He dismissed Iselle with a wave of his wrinkled, papery-skinned hand.

"Good sir," Forrest blurted. "One's tenure in life might perhaps entitle them to some deference from juniors, and you are especially close to the threshold of death's door. However, that does not entitle you to speak disrespectfully of others. No one is too old to practice civility." Forrest's deep voice resonated about the confined space, and his intimidating form made the old man blanch. It was the first time since that early morning that Forrest had uttered a word. The old man gaped at Forrest, unsure how to respond.

"*My* mother says grandfather is older than antiquity! A veritable relic!" the boy innocently, brightly, and loudly exclaimed. So loudly, a few chuckles could be heard from the rooftop passengers. The boy seemed quite pleased to have something to contribute to the conversation. All eyes were on him, and he beamed. The old man glowered at the child. They all bent their heads to conceal smirks.

"Yes. He could even be old enough to regale you with anecdotes about his *direct* and firsthand experiences with the ancient gods," Dorya muttered bitterly, crossing her arms.

There was a ripple of snickers from the four. Even Forrest snorted a little.

And with that, twenty minutes later, they reached Ideyon.

The village itself was old, comprised of dark, stacked-stone houses that leaned now, precariously over the narrow, cobbled roads, cantilevered over the street and sometimes connected by covered walkways and arches that spanned from one house to the next. The streets were a maze, some branching off in rising in broad steps, others were sloping alleyways only wide enough for one person to walk. The recent rain had made the clean streets and lanes shiny in the morning light.

Their chosen inn faced a tiny square with only two market stalls selling some wilted, wrinkled root vegetables, fall fruits, dried meats, Bread and rolls, some feathered game, and freshly smoked trout hanging from the awnings. All around them, voices buzzed, bodies moved, skirts and frocks swung, iron-shod hoofs clattered on the cobbles.

They deposited their bags into the rooms of the inn; both the girls shared one, and the boys another. They wasted no time dawdling about the low-ceilinged, dark-walled spaces inside the inn. They gathered with their cloaks, and the ladies with their bonnets, and they set out upon directions given of the innkeeper, towards the location of the ruins.

It was a half-hour walk, but the weather accommodated them. It was damp from rain, but there were no puddles. The sun shone, but the air was cold and humid. There could soon be snow, Iselle thought. The air smelled like it. Ryle walked beside her; she could sense his boyish excitement.

The road broadened a little and the buildings spread out as they neared the edge of town. They found the entrance to the temple and ruins marked by a pair of white stone pylons flanked by restored river stone walls. Moss flocked the latter, the pylons appearing to be scrubbed. They were met by a cleric who was digging just inside the gate, planting a naked tree sapling.

She wore a simple, coarsely woven black linen gown with a deep brownish-red woolen spencer jacket covering her bust and arms, with a sweet little pleated peplum crossing her mid-back. A high collar closed under her chin. She had the headdress of an order cleric, tinted with the same reddish-brown dye, a wide bird-like construction with wings framing the sides of her head. They exaggerated every movement of her head. The flat of them were displayed like a mating bird when she looked up at the youths as they approached.

She straightened, wiping off her dirt-covered hands. "Best time of year to plant trees, isn't it? They're sound asleep. We lost our old hazel to the first autumn storm, regrettably. So, we are planting one of its children in its place. Fitting, no?"

The four looked on, expectant, but slightly confused.

"It's rare to find students visiting without the rest of their class. Even rarer to find students out and about this time of year. We don't usually let people tour the sites in autumn."

"We came all the way from Rendorff," Dorya complained loudly before the last syllable exited the cleric's mouth. The fear of being turned away set her off. "We had to stay at a shabby old inn, and we haven't had anything to eat since we breakfasted, and that was horrid food to begin with…"

The cleric lifted her dirty hand and stopped her. "I'm not forbidding you. I cannot walk you through the tour, I have duties. We all do, in preparation for winter. It is usual for people to be accompanied by a member of the order. You will be without a chaperone, and you will not have anyone to educate you, nor will you have access to the whole complex. Just the temple of the Three Sisters, which is the nearest. You can come back tomorrow, and we can see if we can find someone who has time to show you the rest."

"We will muddle through with what we are able to do today," Dorya snapped. She then pushed past the cleric onto the stone path towards the temple. The others followed, haltingly and slightly embarrassed, but they followed, nonetheless.

"Don't go any farther than the Three Sisters," the cleric called after them. "No more than half-hour." Ryle pulled out his pocket watch and dangled it on the fob for her to see.

"Half an hour," he affirmed, putting it back into the pocket of his breeches.

The path away from the cleric wound past the monastery wall, where sounds of industrious work emanated, and glimpses of the wide headdresses were silhouetted in the windows, worn by the people rolling dough, and crushing herbs, smashing steamed rice into cake, and scrubbing floors. It was largely quiet, with the occasional murmur of instruction. There were passing scents of food cooking or smoking, a sharp, delicious scent of some kind of berry compote or jam being boiled. There was no idle chat. But all those things faded away as they continued past the modern building towards the ruins of the temple complex.

The gardens that led to it were meticulously kept. The shrubberies trimmed, the ground raked of dead leaves, trees pruned, the ponds scooped free of the detritus of autumn leaf-fall, the silver-grey fish within rippling the glassy surface with their lips in a hopeful search for late-season insects.

The temple appeared from between two cedar trees that were ancient and drooping like two cloaked elderly ladies, swaying in the breeze, their piney scent reaching the visitors before the face of the first temple. The building, imposing and grave, seemed to rise up suddenly in front of them.

The whole of its bulk was supported by ranks of square, fluted columns, wider than a man was tall. Upon them sat a heavy entablature covered in a sprawling frieze, and upon that, a gabled pediment where there stood three figures dominating the triangular space.

Iselle smiled a rare smile. She'd never seen a formal, full-sized temple like this. Not of this scale. Her eyes took in the ancient shapes and figures set against the background of greenery. She felt that all her former passion for the subject that had melted away resurface. Her hand rose and her finger pointed.

"Those are the three divinities of the underworld," Iselle indicated the figures standing abreast on the gable face. "That one is Obraya. She is the goddess that I hear most about, as she is known as the deity of accountability, justice… atonement. Her likeness is in all of my textbooks. The prevailing idea I've found is that punitive type magics we know today come from her. Curses, vengeance magic and such.

"That middle one is the deity that represents hindsight, reflection, clarity, and introspective revelation, Rasseet. Counterintuitively, it is believed that foresight, prognostication, and fate magic derived from her power.

"And lastly, the one on the right, the one with the missing face, that's Tanaju, I believe. She is tied to the concept of regret and change, rebirth, reincarnation. So, you can imagine that the corresponding magics we use today would be necromancy and summoning and that sort of spiritual interaction. It is said one must stand before all three after death and submit to their power before your soul is allowed to return to the world."

"Who are all the little people and things running about below them?" Dorya asked.

"That frieze contains their subordinates. Each group of figures is separated by the acanthus medallions, see?" Iselle explained.

Ryle nodded.

"Those on the left are Furies. See how they have wings like bats? They are servants to Obraya, and they exact vengeance on behalf of those who have come to the underworld by means of being wronged. The middle ones are known as the Sorrows. They have the mothwings. What I understand is they spread wisdom and truth no matter how bleak. And that last group there are the ones who guide restored, healed souls back to the world. They fly on eagle's wings. They are called…" Iselle paused. "Fortunes, or Hopes, or some such. We can allow for a little laxity in the names because they were translated from ancient Vellomme. But it's close enough. I'm sure if one of the clerics were with us, they'd explain it better than I."

"You're not disappointing any of us, Miss Moon," Ryle exclaimed with an effusive smile. "You truly are the fount of knowledge I expected you would be." Forrest rolled his eyes and subtly scowled. Dorya took a deep breath and declared:

"Let's go inside!" She marched around them again and stamped up the nine crumbling steps to the shaded area underneath the temple roof. "Come along!" she cried out, her voice echoing in the cavernous space. A blast of starlings exploded upon the sound of her voice and undulated in a tight murmuration into the surrounding trees. The sound of air whistling through feathers was stark and strange, the closely growing trees stifling the edges of the noise. Around them, as the climbed the steps, they could spy the peaks of other temple gables poking out of the manicured forest. They caught glimpses of other temple entrances between the rows of tree-trunks around the Three Sisters building.

Iselle was last to follow, her eyes gazing up first at the dark ceiling and the stone beams spanning the space, resting on the simply carved capitals of the rows of square pillars, and then her eyes dropped to the dais in the back, the solid walled part of the temple, parts of which had fallen away and had been restored with modern materials. She felt breathless all of a sudden, and chilled. All she could feel for a moment was the warmth of the black widow against her breast—as if it had absorbed all her body's heat and contained it. For but a moment, she imagined it was too warm to be natural, before she regained her senses and took a deep cleansing breath. Her fingers and toes had gone numb and were now tingling. They felt icy, but only momentarily.

Her blood flow surged and returned to her extremities. Her senses were frayed, and she felt removed, or perhaps faint. She tried to gather her wits. She enjoyed sharing all the things she had learned with the others. How rare it had been throughout her existence, from school to school, where she had the opportunity to speak like this. To explain her ideas and share what she knew. She realized that in the weeks she'd been at Whitewater, that this time had been the most communicative for her. Even when she had been friends with Redlan, they spent more time quietly together. She gave no lectures, she only listened mostly to him.

"The other gods, gods from whose magic, it is speculated that black magic, and nature magic, and elemental magic and all the myriad types were borne out of—all of the kinds of magic carried by the gifted—their temples are in this complex," Her voice echoed through the space. She felt like she was having a hard time making sense of her own words. She could see the three up ahead. "There are so many, it's hard to keep track, and some of them have overlapping powers."

The group had spread out. She spotted Ryle, heading towards the arched entrance to the sanctuary. Dorya was ahead of him. She had veered off to the left to observe the statuary that was centered on the floor space between each outer column. She couldn't see Forrest. He was likely exploring the forest of columns. She followed Ryle and stepped towards the doorway to the sanctuary. Immediately visible to her on the back wall, were statues of the three goddesses stood on plinths. Their erosion had been halted by applications of some kind of concrete in the places that had fallen away, veins of whiter stone filled the cracks and bonded them. For some reason, the traces and patches suddenly began to glow. She tilted her head.

What is this...? She wasn't sure if she said it aloud or thought it.

The moment she crossed the threshold; her knees gave way, and her muscles became inert. She expected to feel the stone floor beneath her, but instead, a pair of strong arms immediately gripped her around her ribcage. Her failing senses caught a glimpse of Forrest looking down at her. She felt him pivot her, lift her, cradle her, and before she completely lost her senses, she felt the daylight touch her skin.

CHAPTER 8

Arondon On the Hill was a pleasant school. A large institution, situated on the top of a prominent peak overlooking the bustling city of Endro. It was a city that was not within her own nation, but over the bordering river in the country called Oonil. It was no different. The languages were the same. The food, the same. Some things differed. The waists of the women's gowns were a little lower, the skirts more structured, the hairstyles more extreme and flamboyant.

The building itself was ordinary red granite brick. A simple box of buildings butted up into a square, surrounding a courtyard cloister in the center, and four squat, cylinder towers at each corner with patinated copper onion roofs topping them like coils of whipped cream frosting. There were existing crenelations along the tower tops ringing the base of the roofs, giving clue that this building had been originally used as some kind of fortification.

This school was not exclusively private as the other had been. There were mixed genders here as well. There were local children attending alongside the ones interned from other places. One could tell them apart by the state of their uniforms. Some were made of coarser, cheaper materials. Their wool was thicker and less polished, the cottons woven more broadly. There was a distinct sense of separation of the two groups upon immediate impression.

She was escorted in through the main doors, a footman carrying her trunk. Students were crossing the main hall. They all observed her. Iselle was always well cared for by her uncle. She arrived in her common clothes, which revealed her family's wealth without a single word exchanged, and she was immediately furnished with the finer styles of uniform pieces by the faculty member that accompanied her. She would belong in this school where the clothing placed her.

She was roomed with another girl in the north dormitory floor. She was given time to bathe, and to rest. The students had already had lunch and were well into the second half of their day when she got there. She had arrived at the second half of the school year as well. All of which was an aberration in the established routine for the other students. When the bells rang, and part of the school exited to the streets into town, the rest migrated up to the dormitories. They gawped and whispered at the girl as she padded from the wash chambers to her room, her dressing gown clutched tightly around her body.

In the refectory over dinner, the whole table at which she was sat spoke in whispers, their eyes flashing in her direction, followed by hisses and murmurs.

Their curiosity lasted a day or two. Her roommate, a drawn, pale little slip of a girl named Eenabelle, took little interest and seemed only put out that the empty bed in her room was now occupied by another. She, like Iselle, seemed contained inside of herself and was disinterested in discourse and engagement with others. Like her, she also read a great deal. Had Iselle developed proper social skills, she might have inquired about this as a common interest, but instead, Iselle, appreciating that she hated to be interrupted when reading, gave Eenabelle that consideration, and let her be.

Falling into the routine of classes came with a little time, and by and by, she became used to the place. Her priority had become, like her abbreviated time at Haystack, to seek out the library, so she could learn more about magic. More about the enchantments that made the doll speak and made the bracelet lock upon her. She wanted to know if there were things she could do to stop these attacks from happening or measures she could take to defend herself from the advances of the man who pursued her.

Ryle was a fixture from the start. One she had blended away into the background of her days, like the candelabras in the library, the sound of doors closing, and the undecipherable murmur of the existence of other students in her earshot.

She scarcely gave Ryle her attention—only enough to have him record her daily use of one book or another. He tried to engage her; she walled him out. This was her way.

He was a lanky, awkward boy, with the start of some pimples on the apples of his cheeks, his chin and a few on his forehead. They were red and swollen and some had whiteheads. Iselle tried not to look at his face, for the urge to reach out and pop them all was powerful. She wanted to cleanse his face of them, why didn't he? *Was there a magic that could do that?* She wondered. "A type of healing magic…" she muttered unconsciously under her breath.

"A what?" Ryle asked over his ledger and quill. She noted that his script was sloppy and disordered. He'd printed her name incorrectly. His spectacles were smudged with fingerprints, and the cuffs of his shirt had ink on the edges.

Iselle didn't bother to reply. She simply took the book out from under his hand and left with it.

"Why are you so bent on reading this mind-numbing subject? What use can you derive from…" Ryle picked up the top book on the stack and looked at the title; "…The Variations of the Doon Era Gods by Region and Age?" he read. He grabbed the next: "The Roots of Magic, and The Tree of Arts Gro…" he was cut short as Iselle snatched the book from him.

"Do you interrogate everyone that borrows books from here?" she snapped.

"No. You're the only one that's strangely obsessed with these tomes about mythology. They are worthless. There are no gods, and no root magic."

"How do you know?" she retorted.

"I would know because *I* can do magic. I am mage. A little natural, a little elemental. Nothing mind-boggling or extraordinary," he replied with false humility, and also smugly which seemed impossible. He twiddled his fingers and smirked behind his smeared glasses. "You, however, are not. I have not seen you in a single mystical arts class," he surmised.

"So what?" Iselle shrugged.

He leaned forward on the desk and peered up at her from over the top of his spectacles. "You're jealous of us," he told her self-assuredly.

"Yes. I am," she shrugged, her brows arching. "Congratulations on your profound act of deduction." Her face then flushed with annoyance. "And I'm even more jealous that you think having the ability… the *gift*… to perform elemental and natural magic is *nothing extraordinary*. It makes me sick that you can take something like that for granted and laugh it off like it's nothing." She scowled at him. "Now please list the books, or I'll just take them. I'll bring them back regardless.

"What do you think you will achieve by reading all this? That somehow you will make yourself mage?"

"Whether I achieve anything or not is irrelevant. I am at least trying. Seeking elucidation. Learning. Appreciating. What are *you* doing? You, who has access to the very source of it? Staring at me through dirty spectacles with your spotty face, being so arrogant about having magical gifts, but daring to make sport of me for taking *your* gift more seriously than you?" She snatched her books as usual and sailed out of the library.

She could not know how profoundly her words could mark a person. But she had seen the look upon his face after she rebuked him. She saw his eyes searching as he thought about what she said. She could recognize that he was evaluating her words and realizing that she was right.

Ryle was more thoughtful of her after that. He began suggesting books and compiled reading lists, helping her find texts that were related to her subject—books with stories of the ungifted stumbling upon the ability, given by masters, endowed by spiritual beings and gods. All fiction, but relevant, nonetheless. He found books by admonishing mythicists, and books with intricate studies of unprovable things. He supplied her demands to the best of his ability as library volunteer. With each passing week, he grew increasingly infatuated with the icy little sixth year. She hardly spoke to him. She accepted his suggestions, borrowed the books, and ticked each little line on his list. But in the whole school, in spite of the distant connection they had, it was the only one she fostered with anyone else. The local boy, of middling means, of pimply face and shabby clothes, was the only person who could speak to Iselle and receive even the smallest gesture of reciprocation.

When Iselle concluded her interrupted sixth year of schooling, and was furloughed for summer break, she was left virtually alone, mostly to her own devices in the school. She would eat with the skeleton faculty and the few other students who were also mired at the institute for the summer, and sleep in the empty dorm. She wore a small selection of her own clothing and spent her time alone in the library without the guidance of Ryle or anyone else. She occasionally ventured out into the early summer days, down into the city, to explore and browse the windows and markets.

Going home was not an option. Not this year. Her uncle had said in a letter that perhaps next year, she could briefly come home; risk the exposure, if they could find a way to keep her presence discreet. He assured her that Mrs. Hallwell was in good health, and continued to be employed, and that she would be disposed to visit herself someday. But Uncle Ude would not, for he thought that he too might be cursed with a descrying of some sort. He did not have a means to determine whether he did or not, but he wanted Iselle to be safe. "We are our only family, my dear. We must do what we must to keep the other safe," he wrote. "Until we can find him ourselves, and find some way we can stop him, within the confines of the law, you are sadly conscribed to this state until further notice."

Hence, Iselle was relegated to solitude, and even for a distant, unsocial creature, she was lonely.

It came upon an early summer day, she was walking by the canals, deep in the valley of the city; her school standing above her like a crown on the crest of a mountain. There was a lady there by the water. An elderly one. She was wrapped in a thin, blue-striped sheer muslin gown, a pale blue spencer with gold buttons, and a voluminous cloudy lace-edged cap with two lappets drooping down onto her shoulders, the white-worked ends hanging against her middle-ribs. In one hand she gripped a cane parasol, which she leaned upon as she took slow, laborious steps. In the other hand, she held the lead on a tiny puff of a dog the color of a raven, with two large shining eyes and a little glistening nose. It was so fluffy Iselle could scarcely make out its tail, which was curled up against its backside, or its little legs moving at such speed under it, that it looked like it was floating.

It made her laugh aloud, something that never happened. The old woman glanced over at the approaching girl, and her glistening grey eyes took her in with a wizened swoop, assessing perhaps all she needed to know from the glimpse of her. "You may curb your amusement, girl. Here, take the lead. He's pulling me."

"That little powder puff is pulling you?" Iselle laughed. It felt so good to simply be. She giggled demurely, but she reached out and took the lead as instructed. The little blot of a dog hovered ahead of her, keeping the ribbon of a lead taught. It looked so amusing to Iselle. There was no bend or flexibility to the little dog. It was one solid ball of hair moving all at once, pivoting and bouncing as if it were a bit of fur on the end of a stick instead of a leash. She could not keep from smiling at how comical it was.

"I'm not stalwart and solid like you anymore. A gust of wind could blow me into the canal like a dandelion seed," the old woman retorted. "Hold onto Goblin for me. I've only a short way to go if you would be so kind. You don't look like you are pressed by any obligations, as you are sauntering about the park so aimlessly." She paused and then gave Iselle another appraising look.

"What's your name then?" she barked impatiently.

"His name is Goblin?" Iselle giggled, her eyes twinkling. The dog glided left to sniff at something.

"You should have seen him when he was a pup. No bigger than the palm of my hand, but all teeth, growls, and bites. He chewed up the toes of four pairs of my finest silk slippers. He frayed the corners of almost every piled rug in the house, and his teeth marks are embedded even today in the legs of my favorite slipper-chair. Nobody could catch him; he was the size of a small rat and would scuttle under things every time he'd done something naughty."

Iselle's laughter sparkled around her.

"His little belly, however, was all pink and soft, though," the old woman lamented. "It's hard to remain angry at something with such a tiny pink belly, is it? It's still in there somewhere, underneath all that fur. He sleeps upside down on my lap sometimes and it's there. That pink belly is the only reason I haven't fed him to the wolves." She sighed laboriously while the delight of Iselle's gentle chuckles washed over them.

"Now answer what I asked, you impolite creature. What's your name?"

"Oh! My apologies. My name is Iselle Moon," she replied quietly.

"Ah. A good classic name. Named after the Hevnian empress I imagine?" Her wrinkled face pointed at her; her sharp storm cloud eyes fixed firmly upon Iselle's.

"Yes, Ma'am." Iselle only thought now to offer a polite curtsey.

"Come along then, Miss Moon. Stop that what you're doing there, I abhor such formalities when we have already made our acquaintances. Accompany me to my townhouse then. You may call me Dame Arwey. Or simply Dame will do. There aren't scores of dames to differentiate me from, are there? Or Ma'am, I suppose will do too. If I *must* be a Ma'am."

They walked along the canal, and traversed a tall bridge over it, pausing at its apex to watch together, two narrowboats sailing beneath them. One of them had little black and brown dogs aboard that barked frenetically at Goblin, whose hilarious little ferocious yips and flashing of snarling teeth in response, sent Iselle into internalized raptures. She was so very enchanted and amused by the little thing. She couldn't remember the last time she felt so elated and at ease.

They then proceeded out of the park to the street, and they waited for a lull in the bustle of riders and coaches driving by, to cross the obstacle course of droppings along the cobbles. There, they stopped in front of a large sandstone townhouse with three floors, twice broader than the ones flanking it. There were fine cast iron fences around the patch of land in front of it—more matching balustrades enclosing small verandas in front of tall windows, carved details and trim were dispersed tastefully about its face, with a portico that resembled a tiny temple. A curved mansard roof capped the whole of the house, imposing in diamonds of dark grey slate, with a bristle of chimneys poking out of the flat of its top.

"You will come in for some tea," Dame Arwey said. She did not ask. It was a demand softened with "I'm a lonely old woman," tagged on the end. And even Iselle knew to be polite and accommodating to her seniors, and she too could not deny that such loneliness was her burden as well. She wanted very much to take tea with Dame Arwey.

Dame Arwey opened the iron gate from the walk, and ushered Iselle in. "Go on," she insisted. Iselle complied, the dog leading her up the few steps to the door. It opened almost immediately, and a fresh-faced chamber maid stepped aside and widened it for them to pass. She curtsied politely in greeting to them both.

"Do tell me, Miss Moon—how old are you? Fifteen? Sixteen?" Dame Arwey asked, slowly making her way up the steps.

"Just thirteen, Ma'am." She waited for the old woman to proceed before following with Goblin in tow.

"You are remarkably lovely and poised for a girl so young, I must say. Come along. Follow me. Kattreen, take the dog and have Gale bring us tea in the parlor. We're both parched."

Dame Arwey had a long, winding story which she regaled with a wizened tone, her voice soothing and soft. She told Iselle how she came to Oonil and her house in Endro. As a young child of five, in a family of six girls and four boys, she sailed from Faloneen, accompanied by her father on one of his business endeavors, where it turned out, he would leave her to live with her childless aunt and uncle to stay. None of this had been told to her when they embarked.

"It was because I was the one they worried about the most, you see. I was withdrawn and angry. I had no place in the chaos that was my home. The youngest and eldest consumed all of the time and effort from my parents," Dame Arwey explained.

Her aunt and uncle provided her with a glut of love and attention, a structured life, with nurturing and care she never experienced in a bustling home full of children. The brood shared an exhausted, melancholic mother, and a father with a hot temper and a short fuse to set it off. She transitioned from disorder to serenity. A room and nursery all her own instead of the bottom of her big sisters' bed where they kicked at her and pushed her against the footboard. Now she had a governess that was young and lovely, all the trappings of a well-to-do family with the addition of an excess of indulgences from parents who had wished so greatly for children but who could not have them.

"My aunt, she told me: 'My sister never wanted children, and she produced litters of them. I wanted children with such vehemence and couldn't produce even one of my own. It was despairing to receive letter after letter announcing the imminent arrival of another Newn child. Even after you came to me, she had three more.' And she did!" Dame Arwey exclaimed. "My aunt would throw up her hands almost every time my mother wrote to tell her about the trials of having so many children, or the pains of being with child, or caring for fussy newborns, and shout: 'Fallan needs to get off of her!'

Iselle sat primly in a eucalyptus-green and cream-striped silken wingback chair by the fireplace, across from the Dame. Goblin was comfortably curled upon her lap, a black ball, eyes, nose, ears, all invisible to the eye. He was warm and snoring just slightly.

She was struck by how pleasant the room was, awash in soft colors. Pale greens, powdery pinks, faint blues, rich creamy whites; the paneling on the walls washed in eggshell, with a veritable gallery of similarly soft-hued pastorals and portraits hanging from the rail against them. The rug was made to fit the very edges of the room, and it too was mostly cream with worn designs in dusty-tinted patterns woven in. Iselle saw no evidence of puppy-Goblin's tiny ravagings of rugs and chair legs here. The room was meticulously clean. Every latch and knob shone from vigorous polishing. Not a mote of ash or soot from the hearth soiled the rug. Not a bit of dust marred the smooth, clean surfaces. There was serenity here.

Her hostess doled out the tea from her tea box, while the chamber maid patiently held it. When she was finished, she locked it and carried it away. The Dame then chipped a lump or two off the cone of sugar and genteelly poured the perfectly steeped tea into the stylish, paper-thin porcelain cups.

Iselle could have scarcely imagined that morning, leaving the school, that she would be captive in the parlor of a lonely, rambling dowager with the sweetest little dog perched on her lap like a hand warmer. She was not averse to this, in fact she was glad for the company, and the storytelling. She was glad of the gentility and the politeness, of the slumbering companion on her lap, and the sound of the hearth, and the aromatic scent of was unmistakably birchwood intermingling with that of the tea and strawberry tartlets. It felt like home after many months of loneliness, fear, and exclusion.

She was shocked however, just after the Dame refilled her cup and plopped a lump of sugar into it, to discover that her hostess was mage.

"I'm curious, girl. Why do you have a cloak about you?" The question was non-sequitur. She had been talking about her first husband, and how he nearly gambled them into destitution.

"I beg your pardon?" Iselle, for that moment, did not understand the question. But the Dame's hand rose from her lap, and she made a circular gesture to indicate the whole of Iselle's body.

"The cloak. The veil. You have protection. Why?"

"You can *see* that?" Iselle wondered immediately what type of magic would allow one to see the arts cast by the hands of another.

"Anyone with certain skills can spot it," she waved her hand dismissively. "I will say that these are not common abilities amongst the gifted, to see the magic created by others. It is why I found you of interest to be truthful. I am also *most* curious by my very nature." The old woman bent forward and picked up her teacup by its saucer, taking a slurping sip before clinking it back, and then onto the table again.

Iselle weighed her thoughts on her answer. She did not talk about her situation with anyone. But the wizened eyes of this old woman; her deeply wrinkled face that bespoke a lifetime of kind expressions, humor and laughter, there was so little to distrust in her. She basked in the company; in the prospect of interesting things to be shared. She was lonely, like Iselle.

Iselle let out her breath and reached up to her neckline. She loosened the drawstring of her round-gown and unbuttoned the chemisette that filled the neckline. She then drew out the pendant and laid it on her palm. She presented it with trepidation. She had never shown it to anyone but the professors. The gesture for some reason brought the burn of tears to her eyes. She was overcome with a rush of vulnerability. But also, she felt a wash of relief. For the first time in so long, she could share her burden, and she no longer felt alone.

CHAPTER 9

"Now her favorite hat is ruined," Dorya's voice brought Iselle to awareness again. As her eyes fluttered open, she saw a box-beamed ceiling, and the crown of candles that illuminated the space.

"Her eyes are open," Ryle exclaimed.

"See? Did I not say that it was merely a fainting spell? You said you had not eaten since morning. Here, I will sit her up," a strong male voice declared. "Let's get some of this soup into her. It'll fortify her spirits, and she will be ready to go back with you in no time."

Strange hands fell upon her, and she visibly cringed. She saw Forrest appear over her, and he brusquely, and silently pushed the person away, and he sat down on the edge of where she was placed, and he put his hands out for her to take. His fingers wrapped around hers and he held firm while she pulled herself up into the seated position.

"There," he said quietly. She blinked up at him; his face was taught, and his lips were in a hard line. "You should eat. Your countenance is alarmingly peaked and pale." He got up and helped her swing her legs off the chaise upon which she sat. She was in a room she did not recognize, and there were several people there she did not know amongst her friends. The people were all clerics. They had brought her to the monastery.

A lady gave her a double-handled mug, containing a watery soup with little bits of vegetable floating in it. She took it and drank it. It was the polite thing to do. It was thin and could have used some salt. Once she finished, she was helped up onto her feet, where she wavered a spell, but did not falter, as Forrest had a firm but respectful grip on her left elbow. The lightheadedness and wooziness lingered for a moment before she was able to shake it away and regain her senses.

A little realization came to her as she steadied herself. She looked up at Forrest. She didn't mind him touching her. He was always respectful when he did. He did it only out of necessity. Handing her up and down from the coach, cupping her elbow. Guiding her to his side that was away from the bustle of traffic or walkers. He rarely touched her hands. It was always her arm or her elbow. He also stood in between her and others often when there was the chance she would be jostled or bumped. It was always done with an impassive, detached air. As if to do it was as natural as breathing—to be attentive without seeming attentive.

"Are you better?" Dorya asked. She stood in the back, nearly obscured by the other people in the room, holding Iselle's only remaining hat, which was indeed ruined. It had fallen into a puddle of muddy black water, it seemed, and the pale green silk was discolored irrevocably, and the feathers were soddened, and the brim was bent.

"I am," Iselle replied. She did feel better. She put her hand on Forrest's arm and shook out her skirts, so they were not wrapped around her legs. "We should go."

"Should we go back to the temple?" Ryle asked.

Best not, little girl. Best go back home. There's so much to see, so much to take in. Let's be finished with temples.

Iselle's mind was fuzzy and still slightly off from the fainting spell. She willed her internal voice to stop its ramblings.

Forrest's brow slanted down. "I am troubled by your lack of consideration," he said to Ryle. The younger man balked at the truth of it and frowned.

"I am sorry," he said.

"I think we've seen what there is to be seen today. If you wish to return tomorrow, that can be discussed. We should go back to the inn. We should have some dinner, and rest in the common room, so that Iselle's strength can fully return." Forrest said this in a way that was firm and inarguable. He moved to the door of this room, and before opening it, he turned and thanked the clerics for their kindness. All the while, Iselle held onto him for stability.

On the walk back, Ryle moved to Iselle's other side and drew her hand onto his arm as well.

Push that one away. He's pathetic. Don't let him do that, he'll think it's permissible.

He apologized for allowing the distractions of the temple to make him miss her fall and told her he hoped she was recovered. He watched her with his wide, earnest eyes, and then glanced fleetingly, and repeatedly at Forrest, upon whose arm Iselle continued to rely on.

The inn, in all its age and small rooms, was a cozy retreat after the walk and the ordeal. The girls stripped off their uniforms and changed into the lighter gowns they'd brought with them in their shared tapestry bag. Dorya wore a pale-yellow linen bib-front gown, and Iselle a deep wine-red gown of polished cotton. Simple attire, their hair changed into easy, loose buns atop the crowns of their heads. They donned no jewelry, no adornments. They had solid cotton fichus; scarves of light cotton, tucked into their necklines, and long sleeves.

So fortunate, these fashions. Without forced shapery and starched follies. Women have it quite nice, these days.

Dorya's eyes fell upon the pendant as they changed.

"I've seen that on your neck a great deal. Does it have significance to you?" she asked.

Iselle jumped a little, knocked from her reverie. Dorya pointed at the small black lump that was at present, being tucked underneath Iselle's layers.

"It does," Iselle replied succinctly. She could tell by the flash of frustration on Dorya's face, that it was not a satisfactory answer. But Iselle offered no more.

They joined the young men in the common room. Forrest read quietly near the small fireplace, Ryle was staring out the front window at the square and the rain that had begun to fall. He stood the moment the girls came into the space.

Not him again. Insupportable.

"We must be the only overnight guests," Dorya observed.

"Yes. Thankfully," Forrest snorted. "They just notified us that they will be serving the meal in the other room there at the sixth toll. The girls glanced at the old clock on the wall, with its iron pendulum ticking back and forth. It would be nearly an hour until then. They were all famished.

"I fear I might have ruined our excursion," Iselle murmured shamefully.

"Nonsense. We saw a temple. Even the one is enough." Ryle was adamant in his tone, even though it was tinted with forced enthusiasm. "I even managed to get a wax rubbing of one of the wall etchings in the sanctuary," he added. He clearly hoped to return to it.

He's selfish. His disappointment is thinly veiled—he has resentment for the fainting.

"What could this trip possibly add to the information you already had access to at the library?" Dorya asked suddenly, defiantly. "Honestly, if we were to go somewhere new and distant, we ought to have simply chosen it for the chance to join a party or event, a ball perhaps—and evening of cards or music. Something *normal* young people do. All this scholarly nonsense is unbearable. All it's done is to tire Miss Moon to fainting. And the temple complex isn't even fully accessible." Dorya's obstinacy was charming.

"The shadow-girl makes a valid point," Forrest muttered without looking up from his book. Dorya clicked on her tongue and rolled her eyes.

"The excursion was *my* suggestion if either of you might have forgotten. I thought seeing the temples would spark some more insight into the ancient gods, and why we might suppose that the magic we have today came

95

from them." Iselle sat down on a small hassock whose upholstery had long seen better days. The heavy tapestry had worn down to threadbare at the corners. It sank quite deeply when Iselle's slight weight pressed upon it. It made her tip back and fall into a clumsy hunch. She crouched there, looking cross.

"I should have warned you about that," Forrest said, deadpan, licked his finger, and turned the page of his book. He looked dissatisfied by what he was reading.

He closed his book and put it back on the shelf with the disorganized, higgledy-piggledy selection of other books—a collection likely gathered as forgotten possessions of passers-through and taken from abandoned homes as there was not a single tome amongst them newer than 70 years old. He crossed his arms, furrowed his brow, and tilted his head.

"I have kept my opinion in regard to this project of yours, Ryle, to myself, as I am merely present with Miss Dorya, as a chaperone. However, I am compelled to ask, after watching Miss Moon suffer such a thing as she did today, all for *your* benefit... Has anyone ever presented evidence that magic did not exist before this particular divine pantheon? Where did magic come from in the places in this world where these gods do not exist? Wouldn't magic only exist where they once did?"

Ryle looked at him, irritation plain upon his expression. "These are questions I hope to address with this paper. I intend to search outside of our historic records, to those beyond our homeland. I will compare their pantheons to ours... There could be different gods by name and by understanding by different people, but they could be the same gods..."

"There are places where there have been no gods. No concepts of gods at all. Is there no magic there?" Forrest countered.

Ryle opened his mouth to reply but nothing came out.

Idiot.

"Magic would *not* have divine origin if that were the case. At least not originating from entities *we* identified as divine." Iselle frowned from her crouched position, stuck on the squashy hassock. She looked deflated. "I don't know why I deliberately ignore that there is a world beyond our lands... History that is not our own. Gods that are not our own." Iselle said, her voice, a little despairing.

She already had convinced herself there was no such thing as root magics. No such things as real gods. Why did she persist in seeking something to prove herself wrong? Her hope, her nonsense ideas from Arondon, all of these things that had wasted her time did not fade. She hated that a part of her clung to it still. She hated that she allowed her defiance of Forrest to mire her again into this fantasy.

"That is why you cannot rely on myth to prove anything," Forrest said to her. "Even *you* said that back at the Academy when you decided to come here. I don't recall your exact words, but you said the like."

Iselle nodded. He was right.

"I understand by what Ryle said that this is a particular fascination for you, Miss Moon. I understand Ryle's motivation to discover perhaps a thread of truth—some evidence for it. But can we not admit that none of this is rational?"

"I agree. I sometimes find myself seeking out the irrational, because it's easier than admitting that I don't know, and honestly, I want to believe I *could* know." Iselle exclaimed. Her eyes were glassy.

"Miss Moon, no matter how much it comforts you, you know magic is just magic. It has existed as long as we have. It is a natural connection some are privileged to possess. It is not endowed upon us by divinities; we are born with it, or we are not. Just like some of us are born with the ability to create art, or born skilled in ciphers—with blonde hair, or birthmarks. We know this by the family lines where this trait perpetuates itself."

"We are not even unique to possess a connection to the mystical. There are red-crested raptors that can open shifting portals to catch prey in flight. The grown moropus cow can cloak itself and its young from our world when it detects a threat. Is that not magic? There are barely any people who can do those things, even amongst the most powerful of mage." Forrest looked at Iselle in earnestness. And she peered up at him from her crouch, her arms wrapped around her knees. Her eyes were misty now.

He's not wrong. The gloomy fellow is rarely wrong.

When they were called to supper, Forrest helped Miss Moon up from her bottomless hassock, and they walked into the small room where three small tables for four were situated. They ate the bland cabbage and pork soup and partook of a slightly stale round of bread. Throughout the meal Ryle stared at Iselle, who looked at nobody.

"Perhaps we should just go home with the first morning stage," Iselle said over her soup. "I don't know what I was thinking. I don't know what I've ever been thinking. I had accepted before this that these ideas were ultimately nonsense. I don't know why I keep expecting that to change." She stood and walked to her room.

Dorya followed her, and she sat patiently, kindly, watching her friend disrobe of her layers of garments and pull her nightgown on over her shift. Dorya did likewise, and as they let their hair down, and brushed it, and Iselle plaited hers into a long raven rope that hung heavy on her narrow back, her smaller friend grasped the bent, soiled bonnet from the small credenza and looked upon it with pity.

"The bonnet, it can be straightened. And I can pull off the silk from the frame and wrap it anew. We can go to the milliner when we return to the academy and buy some new feathers and embellishments. It can be made whole again."

Feathers and festoonery won't make anything whole again, my tiny friend.

Iselle's hands paused from tying the end of her braid over her shoulder, and she stared at the hat.

Suddenly, she was overcome with a sorrow she could no longer contain. And she covered her face with her hands and began to weep inconsolably.

CHAPTER 10

The old woman reached down for her eyeglass pendant and lifted it to her eye.

"Ahh… Bloodstone. And the widow," she whispered. "Clever. Your practitioner was close to my age, I imagine, or a well-trained adept of one. This is old magic. A practitioner of death magic."

"Death magic?" Iselle repeated, her tone several octaves higher than the Dame's. Her arm retreated and she clutched the pendant to her breast.

"Mm… Yes," the old woman said, leaning back. "That stone emanates death. When you wear it, you are made dead, in so many words. You *are* alive, don't look so shocked and fearful, dear girl. However, in the perception of the mystical plane, you are no longer alive when that stone is on your body. It emanates no life. No emotion. No energy. Undetectable by any magic, as a living creature, you are inert and absent in all aspects, materially and spiritually. You are a specter.

"It is indeed a stroke of genius if I say so myself. There are lots of protection tokens and changing potions to be created, but most of them are not lasting, or easily overcome by even barely competent mages if they can recognize them." Dame Arwey paused. "May I ask what kind of threat you face, child?" Her demeanor was sympathetic and imbued with concern.

"I am not certain. I've seen enchantments from him. But… I'm told that he can see me wherever I am if I am not wearing this." Iselle unfurled her fingers to look down at the bloodstone spider, the deep, dark red veining cutting through the fathomless grey stone. The finish was matte, and soft. It felt so warm in her hand. She tucked it back under her chemise, buttoned her chemisette, and drew her neckline closed again.

"Descrying spells are not hard to make. Not much so for those with enchantment skills, however. I don't think this is what he has done. Whatever he's done, it *must certainly* be easily removed if discovered, as Enchanters are not particularly powerful. Destructive, they can be, yes. But powerful?" the old woman murmured. She waved her hand dismissively, unimpressed.

"*I* am not gifted, Ma'am. To me, all that are mage are powerful. Against those things, I have no defense. And I might add that the danger he presents is not his magic. It is his obsession." Iselle's hands fell softly back upon the puff of black fur in her lap. It shifted a little and then uncurled his body. He then twisted expertly, exposing a small patch of hairless, pink skin. The infamous pink belly had been displayed. She scratched it, smiling slightly at the absurd little thing. His little feet were finally visible, complete with tiny paw-pads the color of ash. She touched them with a whimsical smile. Goblin did not mind. He stretched out his little legs and toes and made a little grunt of contentment.

"I see." The Dame's dismissive tone melted into something else. Something graver. It was clear she understood the depth of what Iselle had told her. She shifted in her chair, her fine fabrics and shawl crumpled around her slight, rickety frame. Iselle imagined underneath all these rich garments was little more than a bundle of sticks. "Then you must visit here often. Heecham House might look like naught but sandstone, but all of the external walls are lined within with briny-bricks. You can be at ease here. My uncle was a powerful man. He needed protection."

"I am most grateful, Ma'am," Iselle said.

"Where do you live in town, dear? Mekkahm square? Uldon circus? You seem well-raised, well-turned out, from solid stock…"

"I am not from here," Iselle replied. I am Mirithrian. From a place called Ecklo. I am away from my home, because of the *situation*…" she stopped herself. "I am instead schooling at Arondon On the Hill."

"Now?" the old woman asked. She leaned forward, picked up a tartlet, and served it onto a delicate plate, lifting it and offering it to Iselle. She took it. Her lap-companion, smelling the treat, flipped back over, and sat up, his beady little eyes wistful and his shiny little mushroom slice of a nose twitching. *Goblin, indeed*, Iselle smirked inwardly.

"Don't feed him any of that. It will upset his little tummy," Dame Arwey commanded waving her finger at Iselle. She then shifted her weight. "You are staying at the school with hardly anyone there?"

Iselle nodded. She picked up the tartlet and bit into it. She closed her eyes at the bliss of the flavor, the sweet custard, the fresh strawberries, the crisp, thin, slightly sweetened crust. She ate it in two bites and put the plate back. The pup sniffed her hand for crumbs. The Dame, in the interim, gaped at her.

"That will not do. You must come and stay *here*," she concluded decisively. "You should not be alone."

"Ma'am, you scarcely know me, we have only known one another for perhaps two hours. You should not be so quick to invite me into your home." Iselle was astonished by the impulsiveness of a person who ought be the opposite by merit of her age alone.

Had she told her too much—as to invite the elderly lady's pity? She inhaled and then exhaled loudly and patted the dog's head absentmindedly. There was such temptation to escape the solitude of the school, but she did not wish to be pitied.

"I am not inviting you out of pity," the old woman said. Iselle's eyes rolled up and widened. "My magic overlap in the arts of spectral, black, and psychic skills, my dear. My inner perceptions see a great deal more than what merely what meets the eye. That is how I can see your death cloak. I can also see your purity. Your loss. Your loneliness. Your vulnerability. Your discomfort with the idea of being something piteous. That is not in the slightest the case, my dear.

"I also see a fierce desire to stand up on your own. I suppose it's because you have had few to rely upon to protect you. Except for that little bloodstone token, you received from a sister in the old arts, what help have you gotten?"

Iselle dropped her chin, looking down at the dog. "The professors have been attentive. In my last school, they ensured I remained safe until I was able to escape."

"But he *found* you." Dame Arwey's statement was grim and knowing.

"I was not entirely comprehending then, that the token had to be on my person at all times," Iselle replied. "I have learnt my lesson. It hasn't come off my neck since."

"Does he come to you when your cloak falls?"

"I receive things from him. Enchanted objects." Iselle explained. The old woman stared at Iselle blankly and then said:

"Stay here. We will go by coach immediately and fetch your things. You will come and stay in this house. I will not brook any objection."

"I must consult my uncle first," Iselle interjected.

"Then you will be a guest until your uncle approves for you to be a resident." She got up and clacked her cane across the room to the door.

Iselle suspected that the intent of her patroness was both altruistic and kind, but also a little bit selfish. *Not bad selfish*, Iselle thought. An old dowager, a lonely widow, was perhaps wanting a companion—she desired to help, but she also delighted in having Iselle about. The girl could not deny her motivations were similar. She liked Dame Arwey very much, but she also wanted her company. She felt guilty thinking these things, but the Dame made it better in the coach up to the school.

"I'm not the kind of person who thrives in solitude. I think you are used to it. But perhaps, in this arrangement, we can satisfy our own need for acknowledgement, for conversation, or even silence in company, eh? You mustn't worry about the motivation, Miss Moon. Just be comfortable with the outcome," she told Iselle. The girl nodded in consent.

They had indeed, in that very afternoon, arranged for her to come and stay as a guest.

Uncle Ude was thoughtful enough to allow her to stay for summer—and a serene and comfortable season it was. More than the girl had known since she left home. Since before she had experienced the misfortune of meeting Mr. Lacklow.

There was a tranquility and ease that she experienced in the day to day with the old woman. They would assemble puzzles in the evening together, and Iselle would read novels aloud for them. She took lessons upon the piano forte, and they immediately gave up, for she had no ear for music. Most times were quiet, peaceful—an escape from the constant sense of fear.

They explored the parks; they visited the museums and hothouses of the town. They visited with the Dame's closest circle of friends and some ancient crooked old women that the Dame called her coven. Together they attended concertos and operas. It was the closest to normality the girl had experienced in what felt like eternity. She was not accompanied by anyone of her age. Just old ladies, and the occasional elderly, bent and shuffling gentleman. She made no objections, nor wished for anything more. She was, for this brief, fleeting summer, so incredibly happy.

When school was scheduled to resume, the Dame was most put-out, and asked her to attend as a local, and to return at night as many of the students did. But her uncle's wishes were that she remain under the supervision of the school faculty for the academic year. He wanted regular reports of her wellbeing. He objected to her living permanently with someone he had yet to meet, with no qualifications to recommend her. "Summer is enough," he wrote. "The faculty is equipped to protect and watch you."

Iselle's correspondence with Uncle Ude was kept to a minimum on the off chance there was some kind of enchantment or spell in play that could reveal her location. They also corresponded through his law office instead of his home. He only wrote once after his approval letter for the summer stay. He was concise and spoke with finality. What she had described of the Dame did not suffice for him to entrust her permanently into her care. "She is elderly, and you say mage, but she is also frail. What could a little old lady do to protect you if something happened? Bricks imbued with salt will not be adequate. I apologize, my buttercup, but you must go back when classes resume. You may visit with her on your free days."

And so, she returned to live at Arondon.

Iselle's small respite in the salt-lined Heecham house ended. She moved back into the dorm the day before her seventh year began. It felt different now. Hollower. Lonelier. She moved into a new room.

In this new year, there came fresh faces. One of which was a girl who had come to intern along with the other out-of-town, more well-to-do students. She moved into the girls' dorm the same night Iselle returned.

She was a tall, lanky girl of southern descent with fiery red hair and bright emerald eyes. She was as pretty as Iselle, if not more. She took an instant dislike to Iselle. The moment she saw her in the refectory at dinner, a sneer crossed her face. She sat across from her, ignoring the multitude of empty tables. They neither spoke to one another. When Ywynne, a girl that Iselle knew, who too had arrived early, entered to eat, she sat down with them. The new girl spun up a lively conversation with them, introducing herself as Minnaryth to Ywynne. She made a point of being exclusive of Iselle, who herself did not care much at all.

Iselle was not unaccustomed to this. Girls seemed to sometimes simply hate her the moment they saw her. It made no real difference to her. But she did wonder sometimes in passing what it was that spawned such dislike in her.

It wasn't a need to feel accepted that upset Iselle. It was simply the need to endure the unkind behavior of these bullies.

Minnaryth was particularly mean. At first, she did not speak to Iselle. Instead, she went about the school telling others that she heard Iselle was the daughter of a scarlet woman and an unknown father.

But as the weeks wore on, she was more direct in her attacks. "Stop staring at Endris. It's disgusting how obvious you are. Such a shameless flirt. He's not interested in a lowly parentless trollop like you, no matter how much you try to make yourself pretty for attention."

Iselle could scarcely begin to assume why girls like Minnaryth acted this way. She pitied her, for all her anger. She disliked her for her privilege and her ability to take the gifts she had for granted. To be so free, and so well turned out, and yet to be so bitter and angry. Did she have troubles that made her so? Things too humiliating to speak of? Iselle did not know. Perhaps she was simply too spoilt to know how good her life was.

All she knew was that Minnaryth hated her. She hated that so many eyes followed Iselle—that boys blushed over her. That other girls swooned over the quality of the silk of her garments, her fine shoes. She didn't care that Iselle demonstrated not the slightest interest in any of that. It was enough that this was all somehow taking something away from Minnaryth. She pondered often upon why this girl was so full of ire over Iselle. She could not wrap her mind around it. She could not in any capacity, find any justification for it.

Iselle had only been sitting at a desk, staring out the window. Endris wasn't even in her line of sight. She had centered her gaze directly at Minnaryth, chin resting in her hand, and simply held her eyes there until Minnaryth looked away. She made no expression—no response except overt impassiveness and even boredom, which only served to make Minnaryth even more determined to be hateful.

The Dame asked her how she was faring with her studies and if school was tolerable. "A girl as sweet and lovely as you must have many friends," the old woman said warmly over a meal.

Iselle had accepted an invitation to dine and play cards at the townhouse at the endweek. This was rote, these days. She spent all her free time at the townhouse with the Dame.

"No. I do not have friends. I don't know why. Perhaps I'm not sociable. I lack some skills. I invite cruelty from some. It is especially bad this term. A new girl has come along, and she is insufferable. The things she says to others about me, the way she treats me... She shuts doors in my face and goes by my desk for the sole purpose of sliding everything off of it when she passes. I don't engage her; I don't speak to her. I don't even look at her unless she needs to be challenged. I'm not interested in her."

The Dame laughed at the observation and waved her hand dismissively.

"You are at a mixed school. You are competition, my dear girl. Especially for the pretty ones. They're jealous of your particular beauty. You will draw all the attention away from them. And where there are boys, there will be stiff opposition for their favor."

"I don't care about boys. I don't care about girls. I just want to be left alone." She thought of Ryle, who was truly the only person at the school who was polite and kind to her. He had reappeared at the beginning of the term, volunteering at the library. He was *sort* of a friend, she thought.

"Don't mind them, dear. You are good and kind and you don't need them. You have me." And that was that on the subject, with the Dame.

Iselle had been so careful to always have her talisman on her body, close to her heart, ever a comfort that as long as she could feel its weight on her neck, she was safe.

The moment of mishap came at the very end of the school year. Iselle fell deathly ill; so ill that a physician was called to the school into her dorm. Her fever was so great, the doctor ordered that she be brought down to the icehouse, and for her to be plunged into the meltwater pool to bring down her fever.

She was stripped completely of all of her clothes and her jewelry by the nurses. Her things had been thrown into a basket and set aside.

She was submerged and held there until her skin felt cool to the touch. The ice-bath successfully chilled the fever out of her. For two days after, she was not present or conscious enough to know the situation. When she awoke at last in her own bed, it took more time for her to collect her wits— to be strong enough to take stock of herself.

First, she wallowed in self-pity; for nobody knew she had fallen so seriously ill, and there was nobody who loved her there to see her through it. Her hopelessness sent her into a fugue.

And then she realized her token was missing, and her misery deepened.

The basket with her items was located with her effects within it, and the pendant was restored to her neck.

After a few days of recovery, she was allowed to rise from bed. The doctor encouraged her to go out into the sun and breathe fresh air. She was excused from classes and encouraged to do restful, wholesome things.

She was able to do little of either, and was instead plagued, in her weakened state, by Minnaryth instead. Small aggressions, seemingly harmless, added up with each passing day. An inkpot mysteriously overturned onto a note page left unfinished on the table of the library, an anonymous accusation of theft soon dismissed, rumors of impropriety connected to Ryle, her door kicked deafeningly in the middle of the night.

Iselle's despair, although not outwardly perceptible, was at its lowest she could ever recall, and thoughts crossed her mind that one never ought to think. Thoughts of being free of this loneliness, this torment once and for all. She wept each night and wasted away in her bed. It was not particularly the persecution from the bully that drove Iselle to this dark place. It was the hopelessness of her situation. The fear. The emptiness.

However, a letter like a ray of hope, was delivered to the burnished silver salver, on the tiny shelf by her dorm room door. It was written in Uncle Ude's hand. Unexpected, and much needed. She opened it listlessly in her bed and drew the candle closer to read the spidery script that skittered across the page.

Buttercup, the faculty has informed me that you have been deathly ill. This is most alarming, and that you have suffered alone is even more so. For that I cannot even begin to express my regrets to you. You deserve so much more than what you are enduring in solitude. I have been corresponding with your Dame Arwey, and she will be coming to collect you for the summer. You may stay with her for the season, and for however long you like afterward. She has assured me that you are in hands as able as those of your school's faculty and promises to care for you well. She will come to fetch you on the last day of school. You should remove yourself from the school residence entirely. I have sent some funds to the Dame for your lodging and care, despite her insistence that I do not. The Superintendent is petitioning the crown for aid on the matter of Mr. L. I have looked into shipping companies and have found no such name in the list of owners. We are toiling away at it, my dearest girl. Stay strong, and hope alongside us that you will be home soon. In the meantime, you may stay with the dowager.

Be safe, my child.

Uncle Ude.

Dame and Goblin, the sight of them lifting Iselle's heart, came to fetch her in a stylish open barouche as promised.

Iselle could only sigh with relief as the coach left the drive, where Minnaryth and two other girls were walking. They watched her leave. *At least*, thought Iselle, *I will not have to look at her after classes.*

And so, it was. Until the end of the year, Minnaryth remained only a daytime problem. Without access to Iselle at night, there was more peace. No more sleep disturbances, no more pranks and incursions into her private space. The nonsense was relegated only to the daytime, during school. And those were reduced as well, as the redhead's classes were not aligned as much with Iselle's this year. Iselle only needed to be more vigilant in the shuffle of people between classes, and to find the quiet spots in the shared areas as to not be found—and after all her experiences, she'd become quite adept at finding those little sanctuaries. The end of the school year was in turn tolerable, and after each day, to return to Heecham, even blissful.

The day of the summer arrived with a luxurious ease. Iselle was spared being awoken for the daily morning ride in the coach to school. With a sigh of pure delight, she draped about languidly in her bed on the second floor of the Heecham House. Her windows looked over the quiet street. They had been unlatched and parted to let in the evening air, and the sheer cotton panels with embroidered edges, which shielded her room from the view of the houses opposite, ballooned with a sudden, slightly sultry breeze. Outside, songbirds and magpies peeped and cawed, even over the sound of people and horses on the still marginally quiet street.

Iselle's room was humble in breadth, but the walls were tall, and the ceiling lofted. She had a simple bed of curly maple, a headboard, a footboard, the tops shaped like a recurve longbow, elegant lines, a single five-petaled rose carved into the apex at the centers. The blanket was a quilt of old-fashioned printed fabrics; broadly tessellated floral motifs across solid backgrounds, some with exotic birds and fruits. The pattern was a star that radiated outwards. It was at present rumpled at Iselle's feet, as she had chosen to use only the underlying flat sheet to cover herself. The night had been sweaty and uncomfortable. How she longed for the cool air off the lake at home. The scent of everything green wafting in through the tall lancet windows each summer morning; the shrieks of the peacock intermingling with the titter of little birds. Sometimes the sound of shot, as Uncle Ude and Grimm had gone to bag a rabbit while the mist still hung over the grass.

She rolled onto her side, and just as she did, the door opened and Kattreen entered carrying a small pot of tea and her cup and saucer upon a tray. "I would urge you to rise, and join the Dame for breakfast, but it seems she's decided to follow me in this morning. She's right at my heels," Kattreen said wryly. She was such a slip of a thing, with dark hair and glinting eyes the color of caramel. She was exceedingly kind and comfortable with Iselle. She swept past in her black skirts, to the little table by the window. As she did, Iselle saw the flash of something black whisk across the rug, and Goblin popped up on the edge of her bed out of seemingly nowhere and ran up to her face to assault her with stinky licks on her nose.

"Yeurgh, your breath is foul, little dog," she exclaimed with a giggle.

"I've never seen the little thing take to anyone as well as he's taken to you," Dame Arwey exclaimed loudly, pushing the door wide open and hobbling into the room. She'd told her this several times already. She clacked her cane across the floor towards the girl and the exuberant dog.

"You should rise at once. Kattreen has laid out a lovely breakfast, and after that, we will go to the shops."

"Already?" Iselle whined, throwing her legs over the side of the bed and sitting up. "It's only the first fully free day,"

The Dame had decided that Iselle wanted for variety in her limited wardrobe. She was determined to introduce Iselle to a wider society with girls and boys closer to her age. She told her this over twilight cordials the prior evening, shortly before bed.

"I wish to see you with worthy girls who aren't nasty, jealous little shrews. You should be in the company of quality, properly turned young ladies, because those are your *true* peers. Not the worthless chaff at your school." She sipped the ruby liquid from her tiny, faceted crystal goblet. The drink stained her wrinkled mouth red, which puckered at the taste of the dry wineberry-infused liqueur.

In spite of Iselle's insistence that she wished no such thing; the Dame was enthusiastic and motivated to assist her with elevating Iselle's stylishness and her social circle. It all seemed irresponsible—to have her out so much. She protested.

"I will gladly buy some new clothes, but nothing more, please Dame," she begged her.

"I will protect you from any danger…"

"No, it isn't that. It's that I have no interest in society. I'm young still. There's time for that later. I just want quiet now. A dearth of people instead of a glut. Peace instead of forced conversation," she added in a quieter voice. Goblin jumped onto her lap, and she ran her fingers along his shiny, dense fur. She already feared that there would be a package or some sort of ugly surprise waiting for her because of her time without the necklace. No such thing had occurred as of yet.

"Very well," the old woman exclaimed in a burdensome sigh as if Iselle were depriving her of some delight or another. "We will go to the shops on the morrow. Only a few things…" she assured her. "…and no ballgowns."

They set off to shop soon after Iselle was rousted from her comfort by the old woman and the dog. Kattreen dressed her simply and tidied all the underpinnings that peeked out of her neckline and set her hair up upon her head in a plain, easy arrangement. They descended to eat a hasty breakfast, as the Dame was eager to set out.

Both gleeful and free, Iselle took in a great big breath of summer morning air, and boarded the coach, handed in gently by the footman. Goblin was already happily ensconced on the Dame's lap, the top of the coach was folded down so they could take in the sun, and it was setting out to be a glorious day.

The city was just waking up, and there was already light traffic as they exited their little corner of the residential area and joined the current of movement that flowed along the main street. The coach turned westward. The sky had not the slightest cloud.

It was not long before the barouche landed at a free spot of curb in the Eysthale Centre, where most of the best fashion houses were located in tidy, elegant rows of shopfronts and apartments three or four stories high. All of these were set against a wide walk, and street with smooth cobbles and a brisk traffic of coaches and riders' ceaseless hollow tympani of iron-shod hoofs.

They arrived at a milliner's shop first. There, in the window, Iselle spotted a bonnet of the palest green silk; so pale it was almost white. It had a fluffy ostrich feather the color of raspberries arched over the brim, and a festoon of small fruits and berries in similar values bunched along the crown nestled in small shaped velvety leaves. There were plaid magenta, pink and sage green ribbon cockades at the sides, and matching ties hanging down. She grinned, her air so easy and happy.

"Ooh, Dame Arwey... I want that one!" She pointed at it in delight. They passed through the door excitedly to try it.

The plan was to visit here and then ride to the modiste at the end of the street to have some dresses made to order, to buy some gloves and other sundries. They returned to the barouche, which was waiting only a few steps from the shop front. There was already a heavy stream of walkers and shoppers flowing around them, and the street was thick with riders, coaches, and drays. The noise of it was deafening, and it was a great deal to take in for someone who preferred quietude.

The Dame seemed quite undeterred by it all and forged her way through like a sailboat against the current. Iselle followed in her wake.

Iselle was about to be handed up into the coach after the Dame had been helped into her seat, and the hatbox stowed beside her and Goblin, when she was suddenly yanked away with a small squeal of alarm.

A forceful grip took her arm, and she was dragged into the crowd on the walk, stumbling and tripping on the legs and feet of the people walking. She didn't see that it was him until he pulled her into the archway of a livery that was set back from the walk and the people, and seized her by the shoulders and with violence, threw her up against the wall.

His face was a mask of rage and desperation. "Here you are, you little minx, I have had enough of your evasion! What is it that blinds you from me? What marks have been cast upon your skin to make you unseeable?" He pinned her with his body, and he freed his hands to reach down and lift up her skirts, to expose her legs and thighs, and then her belly.

She shrieked in terror, squirmed, hit, and kicked at him, and that only served to further enrage him. He drew back long enough to wind up his arm, and swung his fist, hitting her so hard, she hurtled to the pavement.

The pain was shocking, and it made her ears ring, and for a second, even the din around her was reduced to a faint ringing. The force of the strike traveled through her skull and stunned her. She was senseless for a brief moment.

Her shriek had drawn the attention of a horseman in the livery, and as Iselle gathered her wits, propped herself up on her hands, she made to crawl away between the legs of the people who were drawn by the cries. She heard a hard smack, only this time, it was Prentiss thrown to the ground.

His eyes immediately locked upon her when he fell. Another man interceded, and they both thrust him down as he tried to stand. They shouted at him and kicked at him. Iselle felt gentle hands fall upon her, kindly pulling her skirts back down, and helping her rise up onto her feet. A middle-aged gentlewoman made soothing sounds at her and took a kerchief from her reticule. Iselle's nose was bleeding, and her cheekbone throbbed. Her tears diluted the blood and ran down her cheeks and chin as she sobbed uncontrollably. She accepted the dainty cloth, and pressed it against her nose, glancing down at the blood that had dripped onto the bodice of her gown.

"Why do you insist on obeying the people who seek to keep you from me?" he screamed at her from his prone position. "You should *not* anger me. You should *not* run from me. I don't know what I'll do if you continue to defy me," he shouted desperately. "I don't *wish* to harm you, I hope you do not force my hand, girl!"

"*Sellemeket heevlak benneteket, oossitek meg eet a zornyeteget!*" The words were made with a forceful woman's voice that sounded familiar to Iselle, but not wholly. There was a quality to it that was foreign. Her eyes, as everyones' nearby, fell upon the Dame herself, so smartly outfitted in her pink roll-printed gown, her cashmere shawl about her shoulders, and tall bonnet—and there she was, arms outstretched, no longer looking small or spindly, but instead was fearsome and infuriated. Like Mrs. Hallwell had been that day.

To Iselle's astonishment, at the utterance of these old words, the small black shape of Goblin that was perched on a pillow on the barouche seat behind the angered old woman, began to swell and grow, like a cloud of viscous black undulating oil, until it was as large as the coach itself, and the blot exploded into a flock of smoky shapes that flew at Prentiss Lacklow like a swarm of enraged bees, winding through the crowd. They enfolded him in their formation, and lifted him, bloodied and flailing, off the ground, and carried him away, screaming over the rooftops of the city.

When Iselle's eyes dropped back down, she saw the face of Minnaryth, who had somehow made her way through the crowd, holding a hatbox of her own. She sneered again. "See what your dirty whorish flirtations bring you? The attentions of such beastly men," she snarled. Iselle's vulnerability melted away, and in its place, fiery defiance materialized.

"You must truly hate yourself so considerably, Minnaryth, to be the kind of person you are. I truly, sincerely pity you," Iselle said gently. "To see what you just witnessed, and for your response to be this…" With a benevolent sweep of the eye, she took in the red-faced adversary who had made her so miserable all year before she circled around her to the coach. After all that had transpired in the past minutes, Iselle was met with a rush of realization; of rationality—that this malevolent harridan suddenly looked simply miserable instead of fearsome, and possibly as alone as Iselle was—that likely, all this cruelty was fueled from powerlessness and dejection. She truly felt sorry for Minnaryth. Sorrier than she felt for herself, with blood drying on her lip, and the salt on her face from her tears.

As she turned away, there was the Dame, who had let her arms fall back to her sides. She looked frail and wispy again, and shuffled to Iselle and took her arm.

"Are you injured?" the old woman asked.

"Nothing that isn't tolerable," Iselle replied, a little beside herself.

She eyed the old woman, trying to see where the power and intimidation that had only just infused her and made her seem invincible, had hidden itself again. But the old woman revealed none of that. She said: "Pull yourself together and get into the coach, my dear girl."

Dame Arwey patted Iselle's hand. "You can remain here no longer, I'm afraid. My Goblin won't kill him or harm him—only provide distance and confusion. But that animal won't be away from you for long if you stay here. I've seen that look in a man's eye before. It is not to be trifled with. We will find other ways to remain friends. I will find you a safe place to stay until we can arrange for you to depart securely."

As Iselle climbed into the coach after the Dame, the swarm of inky bees returned in a graceful murmuration, and they coalesced on Goblin's cushion, once again forming the black, sweet-faced blot of whatever he was; for Goblin was *something*, but he never was just a dog. With a decisive shake of his head, snort and a wag of his little curled tail, barely distinguishable from his dense velvety, raven coat, he plopped his little behind on the cushion, parted his little mouth, his tongue lolled out over his bristle of snowy teeth, and he panted happily, his tiny eyes glistening with what looked like humor.

CHAPTER 11

Forrest was late to breakfast. Ryle said he had left the room early. Outside, the rain was battering the street. The six horses tied outside, waiting for the stage change, were draped in oiled leather and they hung their heads against the torrent, water dripping from their muzzles and manes.

The three were dressed in their common clothes for the journey home. They learned from the trip out, that it would be best to be comfortably attired for long, arduous time inside the coach, sitting and jostling. This was a lesson Iselle already knew from her many travels—but had somehow forgotten this time, in her excitement for the excursion.

The breakfast was a vast improvement to the watery cabbage and pork soup of the evening before. It was ordinary, rustic farm-fare, but there was not a crumb of it that wasn't delectable. The butter was freshly churned, sweet, and creamy, the bread freshly pulled from the oven with a flaky, crispy crust and broad, bubbled crumb within. There were soft-boiled eggs with vibrant, fat yolks, plump perfectly seasoned sausages with mustard, and tiny pigeon pies.

"Mr. Outvallen is going to miss this breakfast if he doesn't return soon," Dorya's mumbled around a mouthful of food. Even Iselle, who still seemed to be lost in a bit of a melancholy, whose eyes were still red and puffy, tucked in greedily. Only a moment after Dorya had spoken, Forrest bustled in through the archway, his hair wet from the rain. He glanced down at the food and seemed satisfied by the sight of it. With perfect timing, the innkeeper's wife arrived with a fresh pot of tea. Forrest sat down, after glancing at Iselle.

"Your eyes are bugged out like a toad," he grunted at her, his wryness just barely detectable. She let it pass, because as the others might think it was Forrest being rude, she saw that it was his dry, prickly humor—it was an effort to provoke her defiance—to make her herself again and lift her out of her despondence. She knew this now, her eyes lingering on his face as he took in the breakfast before him. He served himself and ate.

When they finished eating, the girls fetched their tapestry bag, which Iselle carried and donned their redingotes. They came down the steps just at the toll of the ninth bell. The stage was parked in front, covered in leather tarps, with no passengers inside. The horses hunkered against the torrent. The coachmen were nowhere to be seen.

"Let's get in there," Dorya sighed. "It's best that we didn't return to the temple complex. Imagine touring it in this rain…"

Iselle could only agree. They opened the door to the inn and balked at the pounding rainfall. Dorya bolted for the coach, and opened the door herself, climbing in. Iselle took a deep breath and was about to step out into the rain when a shadow fell over her. She glanced up to see a large hunter green umbrella lofting above her. Holding it was Forrest. He had another one, furled against its cane, clutched under his other arm. "Shall we?" he asked.

Forrest was even handsomer in his common clothes, Iselle concluded. He wore a soft, broad-brimmed leather hat, and a long-coat with three capelets on his shoulders, making them look broader than they already were. The rain beaded off the wool on his left shoulder and trickled off the brim of his hat. The umbrella covered her. He walked beside her and led her to the coach.

The trivial things are more telling than the grand gestures, are they not? They can be such selfish, conniving, and duplicitous creatures. This one is not.

Dorya rolled her eyes at him when he handed Iselle in. "You went out early this morning to buy umbrellas for the few steps between the inn and the coach?" she barked scornfully.

"We have two transfers today," he replied levelly. "I am not amenable to hours of complaints when you are both soaked to the bone and are forced to sit in this coach in wet clothes," he added sharply. She clapped her mouth shut after his retort and flung herself back into the seat and frowned. Forrest climbed in and settled himself and the umbrellas in place next to Iselle.

"Where's Ryle?" Dorya inquired, slightly bitterly.

"He's securing a small hamper for us, so we don't starve this time," Forrest explained. "If we do anything of this kind again, perhaps we can plan it out a bit better."

Ryle's body caused the coach to lurch as he came inside, brushing everyone with rain from his greatcoat. Dorya complained as he shifted about, getting the basket of food stowed away. He took off the coat and laid it on the free space on the bench, sitting across from Iselle. He smiled at her.

"We are better off abandoning our excursion, with this weather," he exclaimed.

"I already said that," Dorya mumbled. "Iselle, you're not wearing the bonnet... did you leave it?" Iselle pushed their bag down under the seat.

"Yes. The innkeeper's daughter wanted it. She would refit it."

"Why did you give it away? You seemed so distraught that it had been damaged," she persisted. "That was far more severe a reaction than one would expect for the loss of a hat. I've never seen anyone cry over one before."

Forrest's chin once again turned slightly towards Iselle, but he said nothing.

"I liked that bonnet a great deal. It's the only one I've kept over the years. I had a special attachment to it. I've had it since Arondon On the Hill," she glanced at Ryle. "It was a purchase I made before I was forced to leave."

"Ah, yes. The much discussed, *mysterious* removal of Miss Moon," Ryle cut in. "There was talk of an attack. I did not hear much detail of it. I had forgotten the hullabaloo that followed your departure. That redheaded girl, oh, I forget her name, would not cease her prattle about it. There was nary a soul she didn't regale the tale to. Even me."

The redhead should have been the one to suffer. I hope her life is a misery.

Iselle remained pointedly silent, biting back anger at her own thoughts. She was startled by the lurch of the coach as the coachmen arrived and climbed all over it in preparation for departure. They verified the passengers' tickets and secured the doors.

"Were you truly attacked? By whom? I've wondered about that. And there was rumor of some rash act of magic. Of you being stripped nude, of all things, in front of countless eyes, and of a man striking you and then flying away. It all seemed like wild speculation rather than truth."

Iselle's brain filled with terrible thoughts. Violent images of ways to make Ryle cease his prattle. She bent her head and pinched her eyes closed.

Shut your vapid mouth or I will kill you!

Forrest was deathly still as Ryle rambled thoughtlessly.

"It was nothing so mysterious or extraordinary. I was robbed, nothing more. I know nothing of magic things or flying men. Minnaryth was a notorious liar, and she was particularly heinous towards me," Iselle snapped out her lie a little too quickly, a little to vehemently, a little too angrily. She bit back the force of her bitterness, the urge to weep searing its way into her eyes. She bit it back.

The coachman clucked his tongue, and the horses began to move. It seemed a miraculous act that this lumbering, heavy stagecoach and its six horses could navigate the narrow streets of this ancient town as it did, but it managed, and soon they were back on the main roads, bouncing and jostling through the muck and the rain, progressing slowly towards Whitewater.

The stage made its first stop after four hours, and while the horses were changed, the group disembarked to stretch their legs, both girls huddled under one umbrella to cross a broad driveway, and Forrest used the other for himself. Ryle wore a hat much like Forrest's and stalked quite comfortably through the downpour. They went into the inn to await the change. There, a young woman also waited to embark with the group. She observed them quietly, clutching a small bag in her lap.

Iselle was morose and ensnared in her own thoughts. It was more than her usual detachment. There was a wrinkle to her brow, and a sorrowful air of disquiet about her. She sat down on the bench built into the bay window, and watched the new horses being lashed to the conveyance. The woman examined her intently; Iselle could see her eyes upon her in the reflection of the window. She turned and confronted the stranger with a glare. The woman only offered a soft, kind smile. There seemed to be understanding in her eyes; for what Iselle could not know.

But as more passengers for the roof seats arrived, and the inn's common space grew crowded, the four decided to return to the coach and wait it out there, and the woman followed. She sat next to Iselle, wedged by the window, and Forrest, as usual, took the spot on her other side.

When the rooftop passengers were aboard and huddled under their collective umbrella cover, the coach embarked on the second stage. With the fifth person inside the coach, the ease and informality of Iselle's conversation with her friends ceased. The stagecoach rocked, and Iselle jostled against Forrest and the woman. She was tired, and even in this uncomfortable state, she nodded off. She felt heavier and heavier, and leaned against Forrest, whose steady warmth further lulled her into sleep.

Her consciousness seemed to fade in and out. The din of the coach, the ring of horses' hoofs on cobbles, the voices and laughter of the rooftop passengers; they were present, but behind a scrim-like veil that sometimes billowed open and allowed the noise to intrude upon her peace. It was within that surging and weakening hubbub; she heard an ominous voice, unsure if it was hers or someone else's.

"Her departure is imminent, and darkness comes in her stead," it whispered. "Don't give in to it quite yet."

The second stage was longer, as one of the horses of the team that was to replace theirs had gone lame, and there were no spare animals to work in its stead at this stage. The passengers disembarked at the waystation, while the coachman and his people sought out a suitable carriage-horse to borrow. They were told to be ready to depart in two hours.

The waystation was an unwelcoming space for the passers-through. There was an area inside, annexed to the carriage-house and stable that had some benches for waiting passengers. The benches were hard, and the space was low, dark, and cramped. Especially with the damp bodies of the rooftop passengers added to the mix.

This was a largish town called Frindil, and the four decided to rely upon Ryle's fine pocket watch, and to use the time it provided to walk around the nearest areas of the city. They were allowed to leave their things in the coach, and were about to set off, when the woman who'd ridden in the coach with them, approached Iselle, and quietly asked if she might accompany them.

She fell in step beside her.

"I should have introduced myself properly to you in the coach, I am remiss," she said in a soft voice. "I am Miss Amma Metrelees," she reached out her gloved hand and shook Iselle's hand. She ignored everyone else. "I would be so happy if you were to allow me to join you on your excursion, and escape this place until we depart again," she asked.

She wasn't much older than the four. She was likely three or four years their senior. She had a serene air about her. She was rather pretty; she seemed terminally shy, a woman with soft reddish-blonde hair, with large green eyes and like Dorya, she had a sweet sprinkle of freckles across her nose and cheekbones. Her garments communicated a woman of competent means, unmarried by how she was turned out. Her wine-colored kid gloves hid any confirmation of the absence or presence of a ring.

Without much ado, she was absorbed by the small cortege, clinging to Iselle's side as the five dodged traffic to explore the nearby shops and market in the broad square. The weather was still soggy, but the rain had stopped for a bit. The cobbled streets were riddled with puddles and slicks of mud from the dissolved street droppings and detritus. The girls lifted their hems and hopped over what they could. Forrest followed like a shadow, the umbrellas under his arm.

Ryle almost immediately deviated to a bookseller shop. The others followed Iselle, until she spotted a stationer's shop with the prettiest storefront she'd ever seen. She could see from the large window that the warmly lit space had a plethora of items of interest.

Iselle couldn't afford to add to her meager possessions. She relied entirely on circulating libraries and those of her schools for books. Stationery, however, always fit in her single bag. She could never get enough of it. It was neither heavy nor bulky, and she loved new writing tools, watercolors and drawing implements and paper. This was therefore one of the few indulgences she allowed herself.

"I want to go into that shop," she declared. "I'll be quick!" The others nodded. They had resolved to stay within the market square so that they wouldn't lose one another. Dorya had no interest in quills and paper and pastel sticks. She went straight for the milliner shop.

Iselle and Amma went inside; Forrest, unheeded, followed like a looming shadow. Inside, the scent of freshly made paper was overwhelming. Iselle's eyes took in the blank bound books, the stacks of different papers and vellums, the large case with stacks and rows of vibrant watercolor pastilles arranged in the spectrum, the drawers of pastel sticks, oil, and gypsum likewise, rainbows on a rainy, dreary day.

There were pots holding shuffles of uncut quills, and a case of quill cutters of metal, but adorned with handles of ivory, ebony, mahogany, inlaid hardwoods, mother of pearl and some were even wrapped in soft stones. These are what drew her first. She wanted to cut her own quill-tips, in spite of already having several such unused, fully prepared writing implements in her room at Whitewater.

The counter was manned by a silver-haired, tall, lean, handsome gentleman with a superior set of pince-nez spectacles balanced on his fine nose. He saw Iselle, and his eyes sparkled, and his initial chilly frown melted away at the sight of her beautiful face. "Good day, Miss. How might I be of assistance to you?" He adjusted his pale cream cravat. His eyes also traveled to the ominous character standing behind her holding two umbrellas and staring at the man with no expression at all, which likely looked scarier than if he were glowering balefully instead.

"I've wanted my own quill cutter. Which do you recommend? And could you kindly demonstrate how I might use it?" She asked this with childlike excitement, which was very much unlike herself. "Quality ones are so hard to find."

"I have an excellent producer, who, as you can see, is most creative in his material choices. Which draws your eye most? I will show it to you." He reached down underneath the glass case and pulled out the tray containing the array of tools. He placed it on the glass, and watched with satisfaction as the lovely creature scrutinized his selection.

Iselle's eyes swept the case, eyeing each piece that rested on the green velvet tray. They kept going back to a cutter of silver-toned metal with handles made with pearl of some kind, shining with mottled deep blue and greens with veins and splashes of gold, dusky rose, and black.

"Ahh." the seller exclaimed as he watched her gaze fall back upon the piece. "That is abalone. It is a shell of a south sea variety, where for some reason, the colors are darker, more vibrant, and intense than others. This is my last one until the next shipment. Here, allow me to show you…" He reached over the tray and plucked the piece up. He opened the clipper side. "The shape of the tip is important. The width of the nib, the taper of the cut. As you can see, this is a delicate, refined shape with a slightly broader tip. And here is the trimming knife," he pointed at the small cutter on the opposite end, where it swiveled out from its little berth. He plucked a quill from a nearby pot. It was a large remige feather from a plum-tipped turkey.

"Now watch me," he said, delighted in her undivided attention.

The feather had already been properly cured and shaped, but the vane and afterfeather wasn't trimmed or styled. He used a shining pair of scissors, and with a practiced, elegant hand, he cut away much of the feather on the lower inner curve and then trimmed the other side into a graceful taper, leaving the arched tip with its deep iridescent plum that edged the greyish black feather. He then shaved any remaining fibers near the shaft and demonstrated how to use the clipper on the tool to create the desired nib, and trim away the unwanted side with a slice of the pivoting knife.

"It will take a bit of practice to get it exactly right. I suggest you take a few of those goose feathers to start. I will give you this, if you purchase the tool today," he proffered the plum tip quill he'd just made.

She nodded decisively.

"Here," he said, "try this first, to see if the width of the nib agrees with you." He took a piece of paper he used for scratch and put it before her with a little pot of ink.

She printed her name, with only one shudder that splattered a little ink. It didn't deter her. She knew how quills needed to be broken in, like most everything else. She had a few she needed to freshen up the nibs, and she decided this is the tool she wanted.

He set it aside on top of a little drawstring bag, and she then flitted off to find other things while Miss Metrelees browsed colored inks and sorted through them. Iselle's eye had been on one of the half-calf journals displayed in tidy rows along the top of the shelves, each type with one facing front for the customer to see. She stepped up on the little stepstool and stretched as far as possible for her small frame but could scarcely touch her fingers to the spines.

She startled when she felt a field of heat wash across her back, and she saw Forrest's large, elegant fingers reach up over her head. His voice, which spoke only inches above her, asked: "Which ones do you want to see?"

"The green calfskin with the gold and red marbled paper," she replied, unable to hide a tremor in her voice. She dropped her hands and waited for him to grip a volume and bring it down for her to see. She took it in her gloved hands, and he withdrew so she could step down from the footstool.

She gave him a faint smile, and bowed her head in thanks, circumventing him shyly to bring her book to the counter.

"This will do," she told the seller.

"I should hire your betrothed, so easily he reaches those top shelves, eh?" the seller laughed. Iselle said nothing in reply, but her face flushed with embarrassment at his assumption.

"That'll be two Silver Troys," the seller exclaimed. Iselle lifted her little reticule designed to look like a pomegranate and dug about for her coin purse.

Amma slid up next to her, clutching a bottle of teal ink. "Your man is truly gentlemanly, isn't he?" she whispered with a smile. She glanced at Forrest, who patiently hung back, waiting by the large window. Iselle felt no need to argue about the assumptions they made about her and Forrest. She thought making a fuss would only further convince them they were right. And truth be told, he was indeed gentlemanly. The most gentlemanly anyone has ever been towards her before. He was attentive, thoroughly thoughtful and kind without demand. *He and his umbrellas*, she thought, hiding a smirk.

The door then jingled and Dorya burst in. "What's taking you so long!? Iselle, there's something I want to show you. Hurry!"

Iselle paid her two pieces of silver. Her purchases were hastily wrapped in brown paper and tied with a carrying string. When that was finished, they followed the exuberant Dorya back to the milliner. She led them all inside, grasped Iselle's arm and dragged her to a wall of box shelves containing a selection of bonnets artfully displayed on turned wood hat stands in each little cubby. She pointed to one in particular, with a joyful look on her face. "See? It looks *so* much like the one you had. It's a little softer, and dustier in color, but the same scheme. The same colorways, similar shape. It even has plaid ribbons. This one is more of a capote that it is a bonnet, but it's so lovely."

It *was* lovely. It wasn't the hat she bought with Dame Arwey that gave her so many happy memories of her summer and school year visits with the old lady. How she missed her and her strange little dog. But the colors and style of the decorations were so similar, she was overcome with a rush of feeling—not simply because of the memories they invoked, but because of Dorya's thoughtfulness and her sweet nature, where she would think of Iselle's so kindly.

"You should buy it!" Dorya exclaimed, interlacing her fingers in front of her chin in unrestrained delight. Her eyes were bright and wide, and her dangling rag curls in front of her ears sprang from her enthusiasm. "I would buy it for you, but can't afford it," she said with a bit of shame.

"You don't need to buy me a hat, Dorya. You are too good," she murmured.

She glanced at Forrest, who was staring down at a display of men's leather gloves, the umbrellas still tucked under his arm. She then looked at Amma Metrelees who stood behind them all, peering shyly at them both with interest with an encouraging look on her pretty face. Iselle turned to find the milliner, who had crept up behind them at some point in the conversation.

"May I try it on?" Iselle asked. Dorya's glee was barely contained, that she had helped Iselle find a new hat. She clapped her hands in delight and hopped a little on her delicate little booted feet.

They were walking back towards the street that led to the waystation when Ryle found them. In his hand, he gripped a stack of four brown paper-wrapped rectangles tied together with string. "What excellent timing," he called out happily, waving at them. He jogged to join the small retinue on their journey back to the coach. His coat swung elegantly behind him.

"Miss Moon, your new bonnet is most fetching!" he declared, walking beside her. The rain began to spit again, and invariably, the umbrella sailed over Miss Moon, and Forrest handed the cane to her, and Amma Metrelees nudged in beside her underneath its cover. He gave the other to Dorya while he and Ryle walked unprotected. His expression had gone from unreadable to irritated.

It was still early, but there was a new horse there, being tacked up with a harness and added to complete the team of six. They were relieved they would be underway soon, and to have returned from their excursion in a timely manner.

They asked permission to load into the coach immediately, and it was granted. They piled in, Forrest once again, thoughtfully handing the women in. He settled next to Iselle, and Ryle sat across from her.

Dorya reached down and pulled out the little hamper they'd brought with them. "I'm famished. Shall we eat something?" She began to riffle through the food items. Outside, another stage rumbled in loudly, halted with a squeal of a brake and a clatter of hoofs, and emptied itself of its small horde of passengers. The filled up the area around their coach, and their voices and noise were deafening.

Ryle fumbled with his purchases while Iselle tucked hers away into her bag from under the seat. "Miss Moon," he began. He pulled one of the packages from the stack and presented it to her. It was the smallest one. She froze; half hunched over from pushing her bag underneath the bench again.

"What's this?" she asked. She straightened, hesitantly accepting the package. Her face must have grown paler, as Forrest scrutinized her.

"A gift," Ryle replied, his chin held up with confidence.

"I…" Iselle's eyes flashed down at the package. "I deserve no gift." Her voice suddenly taught and anxious. She proffered it back to him, but he ignored that.

"Gifts aren't given because they are deserved. They are given to be given. Open it!"

Iselle glanced with trepidation at the packet in her hand, and she pursed her lips into a straight line. Her hand hesitated. Her body stiffened.

Forrest looked on, ever impassive, but watchful. She took a breath and held it. She haltingly loosened the string, and the heavy paper unfurled on its own. She seemed to anticipate something from the act. But nothing happened. She exhaled and took another deep breath.

Her fingers gingerly drew open the edges of the paper and she peered at the contents. It was a tiny leatherbound book with a gold letter title impressed into the cover. *A River's Winding Path – Poetry by Imrid Fall.*

"Fall is a luminary from the turn of the 8th Epoch," Ryle loftily explained. "He's a great poet from my region. His works remain quite popular."

"I see," her voice cracked. "Thank you. It is unnecessary to give me gifts. I feel that I have now been burdened with the obligation to return the favor," she muttered, not realizing what she said might be construed as rude. It seemed to have no effect on Ryle.

"To single out one lady and ignore the other lacks consideration." Forrest muttered, his brow slightly furrowed.

"*You* bought her an umbrella. And besides, I am allowed to demonstrate my admiration of a lady with gifts as I please," Ryle retorted with a touch of ire. His expression directed at Forrest was sour.

"Oh!" Doyra blurted, sitting up abruptly, holding a paper-wrapped sandwich in each hand. "Did I just witness a confession? I think he just confessed!"

"I bought umbrellas because it was raining." Forrest said in a bored, exhalation, crossing his legs and his arms.

"If this is a gesture of admiration, Mr. Ryle, I cannot accept it," Iselle interrupted. She reached out her hand holding the open packet. "I cannot consider such declarations at this time. It is not convenient. And although I do enjoy your company, I am unable to return such feelings." The group was momentarily silenced by her response.

"Iselle, did you just turn him down in front of everyone?" Dorya asked in shock.

"He *declared* it in front of everyone," Iselle replied. "Why would I wait and prolong his misunderstanding of our friendship? I value Mr. Ryle... I did when we were younger, and I do now—but he truly knows nothing about me, even if we have a history at another school. We are different people now. He doesn't know me, and I don't know anything about him. We haven't been acquainted for even a week..."

Being kind with words will achieve nothing. Speak your true heart. Tell him you revile his advances. That he makes you sick to even think of it.

"You have no sense of decorum, my friend," Dorya said ruefully. She patted Ryle's arm compassionately. "Give it time, she might come around."

"I would think as her dearest friend, that you would respect Miss Moon's feelings on the matter," Forrest grumbled.

Dorya scowled at him. "And you, you are a tiresome curmudgeon," the little creature snapped.

Iselle glanced at Forrest, her eyes lingering on his grave features. She then dropped her gaze. Ryle had not taken the book from her hand. She reached out and placed it upon his lap. He looked away, almost pouting like a boy.

"Perhaps everyone is a little tired and curmudgeonly, it's been a long day already and we're only halfway through it," Amma Metrelees said in her soft voice. Her encouragement seemed to fall upon deaf ears.

Iselle gleaned from the fifth cabin passenger, who spoke so quietly, so genteelly and unobtrusively as to not disturb the others who slipped in and out of fitful sleep as they rode along, that she too was to disembark at Rendorff.

"I will gladly meet with you as often as I can, Miss Moon. I have found your company to be most pleasant," she smiled. "I am excessively shy, I'm afraid. I have never been of the sociable type. I can see in you, the same kind of reticence. I feel at ease talking to you."

"That is kind," Iselle said in a whisper.

"Shall we be friends?" Her sweet, open face, her wide-set eyes and shining locks inside her burgundy bonnet were attractive and earnest.

At the next transfer, Amma Metrelees had fallen asleep, and everyone partook of the remaining food unpacked from the hamper, not bothering to exit the coach. New passengers bustled their way aboard and lowered the vehicle on its suspension by the sheer weight of them. This time there was a squalling child that did not stop yowling for at least an hour. By the time the group reached the shabby inn at the exchange, they were downright miserable.

CHAPTER 12

Stonegate at Enderell. She read it from a scrawl of ink on a small card given to her by the secretary of Arondon before her departure. In spite of the scholastic year having ended, the school had taken the time to assist Iselle with the transition.

She clutched it in her gloved hand, her eyes downcast. It was here she was soon to land. The only thing that made this place even remotely appealing at all was that it was located by the Erelin Sea. It sat on a rise overlooking the rooftops of lower-set homes, which were set upon a switchback road that led down to a tiny waterfront city, with a small harbor.

Beyond the seawall, the waters sprawled out as far as the eye could see. There was a busy shipping lane along the coast, and ships, festooned with sails in cloud-like clusters, crawled along the horizon against a boulder-grey sky. She clutched her reticule on her lap and gazed impassively upon the landscape that passed her by, the plaid ribbons of her bonnet catching a gust of sea air through the open window of her coach.

From Haystack to Arondon, from Arondon to Enderell, to an unnoteworthy finishing school and the edge of her world. The idea of it was intolerable to Iselle. It had no true curriculum of any kind. Just subjects that were frivolous and meaningless. The genteel arts are what they specialized in, as the Provost of Arondon had told her before she left.

"You are already an accomplished young lady. Your uncle guided your education well, but it cannot be harmful to be polished. Especially as you come of age."

She rolled her eyes. She didn't want to be accomplished or polished for anyone. She bit back her frustration and tried to keep her composure as they approached the new institution.

The coach brought her around the broad circular drive to the doors of a large manor house and slowed as the horses drew to a stop. To her shock, standing on the steps was none other than Mrs. Hallwell. She stood there, her tan-gloved hands folded primly against her ribcage, wearing her midnight blue redingote with the delicate dagging along the capelet and peplum and two rows around the hem. Iselle had watched Mrs. Hallwell stitch the rouleaux onto the breast and down the front in a delicate leafy pattern. The sight of it made her eyes suddenly sting with tears.

Her tall black bonnet was aflounce with feathers as white as clouds, and her face was delightfully framed by a flurry of ruffles from her cap. Her silver side curls bobbed in the wind.

An involuntary noise rose up in Iselle's throat at the sight of her, and she felt the tears welling up in her eyes. She opened the door and jumped out before the coach was fully halted and without reserve she ran into the governess's arms and began to weep.

"Good gracious, you've grown so. You will be turning fifteen soon, won't you?" She felt the woman's arms encircle her and the heavy reticule on her wrist, that she kept everything imaginable in, thump against her back, which only made her weep more. "Mrs. Hallwell," she said between sobs, over and over again.

"I have come to stay with my family here, as there is nothing to do on the islet in your uncle's employ without you there," she said lamentingly. "He would not release me, as he had it in his mind that this flight would be over soon.

"It was *my* recommendation upon the last letter to your uncle that you come here. I know it isn't ideal for now, but it will allow me to see you and even teach you, since there is little to be found in subject matter here that is useful for anyone with half a mind. There are no schools of note here, this is the best I could do on short notice."

"I'm so happy to see you," Iselle sniffed, leaning back to wipe her eyes with the heel of her hand.

"What a lovely bonnet, Miss Moon!" she exclaimed, her wizened face surprisingly full of joy at the sight of Iselle. She cupped the girl's blotchy cheeks in her hands and gazed happily at her.

"I've missed your face," Iselle bawled anew. "I'm sorry I was so naughty and obstinate!"

"I too missed your face, Miss Moon. And one must expect any young child with such a bright and inquiring mind to want to challenge the existing state of affairs. You mustn't apologize for being what comes naturally, little Miss Moon. Well... Not so little, now. Quite the young lady you are becoming!"

Iselle sniffed, and Mrs. Hallwell lifted her wrist, reached into her overburdened reticule, and took out a kerchief. Iselle took it and daubed away her tears and snot.

Mrs. Hallwell clasped her hands together and tilted her head. "The long-term plan, if all goes well here, is to transition the both of us to a townhouse your Uncle will rent, to finish your education in private. We can be safely distanced from all that wretched misery and employ both of us with a purpose while also keeping *you* safe."

"Will *he* think to find you?" Iselle asked. She avoided speaking his name. She understood how irrational it was to think so, but she could not help but worry that he could somehow hear it if she did and find her.

"He doesn't know who I am or where I am from. Nobody does. Anonymity and insignificance as a poor widow have their advantages," she lamented.

"You are not insignificant," Iselle said in a broken voice.

"Now. Tidy yourself up and try to compose yourself. Let's go inside. We shall introduce ourselves to the lady, and the girls in her care. It is, I suppose, of an advantage that this is not an academic school as there will be others here during these summer months.

"I've secured you your own room, so you won't have to share with *anyone*." She put her arm around Iselle's shoulders and led her up the last few steps to the door. Mrs. Hallwell knocked, and it was quickly opened by a black-clad lady with a bright white mob-cap.

They were ushered into a large foyer, which felt no different than any other entrance to any other large home. It did not feel like a school or look like one. Immediately to their left was a dining room with a long table and eighteen chairs, and to their right a formal parlor, both opposite with the same large doors, which stood ajar. Both rooms were empty of people. There were some sounds of life about the space; some girls' voices from upstairs, and clattering from the kitchen below floor.

Mrs. Hallwell and Iselle were guided past the flight of stairs that poured its landing onto the center rear of the vestibule, to another smaller parlor on the right side of the house, behind the formal space. Inside was a woman of about fifty, with streaks of silver running through her jet hair, giving it a steely grey appearance. She was slender and erect, with her head held high and her chin pointed slightly upward. She peered down her nose at them when they entered, and she rose to her feet.

She wore a silver-grey day gown of silk, with a slight train, meticulously pressed, precisely sewn, with cream-colored lace cascading off her mid sleeves just at the bend of the elbow, and her neckline was filled with a ruched sunburst of a chemisette, with a matching ruff pressing up against the bottom of her sharp jaw. She wore a cap of the older style, with great volume, and dense gathering, the ruffles creating a slight heart-shape around her face. Two large teardrop pearls dangled from her ears. A pearl-crusted chatelaine with myriad tools and keys dangled from the high waist beneath her small bust.

"You must be the infamous Miss Moon," she intoned in the accent of a patrician woman, with precise enunciation and a stiff upper lip— garnished with a passively aggressive lilt of disdain.

"*Infamous?*" Iselle repeated, confused.

"You were sent from an academic school to a finishing school for a reason, I venture. Such a transition is never made without questionable circumstances. Add to that, the urgency of it is troubling as well. Thankfully, you finished your eighth year with excellent marks, according to your former Provost. You will begin your ninth year here. However, I will stress that any defiant or rebellious behavior will not be supporte…"

"I beg your pardon Mrs. Beyz, I must intercede and relieve you of your misunderstanding regarding Miss Moon." Mrs. Hallwell was having none of Mrs. Beyz's prejudice. "She neither incites nor seeks conflict. She was not sent here because she created any difficulties. She is here for her own safety. I will not allow her to begin in her new school with these kinds of misconceptions in regard to her character. She's an exceptional child, with remarkable manners and intellect. This school came highly recommended, and that is why I endorsed it to her family. I do hope that her experience here will not be colored with complications before it even begins."

"I see," the woman's eyes took in Iselle and all her youthful beauty. "I will speak with my secretary for the miscommunication, as she was largely responsible for the intake. As for you, Mrs. Hall, I believe?"

"Mrs. Hall*well*," the governess corrected her.

"Ah, yes. Hallwell. I understand you are to be assisting in Miss Moon's daily lessons and that you have arranged for your own pay on the matter, as we are not employing any additional instructors at this ti…"

"My wages are settled with my employer. I will assist here in a private capacity to supplement Miss Moon's daily academic responsibilities until further notice."

"I do hope you will not have a great many requirements in terms of space and resources. We are limited in our means, and it is already unfair to the other girls that Miss Moon will be receiving special allowances."

Iselle knew her governess well. She had been her instructor since before she could speak. And she was well aware of the signs that she was growing increasingly irritated. "From what I gather from my employer, your school is being well compensated for said *special allowances*, Ma'am," Mrs. Hallwell cut back sharply.

This interaction with Mrs. Beyz did not bode well to Iselle. If it began with this kind of icy exchange, and such predisposition to dislike both Iselle and Mrs. Hallwell, it was indeed discouraging at the onset.

The Lady set her lips into a hard line and submitted, "Very well, then. We will have the girl shown to her room. She can begin classes starting tomorrow. She can come down at the sixth bell, and join us all for dinner, and for introductions. You may return at the ninth morning bell. That way you can familiarize yourself with Miss Moon's daily itinerary. Off you go with Ms. Rands then, girl. Good day, Mrs. Hall."

"What a deeply foul woman," Mrs. Hallwell hissed as they left the room. "We will expedite the townhouse and get you out of here as soon as possible, dear girl."

Mirianne was an amazon of a girl, tall, with a solid, imposing, and muscular frame which in no way took from her feminine beauty. She had the appearance of a warrior, with broadly set eyes of leafy green, set in a prettily heart-shaped face with a narrow, dainty chin and the tiniest, prettiest, pert little nose. Her hair was as black as Iselle's but like skeins of pressed silk, catching the light with values of blue and black, like a raven's feathers. She towered almost two heads taller than Iselle. She was a strange creature—a curious one, with a particular fascination with Iselle the moment she was introduced.

She had been chosen to give Iselle a tour of the house, to show her the classrooms, the garden, the dormitories, and the kitchens. She interrogated Iselle as far as she could muster given Iselle's predilection for stonewalling. But her interest in the new girl was cemented from that initial moment, and she dedicated her following days to shadowing Iselle.

On a morning where Iselle emerged from her room wearing her hair styled as she often liked, with a milkmaid plaited crown, the rest of her hair hanging free behind it, Mirianne saw her, and by the time Iselle arrived at breakfast to join the other thirteen girls, Mirianne too had a milkmaid braid like a diadem around her head.

In the middle of the second week, Mirianne asked to be included in the sessions with Mrs. Hallwell, expressing a sudden interest in mathematics and language arts. She spent the day throwing little tantrums when she was denied this by Mrs. Beyz. She bullied two girls and threw another's pencil bag across the room for no other reason.

If Iselle wore a tucker or a fichu, Mirianne did the same. If she wore a sheer overdress, or a roll-printed gown, or a jumper, Mirianne did so as well. After a month, it became tiresome for Iselle, who preferred to be mostly left alone. There was something unsettling about the whole matter. Iselle had been told that imitation was flattery, but Iselle only felt as if her identity, which was already so squashed by her current situation, was being pillaged. For what reason, she could not know. It caused her increasing anger and discomfort with each passing day. Why would she want to be Iselle? Why could she not go and frame out her own identity and leave Iselle alone?

The other girls were rather standoffish of her to begin with. Adding to that, the most noticeable character amongst the girls turning all of her attention upon the newcomer, taking out her frustrations upon them for things that were connected to Iselle; it made for a less-than-stellar situation for the newcomer, who already did not like this school.

The teachers were vapid and artless, fixated upon nonsense instead of ideas—upon appearances over substance, and who took no interest in the brightness in the eyes of the intelligent, sharp girls who sought and deserved so much more than what they were receiving. This school was a fading vestige of a different time. Iselle hoped it would die out as soon as possible and she would be free of it.

Mrs. Beyz was another matter altogether. The widow was an insufferable snob, who was clearly someone who abhorred youth and children, but who had no other recourse to maintain her home and the lifestyle she preferred, by opening it up as a finishing school. She could not keep her home without her husband to fund it. She was an angry, bitter woman, disposed to distrust and dislike anyone who was not deemed worthy in her eyes. It seemed as if the only people she valued were pretentious, lofty people like her. Some of the acquaintances that floated through during Iselle's time at the institution alluded to a time when Mrs. Beyz was not like this.

After Mrs. Beyz had rebuked and ridiculed Iselle in front of the girls and the guests, for not knowing how to play at the piano forte, she was reassured by one of the visitors.

"She's always been a bit of a social climber," the husband of one visitor whispered to Iselle that evening in the parlor gathering, "but she was not always so insupportable and soured. She had hoped for a better situation, but the loss of her husband, and his ill-management of the estate had prevented such a thing and forced her to make do. Do not take her sharpness to heart. It isn't about you or any of the girls. It's founded in her own self-loathing," he said. And then he proceeded to clap lazily when Miss Orbry concluded her display at the instrument.

The discovery that both Iselle and Mrs. Hallwell shared was that it seemed Mrs. Beyz hated all the girls, not just Iselle. Her sharpness and biting remarks were not restricted to her. She accused without foundation, assumed guilt without evidence, and thought the worst of any one of them, regardless of how well-behaved and turned out the girls were. She simply did not like any of them. The feeling, universally in the house, was wholly, and unreservedly mutual.

It made for a deeply hostile atmosphere at Stonegate. It made facing each day a trial. At least at other institutions, Iselle had academics and learning to focus upon, even when things seemed hopeless. Here, she had nothing except for Mrs. Hallwell. She wanted to leave this place as soon as possible.

The process of finding a suitable house unfortunately took longer than anticipated, as Enderell, being a fairly well-to-do seaside town, was a desirable location, and there were few homes that were of quality to let. The lack of housing might have presented a little bit of a challenge for the ladies, but there were at least some distractions in the interim.

Iselle was finally able to meet Mrs. Hallwell's family. Although they were not wholly immersed in poverty, they lived quite modestly.

Mrs. Hallwell described their little 3-story city house, which was wedged between a saddler's shop, and a grocer. She said it was noisy from first light every day, horses clattering up in their steel shoes, the grocer's shouts, people standing in front of their narrow house at all hours talking loudly. The tiny sitting room was only a sheet of glass panes from the street, and even with curtains there was little privacy from the throngs walking by. The rooms were low, and the stairs narrow and steep. There were no servants, there was only the family. There was no chair for Mrs. Hallwell to sit in at the tiny dining table in the room off the stuffy kitchen. She would wait to eat when the family was finished.

The sleeping situation was particularly troublesome. Mrs. Hallwell shared a room with her sixteen-year-old niece who was less than pleased to have her share her small room and the humble bed therein with her aunt.

Mrs. Hallwell did not speak of it the day Iselle set out to visit with them, but there were hints in the conversation as her niece gazed dourly and accusingly at Iselle.

The family had taken great pains on their appearances, donning their finest for the excursion that had been planned. Iselle had invited them to take tea at a large glass-house aviary by the sea, where there was also a tea-room where patrons could sit and watch the myriad colorful birds flit about the vaulted space and light upon the mature trees enclosed in the elegant filigree of iron and glass.

Mrs. Joons was a frail, wide-eyed woman, whose poor upbringing made her especially retiring and shy in the presence of the fourteen-year-old poised and elegant Iselle.

Mrs. Hallwell's brother, the patriarch of the family, was slightly older than the governess, and looked remarkably like Mrs. Hallwell, complete with the same disaffected dissatisfaction with everything and anything. When they stood side by side, both gazing with the same face, unimpressed at the rainbow of feathered creatures fluttering about before them, Iselle could scarcely keep herself from laughing.

Accompanying the parents were the three daughters, Miss Evleen Joons being the eldest and the one who was beset upon by her aunt's presence. Then there was Moria, who was nine, and Halline, who was four, and in Iselle's estimation, the best of all the Joons. She, like her mother, was immediately deferent to Iselle in her fine clothes and handsome bonnet. But it wasn't a submissive kind of respect, it was an adoring one. When they met outside, and introductions were being made, Iselle felt a small hand insert itself into her gloved one, and she peered down to see a small, beaming face peering back up her with broad, bright eyes.

"Well, hello, little Halline." Iselle said.

"H'lo." She radiated a broad, toothy smile. She was so preciously adorable.

She did not let go of Iselle's hand at all until they were seated around a broad table, and the child's eyes were distracted by the birds. She kicked her little feet while she ate her hot cross bun and sipped her tea from the cup while gripping it with two hands. Iselle was wholly convinced there was little else in this world as sweet as this child.

What was evident from this meeting was that Mrs. Hallwell was a disruption to their family routine, an encumbrance on the wellbeing of the family, an obstacle to the peace of the marriage, and the eldest girl was deeply put out by the intrusion in her life. She made passive aggressive comments about how eagerly she hoped her aunt would return to gainful employment and her independence, veiling it as a desire for her aunt's happiness rather than her own. The insult to injury of it all was that Mrs. Hallwell was indeed well-compensated for her work with Iselle, and she contributed generously to the household finances; but that was not enough to quell their collective discomfort with having an intruder in their small, humble home. Iselle felt quite sorely for Mrs. Hallwell. *How uncomfortable it must be for her*, she thought.

Iselle took mental note of it all, and was insistent in her letters to her uncle, that they find a house for them as soon as possible. Mirianne's strange obsession with her was also weighing upon her mind, and she was growing increasingly uneasy with the fact that she waited outside her door each morning and shadowed at her heels at every chance.

The house agent was diligently doing their work, but nothing had come up that was suitable for the two ladies yet. For now, Iselle was resigned to remain at Stonegate, to be plagued by Mirianne, and Miss Joon and her family were left with their current dissatisfying situation indefinitely.

CHAPTER 13

The failed excursion opened Iselle's eyes to one especially important fact. There was something inherently different about Forrest. There was some unidentifiable quality that made his presence unthreatening to her. Although he was as prickly as a hedgehog, and his personality was stiff and indifferent to her, layered upon that, there was a casual attentiveness that seemed both directed and undirected. He made it rote, to open a door for her, to cover her with an umbrella, to hand her into a coach, to reach for things outside of her grasp, to be attentive without being attentive. It wasn't affected. It wasn't performed to impress as would the acts of other men; it was simple consideration for a person he chose to recognize as deserving of it.

The more time she spent with him, the less wary of him she became. His attention was undemanding, even comforting, especially after his gentle, nurturing actions at the temple.

He took his meals with Dorya and Iselle. He remained mostly quiet, but his acts of consideration continued, even if sometimes they were accompanied by acerbic criticism or irony to keep up his façade of ambivalence. If he was nearby, he opened doors for her and assisted her with her chair when sitting to a meal, if he arrived before her. He walked a step or two behind them if he was disposed to do so. He became a looming but protective presence to Iselle. She wasn't quite sure how, but he had somehow insinuated himself into her life and she could find no solid objections to it.

This bothered her to a degree, because she never invited him, he appeared entirely on his own, and changed everything he did routinely to do so, confounding all of his friends and acquaintances. And most befuddling of all, was that this behavior from any other man would be alarming to Iselle. But Forrest managed to do it all and still be unthreatening. The more she mulled it over, she concluded she simply did not understand him or his behavior, but she accepted it, nonetheless.

Just that very morning, Iselle came out of her classroom and was assailed by the attentions of a freshly new student, a young man in his final year.

"Well, hullo, Miss…" he said, his bright hazel eyes and rakish hair, along with a squared and chiseled handsome face and perfect pearly teeth, likely lent him the confidence to approach her as he did. He looked at her expectantly, awaiting her name. She simply turned away and continued walking.

"My name is Theade," he declared, stumbling after her. "And you are…"

"Disinterested," Iselle replied curtly. He was not deviated by her coldness. He continued to follow her. She continued walking, shrinking away from the fellow with increasing trepidation and fear.

"Miss, wait a moment…" he reached up and hooked his hand upon her shoulder, and faster than Iselle could pull her shoulder away, there was Forrest, with his hand slapping Theade's violently away from her body. The force of it made the man stumble a few steps. He immediately squared to Forrest, who seemed to grow and widen, his ears growing red and his face setting into hard lines and a rippling jaw.

"Best you keep your hands to yourself," Forrest growled. "Where did you learn that it was acceptable to touch a lady you don't know? Were you raised by vulgarians?"

Forrest's only close friend, Meddin, came darting from somewhere, right into the middle of the small but prickly exchange and moved his body to make a barrier between them. He lifted both his hands and smiled amicably, but his warning was not so much: "I don't know who you are, my friend, but you best not stir up this walking bees' nest. You need not discover first-hand why this man has a terrifying name at Whitewater. I say this for your own good," he said laughingly, but also quite seriously.

Theade's eyes assessed Forrest, whose demeanor was still just a hair's breadth away from jumping on the fellow and pummeling him to pulp. Everyone but this young man knew of Forrest's fearsome repute at the school; of his multitude of brutal interactions with other young men, where he would leave them deeply injured. He fought like an animal, thanks to his father's oversight. And his temper with other young men was paper-thin.

He was normally passive and still; but he was always on the simmering edge of aggression; one breath away from it if it was called for. Accompanying Miss Iselle about the school; his presence around her continued to deter other young men. But this day, a new student needed to learn a lesson that the others already knew.

Iselle had experienced possessive aggression over her before. That was for certain. But this was not possessiveness. This was someone who knew she was deathly afraid of men, and who was shielding her from them. Protecting her peace of mind. And for that, she was immensely grateful to Forrest.

Ryle's presence diminished significantly after his failed confession. His fervor for academic pursuits alongside Iselle had disappeared along with his presence in the little cadre of friends. He had not returned to spending time with them, and instead, Forrest's friend Meddin slid into the little group, and showing, in Iselle's opinion, some measure of interest in Dorya.

He first came a week or so after their return. They were planning to take tea in the University's common room when he almost materialized like a ghost behind them as they walked from the quad on a brisk day. The sun was shining, the sky a sharp blue, the air was frigid and there was the sense that it might snow once the clouds came in. Iselle hoped so. She loved snow. It reminded her of home. She hoped for it every day.

"I heard you all set out upon an excursion," Meddin's voice startled the three. They stopped to turn 'round and look at him. "Why didn't you invite me, Forrest? Am I not your closest friend?" he asked.

"Who told you that you were my closest friend? It wasn't me." Forrest replied. He then began to walk again, and the girls took the cue and went ahead.

Meddin brushed off Forrest's words and fell into a pace beside him. "I would have liked to go. Nobody asked me. In fact, you've been nowhere to be found of late, and everyone says you're hanging about these ladies. No disrespect to you, ladies, of course," he added.

The girls gave him assenting nods and then glanced at one another.

"You're not the type to participate in these kinds of excursions or whatnot. I might have been greatly amused seeing you with these lovely ladies. And that fellow, the Natural Arts practitioner... the one with the middling skill and a predilection for parlor tricks..."

"Ah, you mean Ryle Kloze," Dorya exclaimed, nodding.

"Yes. With Mr. Kloze. I cannot see you tolerating that sort of mediocrity for any measure of time." Meddin blathered. He gripped his hands behind his back, his class robes rippling on his long legs with each stride. Dorya had to lope every few steps to keep up. "I can do summoning magic. Let that untalented buffoon try *that* kind of magic, I say. We can all have a good chuckle." Faced with no response, he continued.

"I refuse to be excluded, and demand compensation for being snubbed for an inept parlor magician!" he insisted.

"Then we should go off campus this endweek. This time for something diverting and joyful. No pointless scholarly pursuits! The weather might cooperate. There's a fine park attached to a great house only a few miles from here. We can pack a picnic, and go walking," Dorya suggested.

"Yes! We should go!" Meddin wholeheartedly exclaimed. He laughed merrily at the suggestion. He nodded in approval to Dorya, who blushed and giggled.

Iselle thought on it for a moment and then said: "I cannot deny the appeal. It would be nice to dress in our own clothes, and enjoy the nice weather before the winter gloom fully sets in. No prolonged coach journeys, no rain, no bickering. I would say we would delay it a week or two, to recover from this last misadventure. But we don't have many opportunities for bearable weather to choose from. We already had so much rain last week."

"The sage predicted cold sun until the end of next week. Then the rain sets in." Meddin added.

Iselle climbed the stairs to the main hall, and Forrest preceded her to pull open the large door, allowing them all to pass before him. The place was chockablock with students just freed from their final classes of the day, gathering to take tea, and enjoy their free time before dinner.

The group made for the mixed common room left of the main vestibule to sit in one of the various clusters of worn leather chairs and scuffed tea-tables. They chose one little gathering spot far from others near the rear fireplace. It was here where they had ordered their tea to be delivered. They warmed their hands by the small fire, which was devouring the dry moss on a recently added piece of oak. It snapped and popped soothingly.

Iselle thought about inviting Miss Metrelees to this planned picnic, but she supposed her calm, timid nature would not mix well with the general mood as there was a strong vibrant excitement amongst them. At least with Dorya and the exuberant Meddin.

Don't invite nobodies.

She had yet to make a visit with her new friend as she had promised. Amma had said she would send a card with directions soon and had not yet done so.

"Should we invite Teena?" Dorya suggested. She was a playful, kind girl who often sat with the two girls in Risk Analysis, one of the few classes Dorya and Iselle shared. It was primarily Dorya who fostered the friendship, but since the two girls were so often together outside of class, it was inevitable that occasionally, their company included this plump, red-cheeked, cheerful girl.

The school's server arrived with the pre-ordered tea settings as they had planned, alongside other orders crammed on the cart. She wheeled it to them, and the server began to distribute the food and teacups around the low table.

"In that case, we should invite Dellan as well," Meddin said conclusively. "We cannot have one chirping bird without someone else eager to listen to it." He bent down and began to pour the tea before the server had finished putting the tiered platters and large plates full of buns and sandwiches.

He had not been invited to join them, but he took the extra set of dishware, a cup and saucer and silverware from the cart from someone else's order and had successfully infiltrated the gathering. He moved a chair over from another grouping of seats and sat down to enjoy the meal with them, while the server slowly laid out the food.

Iselle leaned back in the chair she had chosen and positioned herself comfortably in and pictured the coachful of people cheerfully riding along in the chill of late autumn with the top parted in two like a book and folded down; everyone flushed from the chilly air and excitement. She could scarcely keep herself from grinning like a delighted child.

How thrilled she was at the idea of joining a party of young people to do something diverting and indulgent. She had dreamt of this so often; having been left behind so many times by other groups of friends at school, while they went to picnics and card games, on long horse rides, to country dances and balls in little knit groups. Her experience with friendly company was limited to the Dame's social circle, which were mostly elderly and impaired—to her quiet moments with Redlan, or the ones shared during theater class. She could scarcely withhold her excitement as they planned. Like Forrest, she was outwardly calm and watchful. But inside, she was brimming with glee.

"The place can be boisterous sometimes, as the Imridan college is all male, and also within riding distance." Forrest murmured.

Iselle brushed one of the curls that hung loose on the side of her face behind her ear. "I suppose we merely assumed *you* would be accompanying us too. Forgive us if we presumed too much. However, I would think with *three* gentlemen present in our party, we would not be subject to too much interference by others. But if you do not wish to join us..." She glanced down at her hands. She continued timidly before Forrest could mumble an answer.

"I want to go *very* much. I've never been on this kind of excursion before. I've never had a circle of friends with whom to share things like this," her words were halting and lacking confidence. Vulnerability was not something she demonstrated often in her rare interactions with people. She put up a mask of haughty indifference on most occasions, or stubborn defiance when it came to Forrest. But she had started getting used to him. It worried her, because she'd never felt that way around a man, but there it was.

"If I am wanted, then I will go," he allowed gently, he looked upon her from the sides of his eyes as he picked up a teacup and drank. Meddin reached out and liberated the cart of two more plates of treats just before it was wheeled away and they all tucked into the food and tea.

"Then it's settled," Dorya exclaimed, giving a little hop of delight in the chair she'd chosen. She gripped a tiny cake, which had a perfect little crescent-shaped bite out of it. She looked brighter than she'd been in a while. "At the 10th bell tomorrow, let's meet in the cloisters." Her eyes twinkled with pleasure. "I'll work with the kitchen to supply the meal. We only need a hamper, a rug or two, and a carriage of some kind, to carry those things and the lot of us."

"We can use my Landau from home. I can secure a driver," Forrest said between bites of plum cake. "We will need blankets for the coach, it will be bracing."

"Consider it done!" Meddin said. "I'll bring some diversions."

Forrest, as impassive as always, watched Iselle. Amid the air of good humor, his eyes softened at her easy, reserved smile and exultantly sparkling eyes.

On the most part, her unpleasant, intrusive thoughts, her hidden rudeness, were quelled by these happy plans. For that, she was relieved.

Forrest stared, incredulous, at Iselle. He'd never seen her like this. He was without words. This was unfamiliar and terrifying territory for him. Iselle was frozen with terror. Her face was ashen and her hands trembled.

"It's gone. I've lost it…" she whispered. There was a frenetic, almost panic-stricken desperation to her voice. "What will I do?" The expression of loss and bewilderment on her face cut right into his heart. She then proceeded to weep again, utterly despaired, hiccupping and sobbing both. He watched from the coach as Dorya led her to the dormitory, with Teena scuttling behind them with an expression of concern upon her brow. Miss Moon was crying all the way back to her dormitory, and her hand had been trembling when he took it to help her down from the coach.

Her fear and distress had stunned him—washed over him like a great wave and drowned him in her emotions. He had always remained respectful of her feelings. He had stayed out of her head. But these emotions were too strong. Too powerful to be contained and they swept out of her like a deluge and carried his rational mind away.

Only now, as her inconsolable feelings receded from his mind, could be take stock of what happened. As they rode the conveyance back to the livery, Forrest gazed with puzzlement into the ether, deconstructing what he could recall from the flood of emotions.

"What could possibly be so important about a trinket?" Meddin snorted in confusion. "Dorya told me she wept over a bonnet. I cannot fathom why the loss of a little bauble would evoke such grief. Is it normal for women to have so great of an attachment to paltry things?"

Dellen looked on in uncertainty. Forrest did not offer Meddin the dignity of a response, and he jumped down from the landau before it turned onto the drive leading to the men's dormitory and headed for the livery on foot.

It was already half past three. It got darker sooner, so he didn't have much time. It took him only a few moments to hoist a saddle onto the back of his horse, girth it up, and strap the bridle onto its head.

He was moving off the campus and back towards the park at a gallop only moments later.

The morning had started off so splendidly. They met at the cloister as planned. He had been so struck by how lovely Miss Moon was in her own wardrobe. She was appointed in a sheer white round gown with a sky-blue linen underdress, with a sapphire ribbon tied around her high waist.

She had her new hat on, shading her face over an organdy ruffled cap with a veil as light as air over it. A chemisette with a small ruff filled her neckline and encircled her neck. Her hair was gathered up under the cap, and a few locks of her hair hung down on each side of her face. Her boots were dark slate blue. She clutched her little reticule that looked like a pomegranate. She drew on a little wool spencer jacket the color of night with bronze buttons onto her arms. The peplum flounced at the mid-back when she walked. She looked like a fashion-plate from the magazines. Perfection.

He did not see anything else but her. The rest of the world faded away. Not even Dorya's effusive chatter with Teena could draw his attention away from her.

The coach arrived almost immediately, and Forrest handed her and her friends onto it before loading up the rug and hamper of food.

The ladies settled in on the forward-facing seat, and the young men took the opposite. They soon set off. Meddin was cheerful and expansive, capturing the ladies' interest, regaling them with absurd stories of Forrest and his rudeness and coldness being a shock to one person or another, of a few of the fights early on that cemented his reputation as a hellion, while Dellan sat grinning. Miss Moon seemed more interested in the landscape; the falling leaves, the pine-scented air, and the flocks of sheep in the brown-mottled fields as they departed from greater Rendorff and headed to the park.

It was a cool, dry autumn morning, as the sage had promised. Iselle caught Forrest's eye once again. She even gave him what was just the wisp of a smile. He seemed as impassive as always outwardly. Inwardly, his heart felt warm and happy.

It was about half-hour on the main road and another few moments on a long drive before the walls of shedding trees gave way to a manicured lawn with a trout pond in the backdrop. There were groves of oak, chestnut and beech, some ash and the road were lined with towering poplars. Far in the distance was the great house that belonged to the park nestled in the cleave of two small hills.

They chose a spot by the pond, and the coachman helped them unload their sundries and lay them out on the rug under a broad beech tree. He then withdrew to wait with the landau on the road.

Meddin produced a shuttlecock set from the supplies they brought. They took turns using the two racquets. Iselle was quite terrible at it, but she actually laughed and squealed several times when the birdie flew at her and she strived to hit it back. Her cheeks were flushed and her alluring eyes gleamed with delight.

They circled the pond as a group. Dorya, in her red gown and mustard boots, gingerly scuttled about the water's edge to catch a frog, which she did, and displayed with unfettered delight. Miss Teena squealed and ran away, hiding behind Forrest, who only stepped away from her when she came too close.

"I shall name him Grog," Dorya declared, holding the frog up high. In a flail of frog legs, Grog made his flying escape, landing with a plop in the watery bank of the pond.

"Oh Grog! You've abandoned me!" she cried. They ended their journey under the tree, sinking onto the rug, and opening the hamper to liberate it of its charge.

A bottle of cider and another of strawberry cordials were uncorked and served in thick glass goblets. They partook of cold pork pie with mustard, the creamed cheese, goat's cheese, watercress and brined salmon sandwiches, wheels of rice stuffed with pickled vegetables and braised beef, hard cheese and sliced smoked sausage. They ate from delicate plates. They devoured scones with jam and small iced cakes.

There was one last rousing game of blind man's bluff before they packed up.

They rode home in pleasant conversation all the way to the edge of the Whitewater campus, until Iselle's hand reached up to her neckline, and she froze. She gasped and began to clutch frantically at her decolletage.

"Where is it?" she asked, eyes washed with alarm.

"Where is what?" Miss Teena replied.

"The bloodstone widow!" Iselle exclaimed; her eyes glassy. "It was around my neck. It's always around my neck…"

"I didn't see a necklace…" Dorya said. "Perhaps you forgot it in your room."

"I wear it *always* under my garments. I must have lost it when we were playing. Or walking." Her glistening eyes welled up and tears fell onto her cheeks. This was something Forrest was unprepared for. Empathy had never been his strong suit, but when it came to Iselle, all those rules meant nothing. The sight of her tears constricted his heart and sparked something inside him. He wanted to reach out and pull her into his arms and soothe her. He could not see her suffering. He wanted to do something—anything to make her at ease again. The sight of her weeping was too much to bear.

"We can go and look for it upon the morrow," Dorya assured her, not recognizing the depth of Iselle's anguish. Iselle looked *anything* but assured.

CHAPTER 14

"What is that?" Mirianne asked, pointing to the dark lump underneath the thin fabric of Iselle's nightgown. She had pulled on her dressing gown and padded in her soft tapestry slippers towards the kitchen gripping her single candlestick. She was thirsty and had emptied her carafe. Mirianne heard her door open and immediately exited her room to accompany her. They walked in the weak, yellow light of the sconces, which had yet to be extinguished by the chamber maid, and that of her candle.

"Oh, it's a gift from my uncle," she replied distractedly. She kept walking.

"May I see it?" Mirianne asked. Iselle toyed with simply saying no, but that would only seem odd and excite Mirianne's curiosity even more. She quickly lifted the chain to expose the little bloodstone spider. Mirianne's eyes widened.

"It's so pretty, but unusual. I've never seen a piece of jewelry made to look like a spider!" she exclaimed. Iselle tucked it quickly back into her neckline.

"It's just a charm my uncle secured from a Sacred Order priestess, it's supposed to bring me good health and fortune," she explained. "I really only wear it because it reminds me of my uncle whom I miss dearly," she lied.

Mirianne nodded and in the shadows, her face soured a little. "My father would never gift me something like that. He doesn't care if I live or die. He was itching to send me away first chance he got. He doesn't like any of us children," she sighed woefully.

"I cannot imagine," Iselle began but didn't finish. She glanced at Mirianne from the side of her eye. "I only have my uncle. My parents aren't here anymore. And I have no near family. As pathetic as that sounds, being deliberately sent away must be much worse," she added. She could see Mirianne responding to the empathy with a shine of tears filling the brim of her eyes.

"Yes, it is difficult to not be wanted." She sighed again, this time tremulously.

"May I ask about your mother?" Iselle ventured.

"I don't talk about her much. She is there but she isn't. There's something amiss with her. There always has been. Father said a brain fever made her the way she is. My eldest brother said it's because my father struck her."

Iselle was appalled. She was irritated by Mirianne's fixation upon her, and her desire to become her. It reminded her of Prentiss, but in a less lascivious way. But she now understood a little, perhaps, why Mirianne was the way she was. She bowed her head and stared at her hand gripping the candlestick she carried. "I am sorry, Mirianne."

"It's not your fault, you have nothing to apologize for," she sniffed. She used the back of her hand to wipe the tears from her eyes.

They went into the kitchen, where they found Imilla, the chamber maid, and she poured them some boiled water from the urn and sent them packing. "Be quick, I will be snuffing the lights in the hall soon," she called after them.

Mirianne went back to her room, and Iselle retreated to her own, and she drank her still steaming water, blew out her light and went to sleep.

Morning came with the bell. Iselle rose and washed her face and toweled it off. She drew off her nightgown and made her way to the chest, where a small pile of shifts was folded in the drawer. She shook one out and pulled it on, and at that moment, she realized something was wrong. Something was missing.

It was the weight of the chain on her neck. Her hand flew up and slapped the front of her chest where it ought to be, but nothing was there. A wash of panic befell her, and she threw on her dressing gown and ran out of the door. She retraced her steps from the night before, but nothing was to be found. She ran back to her room and searched the floor and under the bed and furniture, but again she found nothing.

She repeated her path to the kitchen and back once again and came upon Mirianne who was exiting her room. She had a peculiar look upon her face, seeing Iselle so panicked and disheveled. "What is it, Iselle?" she asked, crossing her arms.

Iselle straightened from her hunched posture, as she had been scrutinizing every inch of the rug, and under the demi-lune tables by each door, the salvers for calling cards and notes upon them. She stiffened at the look in Mirianne's eye.

"I've lost my necklace," she said measuredly, her head turning slightly, but her eyes fixed upon Mirianne's face.

"Oh dear," Mirianne said exaggeratedly, "wherever could it be?" She placed her fingers lightly on her chest in what seemed like feigned shock. She then turned silently and strode towards the stairs. Iselle was certain she saw a little satisfied smirk on her face as she turned away.

"I would think it ought to be said that to make such an accusation is very grave, Miss Moon, yet you continue to make it, and there is no evidence of your claim," Mrs. Beyz articulated with a sharp, unforgiving tone. "The room has been thoroughly searched, as well as all of Mirianne's private effects, and it has yielded nothing! Why must you insist on perpetuating this grudge against Mirianne? Have you no consideration how this might adversely affect her?"

Mrs. Hallwell's already angered face only grew redder at the immediate idea that Iselle was fabricating anything. Mrs. Hallwell understood the risks of the amulet being missing. She was furious that the Lady was allowing so little action to be taken.

"If Miss Moon has reason to believe there has been a theft, I believe her…"

"Of course you would, Mrs. Hallwell, you are in her employ, your loyalty to her is a given," the Lady snapped.

"I've known this girl most of her life, Ma'am. She is not disposed to accuse anyone of anything if she has no reason to. She is not spiteful or mean. She lost something deeply important and precious to her, and she has reason to believe it was taken!" Mrs. Hallwell shouted this. "I will not have you accuse her of untruths when she has never, ever given you reason to suspect her to be capable of it! It's been four days, and you have yet to interrogate the girl about it!"

"The staff is searching the house for the item. The students have been restricted, and any outside activities have been suspended until the matter is resolved. But I must put to question any accusation; for if it is erroneous, it could have dire effects on the life of the accused, especially here, as the girls can be extremely hard on one another." The lady stood and sailed across the room in her dark grey silk gown, her train following behind her with a hiss on the piled rug.

There was an interruption, as someone was rapping upon the door of the lady's preferred parlor. "Come in," she said brusquely, pouring herself some apple brandy.

A girl poked her head in and then the rest of her body followed, squeezing through the narrow crack in the door. She closed it gingerly behind her. It was Reeni, the youngest of the girls, a dark-haired, olive-skinned child with bright hazel eyes. She curtsied to the elder ladies and gave Iselle a repentant look.

"Ma'am. There is something I must say, but I fear I might suffer reprisal for it," she whispered. "But I cannot hear Miss Moon being reprimanded again and again, for what she suspects, day after day, and not speak up."

The older women stared down at the girl.

"What is it, Miss Bean? What sort of reprisal would you anticipate, and from whom?"

"Miss Hamm, Ma'am." She said this meekly, anxiously. "She has been ever so cruel to me before, she mocks me relentlessly about my name, and she has struck and kicked me. I want to say, but I fear that if she finds out, she will hit me again."

"Girl," Mrs. Hallwell said gently, "If she is exposed, we will not say who did it." Reeni looked at Mrs. Hallwell, then her eyes shifted to Iselle, and they were rueful.

"Mirianne told me she took it. The necklace. She was laughing and boasting about it to me and Ybria two mornings ago. You know how Ybria longs for the confidence of a friend, she would never tell of it. Mirianne said she snuck into her room in the dead of night, Ma'am, and took it right off Miss Moon's body. She said she would take the thing and throw it in the lake, because she found Iselle's air so detestable."

Iselle pondered briefly as to why girls like these had such fixations of throwing things in lakes. But Reeni continued.

"Since there are restrictions, we could not go to the lake. So, she is hiding it. She has it in the pocket under her skirts, Ma'am. She showed it to me just this morning. She keeps pulling it out, smiling at us, and returning it into the pocket."

The Lady pivoted on her heel and moved back to her chair. "Best that you are being truthful Miss Bean. If we find out you are not, there will be consequences." She plinked down her glass of brandy on the side table and rang the bell which hung nearby.

"Fetch me Miss Hamm," she hissed at the servant. The girl curtsied and fled.

"You go now," she ordered Reeni. The girl did not dawdle, and scuttled away through the door as quickly as her legs could carry her. Iselle had heard the jeering of Miss Reeni Bean's name from a few of the girls. Iselle would never partake in such contemptible behavior. Apparently, her common consideration prompted a positive outcome, to bring her an advocate at this terrible time. She could not, however, stop herself from finding something amusing in that Miss *Hamm* and Miss *Bean* were not friends.

A few moments later, Mirianne was led into the room, and she peered at Iselle with an overly expressed, affected look of confusion for the summons. All mirth left Iselle when she felt the heat of Mirianne's spite.

"Empty your pockets." Mrs. Beyz commanded, "…and empty them completely, you will pull them inside out, and through the opening of the skirts. If there is nothing in your hand, Miss Hamm, I will have Inri come and strip you to your shift right here if I must."

Mirianne hesitated, calculating her options, while her hands slipped into the slot in her skirts, and found the pocket resting against her right leg. Her hand moved inside the pleats of pale pink fabric. Her eyes rested on Iselle with an impassive gaze.

And then her brow knit, and her lips twisted, and she withdrew her hand, and in one sweeping move, she threw the necklace into the fireplace, which was vigorously burning a new applewood log. "You can have it!" she shrieked. "You imperious, self-satisfied, pretentious tart!"

The fire ballooned as if moss tinder had been thrown into it. Mrs. Hallwell rushed to the hearth, and with the poker, leaning away from the heat and the flames, lifted the necklace out of the blaze. As soon as it was lifted, the fire returned to its quiet state. The bloodstone glowed in a preternatural way and hummed like the wings of a beetle. Mirianne and Mrs. Beyz were so rapt in the situation, they did not notice the signs of magical power.

"You don't deserve gifts! You don't deserve anyone giving you gifts! You don't deserve your uncle or your governess and your *special* classes," she spat and hissed. Her tone then went to mocking: "…and your room *all to yourself*! So *special* and haughty. You deserve nothing!" she screamed, stamping her feet. "I HATE YOU! You and your false empathy! You and your lofty, snobby face!"

"Go to your room, Miss Hamm, and do not come out until you are told you can come out. I will reflect on what ought to be done about this. We do not tolerate theft and disrespect in this house, young lady. Go now, or I will call Dekkins in and have him carry you there himself and lock the door." The lady drank from her glass and offered no apology or consideration towards the girl she had only moments before, derided for having suspicions.

The governess and Iselle left the parlor behind the girl as she pushed past them, and paused at the foot of the stairs, watching Mirianne stamp up towards her room. She said nothing more, nor looked back at Iselle.

Mrs. Hallwell took out her kerchief and wiped the sooty necklace clean. Her fingers were already dirtied by it. The stone had gone back to its normal state, and the chain was no longer glowing hot red. Her kerchief was slashed and splotched with ashy streaks when she was finished. She handed it to Iselle, who put it on and gazed at Mrs. Hallwell with frightened eyes. "Is it too late? Should we have gone the moment it was lost?"

"You would have been exposed wherever you go, then. I have no idea where one could find someone to make you something like that token. I wouldn't even know who to seek out to do it. Perhaps I should take you to an inn for now. Keeping you here at the school seems inadvisable with such acrimonious feelings floating about, not to mention the neglect and animosity from that detestable woman. Go and pack your things. I'll wait here."

Iselle obeyed. She climbed the steps after Mirianne and made her way to the corridor where the rooms were situated. There, she put her now meager belongings into a tapestry bag. Her trunk had been left behind at the Dame Arwey's house, and her belongings pared down to fit the large bag. The rest were sent home to Ecklo.

She disrobed of the school clothes and dressed in her own. She put on her bonnet and her redingote and was out of her room in less than twenty minutes.

As she lighted from the landing that brought her to the mezzanine above the foyer, her hand flew up to her mouth to mask a scream. Mrs. Hallwell lay upon the ground, curled into a ball, holding the side of her head. Mrs. Beyz was running back to the parlor and managed to get inside before shutting the door behind her, holding it fast against none other than Prentiss Lacklow. "WHERE IS SHE?" he yowled.

Iselle keenly recalled his anger at Arondon, but it paled in comparison to what she saw now. His eyes were wild, wide, and looked downright crazed. His face was beet red, and his lips parted to bare his gritted teeth. A bell began to ring relentlessly somewhere, and seconds later, the servants began to appear from their hidden corridors, and a panic ensued.

"Get the girls to safety! There's a madman!" a voice cried out from the parlor. The servants scattered, some vaulting up the steps past Iselle, some into the hidden doors. Girls who had been nearby were squealing and vaulting down the stairs past them all, and out the main door.

Mrs. Hallwell clambered to her feet. There was a trickle of blood coming from above her ear, and the side of her face was hot red. She staggered and then fell onto her hip, but her eyes traveled up to Iselle. "Run," she mouthed.

Dekkins, the stableman and his two hands, shoved open the double door, and barged into the house, carrying a smith's hammer, a pitchfork, and a shovel. They went straight at Prentiss, who retreated, wild-eyed towards the parlor, and kicked the door open, causing a scream of alarm from within. There was the sound of another door being battered as the men followed him inside.

Iselle took the chance to scurry down the stairs with another of the students and a teacher and ran towards the front door. She hadn't even gotten one foot out when she heard: "There you are..." It was a sinister growl. The door slammed shut before she could step through it.

Mrs. Hallwell tried to approach her, but tripped on her own skirts, rising again and holding her head.

Prentiss had come from the formal parlor that adjoined the room where Mrs. Beyz had been.

"Go!" Hallwell shouted at Iselle. She lifted her hand, and Iselle felt something bind her, enrobe her, and her feet lifted off the ground. Both of the front doors swung open, so hard they clattered loudly against the wall, shards of wood slivering off of them, and Iselle was thrown quite forcefully out onto the gravel amidst the panicked gathering horde of girls. Her bag rolled a few steps away. Iselle retrieved it, hugging it tightly to her chest, eyes wide as she watched the scene unfold. The house was spilling out its occupants from every door, and they milled in alarm and astonishment at the scene evolving within.

The room around Mrs. Hallwell groaned and shuddered, and the crazed man paused from his pursuit of Iselle because of it. Mrs. Hallwell stood at the base of the stairway with an expression Iselle had never, ever witnessed upon her face. Her body was rigid, and her arms held out from her sides, with her palms facing the madman. Through the now broadly open doors, it was like a painting from a storybook. The room shivered and the walls bent. The stone on the exterior of the house chipped and trembled.

"Best you pay attention to *me*," Mrs. Hallwell hissed at Prentiss, whose eyes had turned back onto Iselle. "*She* isn't about to kill you. *I am*." Her voice was both a growl and a whisper, two voices, both that shook Iselle's bones. *Her eyes...* Iselle glimpsed the white orbs, no more iris, no more pupils, only plain white. Iselle hiccupped air, as she had forgotten to breathe, as the girls around her exclaimed their shock and amazement in squeals and weeping.

"What are you?" Prentiss muttered. He swung his arm back, he made a cup of his hand, he threw it forward. The log from the hearth in the parlor, covered in flames, sailed through the shredded door at Mrs. Hallwell. It fell upon her skirts, and they caught aflame. Iselle heard herself shriek in terror.

That was when the situation became incomprehensible. The governess's body bent back like a longbow, and her feet lifted off the ground and a concussion of something, a wall of... *something* came out of her like a sphere of destruction. It radiated out, carrying the fire that now enveloped her body, and blew out the walls and what remained of the doors. The girls all screamed and some fell onto the ground in little fetal heaps, with their hands gripping the sides of their heads. Mirianne was amongst them, shivering and mewling in fear.

Iselle watched Mrs. Hallwell, as below her floating form, the floorboards peeled up and away from the joists and shot away towards Prentiss. The front of the house was open to the outside now, debris scattered with flames flickering upon them. Prentiss was standing on an intact piece of the floor, holding his arms up, and bent a door into a shield against the conflagration.

Mrs. Hallwell, visible now as but a dark cutout of a shape in a blinding veil of hot white fire and rage, threw out her arm and sent Iselle flying even farther away from them. The fire around Mrs. Hallwell's now blackened form first retreated into her as if being sucked away, then exploded in a golden white blossom from her body and unfurled into a storm. It devoured the house. Iselle heard her voice in her head. *"RUN when I tell you to RUN!"*

Again, Iselle was swept up in the invisible hand, and it picked her up and carried her away farther this time. She could hear Mrs. Hallwell's tortured shriek from the effort of her magic, which grew farther and farther away. The fire grew tinier, yet whiter and brighter, with miniscule silhouettes of her classmates running away against its impossible light.

Mrs. Hallwell kept him occupied long enough, and with bag containing her few precious things left in the world clutched tightly in her arms, and her miraculously intact bonnet, Iselle did exactly as her governess bade. When she was dumped and rolled onto a grassy field at the edge of the city, she clambered to her feet, got hold of her senses, giving the hot white ball of flames that had been Stonegate in the distance, one last glance—weeping streaks down her face, she jogged towards the town down the coast, to find refuge as quickly as her legs could carry her.

CHAPTER 15

Forrest's horse was lathered in sweat and foam when he arrived at the beech tree. Its breath and snorts were heavy and fast. It was already dusk, and the light was tinted orange. The ground was littered with leaves. They'd had such fun kicking about in them, making them crunch beneath their feet during the early day.

He dismounted before the horse had come to a halt, his feet striking the soil with a thump. He left his horse to stand on her own. She dropped her head and caught her breath, her nostrils wide in desperation to cool her lungs. He walked to the area where they had picnicked.

He knelt. His gaze slid across the serenity of the place. He closed his eyes and inhaled deeply, filling his lungs with the fall-scented air. His hand fell down to his side, and he slid his fingers under the leaves, pressing his fingertips onto the soil. He thought of Iselle's distress. Her glassy eyes. Her reticence, and the secret that made it impossible for her to explain why she was so scared.

He homed in upon the unknown source of that anguish—he filled his mind with it. He was looking for an object he had never seen with his own eyes. He did see the shape of it in its value to her. He saw its weight in her sense of loss and other feelings she emitted, remorse, loneliness, terror, hate.

He grasped onto those things he had sensed in her. He used them like a casting mold to create a form around the absent object, and the intensity of her emotions created a sharp, detailed shape. He took that from his senses, and he channeled it into the earth. Into the roots of the tree. Into the humus and the shallow waters of the banks.

The ground shivered a little. The leaves rustled. The birds chittered and the pond grasses hissed with the sound of a sudden, gentle breeze that rippled the pond's surface.

He felt it now. Like she did. The comfort of a smoothened stone. Warmed by her skin. It was cold without her. He rose gracefully to his feet and like a compass finding true north, he followed the pull—the need of this object to be returned to its place against her heart.

His boots tread through the grass, along the edge of the pond.

They had picked cattails. The men had dueled with them, causing a veritable snowstorm of seeds to enshroud them.

She had squealed, laughed, and ran away as they waved the stems, leaving wakes of fluff. He had never seen her so free and happy. Miss Teena had hidden behind her, and Iselle nearly fell over her trying to get away.

He stopped here, where the grass was still dusted in the cattail seed. The empty mold suspended in his senses called for the object to complete it. It was here. He knelt again. "Speak to me… I will take you home." His spread fingers dug anew into the dark, damp soil.

It spoke to him. It was an object of magic. A talisman. And it needed its ward as much as its ward needed it. He closed his eyes and focused upon its magic.

There was a slight rustle of movement in the tall grass, and against the darkening reflection of the water, from the sward, something moved. Something rose up, encased in a sensory mold, the air shimmering around it, the broken chain dangling from the filigree cage that contained her talisman.

He unfolded himself to his lofty height and walked lithely to it. He reached out and turned his palm up underneath it. He willed the mold away, which dissipated. The bloodstone spider dropped into his hand, the chain piling upon itself onto his skin, and his fingers closed around it.

In the lingering light of the evening, he opened his fingers and studied it. He knew what bloodstone and what the spider meant to magic users, as individual things. The talisman itself vibrated with the power of a magic he had never felt before.

She could not be without it, if this was the case. He tucked it securely into his breast pocket, and just as the sun set, he was back on the road, pushing his horse urgently back towards Whitewater.

There was a knock at Iselle's door, and a person she hardly knew was standing there when she opened it. It was a girl she'd seen passing from the first-floor rooms. She was in her night gown, with her dressing gown hastily pulled on. She clutched the ruffled front closed; her strawberry blonde hair plaited into a long rope on her shoulder.

"There's a visitor for you," she hissed in a whisper as to not alert the proctor.

"We can't *have* visitors…" Iselle muttered stupidly. She then rolled her eyes at her own denseness.

"He knocked on our window. He's waiting by the rear door behind the linen room. Tell him to go away before we receive demerits," she grumbled. She then tiptoed away.

Iselle drew her own dressing gown on, closing the frog under her bust. She slid her house slippers onto her bare feet, and stole out of her room, down the rear stairs to the lower floor. She saw nobody in the service corridor and moved to the back door that led to the steps up into a little enclosed garden.

She opened the door warily and saw the silhouette of Forrest cast against the moonlit sky. She climbed the stone steps up to the landing and peered at him in puzzlement.

"Forr.. Uh.. Mr. Outvallen! What brings you here?" Iselle asked.

Even in the meager light from the corridor behind her, Forrest could see her eyes were swollen from weeping. He reached into the breast of his frock coat and withdrew an object from his pocket.

"It was in the reeds, where I soundly defeated Meddin in battle." He reached for her hand and lifted it, placing the talisman on her palm. She stared down at it incredulously.

Relief washed over her in a visible shudder, and he watched her eyes tear up again. She sniffed and wiped her eyes with the heel of her hand, still clutching the bloodstone widow, the broken chain swinging from between her fingers.

"How?"

"*Intuitive locus*," he said to her. He waved is hand and the chains lifted as his hand did. "If I could not mirror your feelings, I might never have sensed it."

She didn't understand a word. But she gathered he used magic. "I did not know you were mage," she whispered.

"Unlike most others, I refrain from wearing it on my breast like a medal. I prefer to keep it under the cuff. But you did know I studied the track, didn't you? Did you not put two and two together?" he said admonishingly in his usual way.

He was startled into silence by a sudden soft warmth on his right hand. He looked down to see hers clutched around his fingers. She sighed shakily and a tear fell onto her cheek and rolled down to her chin. "Thank you. I cannot express how meaningful this is," she uttered through her soft sobs.

He used his left hand with some difficulty; to find his kerchief in the hip pocket of his frock coat—as he would not have broken her grasp if his life depended upon it. So, he sacrificed his dignity fumbling clumsily for the piece of cloth. He proffered it to her. Sadly, she dropped his hand to accept it, and she daubed the tears from her face.

"You have the very depth of my gratitude, Mr. Outvallen. To go all the way back there… to search for what would be but a bauble to you."

"Think nothing of it," he murmured. "Will you be safe and assured now?"

"I am already. I need only a new chain so that it can be here where it belongs." She pressed her hand to her breast.

"I believe I may have one you may use. It is however made of zargun. So, the chain is black. That isn't what women usually prefer, but it is strong and light. I will bring it to breakfast." He then abruptly turned and left.

Iselle sat in her room by the fire, her uneaten supper Dorya had arranged for her sitting on the desk beside her. Her knuckles where white, she clutched the widow so tightly. *Was it too late? Was nine-hundred miles and a stretch of angry sea far enough?*

The fear would not pass. The fear never passed. Even when she was not exposed without the protection of the talisman—even leagues and leagues away from everything that was familiar. The fear was her constant companion. It felt as if he embodied it. The fear. Like it was *him* that hung over her, around her, looming like a black cloud. And that is what he wanted. That even when she was not within his grasp, she still was.

She rose only for the single step required to reach her bed, where she crumpled into a fetal position atop the covers, curling herself around the bloodstone in her hand. She fell into a fitful slumber, thoughts bubbling up between waking moments.

Would she have to leave Whitewater now? Had he seen through her eyes? Had her body sent out some kind of signal to lure him? Could he suss out her whereabouts from her daily activities? A heavy weight of dread fell upon her. Another icy fear gripped her—could he have seen her friends?

Her chest felt like the weight of innumerable stones crushed her. Tears began to fall. Could she love nobody? Could she never know friendship again? Was she a curse to anyone who cared about her? Was he determined for her to never have anyone except him? These thoughts suffocated her and devastated her. She succumbed to the sobs.

It was so rare for her to have friends. The thought of having to leave here crushed her. The thought that any one of her little circle would be endangered because of her shattered her. This was the happiest she'd ever been since the curse of Prentiss Lacklow came into her life. Would he destroy this too?

CHAPTER 16

Redlan adjusted Iselle's crown and stepped back to take in the full effect of her costume. "You make a terrifyingly beautiful villain," he said in his gentle voice, with that wry smile she'd come to love so much. He was so… *pretty*. Willowy and graceful, with fine, delicate features, flawless milky skin, perfectly formed lips, and a soft, feminine jawline—his eyes were tilted like a cat's, dense with lashes that matched his jet hair. He had his trimmed coiffe shaggy and wild, and it had a bit of a wavy curl to it. He was the first person aside from Uncle Ude that she loved to this degree. The sight of him filled her with joy. Even if she didn't show it.

He understood her. He knew he was precious to her, as she knew she was to him.

He was dressed as a footman, complete with the old-fashioned cutaway frock coat, with pleats at the base of his back that swung gracefully when he walked. He looked handsome. "Would that I was at least cast as your handmaid," he lamented only hours before, as they laid out their costumes and styled their hair. "I would be twice as lovely than the girl who has the role, what's her name again?"

"Ahtri," Iselle answered.

"Ah yes, Ahtri. Abysmal choice. I would carry her costumes with infinitely more grace and aplomb."

Iselle giggled and gently smacked his arm. "Stop, Ahtri is lovely," she chided.

He exhaled laboriously and shook his head. "Why must you be so kind?"

"I need to be kind, if I am your friend," she retorted.

"Actors to the stage for scene one!" the theatre arts teacher exclaimed, clapping his hands. Iselle looked over her shoulder at him, and then back to Redlan.

"See you in scene three." She turned away, and scuttled up the steps to the stage before the curtains were drawn.

Arrowood was the place she would know the longest. Three years. Three years of familiarity. Of relative peace. Of even a small sense of security.

She had arrived at Mellodon, a city on the strait of Omire, alone, with little to her name than what was contained inside the bag gripped in her gloved hand. This place was as far north of home than Stonegate had been east of it. And she would still need to travel a little farther inland. To the Fern Highlands, deep in the mountains where it was cold all the time.

After the fire at Stonegate, she had taken refuge in a Trinity Temple by the sea, and sought the aid of the clerics, who had kindly taken her in. She fled until darkness after she had been tossed so roughly onto the pasture, hiding in a nearby vacant cow-barn until the sun set. At least there were heaps of old, musty straw to sit in. She had even been able to close her eyes and sleep away her despair for a while.

She knocked at the gate of the sanctuary; they spied her in her state and let her in—the women's hands bracing her and patting her arms and body to see if she was injured. She was led to a room, her sooty and torn gown removed, and her coveted bonnet was untied and taken off of her. She was given a hot bath, and they tried to soothe her quivering and sobbing away, as the wash of kindness and generosity from the women overwhelmed her.

While she stayed there for two weeks, she sent letters by relay to Uncle Ude through his law office. She was relieved to learn that he was well. She worried that Lacklow would harm him to get at her. But he was thankfully focused entirely on her. When she expressed her fears, he assured her he was well-protected.

She asked after news of Mrs. Hallwell. The response made her weep anew. Mrs. Hallwell was alive. She was, however, blinded—her eyes a marbled white, and magic-scarred—her hands and wrists stained with a filigree of ancient magical symbols, an intricate tattoo the color of burnt umber. Her family line's magical mark had also spidered out along her neck in unknown words and pictograms. Her uncle explained it was a result of the powers she possessed being cast without training or control, ruled only by her anger and emotion. She had sustained some burns as well. But Uncle Ude had not elaborated on her physical injuries from the fire. Iselle was deeply regretful of Mrs. Hallwell's state. She felt entirely responsible for it. But she could not help but be humbled, and grateful that Mrs. Hallwell cared so much for her that she could evoke, on Iselle's behalf, the powerful emotions that would create such magic.

She was convalescing at an Ivlan sanctuary, where Uncle Ude had secured her a room and ample care. Uncle Ude was optimistic that their magic could heal her eventually, and he expressed his thankfulness for her sacrifice. "We owe Mrs. Hallwell everything," he told her. "Mrs. Hallwell continues to disregard her own injuries and only wishes to hear that you are safe. She is only to be loved and commended for all this," he added.

He warned Iselle she should not remain for long where she was. It was not far enough from the smoking ruin that was Stonegate House. There was rumor of Lacklow, alive and well with a singed frockcoat, continuing to lurk about the town, in spite of the militia patrols in search of him. It was difficult to ascertain if these mutterings were true.

Expeditiously, her uncle, again made necessary arrangements, and this time, he put her on a ship to cross the straight of Omir to the high north, to take her to Mellodon, and from there, up the mountain to Emdroth, the small remote city where the yawning archway of Arrowood Academy awaited to devour her. The land journey alone was impossibly long and arduous. She wished only for stability and a warm fire.

It was icy and biting when she arrived, crossing under the archway of black granite. At least she had this to revel in. Iselle was a creature disposed to wintry weather. She felt most at home with rosy cheeks and steamy breath, wrapped in warm clothes against the cold.

Arrowood's towers and walls were made of the broad, tightly fit stone bricks and were dusted in frost, and the windows piercing the stonework cast the warm light. She couldn't imagine how many candles and tallow lamps burned behind the glinting glass panes scattering the edifice.

Around the school's ancient walls, the little city, bright with lanterns and golden-tinted shop windows glistened cheerfully. The coach lurched from the force of the frigid wind, but inside, the heated bricks had kept her warm for hours since the last waystation. The horses that drew her were heavy breeds, made more powerful by the hills and mountains they crossed to get here.

It was a beautiful place, the Academy. Once a fortification, like many of the schools about the empire, but this one was a particularly ancient one. Once the seat of a warlord King, it had all the hallmarks of a palace, and walls to fortify it, and towers to defend it. The rooms were countless, and the passages about it were convoluted, with no sense of order. Stairways and corridors branched off in all directions, leading to all manner of unexpected rooms. It took Iselle a good three months to get the lay of the great structure.

Here was an outstanding school, with students from all over the known world. The classrooms were always crowded, the hallways continuously bustling, and the air happy and jovial. There were so many options for students to pursue—not only classes required to meet common and magical academic standards, but also classes that offered delightful things, like painting, magical creative arts, and singing, music, and even boasted an excellent theatre program. She never dreamed she would ever be able to do these things before.

She kept mostly to herself at the beginning. It was simple to, as the volume of students pouring through the halls and classrooms made it easy to be anonymous. Her prettiness did make her more remarkable and memorable to some students, the usual complement of young men from the boys' side of the institution would seek her out during the day and make conversation as best they could. But Iselle's reserve had distilled to a more thickset potency after all this time, and her rejections were a little harsher; more fear-filled. She could trust nobody, it seemed. Even a little.

Upon joining the 10th year class, she met him. Redlan. A willowy boy with the gentlest of souls—whose ways gave him full access to both sides of the school as he could be trusted in the girls' domain. She met him because he too was unable to go home for a summer break. Here there was no summer to speak of, and the smattering of other lonely students were isolated in this fortress with now empty, cavernous rooms and echoing archways, a world away from the warmth and welcome of the lowlands.

The few remaining students ate together. They mostly went their own ways during the day, some seeking out the common rooms to idle about in, others taking to the town to explore or visit acquaintances or create new ones. Iselle did none of those things. She spent her time in the library mostly, sometimes she went to the market if she felt courageous enough to do so.

When she first arrived, she was not equipped with the warm clothing required for such a place. But she acquired them after a month or two and ventured out to replace the common clothing that had been destroyed by the incident at Stonegate. But even now when the lowlands were sun-kissed and the breeze warm, here, it was cold. Not as frigid and unrelenting as the winter, but cold, nonetheless. She thought perhaps this was where she was meant to be; in the embrace of the mountain's chill, swathed in quiet and warmth.

One particular day, she was about to walk out of one of the many ancillary doors that peppered the base of the main school. They opened up at all levels, to stairwells, and patios, and verandas connected to more walkways and verandahs, to narrow stairways that led down to the bailey in front of the main building. It was at one of the other doors that connected to her route, that Redlan was exiting, pulling a garrick over his spare shoulders, looking like he was drowning in the wool, buried in the capes stacked upon the shoulders. He had a dapper bicorn on his head, and layered waistcoats as was the mode these days, both shades of emerald green. He looked up as she rounded a corner and nearly bumped into him. He barked in surprise at her appearance and the appraised her in earnest.

"Ah… the porcelain-girl," he exclaimed, closing the door behind him. "I've seen you at meals. You're quiet," he observed.

"I haven't seen *you* before," Iselle replied coolly.

"Nobody ever does," he lamented dramatically, adjusting his lapels and tall collar and buttoning the front with his slender fingers. "People tend to look away when someone as beautiful as I am makes an appearance. It can be intimidating, I suppose, to be around such good looks." He drew on a glove, and then another, blocking Iselle's path. "Where are you off to?"

Iselle didn't really want to have a lengthy conversation. "I don't know yet," she muttered.

"Neither do I. But I felt like a pilchard in a whole ocean today. Let us walk together. I won't talk too much," he assured her. Then he thought it over for a second. "Well," he added, "…maybe a *bit* much." He smiled broadly at her and bounced cheerfully down the steps in his shining boots. He appeared very much a dandy.

He waited for Iselle to catch up and then stopped her again and pointed to her hands, which were clutched together in spare little calfskin gloves. "You need a hand-muff. Let's go find you one. You have money, in your little pomegranate there?"

Iselle did not reply, nor did she react at all. She continued on until the walk widened, and she merely fell into step beside him as they alighted into an alley that led to the academy bailey. They crossed it, heels echoing in the vast space. They traversed the great arch in the battlement wall, now empty of the massive door that had surely once rested in the man-sized hinge holes on the sides and proceeded into the bustling city.

The square sat right in front of the opening to the school, and it was alive with a bustling festival of some kind or another, with people dressed as ice bears and broad-fronted moose with massive spans of antlers balancing precariously above the crowd. Somewhere, a retinue of lutists, flutists and drummers were playing music.

"Oh, isn't that nice? It's Lady's Emerald Eyes!" Redlan called out the name of the dance, and began to skip, twirling so the frocks of his coats flared out. He took Iselle's hands, and he drew her to chassé across the square, and he stopped to balance her forward and back, and he setted gracefully around her. It was hard not to smirk at this flamboyant display, the feathers of his hat flouncing with every bounce and turn. Iselle had never been to a dance, or a ball. She didn't know the dances or the music that accompanied them. She stumbled a bit, and Redlan took note.

"Miss, you must learn your dance steps. How will you exist in society if you don't know even the most elementary footwork? Shame on you," he chided her with a playful smile.

"I've never had occasion to dance," she replied.

"Then we shall remedy this. There are dance masters and dancehall events all over town all year. We shall go together so we will never be want for a partner," he said, pausing to take her prettiness in, while taking her hand. He put it on his arm and fell into an energetic walk beside her. "I suppose, looking at you, that you will never be want for a partner regardless," he sighed, scrutinizing her lovely face and form more deliberately. Like a horse merchant examining stock. "I myself, being prettier than most of the girls at these dances, can be a hindrance, as none of them will dance with me."

Iselle laughed aloud and then covered her mouth with her free hand. She decided to keep it to herself that she had not the slightest intention of going to a ball with anyone. The idea both saddened her and filled her with longing. She genuinely wanted to. It simply wasn't a luxury she could consider.

"Oh, look at Pork Pie!" Redlan exclaimed. He made kissing noises with his lips, and in response, there was a small bark. The school's unofficial dog was out and about as they were. He had free rein about the campus and surrounding town. He was owned by no one. But he had access to most places, even inside the school and dorms sometimes, as students would sneak him in. He was universally loved by all. He must have been lonely with most everyone gone for summer.

Iselle's cool demeanor melted at that moment, and her face broke into a smile at the sight of the pup. She liked the sandy-colored dog so very much. The creature wove through the crowds and came to Redlan's call. He accepted some caresses and scratches from both of them. They both knelt and showered him in attention.

Redlan's hand suddenly rose up and he pointed in the direction of the eastern side of the square. "There. We will find you warm hands in that shop!" He straightened and pulled Iselle to her feet by her arm. He bolted towards the destination, dragging her along, swerving through the crowds of people, Iselle giggling aloud for the first time in... *I can't even remember.* Pork Pie followed at their heels, his tail wagging with alacrity.

Iselle knew she loved this friend already with all of her heart, that very night. He could never be a threat to anyone. He felt safe.

Lenteev first saw her when the curtains parted, and the townsfolk applauded the tableau the first scene displayed, with Iselle as the villainous queen Nirall. She sat gravely upon her throne, with the poor subjugated heroine thrown at her feet.

Like Prentiss, he fell in love with her at that moment. Like Prentiss, he fixated upon her at that moment. And also, like Prentiss, he was convinced she saw him and felt the same.

But she did *not* see him. The massive clusters of candles with the reflectors hanging from the ceiling, designed to cast the light onto the stage, shadowed the audience from the actors. This was the only reason Iselle agreed to participate in the performances—because the idea of having hundreds of eyes upon her had made her uneasy. She had only become involved with the class because she had hoped to paint and create scenery or help with costumes.

The teacher had other plans. Her cool, distanced air, her reserve, her perpetual expression of indifference was perfect, he declared. "You, Miss Moon, must be Queen Nirall! The icy, ruthless beauty. Nobody else will do!"

Rehearsals were great amusement for Iselle. She had Redlan, who entertained her endlessly. There were the other student-actors, who had come to like her over the weeks together, to see past her ambivalent expression, and included her in their talk and play, who guided her and encouraged her. The play itself, she only had to be there, to recite her memorized lines as best she could to sound like the character she was playing. However, as the first performance approached, she discovered it was not simply to be performed for the school, but was open to a public audience, and she grew deeply anxious.

Redlan was there to assure her. "Don't think too much about it. You'll see that the audience becomes nothing more than a painting of faces graded into darkness. You must put your trust in me. And I will be there, watching, so if you become fearful, you can just look in the wings, or at your side, and find me."

He wasn't wrong. Only seeing the spectators in the first or second row made it easier for her; the rest faded into the shadow behind the scrim of light. She couldn't help but imagine Prentiss there, someplace in the shadows, watching. Shivers went down her spine, and she would cast her eyes to Redlan, who was always there, and who always had a wry face, or a grin to distract and comfort her with.

Lenteev had watched her with fascination that first performance, this Iselle was not immediately aware of. He had been there from the opening scene to the curtain call. He had lingered in the crowd after the performance to see her come out from backstage, and he attended the numerous performances they held over two and a half weeks. Every time, he stood before her to congratulate her for her stellar acting. She did not remember him, but apparently, he was certain she did. She simply shook hands with the delighted spectators, while wishing herself away from the chaos and the people.

She and Redlan always escaped at first chance, to eat supper at Duckham's, their favorite mixed public house, where they would sit down and voraciously devour whatever meal was on offer for the night. It was cheap food, but largely delicious as the proprietress was an accomplished cook and had worked the kitchens in the residence of the Duke of Merian with all accolades.

The other attraction of this pub was there was a comely young man who played a 9-string mandora and sang to patrons every other night or so; and Redlan was love-struck by this handsome figure. He had the voice of a nightingale, and he sang so beautifully, they would strive not to miss any of his performances. Even on the nights they themselves were onstage during the run of the play.

Lenteev would follow them, and he would slide into a seat in the pub, and watch Iselle smiling so sweetly at her friend, and eating so delicately, and swaying to the music. And he would follow her back to Arrowood and watch until she disappeared into the archway with her constant companion.

Iselle learned about all this, because Lenteev had told her. He wrote to her of it. He sent messages sometimes twice a day, recounting the times he'd shaken her hand, and come near her, and he was sure she had looked upon him with affection. It made her skin crawl. She soon began to refuse any correspondence at all that was dispatched from the city.

She could not think of who he was amongst the many faces she'd seen. Regardless of his apparent dull nature, and placidity, it terrified her. It was enough to light the spark that sent her back to the library at the school, and the Mendoch archive, which was in the city itself, desperately trying to find some answer to give her the power to defend herself.

It was clear at least that Lenteev did not have mystical abilities. He didn't seem to possess much intellect at all, going by the artless nature of his prose, and his appalling writing skills. But her experience with these obsessions told her all she needed to know. She did not want to leave Arrowood. She had Redlan. She was tired of always leaving.

One thing or another inevitably brought Prentiss back into her life. It seemed certain. Her uncle even talked of sending her overseas, now. Now she had this simpleton following her about, sending her letters when even the smallest message or parcel or folded letter gave her such fear.

She considered leaving. She also resisted the notion. She did not feel safe, but she also had been at Arrowood the longest. She arrived shortly before she turned sixteen and was now turning eighteen. She had managed to age past Prentiss' desired time for marriage. She fostered hope, perhaps, that it was finally over. Perhaps he would not want her anymore. She had even allowed herself to hope that he had been consumed by Mrs. Hallwell's firestorm and the rumors of his being seen were wrong. Over time she gave herself permission to grow close to Redlan. Her reluctance to run away, even with another obsessed man looming over her, persisted.

She was, however, left with little choice, as the predictable once more raised its fearsome head.

After a rousing evening at Duckham's, after their sixth theatre performance, Iselle went into her room, and as she was undressing, the pendant must have fallen out of the silver cage that contained it. It tumbled under her bed into her slipper. She went to bed and slept heavily. She rose, feeling the chain still around her neck. Not immediately noticing that the weight was altered.

She attended class. She ate her meals. She studied in the library with Redlan, who was hung over and groggy. They talked about anything and everything. They attended an assembly, and they walked into town. She did not put on the slippers that evening. Or the morning after that. It was the third day when she came into her room after a long study session after supper, and when she slid her feet into her slippers to go back out for a full bath, she felt the object inside her left one. She shook it out of her slipper and her face blanched. Her panic was palpable. She gripped the necklace, its little cage empty of its contents, and she could scarcely keep from screaming.

Arrowood was far from home. But would it ever be far enough?

CHAPTER 17

Forrest opened the door to the coach and placed his hand against the top of the door frame, so Iselle could duck in safely without hitting her head. He then climbed in behind her and sat across from her. He gazed at Iselle's face. She was already so withdrawn as it was, but the past few days, she looked positively panicked and waxen. She had since the night when he delivered her pendant.

He stole her away from afternoon lectures, and proposed they go to the nearby city of Mimreth. He said he needed to have some shoes resoled, and he brought them, although they weren't nearly as worn as he claimed. He planned to take her to the Blue Pearl Inn, where they could partake in a high-end, traditional Miritrian meal of the freshest ingredients. He thought she would like a taste of home.

He dropped off his shoes at the cobbler and then helped Miss Moon down from the coach onto the street. They set off for The Blue Pearl. Mimreth was a clean city, with cobbled streets and raised walkways along the road for pedestrians. There were elevated blocks that crossed the streets here and there, so pedestrians could avoid the puddles and horse-droppings. There were cuts in the crossing stones so carriage wheels could easily pass. It was a pleasant short walk.

Iselle had already visited here once with Dorya shortly after the temple visit, as it offered more shopping options than the town of Rendorff, and it also got them away from the ever-present students of the academy, who seemed to always have plenty of free time to knock about the town and exasperate the citizenry.

Iselle had also finally met here with Miss Metrelees, who had sent a note to the school, inviting her to walk in the garden district of Mimreth.

It was a peculiar visit, as Miss Amma did not invite Iselle to visit her at home, or to take tea. Iselle suspected she was not proud of her home, or she was unhappy in it. Iselle was unsure. She wanted to ask but felt as if it would be of embarrassment to the young lady, as she seemed rather proud. They contented themselves with the walk instead.

"I thought it would be a good distraction, to keep the doldrums and humdrums from filling your head. You seemed most distracted, if not unhappy, last we met. To be truthful, it is why I was drawn to you. I felt *so* for you. I don't know what troubles or burdens you carry. I'm sure the obligations of your schooling and your absence from home, alone, must be most trying, Miss Moon. I hope you will feel open to speak with me about them. Your friend Miss Dorya, she seems kind; but her thoughtfulness lacks depth."

Well, that was excessively rude of you. But you're not wrong.

"I've had some troubling thoughts lately," Iselle admitted. "I have struggled with them. I am certain we all do."

You don't know the half of it. You would never know the half of it.

"You are so kind to offer to accept my confidence. I am unused to entrusting it to others," Iselle said carefully.

"I won't force you. But I want you to know I am here for you. To let it all pool up inside you, and simmer into a viscid mere… none of that is good for a person." Amma stared at her gloves. She turned a small sprig of dried alder cones in her fingers. She'd collected them from the ground as they walked. The path was soft dirt covered in dried, umber-colored evergreen needles. The path was shaded in arches of tree cover, all along the garden-district street.

Miss Metreless was mostly quiet and thoughtful, but curious. She inquired as to why the small party had visited Torem, and upon learning about the temple, she talked a bit about her familiarity with it, as she had grown up in the area. But her conversation was otherwise without direction.

Boring. You're boring and vapid.

"And why have you come to Rendorff from Torem?" Iselle asked.

Miss Metrelees's expression faded a bit, and she sighed wearily. "I am engaged. I am living with a relative for now, until the wedding," her voice seemed distant.

"Are you unhappy with the engagement?" Iselle inquired. She stepped over a puddle and lifted her hems as they sauntered through the town's finer district, with elegant homes set on generous parcels, all meticulously kept, with topiary and guided ivies and trees trained into garden walls and fences. In spring and summer, it would be dripping with life and lushness, Iselle noted. She wondered if this is where Amma lived.

The response was hidden in Miss Metrelees's silence and gloomy countenance. Iselle gave her a look of commiseration, but did not pursue the matter, as clearly Miss Amma wasn't motivated to do so.

"When I am married, I will invite you to my home for a proper visit. In my current situation, I am unable to have guests," she said. She left it at that, offering no further elaboration or explanation.

Iselle felt like Miss Metrelees had other things to say—other questions to ask, but she sensed Iselle's own unwillingness to be too open as well. This was a nascent acquaintance, with two ladies who both seemed unfamiliar with the territory of lasting friendships of trust and confidence.

The remainder of the walk was one of trite conversation; more about their visit to Torem, about the history of the area. Iselle sensed that Amma missed it. That she regretted leaving there. Or perhaps it was all she knew and had little more conversation to offer.

The ladies parted in good spirits. They promised to meet again soon.

That was before the picnic. As of this day, Iselle had yet to receive a renewed invitation. For some reason it embittered her a little. She had perhaps hoped to have a connection of trust for once, where she could be open about everything. For some reason, she felt that Amma had been the one to be that for her. Why, Iselle did not know. But it was what she longed desperately for.

How Dorya would manage the knowledge of it all worried Iselle. She was so full of doubt about the girl. She did not seem mature enough. Sober enough. She did not trust Dorya.

She's all insipid cheer and happiness. Why crush that with your dark mess anyway?

Maybe it was because Amma was a little older; a little more experienced; maybe the sense that Iselle got, that Miss Metrelees would understand and respect the gravity of it all. It would not make her uncomfortable or change her countenance with Iselle. She would not be cruel, dismissive, or disparaging if she knew the truth of Iselle's situation. Iselle felt a sense of loss, for not having secured the friendship like she had hoped.

That stupid woman.

She and Forrest sauntered past the garden district; Iselle relived the moment. She was drawn out of her thoughts as they headed towards the place Forrest had brought her to visit.

As they walked, she suddenly took his arm. He appeared unaffected by the gesture, but she felt him firm up his muscles to support her, and once her hand was locked on, he pressed his arm against his body. She knew he could sense her feelings; but not see her thoughts, but he got an impression of them, because he relaxed a little. He exhaled and looked up at the sky.

"Why do you keep that little chittering creature Dorya about? You are not matched well, as friends. She is effusive and rather without a clue. I would never see her and think for a moment that she would be your friend."

Iselle followed his gaze, and they both watched a raptor catch the updrafts, and circle lazily above them in the sharp blue sky.

"I suppose I can say the same for you, and Meddin," she replied.

He stopped and in turn she did. He did not let go of her hand, and kept it firmly locked against his ribs. He looked at her, as if realizing this for the first time.

"Why *do* I keep Meddin around?" he asked himself mostly. He pondered upon it.

"Because he's easy?" Iselle suggested.

"No," he murmured. "That's not it. He's anything but easy. At least for someone of my character. He might be such to people *like* him."

"Because he's *normal*," she concluded.

"Is that why it is for you?" Forrest resumed walking, and Iselle's pensive, sullen stare returned to the solid ground. She pondered a bit before saying anything.

"I think so," she said. "I'm not normal. Neither are you. Perhaps we both long for the normality we see in others and choose to associate ourselves with people we perceive as such."

"Perhaps," he conceded. "Perhaps that is it. However, I must say in all honesty… normal is most bothersome,"

Iselle suppressed an ironic smirk. He continued:

"They are bothersome how they glide through their days with such a wide-eyed, detached watercolor view of the world. What a privilege it must be to exist as such." Iselle wondered what it was that pained Forrest so; that colored his person with such dour and cold expression. She tightened her grip upon him.

She did not say what she thought, but she knew he would feel it.

You are not bothersome. You would understand. You would not look upon me in a different light than how you see me now. And I would be the same with you. There was a realization at that moment, as she looked down at their feet, treading through the dead leaves and humus of the path towards their destination, that what she sought so desperately in Amma, was already there before her—and this was the reason she had allowed him to cross her defensive walls. She pondered this in silence. Forrest simply walked, clutching her hand warmly against his being.

The Blue Pearl was a low-slung building with a shallow tiled roof and etched glass windows in diamond panes all around the perimeter. It was situated close to the garden district—at its edge. It was set back from the main road, enclosed in stone walls to match the building's stone face. There was an elegant stairway leading up to the double doors which had iron studs shaped like little pyramids embedded in the surface. A doorman stood under the shelter of the broad eave.

Dining establishments in this part of the world were different from those from Iselle's. The Blue Pearl was Miritrian, and that meant it was the sort with which she was familiar. In the south and west, one was subject to whatever the innkeeper was serving that particular day, and there were few dedicated enterprises that served only food. They were usually guest houses, public houses and inns that also served meals.

In Miritria, there were houses dedicated entirely to the service of upscale food—with large, impressive kitchens and schooled chefs, who made dishes that were unique. And the Blue Pearl was such a place here in Mimreth, on the isle of Baranith, Iselle would have been excited to learn this, ordinarily. She was surprised to find that this existed in this place so far from home. It fed into her emotional state, and made her eyes burn a little with the threat of tears. She wanted so badly to go home.

Forrest led Miss Moon past the doorman as he opened the doors for them. Forrest watched her go by, taking in her pale, distracted face. He helped her out of her street shoes, turning them facing out, and then rising to manage his own. The Miritrian hostess, with her familiar black hair and pale eyes, arrived in turn and led them to one of the cozy private dining rooms. She greeted Iselle kindly, and warmly. She took Iselle's redingote and Forrest's garrick and withdrew, and a younger girl then came in after her and put some fresh tea on the small table. She closed the door behind them after telling them that the food would take about half an hour.

Iselle sank down onto the small floor chair, her uniform skirts crumpling around her legs. She crossed her them beneath the voluminous fabric and took the napkin and laid it upon her lap. The place felt familiar to her. Comforting. Even the scent of the materials commonly used in her nation to build and furnish, the plant fibers of the rug, the evro wood used specifically to truss these types of buildings. There was such a place only two miles from her home in Ecklo. Her uncle often took her there in the company of his colleagues. She would eat the delicate foods quietly while the adults talked of business and law.

She should have felt happy, but the place only made her homesick.

Forrest stared at her. He thought it would improve her spirits. When he saw her shrink a shade more and edge even closer to what looked like the onset of tears, he sighed and shook his head.

"I confess I am without ideas, Miss Moon," he murmured a little defeatedly. The table had a prepared setting, along with a pitcher of cool water, the newly brought teapot made of bubbled glass filled with hot tea, and two tiny matching cups to go with it. There were also two narrow, oval plates of the same style, and a delicate two-tined fork each.

"What could you possibly be talking about?" she replied. Her regard was wide-eyed and confused. He reached over and poured her some tea.

"Your demeanor is troubling. What can I do to make it better?"

"When has my demeanor been a matter of your concern? You often make special efforts to disturb it," she mumbled affectedly. She turned her eyes away to the window and looked at the bent little leafless tree and shrubbery outside, which were shining and slick with rain that had begun to pelt the world only moments after they arrived. The water cascaded down a chain from a gutter, into a pot, which overflowed into a small pond by the window. Iselle sipped her tea. She then peered down at her hand, turning the glistening cup with its amber liquid in the light and studying it.

Forrest watched her, his eye trained upon her face. Her graceful neck was exposed as she had turned her head away a bit. A little pearl from her earring dangled prettily against her pale skin. He pondered that she was perhaps the most perfect creature he had ever seen in all of his days. He loved the shape of her jaw, and the curve of the bridge of her nose. It was the looming cloud of despair that hurt him. The sense of defeat and hopelessness, which had always been there, but seemed so amplified of late. Since the day of the picnic. It seemed to pile upon her. She had already shrunk a bit since the trip to the temple. Her determined air had left her, her sharp tongue, her willingness to even acknowledge people, or even humiliate the people that bothered her, a charm he did enjoy very much. She was a faded shade of what she had been only a few weeks ago.

He had tried to be as attentive to her as possible since that day. As someone who was inexperienced with such things, in regard to attentions to a desirable young woman, he wasn't sure if what he was doing was enough. He also didn't want to appear affected or insincere, as being attentive to this degree was not at all what was known to his character.

Her overt feelings he could sense. But the ones that were subtler, the ones that truly mattered, were overpowered by her lowness, her sorrow, and now a bristly anxiety that washed over her whole being. He was tempted to push in—to disregard his respect for her privacy and her boundaries, to invade her head and find it for himself. But he liked her. *No... I think I love her.* He could not do that to her. She would have to trust him enough to tell him on her own.

Yet still he felt close to her. He wasn't sure how to express how he felt. He even knew that she might like *him* a little. She had held his hand and given him *that look* with her eyes. Those deep, indigo, sad, lost eyes.

He felt deeply and fiercely protective of her. He remained close to her any opportunity that arose. He opened doors for her, he helped her with her chairs. He brought her treats and snacks between classes, acting as if he'd gotten too many for himself. He served her from the platters during

170

meals. This was all done with his typical aloofness. His unreadable face. His standoffish air. She remained close to him. She accepted his gestures. She let him stand next to her, and sit next to her, she leaned on him in the coach, she took his arm, and did not recoil in that subtle way she did when she was around anyone else. That meant something. He could not deny it, and he knew what he felt in fleeting expressions of her emotions. A thread of warmth at his presence. A sense of security and comfort when he was nearby. Even now, he had felt a wash of acceptance of him only moments before as they walked. He was sure, to one degree or another, Iselle liked him.

Two nights before, the day after he'd returned her necklace, he went to the dorm to meet her for the walk to the refectory for supper. Her expression was as depressed and bewildered as he'd ever seen when she came out of the building and walked to his side. Her face, when he saw her, conveyed fragility and vulnerability. And as he walked with her through the cloisters, her eyes began to mist over, and he saw her chin trembling.

"Why must you be so kind to me?" she asked in a broken voice.

"I've never been accused of *that* before," he said acerbically. But then his effort to evoke levity in his unique way, or to spark a diverting, biting exchange only melted into concern.

He halted on his feet, and observed that at the moment, she was fraying, and fragile. He took her wrist and drew her over to the smokehouse overhang, where there were no windows, and no people; an area with an open side that was overgrown with shrubbery and shaded by the broad eave of the small building. She sat down on the low stone wall, the waxy rhododendron leaves that crowded against the back of it, surrounding her. There were no words. She simply hung her head and succumbed to the tears. Her sorrow was all-consuming. Forrest could only look on, his heart aching for her.

Then he ventured to comfort her. He wasn't sure how she would react to it; he feared it might revile her; undermine the hard-earned trust she'd granted him. But he moved to sit next to her, and with his right hand, he reached out and awkwardly patted her back. This made her cry even harder. And she leaned forward and cradled her face with her hands, and bawled into them, her shoulders shaking and her voice growing raw from the sobs.

To his shock, she straightened when the surge of tears subsided, and she tipped over and leaned onto him. She turned her face onto his chest, hiccupping from the exertion. He ventured another risk, and rested his arm on her, clutching her right shoulder, and gently holding her there. And there they sat, for at least an hour, missing the mealtime. She, diving in and rising out of swells of undisclosed suffering, he, clutching her close, and realizing at that moment, how much he adored her. He only wished she would tell him what it was that was destroying her.

Now, he watched her across the table, and the food was served; three large platters of daintily designed food, artfully placed in an array of bright colors and sumptuous textures. Food that ought to have sent her into raptures as they were the kinds of food Miritrians ate during celebrations and special occasions. Tiny tarts with flaky crusts filled with savory things; little edible leaves cupping crisp and vibrant salads and poached shrimp; half-shells of briny oysters, crab with creamed cheese on little crisply toasted bread, and plump, perfectly seared scallops topped with bright orange roe, or green onions.

She stared at it all blankly. He served her one of the shellfish.

Her eyes rolled up to look directly at him. It was unnerving to Forrest, and it made him freeze. She rarely made eye contact like this. Now she did with such fixed thoughtfulness.

They stared at one another for a spell. He said nothing. He let her decide what to say. She seemed to be contemplating something, turning it 'round in her head. When she finally spoke, it was barely above a whisper.

"I want to tell you…" she said tentatively, "…but I'm afraid."

He froze, still holding the serving implement. "You have nothing to fear of me—nothing to distrust."

"I'm not afraid of you," she corrected him. "I don't want you to be…" she dropped her head again. It occurred to him how vulnerable she was with him. To everyone else, she was the same cold, hard, bristly hedgehog. Even with Dorya to a degree. "I don't want to endanger you, either," she added.

"Why would I be in danger?" he asked, guileless.

Iselle looked contemplative for a moment. She seemed as if she had decided at that moment.

"Don't speak a word," she told him. "Don't move. Just look." To his shock, she reached up and unpinned her bib-front, laying the two pins next to her plate. He swallowed and bit his tongue. What was she doing?

Her bib dropped down at her high waist and exposed the laced bodice panels that closed the front of the gown. She pulled the laces loose, and the two panels fell away to the side, exposing her stays and chemise. She loosened her stays, and the drawstring of her chemise, tugging them both loose and wide. She shifted and twisted her body around so that her back was to him. He saw a glimpse of the pendant she had cherished so, against her milky skin above the cleft of her breasts just as she turned her now bare shoulders away.

He watched with fascination and astonishment, silent, his fists clenched in his lap as she bared her body to him. He had no idea what this was or what it meant. He did as he was told. He remained still and watched. His neck and cheeks heated up at the sight of her skin. He had experienced some advances before. This didn't feel like an advance. It felt like she was confiding in him. She turned her head, so her chin almost touched her shoulder and looked back as she shrugged the straps and sleeves from her arms. That moment, that image would burn itself into his brain, the depth of her beauty, the curve of her shoulders and neck, the delicate, graceful sweep of her neck. He swallowed again, this time loudly.

And then the back of her dress dropped down.

Forrest's eyes widened as her fair shoulders and then her back was revealed. She let her bodice and underpinnings drop low—to the base of her hips, clutching the front of her gown over her breasts and ribs. She was half-naked in this private room. But it was no longer the nudity that evoked his reaction. What he saw there was beyond his ken. He stared, struck dumb. His confusion and arousal turned instantly to something black and furious.

Scarring slashed across her back in horrific raised, welted tissue, spelling out the words YOU ARE MINE. It had been carved with brutality into her skin and into her very soul and was embossed upon her body forever. The wounds were ragged and edged in redness and bespoke the violence that had been inflicted upon her to create them. They looked fairly fresh.

Forrest already barely contained his ire. He lived with anger, always. It was always simmering beneath the surface. He controlled it. But this. This boiled up like magma; and it took every shred of his magic and his strength to contain it. His eyes flamed with wrath. He grappled his rage down. His magic, fueled by anger could be devastating. He would rather die than expose Iselle to that part of him. Especially in this moment when she made herself so vulnerable.

He glared at the sight before him; her delicate, elegant, flawless body, what had been a plane of unblemished skin, so ferociously scored and marked by the hand of some monster. This perfect, innocent creature, so terribly wronged. He felt it wholly now, her hurt and her fear. She let it pour out from behind the walls she built. He could almost touch it; it became so real to him. Her heart, her pain, her terror fueled his magic. *Who did this?*

He had never been this infuriated in his life. *No. That's not true.* He had been. Fury he buried deep inside himself. Fury that had wrought destruction and shaped the monster he had become. He felt it again, flames licking at the edges of his soul.

"Who did this to you?" he choked through gritted teeth.

CHAPTER 18

Lenteev's body was found stabbed, an untold number of times, floating in the Amadry River by the mill. It was knocking against the water wheel, which apparently had caused quite a bit of damage to the corpse. Iselle found out about it through one of the theatre people, who, like others, remembered his frequent visits during the run. Iselle felt even worse about not remembering his face. Angry at herself for being so oblivious; she should have known better. Had her situation with Prentiss taught her nothing?

Some people even knew who Lenteev was, his occupation, his interests. They had come to know him, and she couldn't even recall the smallest detail about her mysterious letter-writer and would-be obsessed pursuer.

He had been a well-known, talented men's tailor. He had come to the play because he had supplied some costume pieces. The frock coat that Redlan had worn was one of those. He was a bachelor. He made women's hats as a pastime. They were ugly and garish and nobody bought them, so they gathered dust in the window of his small shabby shop while the sunlight bleached the dye out of the silk. She had heard all these scraps of gossip after the fact. Titterings and mutterings all around her.

Now he was cut up like a slab of pork belly and left to be battered by the water wheel of the town mill. Iselle knew to the very core of her being, from the moment she caught the gossip, that it was Prentiss that had done it. This was confirmed by a letter left on the little silver dish on the table by her dorm room delivered against her orders by the school porter.

It contained no greeting, nor did he leave a signature. But she knew his hand by now. Her face grew pale, and her heart raced.

I've dispatched with the parasite that sends you letters and watches you. I found him peering in the high window of the mineral baths, where you and other ladies were reposing. He was doing unspeakable things to himself, aroused by the sight of you. I was overcome with disgust and rage. I could not suffer him to live after violating your sanctity as he did. I will not tolerate animals hanging about you, leering at you, desiring you, because you are mine. It is time for you to become so. It is time for you to cease capitulating to the wants of others. It is time for you to come to me. I've been generous enough.

Iselle tried to contain her panic and compose herself as she packed up her few belongings into the tapestry bag she had condensed her world into. Her hands were shaking, and her skin was cold and sweaty. All these years of flight had taught her that there was no need for the burden of possessions beyond immediate needs, and a few keepsakes. First, she had limited it to a single trunk. Now it was just the large bag.

Her common clothes were few. She would leave wearing the bulkiest items on her back. The wispy gowns were rolled up and tucked into it, on top of her three pairs of shoes and her house slippers. Her jewelry, her sundries, and trinkets. Her extra chemises, petticoats, tuckers, stockings, caps, and chemisettes took little space because the muslin and organdy they were made from was so airy and light. Her tiny spencer took up only a fraction of the room in the bag, rolled up and pressed into a corner. Her two spare stays were rolled together and tucked with everything else. The school uniforms and robes, she left in the armoire. It looked like so little when it was piled inside the thick brocade enclosure.

She put on her redingote and her bonnet. She then seized the vial of potion made by Professor Reetch when she first arrived at Arrowood—a precaution requested by her uncle. It cost him a fair sum. The price of a new barouche and a team to pull it at least. Potion magic was rare, and the effectiveness was dependent on the skill of the mage that produced it. Reetch was well-known for his powerful brews. They were in high demand.

Professor Reetch had given the concoction to her in a vial of black glass with a bright red stopper, which she had kept on her vanity table next to her combs and box of curling rags. It looked like a bottle of scent, or a serum for her skin.

She plucked the round bead-like top off with a little pop, and threw her head back, forcing herself to drink down the thick, bitter, oily blend. She retched but kept it inside her with everything she could muster, in spite of her body instantly rejecting it. She put the now empty vial on her table, picked up her bag and clutched it to her chest.

Professor Reetch was a remarkably old man, with a wrinkled face, and rheumy eyes sunken deep into the folds of his lids. His fingers had papery skin and were bent and arthritic. But he was an excellent sorcerer, and his glamour potions were renowned, and sometimes sold far afield for a great price.

Shortly after her arrival at Arrowood, he had summoned Iselle from the refectory and instructed her to come to is laboratory immediately. It was a bit of a walk, and a bit of a maze to find her way to him. But she managed nonetheless and rapped softly upon the door.

It opened almost immediately. He stood before her in his dark scholarly robes and his round box hat of forest-green, in the laboratory assigned to him and only him, peering down at her from a lofty height for an old man. He was bent with age, but shrunk down, she was certain, from an even more formidable frame. Even doddering and rickety as he seemed, he was still imposing.

Behind him, his laboratory was an organized clutter of cauldrons and beakers, books, and bottles. Two enormous tables chockablock with braziers and pots, mortars and pestles, canisters of glass stirrers and shining, spotless droppers and tiny ladles. There were neat stacks of notepapers here and there, some lined up in tidy rows in front of various work areas. Every wall was lined with shelves, built right 'round the two towering windows that shed light into this impossible space, and around the door they stood in. The shelves were furnished with ranks of jars filled with substances unknown, liquid, powered, dried and whole. The labels were not readable from where Iselle stood. There were skulls and bouquets of dried herbs and flowers, and some shelves dedicated entirely to honeycombs of stacked rolled papers with marked ribbons dangling from the ends, and others with books.

The scent of a small wood brazier fire still lingered in the room, and a layer of smoke, faded and dissipating, hung under the ceiling in a slowly undulating misty sheet, shrouding the two massive chandelier rings that dangled from the box beams.

"I would offer to keep this here until you must make use of it, but I suspect if you must use it, it will have to be immediately at hand, and I cannot always be relied upon to be in my laboratory. You best take it with you." He reached into a pocket of his professor's robe and drew the bottle out, his hand carrying it across the space between them. "Please take care that nobody will purloin it or drink it. It was costly to make and more costly for your Uncle to purchase. He sent the message high priority so that it would precede your arrival." The old man's voice had a smooth, velvety quality to it, but his missing teeth made the words a little slurred.

She glanced at the vial he held before her. "I know it isn't even your first week of classes at Arrowood, child, but your uncle was most insistent that I make this and give it to you at my soonest convenience. I hope you are not troubled being summoned to this end of the great building so urgently, but I thought I ought give it as soon as it was prepared."

Iselle shook her head and reached out to receive the little vial. "It was no bother at all to come, Sir," she muttered. She stared at the bottle. Her uncle had not said anything to her about it, and she was taken aback. "What is it?" she asked. She accepted the thing from him, and peered at it, turning the smooth black glass bottle with the red stopper in front of her eyes.

"It is a concealing potion," he explained. "You must use it when you want to disappear, in a sense. You can become something you are not. You must drink it all. Every drop. And then you must count to twenty and then close your eyes. Envision something that isn't you. An old woman, a cat, something alive. Something anyone might see when out and about. Something innocuous and unremarkable. And then go. Don't linger. Don't lurk about suspiciously. Just go as far as your legs can carry you.

"What you envision, you become. It is a powerful glamour. A curtain of magic even glamorists cannot see behind. But it is limited. You have only two hours or so," he held up two knobby fingers, "before the ingredients are fully consumed and then flushed from your body. I wish for you that you never have any use for this potion. I cannot imagine what it is that necessitates you having it, but your uncle's letter was quite firm and worrisome. You must be cherished for him to provide you this."

Iselle's eyes burned, and she sniffed back her urge to burst into tears. Her throat tightened and she was able to squeak out a gracious thank you to the old man. He sent her away with a dismissive wave of the hand and disappeared into his laboratory. She lingered in front of the closed door for a moment before returning to her chamber. She put it where it would remain for three years.

Now, Iselle recalled what the old mage instructed. She counted to twenty and then took a solemn moment to picture the sand-colored dog that patrolled the campus bailey and its myriad alleys and walkways. It was Pork Pie she had fixed upon as her model. The students had named him such. He was a leggy, rangy slice of a dog that reached knee-height. He had thick, velvety, almost piled fur—a foxlike face with alert, triangular ears. He was furrier around his chest and neck, she remembered. With a coral-colored nose.

She smiled, thinking about his shining black eyes, bright and delighted to greet any of the students and faculty of Arrowood, and to receive pets and scratches, and if he was particularly fortunate, a tidbit or two of food, if he happened upon someone carrying something. For a moment, she forgot her fear. Pork-Pie, known throughout the town as a troublesome maker-of-puppies, brought her joy.

She did not know why dogs delighted her so. She'd never owned one, or even had much contact with them, except her uncle's hunting hound, who lived in the livery and was not the friendliest of dogs. Uncle Ude viewed dogs as working animals, not pets. Goblin had been a delight to her, but she wasn't quite sure he was even a dog. He behaved as one. But he was the only friendly pet dog she'd known.

She had once gone to the breeder with her uncle and was permitted to kneel in the fresh straw in the stall with a litter of the puppies, and she thought she might have died of bliss as the little things hopped around her and bit her cuffs, and tugged at her sleeve, growling and tumbling and gusting their milky breath in her face. She could still hear her own giggles. She was beside herself when they left without one.

She shook herself back to the present. She remembered; "Just go. You have two hours." *No time to reminisce about dogs. Time to be one.*

In the deep of the night, she left Arrowood. She scurried through the streets, holding the bag in one hand, her talisman in the other, clutched against her breast. *Dog. I'm a dog. I'm Pork-Pie.* She flitted like a shadow, moving through town, ducking from one alleyway to the next, scuttling behind the rows of gardens between the boulevards, trying not to appear too obvious in her flight. Trying to look like Pork-Pie, scampering through the streets in search of cats to chase and dogs to meet.

She did not see anything but herself. Her skirts and coat whooshing around her legs as she half-ran. Her white knuckles clutched around the handle of her bag. But her shadow showed something different. What others saw was not what she did.

To the eyes of anyone that looked upon her, she was a sandy-colored dog with pert ears and a bright gaze, trotting around corners, loping across the streets, padding in the shadows, galloping and chasing after riders and coaches in the final hours of the night. As the sun rose, her glamour faded, and the bitter taste the potion had left in her mouth vanished with it.

She arrived at an inn on the very edge of Emdroth, where the city abruptly ended, and the rocky mountain roads were bleak and empty. She arrived in the chill of the early hours of morning. There, she remained until the stagecoach arrived. She sat quietly by the livery stable, where the horses watered at the stone trough. Riders came and went and never noticed her, sitting in the lee of the building upon a bale of straw, her bag clutched on her lap, a scarf she clumsily knitted herself with yarn Redlan had chosen, wrapped around her neck and the lower half of her face.

The stage arrived with its four horses, the cheap seats on the roof swaying with passengers already. She bought one of the two remaining seats on the roof, huddled in beside a large woman and the arm of the side of the bench, feeling the swing of the vehicle more pronounced from the roof, as people got in or on it.

The aromas from the inn's kitchen wafted out from the windows as the passengers embarked, to make her stomach growl. She did not have a great deal of currency on hand, so she could not ask for something to take with her. The driver climbed aboard, and gathered up his bouquet of reins, and with a cluck of the tongue, the teetering coach was underway without incident. Relieved, she leaned back on the narrow bench, her body swaying, elbow to elbow with a woman in an old tweed walking gown, with a black hat and deep green gloves.

She would never run without some kind of communication, or arrangement with the school and her uncle first. But the letter at her door had spooked her. The murder had spooked her. She ran first. She would do the other things later. She had measures in place to help her if such a thing were to occur. But this was the first time she simply ran without telling a soul.

Her hunger was palpable, and when the lady in the black hat took out a sandwich with jam and butter from the bag on her lap, Iselle's voracious gaze upon the food was so palpable that the lady kindly passed half of the sandwich to her without a word. Iselle thanked her profusely. She ate and gave the woman one of her remaining copper Troys. After that, the misery of a rooftop seat seemed to lessen, and the farther she got from Emdroth, and the Arrowood school within it, the safer she felt. The bare mountain roads angled downwards, and they descended slowly into the lowlands, the horses' resistance against the weight of the coach was felt with forward jerks, and the brake sometimes made an unpleasant noise on the steeper bits, and the scent of smoldering wood enveloped the deathly quiet, rigid group of trepidatious passengers. Nobody breathed easily until the road leveled out.

She spent the rest of the six hours of stops and stages and rotating passengers, fighting back tears at the idea of leaving Redlan behind and watching the barren mountain landscape come to life as they passed the timberline, and entered the evergreen forests. She clenched her teeth and tried to keep her wits about her; to suppress the unease and the anxiety all the while.

The coach arrived at the edge of the tiny city of Iveneen, back in lowland, right in a market square in the late afternoon. She disembarked and melted into the throngs of people trying to purchase their goods before the stalls shut down at the evening bell. She found a bank as quickly as she could as they too would close their doors soon, and there she supplied herself of money.

Uncle Ude had been quite keen to give his niece every advantage possible in any circumstance and prepare her properly. That meant giving her access to emergency funds, as necessary. He supplied her with an

Insignia of Trust, issued by his bank. It was replaced every two years, and issued rarely, only to people of exemplary credit trusted by the bank. It had her name, and her date of birth etched in a code that also changed every two years, upon its shining silvery face, along with the emblem of the issuing bank.

With the little coin on a burgundy twill ribbon fob, she could walk into any bank she wanted, and request currency. She had yet to make use of it, as her uncle often furnished her school accounts with enough to supply her essentials. She normally kept the medallion pinned inside the inner band of her bonnet. In an emergency, she would have it on hand.

It was a strange, calming feeling when she walked into this bank, and was met at first with skepticism by the clerk, to only watch his tone and actions change to deference and welcome the moment she took off her hat and presented the insignia. One had to be of some consequence to merit the use of such a thing. She felt, at least in some minimal way, that she wasn't utterly alone on this frightening journey.

Her fresh banknotes tidily tucked away into the busk-pocket of her stays, a few coins for immediate convenience in her reticule, as well as some in the pocket under her petticoat, hanging heavy against her thigh, she stole out into the afternoon to find a place to stay until she could find her bearings and correspond with her uncle.

The next morning, she embarked again, dispatching a letter before buying a fare on another stagecoach. She would go far. As far as it took until she could breathe.

In a trade town called Iridrine in a northwest region, far along the straight of Omire, she finally stopped. The succession of coaches felt eternal. She was exhausted. She'd lost count of the miles and the days, the procession of inns. At this bustling sea-side city called Iridrine, she decided to pause. To retrench and regroup. To rest.

She found a little guesthouse near the town center, situated against one of the briny ship canals, which connected the ocean to the land waterways. The inn was right by the top of a lock. It was also set by one of the many stone bridges that spanned the waterway. It was charming. The walls were made of the same stone of the walls that lined the edges of the canal, and there were windows higgledy-piggledy all over the four sides of the building, with no sense of order to the floors. Inside was no less confusing, with a stairway of unexpected landings, archways with little mezzanines, and rooms set higher or lower than the ones next to them. It all reminded her of the school she had just fled.

All the walls were clad in dark wood paneling, and the candelabras cast all the rooms in a gold-tinted light, at least these warm things gave her comfort—but her overall melancholy was heavy upon her shoulders.

There, she settled into a small room situated just at the bottom of the roofline, where part of the ceiling was angled inwards with the roof. The sky opened up and she could hear the rain pattering down upon it and washing down her only window. She didn't feel wholly unsafe here. She felt somewhat secure that he could not follow. She had come so far.

He could not see her with her talisman. She allowed herself a little leeway. A little hope. He would search for the stagecoach stops. He might deduce she would choose a crowded town or city. So, she would remain in her room as much as possible. She had sent a letter to her uncle immediately upon arrival, and she would wait for his response.

She also took a moment to write a letter to Redlan. She had fled without a word. She owed him at least an explanation. She sat down at the tiny desk in the common room, amid the din of the slightly off-key, unsuspecting spinet being assaulted by an unskilled player, and the younger sister yowling along to the tune. They were both displaying for a handsome gentleman in a banyan and slippers, who was sitting with one leg crossed over the other next to the fire, reading a periodical, and stealing glances of Iselle every other shrill verse.

Iselle used her last sheet of paper, which had been slightly crumpled by the other items shifting about in her bag. She pressed down upon it with the flat of her hand, trying to smooth it to little avail. She used the guesthouse's ink and quill, which was worn and the ink slightly viscous. She fumbled through the drawers for a quill cutter, and found an ebony one with worn, patinated brass workings. It was dull, but it did the job well enough. She felt so out of sorts, so clumsy, so obvious and uncoordinated. As if fear and flight made her into someone she wasn't. She was never without poise. But Lenteev's death had profoundly shaken her. He had killed someone. This was beyond her comprehension. Murder was wholly outside of her understanding. It made her realize exactly how dangerous a monster this man truly was—how perilous her situation had become. Or had it always been such? Had Lacklow always been a murderer? Had she been subject to greater danger than she even knew? She shuddered, and her skin rose into goosebumps at the thought of it.

The gentleman in the inn seemed to be watching her. She could see him out of the corner of her eye, his face turning in her direction now and again. Paranoia raised the hair on the back of her neck. She focused on her letter. She tore off half of her paper with a rule and folded the unused piece for future use. With the slip she left on the desk, she wrote a note to Redlan in tiny script, using every spare inch of the paper, even writing vertically, in the margins.

She made an explanation to Redlan.

My beloved, sweetest Redlan, I assure you that I am safe. I only hope that you will not resent me for never confiding my secrets. I have lived so long with danger; I have grown accustomed to keeping it all close to the chest and not involving the few others that might be near and dear to me. I've been so reluctant to make friends, because my tenure at any place is always so short-lived, and like today, I have had to walk away and leave you behind. The danger always, inevitably, finds me. I can only hope that in this mad, raucous city, in this humble room, until I can depart, I can keep my spirits up. I can only dream that I can escape. I will hide here for now. It is confined, and I have hardly anything to occupy myself. I have only a small window, where I can watch the ducks and narrowboats in the canal and spy into the normality within the homes on the other side, and at clouds in the sky. I miss your companionship already. If I have not said enough, I will say now, you are my dearest friend. I confess I am terrified. I'm so very, very afraid. All I can think of is having you there to reassure me as you always do. I ask only that you remember me as fondly as I will remember you. I have never adored anyone more. I bid you farewell, and perhaps, by some dream, I might find you again and live in a world where it will be safe to just be. With love, my dear, dear beloved friend, your devoted Iselle.

But this was their undoing—this letter.

He found the school—that was easy enough. Her signal grew stronger with each discovery; her very *fear* of him was what drew him. That was the source of his locus spell. He had felt it from the first day, when he saw her upon the road, the perfect girl child, with a face that could not escape his thoughts. He felt her fear radiating, fresh and delectable, the trepidation in her eyes, it was like the finest wine.

And each time he saw her, it intensified. It filled him, and he craved more and more of it, and he wanted her so. He wanted her beauty and her terror. The more she matured, the more her anxiety matured. He could scarcely exist without it. His heart and body felt hollow and empty when she was cut off from him. Whatever it was that shielded her, it killed the fear that transcended distance and cut through the misery that was his existence. He followed, like a hound upon a fox. He liked the chase, and each encounter was increasingly exciting. He was unsure of what would transpire when he had her, but when he did, he would do whatever he could to keep her afraid. It was a sweet elixir without which he could no longer live.

He was drawn to the great school.

She likes to hide in schools.

He even saw her perform in the last show as a terrible queen from the back of the hall. He had traversed a strait and up a mountain to glimpse her on stage. How suited her role was to her. To be that queen. Her face, her air, her manners… all so composed and calculating. But he couldn't feel her fear. He so wanted to know what she had that could keep it from him—to starve him so cruelly of it.

He waited for her to be alone this time. There was a chance another person like that hag was there to keep him from her. To carry him away and throw him in a marsh, or to try to consume him with fire. He had to be a bit more careful now. She had allies. Interfering allies. *He* was supposed to be her ally.

There she was. One evening, after the last bell rang, amongst a cluster of girls, they, riotous and happy, she, subdued and watchful, but still accepted. *She made friends*, he thought, mildly shocked. She wasn't that type of girl, was she? Social and outgoing? *No.* This was the theatre group; clearly they were *obliged* to include her. Prentiss was still surprised to see girls making special effort to involve her in the conversation. He heard her soft replies, the tentative smile barely forming upon her perfect lips.

Hm, he puzzled, tilting his head.

He trailed them towards the city's hot baths. They were carrying sacks with towels and fresh clothes, bars of soap and lotions he could smell even from his distance. They were all a sight, in their simple columnar gowns, little trains dragging upon the pavement of the walk, hair done up upon their heads with curls falling down around their faces, shawls around their shoulders, so little wrapping in this cold place. *The baths are not far from the school, after all,* he thought, a little smile forming on his lips.

How much lovelier she is than the others. Look at how gracefully she moves.

The girls burst into boisterous giggles over some unheard joke. Even Iselle's lips parted, and a bright smile crossed her features. She dropped her head shyly, and one of the other girls reached out and smacked her arm, making some statement that made Iselle cover her mouth and laugh. She was ever so beautiful when she smiled. *I will make her smile and laugh like that. She will be joyful when she is with me.*

He followed. But he discovered, as he slipped through the shadows behind the little retinue of young women, that he was not the only one to shadow them.

It was then that he spotted *him* creeping from doorway to alley, a measure behind them, and only a bit farther in front of him. Prentiss narrowed his eyes, and tucked himself against the building, watching now, the stranger between him and Iselle.

It was without doubt, Iselle, he followed, this interloper. None of the other girls were even near as perfect and beautiful. *It had to be.* This conclusion made Prentiss terribly angry. He bit back his ire, and edged behind them, his eyes now on the man, and no longer upon Iselle.

The letch vanished just before the baths. It took a moment for Prentiss to locate him. He circumvented the broad, stone façade of the bathhouse, and slipped into an alleyway that led around the side to the back of the building.

It was there that he spotted the man crouching down on the top of a retaining wall above the alley, which was just about as high as a wide ventilation window on the back of the bathhouse. Billows of steam rolled from it. Prentiss melted into the shadows of the alley, watching.

After a bit, the interloper stirred. From inside the window, a rousing explosion of echoey giggles arose along with a fresh billow of steam. The pig that hunkered atop the wall like a grotesque, flabby bird, stretched upwards a bit to better see inside, and the light from the window washed across a lurid smile.

To Prentiss's shock, the man made a little grunting noise, and he unbuttoned his suspenders, and the flap of his fallfronts, and pushed them down 'round his ankles. He then squatted, and his hand slid up under his belly, and then his pasty, fleshy, unworthy body began gyrating from his unspeakable act.

The rage that boiled up in Prentiss could not have been more palpable. He clenched his teeth and withheld a roar that was pushing up into the back of his throat. How *dare* such a base and foul thing disgrace his Iselle with his disgusting gaze, or pleasure himself at the sight of her body? *His* body. He had yet to see it, in its glory. Yet to touch it, it was *HIS*.

His hand, as if of its own accord, reached into the large pocket of his great coat, and slid around the thick, plied fibers of the cord he had planned to use on Iselle. He had brought it to hold her fast when he took her away from this forsaken, frozen place. He drew it out of his coat, and his long, slender fingers hastily and expertly looped it into a noose in the dark, his eyes never leaving the debauched animal perched on the wall.

He then returned to the street, and to where the bank rose from the walk, and he crept with great care up its steep incline, gripping the dense, low-growing trees that had been planted upon it to ease his climb. He circled widely, so that he could emerge from the foliage behind the intruder. There was a realization that crossed his mind, that in this place, there was already a worn path through the trees, up the hill to the wall by the bathhouse window. He twisted his lip in disgust.

He slid silently, like a shadow, from the darkness, and in a rapid motion, he dropped the noose over the intruder's ugly head and used his enchantment to make it constrict fast around his neck. Not enough to kill him. Not yet. But enough to constrict his windpipe and keep him quiet until he lost consciousness.

Like a wild pig on a snare, the stranger panicked and twisted. Prentiss dragged him, bucking and struggling, into the trees, away from the window, away from Iselle.

The man was weak, and feeble. It wasn't long before he lost consciousness. It was only then that the rope was loosened. Prentiss packed a kerchief into his mouth, squatted over the man's body, and waited, reconfiguring his fastenings around the heavy person, and readying to roll him down the hillside and drag him someplace else.

When the girls emerged, and made for the academy, the streets quieted, the bathhouse was closed and its workers had left, Prentiss, in his infinite patience, finally emerged from the brush, dragging a bound man behind him.

He lugged him into a nearby livery, where there were only horses and empty carriages. There, he tied the gruesome creature fast to the post, and he contemplated what he would do next; the rage inside him building as the vision of him at the window repeated in his head.

Prentiss pressed his hands to his temples and then roared into his sleeve in anger at the images, sharp and clear, flashing in his brain. "She's MINE!" he screamed through the wool on his sleeve. The horses shifted about in their stalls, awoken by the muffled shout, taking in rattling snorts to catch the scent of these intruders. He could spy the shine of their eyes in the meager light, as they hooked their heads over the half-doors of their stalls and pivoted their ears and gazes upon the activity.

Kill him, kill him, the dirty, filthy pig, he commanded himself. But he hesitated. He bent down and began to slap the man's cheeks and jostle his shoulder.

"Wake up, you foul idiot. Wake up," he hissed.

The stranger stirred. He grunted behind the square of fabric crammed into his mouth, held in by a length of cord. He sat flat on the floor, his upper half propped against the post and lashed to it so tightly, his flesh protruded like a trussed ham.

"Good. You're awake," he said. His eyes examined the pathetic soul, his mouth clamped around the portion of rope Prentiss had wound around his head, pinning it to the post.

He knelt before him, fixing his vengeful gaze upon the man's wide, terrified eyes. He could scarcely see him. A single tallow lantern was suspended from the ceiling of the aisle between stalls. The flame, small and yellow, flickered inside the glass enclosure. It had been deliberately left burning by the livery in case their services were required in the depth of the night. It shed only a tiny light.

"If you speak, I will let you live. If you shout, I will kill you where you sit. I'll slice your head off and throw it to the dogs. Do you hear them barking?" Outside, there were indeed dogs barking across the silent city.

Lenteev nodded as best he could with the ropes holding his head fast to the pole. Prentiss pried the rope out of his mouth and glared at him through the darkness.

"Then talk," he said levelly, in a chilling voice.

The man proved to be of some use before he became the recipient of Prentiss' mania.

He learned about Redlan from Lenteev. The pig knew a great deal about Iselle and this Redlan.

Prentiss had been thorough in his interrogation before he slit Lenteev's throat and then stabbed and slashed his body repeatedly in a blind fury with a farrier's hoof-knife, pouring into this worthless soul every shred of his rage and anger. The image of him at the window made him stab the man until exhaustion. For a spell, he fell back onto his backside in front of the slumped body and caught his ragged breath. His face, his arms, his hands were dripping with blood.

The horses whickered from the scent of the blood, and circled in their stalls, stamping their hooves and pinning their ears. The whites of their eyes were bright in the darkness.

It was done.

Now he had other matters to see to now. His eyes rested on the body in front of him; a few rumples of clothing and bloodied skin catching the spare light of the lantern. Lenteev's desperate terrorized ramble was strangely satisfying to listen to. His fear was pleasing. Not nearly as pleasing as hers, but pleasing, nonetheless.

She likes hats. She gazes at them in shop windows. She would very much like mine if she saw them, she would, I know it. The dandy, the dancing boy with the bicorn hat always on his head, they are so close. They like the mutton stew. They like to listen to the music at Duckham's. They're always together. She is most fond of him. He is most fond of her.

Prentiss didn't like it that they were always together. He did not like the fondness.

If Prentiss had not been so very impulsive, he would have done a better job of hiding the body. But he was depleted after the kill. He had no idea that stabbing with a knife could be so strenuous. He had cuts upon his own hand from the blade. It never occurred to him that this would be the case.

But his arm was shockingly sore after all this. His shoulder blade and his ribs were sore. *I dragged that swine for how far? Of course I'm sore,* he rambled inside his head.

Killing the man had eaten up so much of his anger and sated something inside him for now.

He waited and rested. He bided his time with the horses until the third hour of the morning. He then unwound the rope from the post, threw it aside, and grasping the legs of the body, he dragged the dead man through the street, leaving a gory trail of blood behind him. He dragged him to the edge of the river and kicked him into the languid waters. The splash was rather loud, and it echoed against the walls that encased the city portion of the Amadry waterway. Nobody was awoken. Not here. The only things that were awake were the dogs that barked so incessantly that nobody listened to them.

Prentiss only thought about his drastic and thoughtless actions in hindsight, and how Iselle might be frightened by what he had done, instead of grateful. It never occurred to him, as he washed his body of Lenteev's blood, hunched, nude, over the washbasin in the room of a small house he'd broken into. Furnished and dusty from the absence of its owners, he found refuge here. He had returned to it at the wee hours of the morning and shucked his stained attire and set it all ablaze in the hearth.

He stooped over the washbowl and poured clean, cold liquid from the decanter. It was frigid, as he had only just sluiced it from the well-pump into the vessel. He washed it over his head and face, and he swished his hands in the red-tinted water that collected in the basin at his feet. All he thought at that moment was that he was victorious. That he had won a battle for Iselle. That he rid her of a parasite. He didn't know the body would be discovered as quickly as it was. It only came to him afterwards, after she had run away, that he should have been less grandiose about it. He had let his anger lead him—reckless and instinctive.

She is a fragile and gentle girl, after all. A murder might be alarming to her, regardless of its good intentions. Girls don't understand the sacrifices men must make for them. The acts of violence. They don't understand.

He had not considered any of this. He had been led by his rage and disgust with the intruder—at the pig that deigned to set his eyes upon the woman Prentiss loved, bared in her most vulnerable, most hallowed naked state.

He lamented his reckless, wrath-driven actions, now. He should not have infiltrated her school, and left the note by her door, it was impulsive in misguided. *Too forceful for a delicate creature.*

He pressed the heel of his hand against his forehead and rebuked himself as he ate his breakfast at the table of a nameless public house, his gaze distant.

Now she had vanished. She was gone and it was his fault.

When he had written of what he had done in his note, at that moment, he truly fostered a certainty that she would have *appreciated* the gesture of removing that animal from the plane of existence. He left the note, confident it would send her through the gate, and flying into his arms. He never considered it would make her run the other way. He did it *for her*. He did not understand. He did not understand Iselle. She loved him, he knew this. She was merely immature and bendable to the wishes of others. He knew she would see things his way, if only she would not listen to them.

He was at a loss as to how she had slipped under his nose. Where had she gone? He had been watching the gate of that school for days. It was the only entrance to the place. When he went to her room, she had left only her uniforms behind. Everything else was gone, save for a little triangle of sheer fabric; a fichu to cover her poitrine, that had fallen partly under the armoire. He stooped and picked it up, pressing the airy slip of embroidered material under his nose. He took in the scent of her skin. It was intoxicating.

He dropped his hand with the garment clutched in it, straightened, and examined the room, the daylight cast into the small space upon the emptiness she left behind.

As inconvenient and unexpected as her flight was, he was overcome with a sense of thrill at the idea that she was on the run; and if only slightly, by the idea that the murder would further buoy her dread. He could scarcely wait to taste it. He would catch her. It was inevitable.

At least he had in his possession the information that the pig had given him. This would bring him to her. This would sweeten the hunt.

Prentiss began to scrutinize the male students that came and left the academy. There were many dandies, as was described by the pig, among them. Some were older, some were younger. Some were handsome and wholesome; others were lascivious and predatory against the girls.

He followed them each in turn. Predictably, he came upon the one he sought; a waify, pretty-faced boy who walked to a place called Duckham's one evening, with Prentiss at his heels.

It coalesced for him. He'd heard that name. *Duckhams. The swine had said it... something about mutton... Yes. Mutton and music.* He followed him inside and sat down to watch him. Why hadn't he thought of it? Why had he forgotten this detail? The blatherings of the pig were many. Perhaps it slipped his mind. By the time he had come to this realization, the boy had disappeared. And the music was over.

Why was he so scattered? Was it the prospect of having her, of being so close? Perhaps it thrilled him too greatly. Was it the letting of blood? Why were his thoughts so disorganized and his instincts so blunted?

Prentiss ordered a grog, and drank it bitterly, staring at the tabletop as his thoughts tormented him. At least, he mused, he had found the dandy. But he had some things to do before he did anything else moving forward. He could no longer do anything without money.

Emdroth was distant from home and his bank. He had spent what he had in his purse and was thus forced to perform some enchantments for money, to purchase what he needed; giving a little life to the toys of rich people; enchanting the jewel of a ring to dance in its box, making an old portrait smile and nod. Silly things such as this were his bread and butter.

This is how he subsisted, mostly. Fooling people, entertaining people. It could be profitable to perform such meaningless acts of magic, and he never lived in poverty. He had late purchased the small shipping concern which now made him a nice passive income, as he left its management to a hireling. Thanks to these things, he had a lavish home at Neddham, so close to where she had once lived.

He wanted to expedite bringing Iselle home, to have her at his side where she belonged.

Why didn't her uncle wish that as well? Foolish man, he thought bitterly.

Lately, this place, this cold, unforgiving black-stone-covered place was the farthest he'd come so far in pursuit of his lady. It had taken him days on horseback and by ship to reach it. He'd burnt a set of clothes. He'd bought a horse which also needed livery and care when he was not traveling upon it. He'd eaten at pubs. The whole venture had cost him a lot of money. He needed more money, because if he were going to finish things up here, he would need it to move on.

Prentiss took some time and spent a day or two in the parlors and ballrooms of the town's few social clubs, mingling with the local set, demonstrating little entertaining glamours to attract clients to hire him for more complex enchantments. He was not an ill-looking man, and the ladies flocked to him already for his gifts and tried to seduce him in turn. None of them could stand up to the beauty and elegance of his Iselle. He suffered through their vapid flirtations and happily took their money in return for trite little acts of magic and pursued them no further. It took two nights only to collect clients, and the following days to do his work and make enough.

He took his earnings when he had refilled his purse, and he went to stay at Duckham's; vacating the house he had broken into to save money and have the privacy he needed. There at Duckham's, he waited every night at the table, growing anxious that Iselle was getting farther and farther away with each passing moment he was delayed by the Redlan fellow's absence from this public house.

While waiting, he even tried the mutton stew, which he found to be middling at best.

Redlan arrived at length. Red-cheeked and merry from prior revelry that evening. Like the time before, he arrived alone. The boy wore a navy wool cape this night, and he flung it dramatically off his shoulder and sat down. He watched the musician play, consumed the night's fare, which was venison and potato stew, and imbibed some ale. The boy appeared bereft. He sat, one leg crossed over the other, in his chair, his elbow on the table and his chin resting in his fist, his eyes fixed upon the player.

The musician rose after his last piece, and approached the boy, sinking into the chair that Iselle would have likely been sitting in, if she were still here. The musician asked the young man where his beautiful lady was, and Redlan blushed and denied his connection to be so intimate. "She is only my friend," he insisted, smiling broadly. The musician also smiled at this news.

Prentiss chuffed through his nose and glowered balefully in his shadowy corner. *Liar.*

"She's gone abroad for a spell," the boy added.

More lies thought Prentiss. *And that lutist*, he glared at the handsome man, *he too covets my Iselle.* Is there no man that does not want her? His glare grew black with rage. He would have to keep her away from everyone. He would not let her out of the house. The world was replete with animals lusting after *his* woman. His anger stoked anew; he observed Redlan closely.

He rose from the table and left just after the delicate boy departed to return to the school. Redlan was tipsy on the thick, bitter ale the place served. He walked unsteadily through the busy street to the square, singing to himself, waving at familiar passersby who were still enjoying evening activities. Redlan didn't have the presence of mind to realize he was being followed—that he led a predator straight to his rooms in the dorm.

The streets were crowded. People slipped languidly around them as they moved against the flow of walkers. Prentiss followed closely. Close enough to look as if they were walking together. Nobody batted an eye as they crossed into the courtyard, entered the main hall, climbed the various stairwells, and crossed through the myriad corridors to the boy's room.

When Redlan opened his door and went in, Prentiss simply reached over his head, stopped the door as it closed with the flat of his hand. He then pushed his way into the space, locking the latch once inside. The boy with the cherubic visage turned in confusion at the sight of a stranger in his room. Prentiss smiled cruelly at his pretty face, and advanced upon him. It didn't take much to overpower the young man and slay him quickly without noise. He'd kept the hoof-knife from the livery. It sliced beautifully through the young man's tender skin. *How could she want such a weak, fragile thing?* Prentiss thought. *Oh, Iselle. You disappoint me.*

The boy was so easy to kill. His crisp white, pressed cravat and tunic wicked the blood from his throat and the red shape spread along his shirt front like rose petals unfurling, and his silken frockcoat and waistcoat were ruined. *Her beloved, her beau, this pathetic ragdoll of a man, sprawled upon the floor of his room, his dead gaze peering up at the ceiling.* How delightful this hunt had become. Unexpected rewards of fear had washed upon Prentiss; more potent and defined than those of the Lenteev character.

He casually circled the room, at leisure, and picked through Redlan's belongings. It was on his table where he found the letter, folded and wedged upright between a carafe of water and a faceted glass goblet.

He sank down in the chair, crossed his leg, and unfolded the creased paper.

She only used half a sheet, thrifty girl.

He left smudges of blood from his fingertips on the edges of the paper, obscuring a few of the words she'd scrawled in the margins. He liked her handwriting. The words looked like a soft wind was gusting through them.

She has been gone for eleven days; he mused. Eleven days. She had written no date on the letter, but there were other clues. What crowded place could be inside that radius, counting the letter's journey from wherever that was?

Eleven days, with a message sent from a city with canals, how far away would that be?

CHAPTER 19

"First, he killed Lenteev. He was displeased by the attention he gave me. It didn't matter that the attention was unwanted and unsolicited. Lenteev was *like* him. Obsessed. Possessed. But I don't think he deserved to die like that," she said this in a soft voice.

"Then he killed…" her voice was suddenly strangled. She pulled up the back of her dress, and facing away from him, she hiked the bodice and the shift and stays beneath it, back onto her shoulders. She pulled herself back together, both her dress and her composure. She tugged laces tightly and adjusted her garments with each layer she restored. Meanwhile, she measured herself, took a breath, bit back her emotions, as he had seen her do so often.

"Redlan didn't even *like* girls," she muttered in a broken voice, looking down and then over her shoulder, her elbows waving a little as she tied laces. She tugged brusquely in front, and the back of her gown tightened on her body again, conformed to her graceful shape. Her hand slipped 'round and her fingers pinched the pins from the table. She remained with her back turned to him for an instant longer, pinning the bib back over the laces of her dress closure, and tucking in the edges of her underpinnings that might be escaping the neckline of her gown.

Perhaps she remained facing away because she lacked the courage to see Forrest's face after revealing the ugliness Prentiss had inflicted upon her. Perhaps she thought Forrest would think less of her, and she would see it in his eyes if she turned 'round. He could feel her bracing for disappointment. He caught the whisps of those emotions with his projected senses. He silently willed her to stop feeling those things.

"He was innocence embodied. My only dearest friend. My heart," she said, her voice choking. She tried to collect herself. "If he had not been connected to me, he would yet be alive. I am complicit, and I cannot be the same for you," a sob escaped, and she swallowed it back, covering her mouth. She waited a measure or two before continuing.

"I don't want anything to happen to you, but he might know now, where I am. There's you. There's Meddin and Dorya, even Ryle. I will have to leave again… I have a little time. It took about twelve days to sail here over the Onham Sea with all its inclement weather and headwinds. Add to that travel from Emdroth… Or wherever he was when he detected me," her voice trailed off.

"I am far from where he was. But it's not a great deal of time. Every time he finds me, it always seems so rapid, so speedy after he is able to locate me. I've been postponing my departure, even though he surely saw me when I lost my necklace. I am sure of it, no matter how far I am from home and from him. I don't *want* to go," her voice was strangled again. "But I must. The farther I get now, the better," her voice broke, her head dropped, she emitted a wracking sob, and her shoulders shook. She lifted the top of her wrist to her nose and her eyes, shining with tears, blinked out more to tumble down her cheeks. Her lashes were clumped from the moisture. She was so beautiful, even when she was lostF in abject suffering.

Forrest rose to his full height, looming over the low table, and circled it in two steps. He knelt softly down in front of her hunched, miserable form. He reached up and lifted her chin so he could see her bleary, swollen eyes.

"Miss Moon, I do wish you would not fret so," he muttered in a gentle voice, his eyes warm and kind. "I beg you, please be assured at least that he cannot harm me. You mustn't twist yourself up with worry. I am mage, after all."

"So is *he*," she retorted desperately, her eyes fixed upon his face, so plaintive and concerned, "…a practiced, powerful, and ruthless one. He is a murderer—one that kills with vicious rage. What he did… father said he cut Redlan's thr…" she stopped herself, the back of her hand wiping away the tears. She grimaced and began sobbing again, her wrist over her eyes. "I should leave here. I'm so tired of running, Mr. Outvallen. So tired…" she wept.

Forrest gazed upon her for a long moment, until her sobs subsided a little and she was sniffing and dabbing her face with a kerchief he had produced. Her mood was so low these days, he kept one, always in his pocket for her.

He stayed with her through her catharsis, yet again, soothing her with gentle pats on her arm. When her sobs subsided, his eyes fell onto hers, and he knew that they expressed the feelings he fostered for her, openly and without apology. But she was too overwhelmed to notice.

He rose again, and returned to his side of the table, sinking ungracefully down into the tiny floor-chair, and folding his long legs in front of him. "I can fight too. I'm quite skilled at it, truth be told. I quite enjoy a little viciousness; a little bloodsport; a touch of violence," he said in his level voice.

Iselle recognized the ripple of darkness that passed over him, he felt her reaction to it, as she peered squarely at him. She did not think his assurances were sufficient. She watched him study her furrowed brow and her worried expression. He chuffed through his nose.

"Eat," he said decisively. "You are peaked, and your face is a mess." He shook out his napkin and placed it on his lap. "Then, we will go and visit a family member of mine. She isn't even far from here." He reached over the table and served her a little pastry cup crammed with some kind of meat filling, placing it gently upon her plate. "I went through the trouble to book this table at an establishment that was supposed to make you feel comforted. And look at you," he admonished.

She wiped her nose again with the kerchief, and her eyes narrowed. She took the pastry and popped it into her mouth, chewing as if she could not taste it.

He ate something, making a little *Mm* sound after a chew or two. His brows arched in appreciation. "Not bad," he said through his food. "I could get used to this kind of fare."

He could feel her doubt. She did not believe his flippant lack of concern was real. But somehow, it still comforted her. He rested his mind on that, dwelling just slightly inside her head. There was warmth in her emotion. She looked down at the table. Her plate had an oyster on it still. She picked it up and slurped it out of the shell.

"Good girl," Forrest muttered. "Have some of that. That is particularly good." He pointed at the crab.

She did.

"We shall go and see Niria after we eat every crumb of this. She might have some advice to give," he said. "You will like Niria," he added with a brighter face.

"You bring me this bedraggled little thing?" Niria was a woman of about fifty, with hair the color of polished pewter. She was an exceptionally elegant woman, with strong, aquiline features that had a remarkable resemblance to Forrest. She was his paternal Aunt. She refused to be addressed formally and instructed Iselle to call her Niria the moment they met. She swept the girl with a practiced, deep green eyes, and arched her brow.

Iselle immediately noticed a subtle tone of reticence or trepidation in Niria's body language when she addressed Forrest or came near to him. She stiffened, and her jaw tightened.

"You are a troubled little soul, aren't you? Is this your chosen one, Forrest? Finally, you've expressed interest in a girl. We were all quite worried. He's never liked a girl before," she said the latter in a faint voice as if telling Iselle in confidence. "There was speculation amongst his cousins that perhaps he was a barrener, or someone who preferred his own gender…" When she said this, she revealed just the tiniest shred of malice in her words. She tried to hide it with good humor, but it was there. Iselle saw it.

"Aunt…" Forrest groaned with irritation, coming up behind Iselle, making her look very small with his tall frame and wide shoulders.

"I have often thought *myself* a barrener," Iselle told the lady with a bit of a reproachful look. "I have always foreseen my life to be lived without attraction to anyone."

"And that's changed. Thank goodness" Niria concluded. She let her critical eye sweep over the young man she called her nephew. It was a cool, ambiguous gaze.

Iselle watched her with interest and displayed a neutral expression. The woman's eyes then swept back to Iselle, and she gave her a lingering, amused glance before turning to the window and throwing open the sheer curtains to the view of the park across from her lovely home.

"His mother told me that she was desperate for him to show any sign of romantic interest in anyone. She said she would accept a street urchin as a daughter-in-law, even, as he has been implacable when it comes to avoiding love."

Niria wore a goldenrod and chocolate striped day gown with full sleeves and the loveliest lace chemisette and ruff Iselle had ever seen. She wore no cap, but her hair was fashioned into a perfectly arranged roll atop her head, with a single swath of hair coiled down upon her shoulder. Her parure of gold and amber stones glistened from her wrist, ears, neck, and fingers.

She lived alone in this tall, narrow house only a quarter of an hour from the Blue Pearl on the edge of the city of Minreth.

She moved languidly through the smallish parlor and gestured for them to sit. She watched them as they did. Neither of them argued whether Forrest liked Iselle or not. They both knew from her air alone, that it would be fruitless to do so, and any resistance would further cement the idea with her, as it would with anyone else who knew them.

They chose to sit side by side on an elegant chair settee with graceful saber legs and gold upholstery upon the seat. They faced the lady like an audience, Iselle with her hands clutched demurely on her lap, and Forrest, with his usual air of casual boredom, with his ankle resting on his knee, and his arm hooked over the back of it.

"Now let me see it," Niria said, approaching, and looming over them.

"What?" Forrest asked. She shot him a look of impatience.

"The magical item. Let me see it," she jutted out her hand, palm up.

"I cannot take it from my body," Iselle uttered.

The older woman would not be denied. "Let me see."

Iselle figured she had nothing else to lose. She had already lost it once again. He already saw her, if that is how it worked.

What would another few ticks of the minute hand matter? You're so spineless. Disgusting creature.

Iselle paused for two beats, her brow wrinkling. She measured herself and then reached into her neckline and drew it out. She unlatched the black chain that now held it, the gift Forrest had bestowed upon her.

Niria took it, and examined it, a peculiar expression crossing her brow.

"This is death-magic," she said. "Why are you wearing a death-magic charm?" She walked around the seating area, staring at it contemplatively.

"She must remain unseen," Forrest explained.

"Who would see her? She's a ghost," she said, tossing the chain onto the low tea table. She paced restlessly across the room and pulled the cord for tea. She then sat down at last, taking in each puzzled face with a heavy-lidded, impassive gaze.

"What?" she sighed impatiently at their confusion. Still, they stared, waiting for further explanation. "I can't expound adequately. There's something ghostly, something otherworldly about the girl," she said to Forrest. "Her presence is already faint and almost unreadable. Why would she need that trinket?" Niria waved her hand dismissively.

"I don't understand. He sees me when I'm not wearing it. He finds me." Iselle reached for the black widow and put it back on her neck over her garments.

"Who? Who sees you?" Niria asked.

"It's a long story," Forrest replied with a tone of finality to it.

The lady exhaled impatiently and rose to her feet again.

"What do you need from me then?" she snapped at her nephew. "I can scarcely be of assistance if I don't know what the problem is."

"We need to know *how* he sees her. And perhaps figure a way to stop him from doing so for good." Forrest rose with a swish of his tailcoat, and like his aunt had before, he paced.

"Have you never asked for a mage to help before?" Niria asked.

"Yes. Nobody can figure." Iselle frowned.

"How long has this person been plaguing you?" the woman persisted.

"Since I was twelve."

There was a silence that fell upon the room like a slab of stone.

"I can only try," Niria finally acquiesced. "I make no guarantees. The stone tells me nothing. I will need to cast my eye upon *you*, not your trinket."

She rose again and circled the table. She reached down and took Iselle's hands in each of hers and pulled Iselle up onto her feet.

She circled the girl, and a gentle hum rose up from her chest. It was a strange tuneless drone. Niria scrutinized and examined Iselle. The hum grew more and more resonant, and as it did, Niria's hands rose to hover flat, only an inch over Iselle's body.

She moved them over the girl's form. Along her chest and arms, she stooped to her legs, and then up again, around her back, and finally came to Iselle's head. The tune rose an octave, and her hands trembled a little. Her flattened palms lingered at the side and back of Iselle's skull. "Fascinating," she said.

"Aunt…" Forrest implored impatiently. The sound of his voice made her jump a little.

"Hush, boy," she snapped. She began to hum again. Iselle felt heat emanating from her hands. She spread her fingers, and the heat spread as well. "You are emitting something…" she pointed out.

"There is an energy… no… a call of sorts. It is rooted, entangled with the source of your feelings, in here. Just about here." Her hand lingered just above Iselle's ears. "It is sending out a signal of sorts. Strong. The … *entanglement* is augmenting it." She paused and fell quiet, still searching with her hands, homing in on something just above her temple.

"What *is* that?" she whispered.

What is it, what is it, what could it be?

She leaned her head close to Iselle's and seemed to be listening to something. She cocked her head, the lids of her eyes trembling.

"I can feel your fear now. It is what the entanglement is leeching. Nobody who does this kind of magic cannot be ill-intentioned. He could be an *eater*," she concluded. But she looked uneasy. Her hands dropped. Iselle was relieved as there was an unpleasant buzzing in her brain from it.

"He's an enchanter," Iselle argued, rubbing her head.

"It *could* be an enchantment…" Niria pinched her chin in puzzlement. "I've never seen one like this, inside the brain, inside living flesh. What did he enchant exactly? Is it a parasitic spell? It is quite clever if it is what I think it is. He *could* have an ability like Forrest, but that seems unlikely. But this might be the fuel for his magic. Emotion can be powerful.

"The spirit magic is a trait in our family. It varies how it is used; it can spark *terrible* outcomes if *misused* as with most magic; but it can be particularly destructive to the wellbeing of others if their spirit, their emotion, their sense of self can be purloined and used." She fell still, a dark gaze falling upon Forrest, her brow tightening. Iselle saw a flash of fear cross the woman's eyes. "It can be tapped to control a person, to operate, to manipulate and read secrets, to *harm*."

Niria hesitated. Forrest measured himself. He moved quietly back to the seat where he had been, and sank down, his brow furrowed. He leaned his elbows onto his knees and interlaced his fingers.

There is such darkness of a sudden. What secrets are they hiding? What stories pass between these glances?

Forrest's aunt watched him attentively and coldly for a passing second or two. He deliberately looked away. She then pivoted on her heel a little, and turned her back to them momentarily, and then peered at them over her shoulder.

"Forrest uses his empathy to *form* his magic. To shape it and fit it to the subject. This mysterious person must merely *consume* it if his magic is made to augment a particular emotion. Your fear must be quite delectable to him; enriching and appetizing, if you will, to do something like this."

Niria took a moment to mull over all these ideas, her eyes wide and searching. Her thoughts seemed to be overwhelming her. She shook her head in bewilderment. "This is not normal magic, I must say. To enchant living flesh.." she repeated, trailing off. "How?"

She faced Iselle again, and lifted her hand back to her head, resuming her haunting, discordant song. She clenched her eyes closed and forced greater heat from her hands into Iselle's head.

Stop it.

"Yes. It's like… roots… prying deep into the center of your emotions," she said. "There's another noise. I can't quite fix upon it," she murmured, concentrating.

Stop it, you cow! It hurts, you insufferable bitch!

She focused on the back of Iselle's head, just at the nape of her neck. Her humming intensified, and her expression became graver and focused. Her hands paused, and she abruptly fell silent.

Stop!

Niria sucked in her breath in a dramatic gasp, wrenched herself away as if Iselle had burned her. She recoiled several steps, gazing upon her in alarm.

Forrest gaped at her. Niria's expression was troubled and confused.

Iselle reached up and rubbed her temple. She had her fill of this.

"There's something… Something *else*…" she murmured hauntingly.

Her brow knitted, Niria gathered her resolve and approached again, her hand rising; her eyes clamped even tighter, her focus sharp. She hummed, the sound vibrating intensely. Iselle shifted, uncomfortable with the proximity, the heat, the buzzing in her brain and the scrutiny "Stand still, child… you're mak…"

STOP IT!

Niria yanked her hands away again, this time yelping a little.

"You've hexed yourself!" she accused Iselle with shock, rubbing her hands as if it hurt.

"I beg your pardon?" Iselle remarked guilelessly and confused. She furrowed her brow, fighting back tears. Her head was ringing. "I am incapable of performing magic," she snapped between gritted teeth.

Forrest stood, and he put his arm 'round her shoulders, and enfolded her a little with his body, offering support and protection. Iselle wavered on her feet.

Niria gaped at Iselle, confounded. The pause was long and awkward. The woman shook her head subtly as she worked what she felt in her mind.

"Could the pursuer have cast something else, something dangerous upon her?" Forrest asked.

"No. This is something else. Something only one can *invite* into oneself." She glanced at Iselle with suspicion again, almost accusingly.

"I don't understand," Iselle whispered. "I can't *do* that."

"This is all too strange," Niria murmured. "Too strange."

She pondered upon what she had felt inside Iselle's head and studied her hands as if they had indeed been burnt. Forrest guided Iselle back into the chair, and he settled next to her, his arm still resting gently upon her shoulder. They watched Niria as she ruminated.

The older woman quickly turned and hurried to a small desk in the corner of her sitting room. She took up her quill, dipped it brusquely into the inkwell, and scribbled something down hurriedly. She carried it to Forrest.

"Take her here. I can't read this. But *he* might. The entanglement is concerning, but this *thing*... It is a thing entirely of its own." She stepped back, looking with trepidation and even a little fear upon Iselle, still rubbing her hands.

"But the... *entanglement*... it will draw him here," Iselle exclaimed in a plaintive, frightened, wavering voice.

Let him come then. Perhaps it's time for all of this misery to come to an end.

Iselle hated to hear herself say such terrible things. Not when she had finally found a place where she could belong. People she could become deeply attached to. She bit back a sob, which pressed sorely against her throat.

"I suspect your entangler will be the least of your problems if you don't address that *thing* that is in there. It feels like nothing I've ever felt. It feels... *old*." She stood in her fine slippers and draped silk taffeta, jewels shimmering upon her ears and breast; her hands anxiously clasped and wringing. "Take your young lady to the directions I have given as *soon* as you have a free moment."

"Something *else*?" Iselle repeated.

"It's in Heliddon," Forrest said as they settled back in his coach. He stared at the directions given.

"Something *old*. Something *I invited*? What does she mean, Mr. Outvallen?"

He stared at her blankly.

"I can hardly begin to know, Miss Moon," he replied.

Iselle's mind settled on the thing he'd said to her previously. "Heliddon. That's a bit of a drive, is it not?" Iselle asked. He nodded.

"Eight or so hours, I think, last I went. I did go by saddle, which is a bit quicker."

"Then I should go," she exhaled. "I suppose we need to determine what this added information means. To be truthful, I don't even want to know," Iselle admitted. "I have sufficient troubles to face, now I have something else inside me. Something old. Something I invited," she repeated with a hint of bitterness.

Maybe you deserve it.

The coach began to roll, and they sat in silence, the rumble of the wheels filling the space between them. Forrest gazed upon her impassively. She was aware of it in her peripheral vision, but her eyes were fixed out on the banks that flanked the road, covered in scraggly grasses, and dormant blackberries, with the fruit still clinging, shrunken and inky, to the vines.

"Miss Moon," Forrest broke the quiet. "I know this is not entirely appropriate, but I think you should leave the university dorm for now. You can resume classes later. I know your schooling is important to you. But you should not be so easily found." Forrest tucked the piece of parchment into the breast pocket of his aubergine woolen frock coat and peered outside as the coach bounced along on its bowed suspension, the cab swaying. The sound of hoofs clattering on cobbles and the jostle and noise of it all was somehow soothing.

"Where would I stay? There is no inn at Rendorff." As she said this, she spotted a rider out in the field, over the top of the road bank, riding a silvery white horse. It was a lady, perched prettily on her sidesaddle in a deep gold riding habit and a fine ladies' topper and veil. She thought as the coach slid by, that it looked a great deal like Miss Metrelees, but she was past before Iselle could verify it. She had held hope for a friendship with her. She would have liked to go riding with her. Dorya did not ride, for she was afraid of tall horses, and embarrassed of ponies.

"You can stay in my family's home," he suggested.

Iselle's eyes swiveled to his face; her train of thought halted.

Forrest continued: "It is only slightly under an hour from the school by horse. I can make the journey as needed between home and school. I do not think you should be alone, and I do not think you should flee. I think we can overcome this problem if we find the help we need. I come from a family with a strong line of mage skill. We might be uniquely equipped to protect you."

"I very much doubt your aunt will come within five paces of me now. She looked positively horrified by me," she retorted wryly.

Iselle gazed at him from within the shadows of the coach. The deeply grey day made him darker than usual. His face, so grave, so concerned, was not the face she had grown accustomed to. The acerbic, permanent state of irritation had slipped away, and in its place was a Forrest she did not know as well. His large, brooding brown eyes, earnest and worried, rested upon her.

As they stared at one another, the sky crackled and rumbled, and a sudden downpour began to batter the oiled leather roof of his landau. *So much rain.* Her thoughts briefly returned to Amma and her horse, out in this unpleasant weather. She was perhaps spared, if not invited to ride with her.

That selfish harlot. Would that she withers away from winter fever.

Iselle took another measured breath and tried to clear her mind. She then nodded once to Forrest. "Will your family not see me as an imposition?" She thought about Niria, who looked at Iselle with such fear. She had looked at Forrest the same. She was sure she saw it.

Forrest laughed ironically, just one bark of mirth, and his face melted into a warm smile. It was jarring to see him do this. Her heart quickened at the sight of it. *He has a beautiful smile*, thought Iselle. "Far from it. Be prepared is all I have to say. The imposition might be placed entirely upon you." He sat back, his eyes moving out to the rain-soaked bleakness. They still contained remnants of his grin, and his lips were still set slightly in a knowing smirk.

CHAPTER 20

Iselle gazed out the angled window with its limited view. It was snowing. The kind of wet snow, large clumsy flakes that splotted on the glass panes, pooled on the muntins, and then ran in rivulets down the glass onto the roof. Uncle Ude had just written, and his letter was burnt like so many had done in the past. She left no trace, no matter where she was. She missed Redlan, and the people she thought of as friends, in the art class, the theatre class, the awkward girl who was always in the library; pretty behind her spectacles, but oh so timid and quiet.

She bundled up and decided to face the bleak and joyless weather, the unsticking snow. She would be leaving here soon. Her passage on a vessel had been purchased and she would go south to a place called Rendorff. There would be a light phaeton to collect her in two days. She would attend university on the great island of Baranith. The new year would begin in fall. She would abbreviate her twelfth year. She would live there until school began. It was far. She only wanted to go home. She was so very tired.

She braved the world and ventured out to escape the sense of being suffocated in her little room. She explored shops full of things that used to bring her joy. Stationery, hats, paints, books, magic shops filled with things she could do nothing with, and she found no comfort in those things. She was so deserted.

She returned to the inn, and there she found a letter from Uncle Ude's secretary waiting for her. She opened it before she even climbed the steps to her room. She moved to the front of the common room, where the light, cool and stark, fell upon the script spidering across the page.

Miss Moon. Your Uncle has decided not to keep things from you, although it was much considered not to share the following, as it will be greatly devastating to you. However, it would be of greater disservice to everyone if we concealed this information only to have you discover it later and hold it against your Uncle. He did not have the heart to write it himself and asked me the kindness of telling you. Your Uncle has gleaned from your correspondence the preciousness of your friend, Redlan InDayle has to you. You have mentioned him frequently since you began your matriculation at Arrowood. We regret to inform you that we have heard from the school that unfortunately Master InDale has been found murdered in his room. We understand that there have been two deaths connected to you in your wake. Your Uncle has acknowledged the escalation of harm caused by your pursuer. He has furthered his appeals to the Royal Constabulary and again requested the assistance of their Mage Forces. They have never been quite concerned for your case since it began, but these murders might be the thing to prompt a response at last. We cannot imagine how this news will grieve you, but know your Uncle is doing his absolute best to end this nightmare and bring you home to safety. – Secretary Senior, Hulin.

Iselle could scarcely read past the sentences describing Redlan's fate. She could only collapse to her knees there in the common room and succumb to the destruction and ruin of her heart. Her sobs were raw and hoarse. She hunched upon her knees, rocking in utter agony as she bawled and cried and howled her sorrow, the letter crushed between her stomach and her thighs, her hands pinched between, crumpling the thick parchment. Tears and mucus flowed down her cheeks and her chin; such anguish she had never known.

"Redlan," she coughed between sobs. "Not Redlan! No, no, no, no…."

She barely felt the hands that fell upon her, that lifted her to her feet, the warmth of the bodies pressed against her sides as they hoisted her under her arms and carried her to her room. She could only weep and cry and beg for it all to be a lie. She was tucked into her bed by gentle hands and given sips of water as her awareness slipped in and out.

She awoke still gripping the letter, her knuckles white from the pressure, the grip so hard, her fingers took a few minutes to bend and become supple again. She sat up, remembering suddenly what she had read, and the hollowness inside her yawned further into bottomlessness, and she fell back, weeping anew, and turning onto her side, curling herself up into a tiny ball, and weeping herself back into a fitful sleep.

The next morning, the chamber girl, the innkeeper's daughter, entered the room. Her name was Beatrin. She had always been kind and attentive to the remote girl. She came in carrying a pot of tea and a cup and saucer. She set it down on the table, and knelt by the low bed, where Iselle's back faced her. Her hand fell gently upon Iselle's shoulder. "Miss," she whispered. Iselle had already woken at the sound of the door. She had simply not moved. She felt dead. As if the amulet at her throat had truly made her so. There was nothing left inside her. She lifted her head and barely looked over her shoulder at the girl.

"Go away," she muttered.

"No, Miss. I cannot. I have been told I must rouse you. There is a woman here to see you. She wants to come in. But you should have some hot tea. Come, please sit up." The girl's strong arms laced underneath her, and she helped her sit up. "Here, slide your legs over," she instructed her.

Iselle felt weak and frail. Like there was no strength left within her to function even the slightest bit. But she managed it. Her linen gown, irrevocably wrinkled and ruined, her hair wild with flyaways, her eyes puffy and her nose and upper lip flushed, swollen and red. She sniffed and sat, staring at the letter still crumpled up in her hands. She felt a new welling of tears. She had no idea how her body could still shed them; so empty she felt. Iselle was irrevocably sunken and hollow.

The girl handed her a cup of hot tea, and helped her lift it to her mouth, making her drink. Then she rose and went to the door. "I've done my best, Ma'am," she called out. "I'm afraid it's as much as I could do. She is most shattered and distraught."

"*As much* is plenty. Thank you. If you would kindly wait outside the door for a moment, I would need your assistance shortly." The voice was firm and authoritative. The sound of footfalls creaked across the boards, and the door was closed. Iselle did not lift her eyes.

"I am Mrs. Hulst. I have been sent by your father, a judge…"

"My uncle," Iselle intoned levelly, her air listless and blank.

"Yes. I am a lawyer. I've been asked to take you with me. We will prepare you for a journey. You are to come with me. I will gather your things. I have two constables waiting to accompany us."

Iselle was then changed with the assistance of Beatrin. The girl stripped her bare. She helped her wash herself with a milky, soapy, kettle-warmed water, and a sponge. Her stringy, oily hair was pulled back into a high bun, simple and practical. She was dressed in her plain burgundy cotton day gown, silk stockings with wool over those, enrobed in her warm redingote and all of her things were packed back into her bag.

She rode in a coach with the lady lawyer at her side, and the two constables across. Outside, the weather was frigid, and the sky was grey. She clutched her reticule against her stomach. The smart, cheerful colors of the bonnet on her head seemed to defy her sullen, swollen eyes and her empty gaze. She disembarked at the law office, and followed the lawyer in. The constables took positions outside the entrance.

Iselle was instructed to sit on a bench in the main hall. She lingered in silence as she was left alone there. All about her, clerks and barristers bustled about in their plain black and white ensembles, serious and focused, for once, not noticing her. Her ruddy cheeks and her puffy face hidden under the brim of her bonnet made her unremarkable. She sniffed and dabbed her nose with a kerchief.

But she was not safe here.

He came inside with no resistance; his clothes and his carriage no different than the people crisscrossing the open space. He walked right up to her and knelt before her. The shock and alarm of seeing Prentiss Lacklow's face just there, inches from her, was such a shock, a scream could not even form in her throat. His hand rose up, an affectionate smile crossed his face, and he said: "Come along, my love. It's time to end this eternal chase."

His hand did something. It felt like a knife piercing her temple. She could not know, for her senses wavered and then she fell forward into his arms. He lifted her to her feet. He stooped to take her bag and then turned her towards the door.

She walked.

She walked, but she could not speak.

She walked and she could not run away.

She walked beside him, unable to stop herself.

Her screams were stifled by her own will. She could not obey herself. She felt his arm snake around her back and his hand gripped her waist. "That's it. Come along, we will be free of this place soon enough," he whispered from beneath his top hat. She struggled but could only shriek silently inside her head. A tear fell onto her cheek. At least she could cry.

They exited the law offices. The constables were no longer present.

"There. That did the trick, didn't it? You could trust *them*. But not me," he said, now sounding angry and speaking the last three words between gritted teeth. "Why do you not trust me, my Iselle?" His arm tightened almost painfully around her. "That little trick cost me a good penny. I know you are worth the investment, but you should know that I hate lawyers. They are crooks. I did it for you, though. It got you peacefully out of that inn. It raised no brows. It alarmed nobody. Your exit was natural, and nobody will suspect you are missing for quite a while. Am I not clever?"

He guided her to a high-perch phaeton, and steered her onto it, his hands clutching her waist and lifting her up onto the tall step. His touch reviled her. He climbed up behind her, sat her down and slid her to the side of the seat. He then reached over her for a folded blanket and thoughtfully draped it across her knees. She shivered and tried so hard to gain control of her own body to no avail.

He plopped down beside her and gathered up the reins.

"Hiring coaches is not cheap," he told her, "and the state of these things are always questionable. The suspension of this one is abysmal. Be prepared for a jostle or two."

The horse was untied by a young hand who manned the hitching posts. Prentiss clucked his tongue and drew back his reins, and the horse backed up. Once fully onto the busy street, he snapped the reins, and the horse broke into a brisk trot. "I don't like this place. It's expensive. I'll take you to the countryside. It's not far. I found a little cottage we can use for the night. Then we will return home. We can come to know one another tonight. I can finally show you how much I love you. Then you will come to your senses and stay with me of your own volition."

The coach slid through the streets, weaving around the heavier conveyances, the trotting horse winding between riders and walkers. From the lofty height of the scoop-shaped cab, they swung side to side as the wheels absorbed the bumps and dips of the road.

The business of the highway began to wane, as the density of the buildings lessened. Soon, there was only the occasional rider or walker on the rutted road.

Prentiss was singing to himself, quite self-satisfied. He would look over and peer at her with a loving expression. He was happy. Inside, her terror and dread roiled. Prentiss merely basked in the wash of it as he drove her towards a fate her innocence could not imagine.

Lacklow guided Iselle down in a dusty chair inside a shabby little cottage that hunkered under an osteal old oak off the main road. It was night.

He left her there sitting in the darkness while he removed the horse from harness and set it free in the small stone walled pasture by the house.

He came inside, and looked at her inert form, sitting stiffly in a chair. He lit two candelabras and then knelt by the hearth, silently placing kindling in a neat pile, and lighting it. She sat imprisoned by her own body, silenced. Her eyes were wide with horror. He was still singing under his breath, a soft smile on his face.

"Bring me candied strawberries,
Bring me jellies that glisten,
Bring me songs played upon harps,
Bring me good guests who will listen,
For I am the king of my merry little land,
And all will be yours when you take my hand.
And you will be the queen of my heart,
And we shall never be apart..." he warbled.

"There, we shall warm you up," he said. "It's too cold to do anything yet. We can't have you shivering, can we?"

He rose to his feet, and took off his greatcoat and his hat, then shrugged off his frock coat. He then reached over and pulled off her bonnet. "You look a bit of a mess, darling Iselle. Are you *so* sad?" He ran his thumb along her lower lip. "Are you *so, so* sad, my precious gem?"

Iselle would have vomited on him if she had had power over her own body. He pulled her to her feet, and she stood. "You *must* know we are fated for one another. Why do you run, and hide? I can feel you so strongly now."

Iselle remembered that her charm was in her bag. Beatrin had taken it off her, along with her old clothes, and put it in there. It hadn't mattered then, anyway. She had, she realized, given up on everything when she received news about Redlan. She made no effort to take the necklace from the bag when they prepared her to go. She was without any remaining hope that would have prompted her to, otherwise.

Is that how he found her? No. The lady lawyer was there already.

He answered her question as if he heard it himself.

"I've been seeking. Days and days. You are a silly girl. I had only a few clues. An inn or guest house, up against the canal. But I found you. Walking, staring into stores. I bought you a hat, you know. From one of the shops. I saw you go in and try it on. The animal said you liked hats."

He walked to a shelf and picked up a smart hatbox. Inside was a hat that Iselle had indeed tried on. "It looked quite fetching upon your head. Your beautiful face is framed so well by this lace inside the brim." He put it down, his eyes softening. "I'm not versed in women's things, such as fashion and genteel pastimes. But I will let you guide me. You can help me buy all the things you like. You will not want for fashionable things." He smiled benevolently. She hated his face.

"But before the pleasant things, I must sadly address the unpleasant ones. That will begin with a necessary but disagreeable matter; your much-earned punishment for the trouble you've put me through. All these years of evading me. Hiding from me. You were only postponing the inevitable, and you have cost me a pretty penny. I do not wish for this, but you have forced my hand, truly."

He approached and lifted his hand to the neckline of her simple cotton round-gown. The drawstring ribbon was tied in a neat bow. He pulled the tail, and it loosened. He took her hands and tugged her to her feet. Her body complied. She hated herself. Her weakness. Her pathetic defenselessness against this monster.

He yanked the front of her round gown, to widen it, and then reached inside to undo the drawstring at her high waistline. He then, with both hands, pulled away the lacing of her stays. She could feel his breath on her as he stood so close, a few inches from her, his head tilted down, peering at his work, concentrating on the unwrapping of his gift. Her gown sagged away from her body. Her underpinnings were loose. He pushed layers off her shoulders, and they slid down her arms and body, and crumpled around her feet.

She cried. Her terror made her skin rise into goosebumps. Tears rolled down and fell upon her breasts. She could hear his excited breath, feel it on her skin as he bent in close to inhale her scent from the curve of her neck; she watched his eyes widen as he took in her smooth swells of skin.

"You're eighteen now," he said, his voice quavering. "No longer a child, but a grown woman. We shall join first. Then I will exact your punishment." He said this decisively, as if he had made this decision on the spot. The sight of her body, her vulnerability, the taste of the waves of fear rolling from her being was so arousing, he could not wait.

She heard him groan as he stepped back to take in the whole of her body, in her stockings and the ribbon garters she had embroidered with little blue flowers, tied in bows around the middle of her smooth, milky thighs. Even though she was frozen, hexed, her body violently trembled, and her teeth chattered, not from the chill, but the fear. His hand reached for her, his mouth almost slavering at the full view of her creamy skin, her gentle curves, the swell of her breasts.

She felt his skin touch hers.

"Finally," he whispered almost inaudibly.

Frissons of horror washed across her skin.

His fingers raked across her trembling form, her goosebumps of fear and of cold, she sucked in air and could not cry out what was screaming inside her head and was getting louder and more desperate the bolder he became with his hands, the longer he drew it out, and the more demanding his desire and need for her became. In her head she was screaming.

Stop.. stop, stop.. stop! Stop and then her tongue twitched. And it moved. And it made a sound as she exhaled air through it. "Sssss.. St... sto... Stoppp... *STOP!*" she shrieked. Her voice exploded from her.

It halted him. He looked surprised, shocked, and then his reaction devolved into an expression of rage.

"How dare you command me! How dare you deny me!" he roared. He drew his fist back and swung it across her cheekbone, sending her flying face-down to the floor. The blow stunned her, the pain reverberating in her skull. It was sharp and pulsed with fading intensity until her senses returned. She still could not will her body to move.

However, she could scream.

And she did.

Her cries were shrill and violent, they filled the room and reverberated off the hard glass of the windowpanes.

With all her might, she shrieked and wailed, crying out in terror as he first went to a table, and then returned, straddling her prone form, and he sat down on the top of her thighs. She felt his left hand sink into the yielding flesh of her backside and then the fingers curling into her until it became intolerably painful.

"Punishment it is, then!" he yelled over her shrill cries. "You could have avoided it for a while. I might have taken pity on you if you had been compliant. But now look what you've done! You are *mine*, you ingrate child. You have *always* been mine. And I will make sure you remember it!"

Prentiss's right hand fell, and the blade he gripped in his fingers first drew along her shoulder blade, and he pressed down and punctured through her skin.

The pain was unfathomable. She felt every cut. Every slice. She felt beads of blood rolling down her ribcage. Her howls and screeches of agony sliced through the night.

He was shouting something, but she could not decipher what he said. Her screams cut through his spell, and her muscles slowly began to respond to her brain. They moved where he was cutting, and the agony sliced through her with each stroke of the blade. She was gaining control of her body. She squirmed weakly. She began to slither out from under his weight on her legs.

"Don't you go anywhere, you little wretch. I will have you tonight, I have waited *long enough*!" She heard him through her wracking, wretched sobs.

She felt him root himself upon her backside, putting his entire weight on her. Her back was ablaze with burning pain. She could feel herself rolling in puddles of her own blood, wetting her skin. She could also feel him fumbling. He was unbuttoning the fall front of his breeches. She could feel his want and need throbbing against her body, pressed firmly on her, as he freed himself from his trousers.

His noises of anticipation and arousal made her sick to her stomach. Her anguish grew, and she twisted her body, pain, or no pain, driven by raw desperation, trying to escape from beneath him, all the while, her hoarse, now ragged cries for him to stop and for help and for escape did not cease. The pain in her throat from her screams now stung enough to be noticeable against the agony of her back.

It was at that blessed moment that the door burst open, the latch shattered and the wood splintered away from the casement. Someone came at him in two long strides across the floor. There was the sound of a whip slicing through the air with its welcome song, and then the noise of a brutal strike on flesh.

One, two, three, four times, and the weight pinning her down tipped away. Freed, she could crawl. She clambered to her heap of clothes, and grasped the shift, sitting up with mewls of pain, and pressing it to the front of her body. She scooted against a wall and spied the looming figure of a tall man in a broad brimmed round-hat, a thickly frocked greatcoat swinging, and shining topboots against the light of the fire in silhouette.

He was glorious.

He clutched in his hand a long, tapered horsewhip. A black slash of a line that cut the firelight.

The figure raised his arm again and brought it down upon Prentiss. He whipped sharp, ruthless cracks of penance onto Prentiss's body nine more times, slashing each way like a sword parry, each time the whip elicited a bark of pain from its victim. Prentiss managed to get to his feet somehow and stumbled out the door, retreating into the darkness. The man with the whip immediately turned so his back was to Iselle, and said:

"I will not spy upon you, Miss. I ask that you robe yourself hastily with whatever will cover you. I want to get my men after that blaggard post-haste!"

Iselle lurched gracelessly to her feet, sniffing and crying out in agony as her skin burned and her body ached. The blood that had already begun to dry at the edges of her wounds cracked from her movements.

She hissed and whimpered in pain as she put her shift on and clumsily, with trembling hands, tightened the neckline. She sobbed all the while; sobs imbued with the rawest of agony and misery. When she was marginally covered, the man shrugged off his heavy woolen greatcoat and whisked it around her shoulders. She cried at the weight of it upon her back.

"I'm so sorry, Miss. But you will suffer the cold without it," he said gently. He was a middle-aged man, perhaps in his forties, with a ruggedly handsome face, and eyes that were so exceedingly kind. The sight of his empathy and his concern made her weep even harder. He was so angry and flustered, there were tears in his eyes when he looked upon her bedraggled, and ragged state.

"My bag..." she muttered between sobs. The pendant was in it.

Suddenly, she wanted it again.

She wanted to be safe again.

"I'll have my man fetch it." He scooped her up like a ragdoll and stalked outside carrying her cradled in his arms to a large heavy draft horse so black, just the shine of the yellow light on its eyes from the window revealed its presence. It snorted at the scent of her blood and danced a few steps on its massive hoofs.

He lifted her up and plopped her sitting sideways in front of his saddle, took the reins up against the horse's neck, and mounted. He fixed Iselle in between his arms, kicked his steed into a thundering gallop, clutching her tightly against his body, and carried her away into the night.

CHAPTER 21

Iselle had never understood what being fussed over meant. But the moment she set foot at Chestnut Hill House, she was overcome with the commotion and excitement at her arrival. Forrest's mother, a healthy, short, round woman with a broad, sweet face and plump arms, swooped in like an owl upon a mouse, and gathered Iselle up in her embrace and simply held her close.

"Welcome, welcome you pretty, pretty girl! Come in, come in!" she exclaimed, upon release of Iselle, her warmth and delight pouring from every inch of her person. "I am Lady Outvallen. But you may call me mother if you like," she laughed. "Niria sent word of you only moments ago, but I scarce believed her!" She clucked and tittered, taking Iselle's hands and appraising her, and then cupping her face in her hands, and patting her hair. "So lovely, so lovely!" she articulated over and over again.

She had the deepest brown hair, and kind green eyes, a tiny nose, and the most charming smile. The same smile Iselle had spied breaking across Forrest's face only a few hours earlier. They had only briefly stopped at the university to gather Iselle's things before embarking to his family home.

"I have ordered a nice tea with sandwiches and cakes, and we are having lamb tonight, so if you are hungry, you will not be so for long. Come this way, dear. We shall settle you in as soon as you warm yourself after that ride. You must be cold."

Iselle was never cold after riding horses. In fact, she did not like to wear heavy habits to begin with, because the exercise was vigorous. Her thighs complained a little, it had been a spell since she'd sat sidesaddle. She hadn't done much riding for the past few years. There was no need to at Arrowood. There was no place to go as everything was situated right at the gates of the school; in perfect walking distance for her and Redlan to cross, arm in arm.

She was whisked to a chair in a corner of a morning room where a brisk fire danced. The room was cozy and well-lived in. There was a half-painted watercolor still-life scene on an easel by the window and the subjects of which were still arranged on a table—a pineapple, some apples, and a citron on a crumpled piece of wine-colored velvet. There was a small worktable near the window full of scraps from paper scrolling, there were books scattered about the space, on the tables by the chairs, on the desk in the opposite corner, along with inkwells and a forest of quills in a wide clay pot, papers shuffled about, shelves full of oddities and small statuary wedged between rows of books. Iselle had never connected so instantly to a space than when she entered this room. She loved it more than anything in the world.

"Sit, girl, sit, here, it's lovely and warm by the fire. Forrest, fetch her the green footstool!" she ordered. The tall man complied wordlessly, and walked two steps, and picked up the tiny piece of furniture and brought it, placing it in front of the girl. Iselle's legs were then lifted by his mother and placed like they were made of glass onto a little sage-colored velvet pouf.

A small dog that Iselle had not previously noticed, appeared. It was a lithe, muscular little thing, no higher than her mid-calf, with white fur and brown spots and an intelligent gaze. It had a smooth coat, and bright, chocolate-brown eyes. It leapt up onto the chair with her and wedged itself, uninvited between the arm of the wingback, and her thigh.

"Go away, Pip," she said, shooing the dog, who duly ignored her and rested his chin on Iselle's leg.

Iselle could not have imagined Forrest being so utterly unlike his parent. She was expansive and merry, with rosy cheeks and twinkling eyes. Forrest on the other hand, stood looming as always, his unreadable face back to its normal impassive and unimpressed state.

He was however, brusquely shoved aside by a lithe, willowy girl of about fourteen, with long straight raven hair loose upon her shoulders with but a red ribbon tied 'round her head behind her ears to keep it out of her face. She wore a dusty rose pink gauzy muslin over a white under gown with a ruby ribbon tied about her high waist, the ends hanging down against the back of her skirts. She had pale green silk slippers on her feet, and ribbons winding up her ankles. She looked like candied berries, Iselle thought.

"Get out of the way, you great big brute," she said in a delightful, velvety voice that was the feminine, youthful version of Forrest's. "I want to meet her," she pushed her way through, and threw herself ungracefully into the chair opposite Iselle before her mother could sink her bum into it and gracelessly hooked a leg over the armrest.

"What's your name?" she asked, her azure eyes bright and happy.

"Iselle Moon," she replied, her eyes smiling at Forrest's adorable young sister. She looked a great deal like him.

"I'm Talia!" The girl's eyes sparkled with delight at Iselle's presence, but then her brows slanted, and she continued: "I'm so unfortunate as to be *Forrest's* little sister," she sneered.

Iselle smirked.

The girl's eyes fell onto Iselle's lap. "Well, Pip likes her, so that settles it for me," she declared. "Pip doesn't like anyone. Just us. Forrest sometimes, but nobody *really* likes Forrest.

I like Forrest, thought Iselle, blushing at her own musings.

"Dogs like me," Iselle said softly, her hand alighting on the dog's shoulders, where she petted him. The dog sucked in a breath and let out a sigh that somehow made him melt further into the small space between her leg and the chair.

A maid entered carrying a tea-table, and another carrying an elaborate tea-box. She put the table down, with all its offerings on display. Mother set to work preparing the tea. As she did, Iselle took a moment to look about the room again. The walls were covered with a gallery of portraits. She found one of a person she was sure to be Forrest's father. A man in full regalia of a militia officer, with a massive bicorne with cockades and feathers; the style fairly recent—the shape and composition of his face was without any doubt, the same as the two young people in the room before her. Here was where Forrest got his looks. Here was who he was similar to. He had few of his mother's traits save for the smile she briefly glimpsed. But the sharp lines, the hard eyes, the angles of the face, the noble nose, these were *all* Forrest.

"That's my father," Talia exclaimed. "He was a dreadful monster."

"Talia!" Forrest scolded her loudly and abruptly. The girl hardly even twitched at the bark of rebuke.

"Truly, if you cannot control your words, I will send you out," Mother Outvallen said in a gentle, permissive voice, chipping some lumps from a large hunk of sugar. "You've were told not to speak with such language, girl. Even around your poor aunt, you are utterly careless. Mind your tongue."

"Well, *he was* a monster, and he was utterly cruel to Forrest. That's why he is the way he is, and Aunt knows it too," the girl lamented. "He was rarely vicious to me; I was just a tiny thing. But I heard how beastly he could be,"

"Out!" Forrest snapped. Talia was startled by this reproval, and she glowered balefully at him.

"She *should* know if you are going to *marry* her," she retorted stubbornly.

"Marry?" Iselle said in a small voice, which nobody heard except maybe Pip.

"Out you little vermin!" Forrest howled.

"NO!" the girl shouted in return, balling up her fists and glaring at him.

Mrs. Outvallen handed Iselle a cup of tea, and smiled kindly, as if none of this was happening around her. She then turned and shooed her daughter out of the chair. Surprisingly, the girl complied to the subtle wave of the hand, and between barks at Forrest, she moved in a flutter of skirts and a flash of bright jewel-toned slippers over the arm of the chair.

The mother sat down, folding her hands primly upon her knees. Talia, once on her feet, tried to shove the immovable Forrest, and he simply put his hand on her forehead and pushed her back.

"They can be boisterous; it's something one must get used to. I imagine you aren't used to this sort of disordered behavior. Do you have siblings?" Mother asked.

"No. I lived alone with my Uncle," Iselle replied distractedly, watching the girl trying to stamp on her brother's large foot while he held her at bay with his arm. It was then when Mother intervened. It was not what Iselle expected from the sweet woman.

"That is *enough!*" she shouted in a shrill, powerful voice. The girl fell still, and she looked cowed almost immediately. "Miss Moon is our guest, and we will comport ourselves with civility for the duration of her stay, *may it be long and pleas*ant," she added with a softer voice. She then returned to being stern. "I say this especially to you Talia. Now get back to your studies or I will send you away to an intern school!"

"I hope to play with you later, Miss Moon, when this Beastly Beast of Beasterton isn't hanging over all of us like a smelly carrion bird." She then turned dramatically and flounced out of the room.

"Now, Miss Moon. Please, have something to eat. You look a little fatigued."

Iselle *was* tired. But she was also peckish, and she could not resist the offerings on the table. She leaned forward and took a plate and placed some little things upon it. A salmon and creamed cheese sandwich, a cucumber sandwich with salt and pepper, a tiny tea cake with a sugary top. She then leaned back and ate. Pip didn't seem interested in tea cakes and cucumber sandwiches. She felt his little body heaving and shrinking with each of his relaxed breaths.

"Now that things have quieted, I would dare to ask you; Forrest mentioned in his little note you have some troubles. But I would like very much to know what peril it is that Forrest revealed, that would require you to hide?"

There was something about Mrs. Outvallen. Her air, her comforting gaze, her trustworthy face, perhaps. Or that she was an extension of Forrest, who she now trusted explicitly. As Forrest drew up the chair from the worktable and made it creak as he folded his long body down to sit in it, she ate a bite of a sandwich, and took a sip of her tea, and then she outlined her story, perhaps a bit abridged, and told in such a way that it wasn't as gruesome or terrible. But she told it. Freely. Openly. Painfully.

"Goodness, my child," Mrs. Outvallen said this with eyes brimming with tears. She had been shedding them throughout the narrative. "How you must have suffered."

She had gotten out of her chair and taken her hands at some juncture of the tale, and now she enveloped Iselle in a deep, warm, loving embrace, which only, for some reason, wicked up all the pain in her heart, and made it spill out of her eyes again. She clung onto the woman she had only just met and buried her face into her soft chest and sobbed. Maybe it was because she belonged to Forrest that made her so easy to hold onto. It didn't matter. She had never known this kind of affection and kindness, this kind of physical consolation from another human being. It was magnificent. Such solace. Such warmth, acceptance and understanding. It felt so wonderful to just cry, and to be soothed in such a way.

Forrest looked on silently. His hands curled into fists. His gaze, full of anger. Forrest wanted Iselle to take comfort in a woman who was the personification of it. His mind reeling from hearing her story again, he watched as his mother patted Iselle's back, and hummed gently, and made hushing sounds, "It will pass, Iselle. By and by, my poor child. By and by," she lulled her.

Iselle's sanctuary in the Outvallen family home was a luxury she hadn't known since she left home. Even at her finest school, she hadn't possessed such an inviting, private space. It was a broad room with a connecting one, both sharing the tall, elegant fireplaces of the house. The white stone of the exterior, the fluting and corbels, the graceful bay windows and tall, sweeping gables and the dark slate roof were nothing to the immaculate style and aesthetic of the interior. Like Dame Arwey's home, the rooms were stately, well-appointed, and the ones not most frequented by the family were tidy and formal.

The informal spaces that the family used were welcoming and warm, appealing and cozy. Her room was a mix of both. The scale of the walls and room size was imposing, the tall mantel, the soaring windows with the divided light cast through sheer white curtains, framed in silk panels draped to perfection, the fabric embossed with little gold-embroidered cartouches of leafy designs. The furniture was slightly older in style. The dark stained, heavy wood pieces were out of mode but arranged in such a way that suited the grand scale of the rooms and were freshly upholstered with modern fabrics. In the larger room, there was her bed, commanding, of the old style, with thick posts and a tester canopying the mattress, which was soft and yielding as she liked them.

She settled in quickly, missing the droning professors, the bustle of the school and its students. But it was an acceptable adjustment to move here. She felt welcome and loved. Iselle unpacked her things and settled in for the duration, whatever that might be.

Her first morning, she arose, dressed in a walking gown, and joined Mrs. Outvallen and Talia for breakfast. Forrest arranged for them to go to the place his aunt had directed him. She would go with him this morning. But first, she needed to eat.

Talia was in a cross and unpleasant mood, all a-grumble about her governess and her studies. But she did not direct it at the guest. Iselle heard her complaints upon entering the informal dining room, where there was a small table made to accommodate the family and a guest or two.

"Good morning, Miss Moon," Mrs. Outvallen exclaimed.

"Hello, sister!" the young girl's disposition brightened at the sight of the older girl. "Did you sleep well?"

"I did," Iselle replied softly.

"Forrest sent a note from the school that he will be here shortly to fetch you. You best eat quickly, my dear," mother told her.

Iselle did as she was bade, and she sat down to the lovely breakfast; a humble one for such a fine house. A familiar and comforting complement of cold ham, and bacon, of toasted bread, soft-boiled eggs, of jam and butter, and tiny scones studded with bits of caramelized apple, and freshly whipped cream. She ate hungrily, as if the food itself was reassurance.

Forrest arrived as he promised, in his landau. She was soon wrapped up in her worn redingote and her new hat, ushered out the door and helped into the carriage by her silent, attentive companion. "Dorya said she misses you," he told her as he climbed in. She pursed her lips and nestled into the upholstery.

"I miss her too," she replied in a soft, airy voice.

"Hm," he grunted. He used his knuckles to knock on the coach to prompt the coachman to go. They set off for the arduous drive, neither having any idea what was in store.

As the wheels bounced on the now hard, frozen ground, and the coach cut through the small forest towards the hilly countryside, it finally began to snow.

The directions that were given brought them to a rather lovely two-story house of humble size; a simple box of a shape with a receding hip roof, and windows spaced evenly around each side, a simple but stylish portico over the front door, and a walled garden all around it. It was the house of a gentleman or gentlewoman. The drive was white with crushed oystershells, and it made a pleasant noise as the coach drew into the circle and stopped in front.

The garden was a little shabby and wild. The grass was managed by a goat that wandered about clipping away weeds with its brown teeth. It ignored the coach as it drove up. The shrubberies were also pruned. Likely by the same culprit that was chewing up the growth around the house. The trees shed their leaves to blanket the ground under them, and a naked vine clung to the front of the house.

Forrest dismounted first and handed Iselle down. "Keep warm, Effrid," Forrest muttered to the driver, "Sit inside if you must." The man was swathed in wool and a broad hat. He nodded gravely in obeisance.

Forrest rang the bell, and when the door cracked open, he handed the ancient housekeeper their card. She invited them into what was a fetid and dank interior, dusty and drab, dripping with cobwebs, with dirty floors and puffs of dust aggregated in the corners. The old lady shuffled before them, guiding them into a modestly sized formal parlor, simply appointed, and as dirty and unkempt as everything else.

They perched on the edge of a broad chair side by side and waited for a spell. At length, the door slid open, and an elderly gentleman entered. His hair was snowy white, with mutton chops that were voluminous and fluffy like whiskers. He was hunched, and he moved slowly. He wore an old, patched banyan, and a box-hat, and slippers of thick tapestry fabric on his feet which were brown with dirt. He had a cane in one hand, and to Iselle's shock, a familiar person was supporting his other arm.

It was Miss Metrelees. Iselle took in a breath and tilted her head. "Of all people…" she exclaimed.

CHAPTER 22

Lord Thrait's stablehand had seen to fetching Iselle's belongings left at the cottage, and his landsmen spread out to find Prentiss Lacklow. So far, there was no word of his whereabouts. The Lord was irate, Iselle could hear his shouting and barks of command from upstairs in the room where she was now situated.

Iselle was once again furnished with her pendant. She lay on her stomach, a blanket carefully covering her lower half, while the physician and a Mage Healer, who had been subsequently called in for the strange behavior of her wounds, puzzled over her. She wept in silence, only whimpering when one of the cuts was touched by the attending doctors.

The mage healer had been called because the wounds would not stop bleeding. But some magic had stanched the flow, and now they were cleaning them, and assessing them. "Enchanted knife, most probably," the Healer mumbled, her fingers brushing along the skin beside the deep slices in Iselle's back.

She was a small woman of middle age, remarkably thin, with a deathly pallor and massive green eyes and waves of deep wine-colored hair. Her face, although rather sallow, was kindly in its expression. Her heavy brown robes with the bright gold piping rustled around her as she hung over Iselle.

"Made to mark in perpetuity. It will take some work to set them to normal healing," she uttered. "Hm..."

"I should stitch them." The Physician proposed. He was a thick, heavy man of thirty, with bushy brown sideburns and the cheeks of a well-fed man. He looked confused and overwhelmed by the state of the injuries before him. He had, however, cleansed and purified them with the gentlest of hands.

"No. The scarring will be excessive as it is. She should not have skin riddled with laddered lines in addition to the existing scarring. She is young and lovely. I will close them as best I can. They might take time to fully heal. But these scars..." she sounded despaired. She did not continue.

Iselle's eyes welled up yet again. The Mage healer mitigated the agonizing pain again, when her whimpers grew more frequent. With a gentle heated touch of her hands across the span of Iselle's back, for a few seconds, she did not feel the agonizing reminder of her humiliation and abuse. She could think clearly and make herself present after the ordeal. She appreciated the healer's gentleness and consideration, both of the kind only a woman could offer another woman.

Downstairs, there was another round of shouts and barks from her savior. The Lord was a man with a fiery temper, but he had assured that Iselle was as comfortable as she could be and spared no kindness in ensuring she had whatever attention her injuries required, with no worry about the expense. In the meantime, he focused his rage on the intruder who had harmed a young lady inside a house that belonged to his estate.

The doctor heard the situation from his Lordship. The physician told her of it when he sat her up to drink a foul herbal tonic. "He had been riding back from the village public house when he heard your screams across a barley field. He spurred his horse to full gallop through the dead stubs of dry barley stalks without hesitation, threw himself from the mount, and crashed through the door of the cottage," he told her.

Iselle drank, her face puckered from the awful taste.

There were apparently few things that incited the Lord's anger more than poachers, thieves, trespassers, highwaymen, and people who harmed the innocent. He was renowned for his unforgiving nature when it came to those sorts of injustices and exacted an iron-fist upon the people who resided on his lands and were subject to his rule. This was not to be tolerated.

The physician recited the whole tale to Iselle when the Lord left her in his care. Hearing it, Iselle had never been more grateful for a tyrant landlord than she was at this moment.

When her ribcage and lower back were wound in a thick layer of bandages, she had been robed in her wrinkled nightgown and her care had been passed onto the staff, she was at last able to address the matters she needed to. Iselle first provided his housekeeper directions through her trembling voice and tears, to write to her Uncle. In turn, Lord Thrait immediately incurred the costly expense of using flight messages carried by the Elcreen pigeons—sending a bird post-haste towards the nearest roost to the relay office in Ecklo, then to her Uncle's home.

The hunt by his abundant force of young men, roused from their beds, from the farms and homes in the estate's towns and cropland, yielded nothing but reports of a few sightings. What they did know: the whip had scarred Prentiss across the face; as several witnesses who had spotted him, described a raised, vivid, and bleeding red line cutting diagonally over his forehead, the bridge of his nose, and his cheekbone. It made him noticeable, and with the bulletin with a detailed description, was posted at each town hall and public square, recognizable. Chances were he would flee this place and remain unseen until he could emerge again without this brand upon his face.

The Lord took no chances. He posted his men all about the house. His fatherly protection of Iselle was extraordinary and of enormous comfort to a girl who had been so brutally battered.

When she came downstairs for the first time in two days, being indisposed by her injury, she was led to his sitting room where he reposed in a great big leather chair, smoking a long-pipe. He got to his feet the moment she shuffled in, leaning on the arm of the chambermaid.

"Miss Moon," he intoned in a gentle voice, which was a stark change from the commandeering, infuriated tone she'd heard over the past few days. "I hope you are not too pained to come down here. My invitation was a request only, not a demand."

"Thank you, sir, but I am relieved to be out of the room, if I might be direct, my Lord," she replied, her voice a little hoarse, raw, and strangled still, from the force of her screams. Her throat had yet to heal.

She was guided to a chair with a soft velvet upholstery, deliberately moved from another room for her to sit in. She could not lean back, however, and she sat pertly instead, wincing at the bandages against her skin. She wore no stays, no constricting bodices. She wore a loose round gown over a petticoat and shift, with the drawstring at the waist barely tightened.

"Take some tea, and try to find comfort here," he said sympathetically.

Iselle picked up the cup that was waiting for her on the small table, little curls of steam rising from it. She drank, taking in the dark, masculine room with its deep mahogany paneling, the leather-clad furniture, the warm reds of the designs in the piled rug that covered the floor, and the framed art upon the walls of hunt scenes, hounds, fine purebred horses with shining coats, and still life capturing the bounty of autumn food, including a brace of fowl, on a table in the warm light of a candle. There were shelves of books; and the smoky grey granite of the fireplace, with its mahogany surround and mantel, anchored the cozy space.

It felt like an embrace. A fatherly, manly embrace. She tried to lean back a little, gingerly, she rested against the chair, waiting for the sting from the pressure on her wounds to abate a little.

"You should not feel burdened by the resources I have provided for your care, Miss Moon. Ebrem told me this is what you said to your chambermaid this morning. You do not have to weigh your mind down on such matters. I am not wanting for money, and I have nobody to spend it on." He put the end of the thin, curved stem of his pipe to his lips, and drew, holding the smoke for a moment before expelling it with a puff. Inside the bowl, the fragrant herbs turned orange-hot and then faded.

Iselle was not sure of his motivation. Men were often guided by their wants, in her experience. And they often only made grand efforts when it came to women, when there was something to gain from it. Like an investment. Kindness, generosity, gestures, those were normally reserved for the attainment of a woman's attentions. She wondered if he was interested perhaps, in her. She could only hope this was not the case. She had no attraction, in spite of his generosity and attentive care. He was close to Uncle Ude's age.

But why else would he extend himself so greatly for her? It was true, he had been nothing but a gentleman from the moment he came to her aid. He made no overt advances, nor did he look at her in such a way that would make her think so. Were there truly men of such character beside her Uncle and Redlan? A man with no selfish motivation when acting kindly towards a young woman? She found it hard to believe after all these years of experience of the opposite.

He sat happily silent, one leg crossed over the knee of the other, his slippered foot wagging a little as he mused. He had a fine silk banyan that draped from beneath his legs, and his hair was swept forward onto a handsome brow. He had a thoughtful look upon his face as he stared at the flames. There was not much light in the space, and the fire washed the room with dancing gold. Outside, it rained, and the drops ticked on the panes of the single tall window.

"You have been so very kind, my Lord." Iselle said it meekly. She was overcome a little by her feelings. Her body wasn't the only part of her feeling battered, bruised and brittle. She was laid bare, her vulnerability exposed to all.

"You mustn't dwell too much on my supposed kindness," he waved his free hand dismissively. "I'm only doing what anyone ought to do—what any *decent* man ought to do, when someone is in danger. Would that I had my flintlock on my body, I would have shot him between the eyes." He growled the last words out a little, his face awash with disgust.

Iselle, however, could not be anything but obliged to him. Indeed, she ought to be grateful for all the good souls who had come to her side. Dame Arwey, Mrs. Hallwell, now this kind man. She hated that she had to rely on the compassion and goodness of others to escape the escalating perils she faced.

As she had rested in bed these past two days, she had contemplated this ruefully. Had she no defense against this monster? Was there nothing she could do except hide behind a bauble? Was there no place where she could feel and be safe to live a normal life, and have happy friendships, *and perhaps even love?*

No. She could never look at young men now and not question their motives; or worry they could turn out to be like Prentiss. How could she know on sight if he is a good or bad man? How would she know if he would harm her or not? She had not listened to her intuition then, when she scarcely understood what it was, when she was a child. Now her experience made it so that she felt that way about any man.

Her memory assailed her again, as it had done for days. *The way he looked at me. The way his fingers touched me.* She felt a wave of nausea wash over her. *I don't want anyone to look at me or touch me like that again.*

"Miss Moon, are you unwell? Shall I call for the girl to bring you back to your room?" The Lord sat up, putting his other foot on the floor. He leaned forward, his face awash with concern.

"No, I am better here. I feel protected here." She said this with her eyes filling with tears. He watched her closely, scrutinizing her sorrowful face. His hand fell upon hers, which was on her knee, and she pulled away reflexively. He straightened and apologized.

"My apologies! I did not consider for a moment the misery and agony you must have endured before I intervened at Creekbottom Cottage. I have neglected to think how you would be reviled by the touch of another after what you have endured. I will not repeat such a thoughtless action again," he said. "You are welcome to sit with me as much as you desire if it makes you feel safe, because I *am* safe, and you *are* protected here. You will only experience the same treatment a beloved daughter of this house would experience if one existed. This I promise."

She felt it, his earnest feelings. He understood. She pressed her lips together and nodded haltingly in assent. She turned her head to the fire, where his gaze had turned.

"Now drink your tea, Miss Moon. It will make you feel better. There are healing herbs in it prescribed by the physician. He told me this one will taste much better than the last." He leaned back and put his leg back over his knee, and he lit his pipe anew.

She took in a deep breath of the scented air.

Prentiss had been obvious and unmistakably obsessed from the onset of this disastrous existence. Lenteev had been quiet and watchful. Both, however, had designs upon her. Both desired and pursued her regardless of what she wanted. Neither took her wishes into consideration. To them, she was not a creature with a heart or wishes of her own. She was merely an object they desired. Prentiss felt he was entitled to her attentions; *nay, entitled to me.* Lenteev likely did as well. In her life, there were so few trustworthy men. There was only her Uncle. And there had been only Redlan. And now, there was this Lord, whose actions were, she surmised, taken with only the man's powerful sense of justice and empathy, in his heart. She had no hidden motivations to fear. She sipped her tea, which did indeed taste lovely, and watched the fire, its golden glow washing her with its warmth.

Word came from Uncle Ude soon after, brought by relayman on a sweaty horse. Iselle's Uncle bought her a new passage, to Rendorff. In his communication, he imposed upon the Lord's kindness to keep her there until she departed. It would be a week and four days. Iselle's heart shriveled a bit more, for the news. *Father away. More running. In the state that I am.*

She lowered her hands with the letter in it and glanced across at her host. Lord Thrait had been reading from a book to her, this early afternoon, in the sitting room at the front of the house. Both had looked up at the drive and observed the hasty arrival and subsequent departure of the relay rider. They had paused and waited for the footman to bring the letter to the room. The Lord had kindly waited for Iselle to read it out in her quiet voice.

She existed in a state of pain and anguish alike. She did not leave the house. She spent most of her time in her room. She dwelled in quietude with his Lordship in the afternoons and evenings. She had come to find comfort in the scent of his pipe smoke, and his quiet humming, which he did under his breath when he was reading to himself. She had found peace here. The idea of renewed chaos, of greater change and uncertainty, made her eyes burn with tears.

"Cheer up, Miss Moon," Lord Thrait said gently. "You have more time to rally before you will need to go. It won't be as bad as it feels right now."

"I suppose," she began, "I can take solace in knowing I will no longer act as an imposition upon your generosity."

Lord Thrait's brow wrinkled, and he frowned. "I've told you before, and I will tell you again, this problem does not exist. You are fabricating something to feel terrible about. I am truly, and sincerely *happy* to have you in this house. In all honesty, Miss Moon, I wish I could *keep* you. Like a pet. A daughter-pet," he chortled.

Iselle laughed for the first time in... *oh I don't remember.* "Daughter-pet indeed," she snorted with a smile. The movement made her wounds sting terribly. She contained herself, but her eyes still twinkled for it. The Lord exhaled burdensomely and rolled his eyes up at her.

"Shall we continue?" he asked. Iselle nodded.

"The knife of her prow cut through the tempestuous waters, climbing against the mountainous swells, nearly swallowed in the fluid hollows..." he began again.

Iselle watched him. His lashes were like little dark crescents hovering over his cheeks as he bent his head to read to her.

She dwelled a great deal upon her misfortunes. She languished in her despair. She had reason to, and for that, she made no apology to herself or anyone else. But she reminded herself, looking at this man, who only days before had been naught but a stranger to her, that there were so many things she ought to be so thankful for. For a gravely voice reading her a novel about a ship. For his youthful lashes, and his unexpected humor and almost brotherly, or fatherly familiarity. For the people she could love even in passing, as she drifted from one place of hope to the next. She could love, even if it meant it was fleeting.

As he read, tears rolled down her cheeks. She wiped them away with care, so as to not distract him with her movement.

Three days before she was to depart, there was a card delivered to the breakfast table where she and Lord Thrait were sipping hot black tea and quietly awaiting the chambermaid to set the platters of food on the table.

She had risen in a rather black mood. She'd slept heavily upon the soporifics the housekeeper had put in her evening herbal tisane. She'd rolled over and slept on her back. Her bandages and her wounds had become one. Redressing them come morning was agonizing.

She wore her clothes loosely. She felt ugly and unkempt. Tired and sore. She paid little heed to what was going on at the table. She drank her tea and tried to put the burning and stinging out of her mind.

The Lord accepted the card from the butler, and his brow rose when his eyes fell upon its printed face. "We have a visitor, Miss Moon," he said with a bit of a smile curling onto his lips. "Send him in, Varin," he said to the butler. The portly man half-bowed and exited, returning only a moment later with none other than Uncle Ude.

It took a moment for Iselle to make herself present and set her eyes upon him. And another fleeting moment passed as her brain recognized who he was, and that he was here.

Iselle's exclamation of surprise contained both happiness and sadness alike. All pain forgotten, she got to her feet so quickly, she nearly upset her chair, and she flew into her uncle's arms in a wash of tears and sobs.

"I had business in Allendell, and it wasn't so far that I couldn't simply ride on for a day more," he said in his comforting, stony voice. Iselle clung to him with all her might, her arms laced under his damp, rain-speckled coat around his sides. He patted her head awkwardly. They were never the kind for these sorts of demonstrative acts of affection. But it felt so right, and she never wanted to let go of him again.

Uncle Ude eventually had to pull her off like she was a barnacle upon his hull. He held her at arm's length to look at her splotchy face, puffy eyes, and red nose, and he smiled at her. "Ah, it's good to see you my little buttercup," he said to her. He was all warmth and relief to see her.

They embraced once again. Iselle hiccupped and sobbed against his waistcoat.

Uncle Ude's eyes rose to meet Lord Thrait's, who sat quite comfortably in his chair and eschewed all formality. His eyes grew even warmer. This was the man who'd saved his little buttercup. "Lord Thrait, I cannot express my thankfulness enough to you," he actually choked up a little, and cleared his throat, "...and that you have extended yourself to such lengths for a stranger."

"Nonsense. Here let us have breakfast," he blurted gruffly, and admonishingly. He assessed quietly, the man standing in his private dining room; and the other did the same. They sized each other up. When this evaluation was finished the Lord said: "Sit." He waved his hand to the seat next to him on the round table.

"If I can peel this little rind from my body," Ude chuckled.

"Ah, you mean my daughter-pet," the Lord said. "She is ill-trained, I'm afraid. Hey there, let your uncle go." The man was easy in his air; already comfortable with Ude because he was comfortable with Iselle.

Iselle stepped away, and Ude grasped her face with both hands, using his thumbs to wipe away the moisture from her cheeks. "You look utterly wretched, girl," he said lamentingly. "Wasting away to a little figure made of twigs. Sit down and eat. I am here now." She nodded and returned to her chair. Uncle Ude followed and slid it carefully behind her knees. His eyes were on the bandages he spied underneath the loose neckline of her morning dress. He then exchanged chagrined glances with the Lord.

A servant relieved him of his coat and hat, and an extra plate and silverware were placed upon the table across from his niece. Only then did he sink, with a groan of fatigue into the chair. He was also quite evidently hungry as his stomach roared at the sight of the food when it arrived.

Lord Thrait watched him.

"Business, my foot. What I see is a man who has clearly ridden through the night, possibly two nights, to come here before his niece left the mainland," Lord Thrait postulated with a chuckle, leaning his elbow on the arm of his chair and turning his body slightly towards Uncle Ude with a wry grin.

"What I see is a man who whips rabid animals into submission as diversion," Uncle Ude replied in turn. They both laughed. Uncle Ude's eyes returned to his little buttercup. They were shining, and still sad, despite their momentary levity.

"Would that I had whipped him into pudding," Thrait said regretfully.

"You did well, my Lord," Uncle Ude assured him. "She is worse for wear, but she is here."

Iselle did not often see her uncle take to people at the outset. He was difficult to befriend; he was reserved and often distrustful of people until he slowly became better acquainted with them. But Lord Thrait bypassed the usual hurdles in but a fleeting moment.

It surely was mostly because Lord Thrait had protected Iselle in uncle's stead and done so with heroic aplomb. But there was an air to Thrait's personality that was warm and kind with his peers, in spite of his being rather intolerable to others. Iselle sensed, from the easiness of their one exchange, that this would likely be a strong, lasting friendship. The kind where they would hunt together in the autumn. They would pursue women together at the social clubs. They would lock horns over the billiard table and visit the snug of a public house to drink wine and eat beef. She saw that kind of easy camaraderie in their initial exchange she only saw her uncle share with longtime chums. Her heart grew warm and happy for the prospect of having Lord Thrait in her life some way or another. She became overwhelmed a little by the idea. How she wished it could be true.

She watched Uncle Ude reach for the sausages and serve himself of two. He then seized the pot of mustard and spooned two little daubs of it upon his plate. Iselle reached for the hard-boiled eggs and dropped two onto her uncle's plate. She had composed herself and had resumed eating. She was overjoyed to see him. As she ate, a happy tear fell onto her cheek. Uncle Ude half-rose, reached out across the round table, and wordlessly wiped it away again with his thumb.

The conversation then resumed and almost immediately devolved into an animated debate over recompensation of expenses. Lord Thrait was a stone wall, no matter how eloquently or fiercely Uncle Ude argued.

"Don't you dare blather your courtroom nonsense at me, Moon, I'm not susceptible to legal parlance and argle-bargle," he barked, cramming a piece of toast into his mouth and downing a gulp of coffee. "I won't hear another word of it! She's *my* child as long as she's under my roof, and she's *my* responsibility. Once she leaves this house, you can do whatever you like," he snorted defiantly.

When they'd finished eating, the did not leave the table. More coffee was poured, and Uncle Ude set aside the lightheartedness, and soberly asked for the whole of the story. Iselle, with difficulty, with no shortage of shame and trauma, detailed her rescue. The gravity of it fell over the room. As she described the events; edited a little for the sake of her own humiliation and disgrace, explaining from her perspective what she had seen when Lord Thrait arrived, and how gentlemanly he had been, how kind, and how bravely he had saved her, Uncle Ude's expression to his new friend was one of undying respect.

The two days prior to her departure with the three of them together, in spite of the pain from her injuries, and the memory of the ordeal weighing upon her, were some of the most comforting days she had ever experienced. Those two nights by the fire safely flanked by the fatherly men who wanted nothing more than to protect her, were so precious to her. She did not want to go. She begged Uncle Ude to let her stay.

"My dear buttercup, until we can find that monster, no whip is going to protect you from his magic. That incident caught him by surprise. He was too shocked to retaliate. That whip came too quickly for him to react. He won't allow that to happen again.

"I have been working to find help with the people who are best suited to find and catch him. It won't be the layfolk like us. It will be magic bearers who will defeat him. He has murdered two people that we are aware of and has attacked you violently. He is now a desirable target for the constabulary, and its mage.

"Go to university. A good one. Far away. I make no promises, but we will try our best for you to be free of this madness once and for all. And you can come home."

She was seen off by Uncle Ude, and Lord Thrait. They accompanied her to the port, where they stood upon the pier and watched her vessel move slowly away. She stood at the rail, while the sailors scrambled and scurried to drop the sails. They scrabbled up the webs of ropes like spiders, and the sails inevitably unfurled and ballooned against the wind, and the sharp prow cut through the chop turning away from land.

The two men had almost instantly become friends. She could see their tiny figures, side by side, retreating farther and farther away until she could see them no more. She hoped they would remain friends. She had come to adore Lord Thrait so very much. She already missed them both.

The waters grew wilder as they found the deep sea. When the wind and the rain drove her below the deck, she collapsed into a ball of despair in her tiny cabin, curled up in the little berth of a bed. Her back still hurt terribly. She was so tired of hurting. She was so tired of leaving. Tired of running. Tired of the pendant. *Tired, tired, tired.*

Away from the protection of Uncle Ude and Lord Thrait, she was quickly overcome with fear again. Her vulnerability washed over her like a frigid wave. She focused her thoughts on the good. On the people who'd been drawn into her interrupted life, who'd helped her, soothed her, and loved her. She had to steel herself for it all. The new journey, the new, strange place, the sense of isolation and finding her footing yet again. As she always had, time after time—since she was a but a little twelve-year-old girl, wide-eyed and innocent.

She had never felt safer than in the presence of Lord Thrait, with his long, tapered whip. She would forever remember its whistle and the sound of it on Prentiss' skin.

What concerned Iselle, however, and imbued her with anxiety for her own sanity, were the feelings that had emerged at that particular moment of ferocity. For the satisfaction, the act of violence had given her, could not be normal. Every strike, she counted them, one, two, three four... One two three, four, five, six, seven, eight, nine. Would that there had been more, she sometimes thought. Would that he had been whipped into oblivion.

Through all the pain, humiliation, violation, and misery in that dreadful moment, every single one of those sharp strikes from Lord Thrait's whip, for Iselle, were little punctuations of unmitigated glee.

CHAPTER 23

"Oh! Miss Moon!" Miss Metrelees exclaimed, also stunned to see her here. The old man shuffled on with his companion and slowly lowered himself into a squashy old chair with the shape of his body embedded in the ancient upholstery. The leather was shiny and dark from where his body and hands rested most often. "This is my great grandfather," Amma explained, clutching her hands, her eyes bright. "Of all the places, I would never have imagined you here. I've only arrived lately myself." She took a place behind him, by his left shoulder, her hand resting on the back of his chair.

"Do you know this old man?" Forrest asked Iselle. Her brow furrowed.

"No," she replied. She looked upon Miss Metrelees, unable to hide her confusion. *What a strange coincidence. Where have you been? Why have you broken your promises, and then appeared here like this?*

"You've come to see me upon recommendation of Lady Niria?" the old man asked. He turned and his bloodshot gaze fell upon her. His irises were milky with cataracts, looking almost like pale cymophane stones. He was frail and wobbly. His knuckles were arthritic. "I *know* you," he said in a quavering voice to Iselle. Forrest looked at Iselle again, confused.

The room had no fire in the hearth. There was a heavy chill about the shabbily kept space. The cobwebs on the top of the cabinets moved subtly from a draft. Curios, odd and inexplicable, filled the shelves; taxidermy, skulls of animals, strange little dolls, all with beady little eyes Iselle felt were directed upon her. For such a fine house on the exterior, the state of the interior was a shock.

Iselle's throat felt dry. She cleared it. "I beg your pardon?" She queried.

The house was small, low-ceilinged, the furniture was dirty and old. This was not the place one would imagine a great grandfather of Miss Metrelees would live. Iselle's eyes traveled up to the young woman, who stood still, straight and poised, her own gaze trained upon Iselle with intensity. She was peculiar and awkward. She had been from the first day they met, Iselle concluded.

"Yes. Clear as day," he said, "where did you hide all these years?"

Iselle's eyes dropped back to the old man. She wondered if the old man was in his right mind. Perhaps Miss Niria did not know that he had fallen into senility. He made no sense.

"Lots of old visitors of late," he sighed. "Perhaps it is a harbinger that it will soon be my time to pass onto another plane," he said. "It is a long time coming."

"That one won't go away," he sighed. "Been here all day." His hand rose and he indicated behind his shoulder where Amma stood. "I don't like such visitors anymore. I wish they would all go away. Will you? Go away, that is. I don't like figments hanging about, even if Lady Niria sends you. Add to that, you have a blot of death in tow. The old ones are the worst of all. And Murderers are intolerable."

Forrest stiffened noticeably. Iselle glanced at him for a fleeting second, noting the ripple of his jaw and the lines on his brow briefly knitting. She frowned a little.

"I like my peace. Mrs. Arnd is all the company I need." The old man spoke of the housekeeper who was almost as old as he was, and who clearly was no longer able to do her work well, seeing how dusty and grimy the rooms were. She had let them in and then disappeared into the shadows of his bleak house not to be seen again. She did not offer them tea. *Best we don't eat or drink anything in this house*, Iselle mused.

"What did Lady Niria see, and why did she send me? I don't understand," Iselle asked.

The old man's blind gaze fell back upon Iselle. "She saw the detestable monster that you are. You should not exist."

"Sir!" Forrest began, but Iselle put her hand upon his to silence him.

"Few of us remain who can see such things. The young ones—they cannot fathom it. They were never touched by it." He murmured in his broken, old voice, his chapped lips barely moving. He cleared his throat. There were little blotches of white saliva on the corners of his mouth. His vacant regard rested upon Iselle.

"You are ripe with fear, girl. But if you turn that into anger, you will lose yourself to what is inside you now. Anger like that one," his hand once again rose up and vaguely indicated Miss Metrelees. "If you leave, will the creature accompany you? It must have sought you here. It is why it lurks like a shadow near me. Leave so that it will leave too. And take the death-dealer with you, too."

Iselle's eyes moved back up to Miss Metrelees, who now smiled primly at her, her hands clasped delicately in front of her. She shook her head dismissively, and apologetically for the mad talk was apparently common for the old man.

"Is that all? Is that all you must say after we came all this way?" Iselle suddenly blurted at the old man. She leaned in towards Forrest and whispered: "Why would your aunt send us to a senescent old man?"

Forrest shrugged.

"What else is there to say? You have been claimed by a parasite. From where I do not know; you must have tread into sacred grounds, and your fear, and your magic must have drawn it to you."

"My magic?"

"The thing, on your body. It is an ancient magic, and it's only natural that it would attract something ancient to you. It will consume you. Now take the other ones with you. They do not belong here and neither does your parasite." He got up with a lengthy groan and significant effort, and he shuffled out alone.

Amma Metrelees laughed merrily as soon as he had gone. "I'm afraid my great grandfather isn't as sharp as he once was. It was shocking to see, after so many years of absence from his life. Off you go, then," she tittered. "I shall see to him. I must get to work cleaning this dusty, crumbling heap of despair that this house has become," she laughed uncomfortably. She flitted from the room after the old man. "Let's visit when I'm back at Rendorff," her voice called as she retreated.

The two sat silently in the coach as it drew away. They stared at one another incredulously.

"What happened?" Iselle finally muttered. "What did she mean?"

"Who?" Forrest asked.

"Miss Metrelees," Iselle said.

"Who?" This time the word was inflected with confusion.

"What do you mean, who? Miss Metrelees!" she snapped.

"Miss Moon, I have not the slightest idea who you are referring to," Forrest insisted.

"Did you not see her? Standing there behind the old man, clear as day?"

"I did not see anybody, Miss Moon. Are you unwell?"

Iselle gaped at Forrest, and her brow knit in befuddlement. "Miss Amma Metrelees. She rode in the stagecoach with us from the temple. You truly don't know who that is? Are you teasing me?"

Forrest dropped one of his brows, and shook his head, gazing at her as if she were mad.

"You don't know her? She sat right next to me in the coach. She came with us when we shopped in that town at the exchange… When the horse threw a shoe. She was standing right at the old man's side. Behind his chair. Are you making sport of me?"

"Miss Moon, I am truthfully, in all earnestness, bewildered. There is no such person. There never was. There was nobody else in that room besides the two of us and that old man. There were never any strange women in the shops with us. I accompanied you for that entire day, and I assure you, I would not speak such falsehoods to you."

Iselle, who had been leaning forward on her seat, threw herself back with an expression of uncertainty upon her face. "She was there; I saw her." Her voice was weak with doubt.

"The old man, he kept referring to 'that one,' or some other thing in the room. Is that what you speak of? I thought it was his senility speaking."

Iselle fixed her eyes upon Forrest, looking for a smirk or some kind of sign he was joking. But he looked as solemn and honest as he always was when he was in her presence. With her eyes sliding to the left, focusing on nothing in particular—she directed her mind back to the interaction, and then at all the interactions with Miss Metrelees.

It came to her that the young woman had never been acknowledged by any one of her friends. How had she not noticed? Amma had made herself known to Iselle, she had sat next to her, she had spoken to her. She had invited her to walk and sent her notes at school. The note had been in her tray by the door of her room. Was it not real? Miss Metrelees had been present, but in all truth, present only to Iselle. Nobody spoke of her or to her once. *How could I not have seen that?* Am I going mad? Iselle mused.

"It seems I might have been seeing a phantom for some time," she muttered to Forrest. He watched her with concern. "A phantom that promised friendship and then offered none of it."

"Since when?" he asked.

She thought about it, her gaze without direction and searching.

"Since the day we left Ideyon," she replied. Perhaps that explained also, the odd voice, which she could not identify as her own, speaking senseless, often insolent things inside her head, as they too, began after meeting Miss Metrelees, now that she thought upon it. For that, if it was true, offered relief, as she did not like the thoughts the intrusive ideas expressed. Would she be inside her head? Could it be her presence that had shaken Aunt Niria so greatly?

Forrest contemplated her words, his body swaying with the coach as it made its way back home.

"Could it be that day at the temple, something happened?" he ventured.

"Something did happen. I fainted," she reminded him, but she added: "…for no reason, really."

"We *were* hungry," he offered, with a touch of doubt.

"I've been hungrier and not fainted. I think you're right. I think something happened at the temples. He, and others, have referred to the old ones. The old man said something was attracted to my old magic," she reached up and touched the black widow beneath her bodice. "Is this possible?"

"I suppose we can't know what's possible with old gods, Miss Moon," Forrest said. "But the old man did."

"Then am I beset with a parasite as he described it?" Iselle's voice fell. "Why would a phantom manifest itself as Miss Amma Metrelees?"

"I do not know, Miss Moon."

They stared at one another in incredulous silence. They spent the rest of the long ride deep in thought, contemplating what they might have learned.

Iselle lingered on other thoughts. Of mentions of murderers. Of Forrest's subtle reactions to them. She glanced at him, pale, thoughtful, eyes trained on the snowy landscape rolling by. His grave, ambiguous face was so handsome to her. He was such comfort to her. He was always there. Always beside her. There to steady her and shield her. Who was he? And what had he done?

Eight hours one way, eight hours to return. For less than ten minutes in the presence of a rickety old man who spoke nonsense, and a visit from a figment, as the old man described her. *Figment*, thought Iselle. *I am a figment? A parasite? A monster?* Inside her, there was this thing. Did he mean the entanglement placed there by Prentiss?

Iselle shook out her nightgown and drew it over her head. It was past midnight. They had come home in the thick of the evening, woken the housekeeper to come inside, and gone to their respective rooms, both exhausted. It had been a trying, long day. And it ended with only vagaries for answers.

She sat down on her bed and put her mind back to that day. To the temples. To that moment she fainted. What she remembered most was feeling Forrest's arms grasp her before she could fall to the ground. Feeling him lift her and carry her as if she were nothing more than a bolt of cloth. Of him, shoving the hands of strangers away from her when she awoke.

She had no memory of figments or gods. Only the faintness and fading of her awareness, the heat of the pendant against her breast.

Who is Miss Amma Metrelees?

Iselle crawled under her covers and buried herself into the depths of her mattress. She lay there, staring out into the dim room. Outside, the snow fell silently.

Morning came with a thick, fresh layer of snow. Iselle woke late, and breakfast was brought to her, along with Talia, who snuck in behind the chambermaid, and slid onto the bed next to Iselle. "Good morning my big sister!" she said in a loud whisper. "I don't have any lessons today, so I have resolved to trouble you *all* day!" she exclaimed gleefully. She was wearing a plain dark blue cotton round-gown, no shoes, and had her hair loose and wild. She burrowed under the covers next to Iselle, who, unaccustomed to such informality and familiarity, shrank away a bit. But Talia would have nothing of it, and she wedged herself up against Iselle and hugged her. The bed then jostled again as Pip leapt upon it, stamped a few steps, and then plopped down behind Iselle's legs. He had seemingly snuck in as well.

"I'm so happy you've come. I have always wanted a sister. Forrest is a big beast and isn't pleasant at all. But *you* are perfect, and I will love you *dearly* and all of your little children as well, I will be the best, most diverting auntie in the world!" she exclaimed. "The opposite of Aunt Niria. She is somewhat kind to me, but she is not as kind to Forrest. I will be kind to all your children." She exhaled loudly and scratched her nose.

"I don't know what you see in that looming brute of a brother, but one must not question providence, and be happy that you regard him at all. We had all lost hope for him in finding anyone to love," she continued. "And he surely loves you. I've never seen him fawn so over anyone, let alone a lady."

"Fawn?" Iselle said incredulously. "He does *anything* but fawn."

"Oh, you don't know him. He's as cold as an ice-bear's toes. He doesn't speak to ladies except to insult them. Cousin Neeb told us all about how he follows you about the place like a sullen puppy at university. How he opens doors for you and brings you treats, and how he carries your books, and meets you at the end of each class, and knows your class schedule better than you do. Neeb knows. He's seen him. That's fawning."

Iselle had initially regarded these acts as making himself present to irritate her. Insisting on dramatically taking her books as if he were disgusted by how she struggled with their weight, or he was mocking when opening doors, as if she were some haughty queen he was affectedly serving. But she had always colored him in that light because he was always so cross and taunting when he interacted with anyone else. But she had realized how his prickliness had abated into thoughtfulness over the weeks. How he had so kindly let her weep upon his chest and made no mention or acerbic comment about it afterwards. He had taken her to eat to cheer her up, shown anger and concern at her plight, and he had used the fear he invoked in others to shield her from being pestered by other young men. Was that fawning for Forrest? And what did that mean for her? She was so disposed to be averse to any attention of the romantic kind, from any young man. Why was she accepting of Forrest's supposed fawning then? Why did this petulant, perpetually cross man elicit different reactions from her?

Talia snuggled closer to Iselle, and she yielded to it. It felt nice to be cuddled and embraced so lovingly by Forrest's family. Such tenderness and overt warmth were what she had always longed for. The love of a kind, affectionate, doting mother, the guileless adoration of a little sister. She loved her uncle. But this was a different kind of love.

She was not deprived of the sight of loving families, and demonstrative fondness towards children, mothers who fussed and clucked over their little ones, of fathers who sat in their parlor to talk with Uncle Ude, with their children crawling up onto their laps. The squeals and giggles as siblings and fathers and mothers chased the little ones over the immaculate lawn during the summer feasts Uncle Ude hosted for the neighbors each year.

She had witnessed this many times. Uncle Ude tried to be these things. But he fell short because he was not of that nature. He was not the kind of man who would marry and produce scores of little cousins to brighten Iselle's home. She accepted and loved him in spite of this sense of loss. Because he was always good to her. Because she was his buttercup.

She had never been able to stop herself from wondering how her mother would have been, would she too have been like Mrs. Outvallen? Would her father have picked her up and thrown her up, and caught her as she'd seen Ylly's father do when they were little? How much envy had consumed her upon witnessing that.

Forrest's father had been a monster. And they didn't have him anymore. She patted Talia's head and wrapped her arms around the girl in return. Pitiful thing, she thought. How she could be such a joyful, shining creature, with such a dark stain looming in her memories, Iselle could not know. She only gave her a commiserate cuddle in return.

She met Forrest in the morning room, where he sat reading with his mother. They both greeted the girls as they entered, and Forrest gestured to Iselle to come closer. She approached, and he passed her the book he was reading. He had it open to a page in particular. He pointed to it.

"I puzzled all night over our visit yesterday. I couldn't put it out of my head. It occurred to me to just look it up in a reference book or two this morning—and look what I found. It did not take me long," he told her. He rose onto his feet and leaned over her shoulder to peer at the page, and his finger fell upon a word. The book was a Palaeolexicon; a translation dictionary of sorts for the ancient language of used throughout Baranith, Oonil and Mirithria. She peered at the word he had found.

Metorlees – (met-ÒR-lēs) noun – *translation: vengeance/revenge* - infliction of punishment or retribution exacted for those who have been wronged. Ancient

Eermit, Hendrelon and all Northern Continental and West Isle Regions, Nordmin, Baludri, Asmaneed (primarily).

Iselle's eyes rolled up to meet Forrest's, and the color drained from her face. "Mr. Outvallen... could Miss Amma Metrelees be some..." Iselle paused, as if taking account of how mad what she was about to say sounded. "We were at the temple, were we not?" she asked. "Could she be a *Fury?*"

Inside her head, she laughed and laughed.

CHAPTER 24

There was only one university on Baranith that was of note. Prentiss had been careful to study what existed over the Onham Ocean on this land he had never visited. It was now obvious to him that this was where she would flee. But her fear had flowed into him for an hour or two, strong and fulfilling. He could pinpoint it. He always could. Like a beacon. *Like the beam from a lighthouse, I am here. Come find me. I am far, but I am here.* His preternatural senses homed in upon its direction like a compass. And his compass drew a straight line, and brought him to the shore at Eddoch, looking out across the waters towards the only place it could be. Baranith

He did his research. He found a map and literature about the place, its attractions, and its most prominent institutions. The University at Whitewater was the only thing that stood out to him. Where else would she go, but to a school? It was always a school. *Little scholar,* he mused, a smile crossing his scarred face. *I shall furnish her with books. I do not have so many, but for her, I will buy them. An expense so great is worth it to please his Iselle.* She would be so grateful to him for it. Of that he was certain. She chased learning, and it made her happy. He would make her happy.

He longed for her. For her beauty, for her presence. How he loved her.

Prentiss smiled. He imagined her in his home, *no... our home,* reposing, in the window in the aubergine velvet chair, looking out at the street, perhaps, stitching something peacefully. What an image of domestic bliss he painted. He imagined walking into the sitting room to find her; to see her turn and smile at him, her perfect blue eyes warm with affection for him. His pleasant daydream upended in a heartbeat. *She will be there, and she will stay;* he would ensure she would know fear if she deigned to abandon him. She would not be permitted to. It was just a matter of getting her there. Of that, he was certain.

He forgave her flight all these years because her fear had fed his magic so well—fed his soul, he thought. It was what he desired; her reverent fear, so that she would not defy him. If she feared him, if he had her in his grip, in his home, her trepidation would turn into respect. Like horses, or dogs, fear could keep them docile and instill obeisance. In turn, he would have those emotions always to replenish him.

He walked quietly next to the hired horse, his hand gripping the reins tightly against the bit. The animal tried to shake its head free but was met with a brusque jerk from Prentiss. A sharp breeze crossed them, sending its mane waving, and the tails of Prentiss' riding coat flapping. His cold eyes gazed forward, to the rocky coastal view below. From the bluff he could see the expanse of the Onham Ocean sprawling endlessly to the west. The wind hissed through the needles of the evergreens, and they swayed oceanward. Below, at the foot of the cliff, the small city of Eddoch bustled, fishing boats were returning with their morning's catch, and a bank of clouds crowded on the horizon, grey and ominous. The tide foamed and sprayed against the speckle of sea stacks and stumps bristling in a line from the easterly headland, which jutted from the sea like the prow of a great vessel. The westerly spit was almost overcome by the waves.

The ship bound for the great isle would be leaving soon. It would be another month to depart from this place again if he missed it. It would be a gamble to travel across the strait to Oostridge and to find passage in a timely fashion. He would leave from here, or he would likely be forced to ride farther south, to Narando, at the southern tip of the Gulf of Godsmouth. With the wintry weather affecting the already troubled seas, and the always easterly blowing winds, his window for passage to Baranith was slight.

How this vexed him. He had been so close. So remarkably close to having her at last. His horse threw up its head again unexpectedly and he nearly lost grip of its reins. He yanked down violently, and the wild-eyed gelding danced a few steps and shied away from Prentiss. The man halted it, gathered the rains tightly against the bay-colored withers, stuck his boot into the stirrup and mounted in a flare of his greatcoat.

The animal wheeled under the firmness of his hand, and reversed several steps, its hindquarters dropping, hooves clattering on the stone road. Prentiss tugged down the brim of his hat and dug his heels into the sides of his mount. The horse lurched forward, throwing up pebbles and debris from the force of it. He cantered down the bluff road, towards the city.

He leaned forward against the gusts of wind. His mind washed with thoughts of Iselle—with plans of his life with Iselle. No other man would have her now anyway. Not with his signature so deeply written upon her very soul, he thought with grim satisfaction. He thought how near he had been to her, to having her. He had felt the heat of her body against his own.

He had run his fingers along the goosebumps on her milky skin. He swallowed, his body growing warm with desire. He shook it off, leaning into the turn of the road, his knees absorbing the movement of the horse as it galloped around a slow-moving coach.

She would fill his house with children. Children they would both love as he had not been loved. They would never know the agony of his childhood. They would be happy, plump, rosy-cheeked cherubs, who would adore him, and climb in his lap, and run to him when he stepped through the door, and Iselle, like an exquisite shepherdess at the heels of her little flock, greeting him with an expression of delight and adoration. He would no longer be alone, no longer be isolated. It had always been such for him. From his mother, who vacillated between hatred and neglect, to his father, who beat him ruthlessly. They left him with a feeling of no self-worth. They essentially abandoned him, alone, in his house, to pursue their own ends.

His mother left for good. She was still alive somewhere, married to another man. She took no interest in the life of her son. She had said before she left that Prentiss was poisonous, wicked, irredeemable, and cruel like his father and she would have nothing to do with him. His father remained but was never present. He was a drunkard, and when Prentiss was seventeen, his father was shot dead by his partner in business. He only died after he'd squandered almost all of the family's fortune at the card tables and nearly driven the business into bankruptcy.

Good riddance, Prentiss doleful scowl was black with hatred.

He drew in his reins and stood up in the saddle, the horse slowing to a trot and then a walk, its barrel chest heaving, slick with sweat. The gelding threw foam from its mouth, and more formed around its girth and martingale. Its nostrils were flared, and it snorted in gusts of breath. Prentiss let the animal have its rein and it walked in long paces. He sat down and ruminated, his thoughts lulled by the rhythm of the animal's gait.

The house became his when his father died. It was one of the only assets remaining after the bank and debtors took their share. Prentiss was able to stave off further collections by commencing his trade of enchantments soon after that. He rebuilt the riches of his family name and brought ease into his life, but he brought no comfort. No love. Only emptiness and separation. No friends. No society. Alone against a hard, colorless world. It remained so until he saw her. Her eyes so blue, and her gaze so guileless and lovely. He knew it was fate. For she came into his life when he was prepared for her. He had overcome the destitution his father had bequeathed upon him. He had grown into a man. He could, and would provide a wealthy, comfortable home for Iselle.

I am a good man. I am the ideal man for Iselle. She knows it. She is simply influenced by her family and her friends to act in this way; to spurn me. Deep down, she loves me as much as I love her. And I will keep her in line. She is so easily swayed because of her innocence; she will need to be watched over; she will need to be separated from the people who persuade her so effortlessly.

He had invested a great deal of thought on the idea of killing her uncle and that governess with her unchecked, untrained magic. It had crossed his mind countless times. But he knew that those would be unforgiveable acts—the one thing that would make her hate him—and he did not want to make her hate him. He would have to cherish them as she did. Or kill them without causing suspicion that it was he who had done it. It was still a matter of debate in Prentiss's mind.

Her love for me needs to be steadfast, like my love is for her. I might permit her to visit her uncle in time when she's been with me long enough to affirm our love. To form the attachment, he knew she would feel once she was established in her proper place by his side.

He arrived at the shipping office by lunchtime, leaving his exhausted horse at the livery and walking the four city blocks to the sea-facing building. He reeked of horse sweat, and his coat tails were soaked in it. Indifferent to it, he proceeded to book passage aboard the Willogen.

He was told by the ship's captain, who was sitting at the shipping office, sharing a jug of grog and some cheese sandwiches with the clerk, that it would be between eleven or fourteen days to get there, depending on the winds—the latter, most likely with the looming storm and the winter conditions. The Onham Sea was infamous for its easterly gales, blowing as headwind to westward ships, and rough waters. The ships that came from the isle arrived quickly, as their sails caught the tailwinds and cut through the whitecaps like a knife through butter. At least, he thought, he would have her home quickly once he found her.

"You have five days before we set sail from Baranith back to the mainland. You best get your business tied up before then, because it will be a few weeks before we make the crossing again." The lady captain, a native of Erdoone by the hawkish shape of her face and snow-darkened skin, said to him. She was handsome, in her merchant marine uniform. Her bicorn sat on a bench beside her, along with her gold-buttoned coat. She studied his face, scrutinizing the scar cutting across the whole upper half of it, still enflamed and prominent, with dark scabbing on the crest of his forehead and the cut on the bridge of his nose.

The clerk sipped the clay vessel loudly and then lowered the mug to the desk. Around them, the dark, low, wood-paneled space, cluttered with its heavy desk, the shelves, heaving with shuffles of paper and ledger books, was warm and oddly welcoming. The fire was low in the humble little hearth embedded in the side wall near the desk. The lamplight did little to brighten the space, and the cold light of the broad front window only chilled it.

"There's an inn four buildings west. I can't guarantee there will be vacancies, but if you're timely, there might be. The ship will depart on the morning tide." He looked briefly at a chart pasted to his blotter. "The ninth bell would be a prudent time to board." The great clock on the back wall chimed.

"My thanks," Prentiss muttered. He dropped the Troys to pay for the passage on the desk, and seized the receipt the clerk had scribbled, and shook the breadcrumbs from it, stuffing it into his pocket. "Good day," he tipped his hat and bustled through the door.

The shabby little building of the inn swallowed him, and he found himself inside a similarly low and dark space. There, the squat little man in ill-fitting clothes welcomed him. He secured the only available room, a small sloping attic space with a drafty window. He set down his bag, and descended, hungry.

While he ate, he watched from the large window to the street, while the storm advanced, until the view of the ocean was completely obscured, and he could only see the faint indications of swinging masts, undulating ropes dripping from them, flapping tarps, and people, huddled under their woolen coverings and hats, scurrying against the spitting rain. No umbrella would survive such winds. Somewhere, the wind tolled a bell.

He made inquiries of the people in the inn's public house, eating rich tomato-tinted cod soup and the flaky, buttered roll served with it. It was a large serving in a hefty stoneware bowl. It was delicious. He found out what he could from other patrons between sips, easing their cool demeanors with small enchantment spells to humor them.

He learned a little about the whitewater university, about the area. When he finished eating, he took to the common sitting room, staring at the lively fire, visualizing the glee upon her face at the sight of him at last. *She has surely missed me. Yes, I punished her. But she knows that it was deserved, and she will repent. I will not hold the scars I now bear against her. It was not her doing. I will someday find him, and I will do what I did to that animal Lenteev to the man who marked my face. I do not have time for revenge right now. I must find my woman.*

In the evening, he bent over the spindly stand that held the washbasin. He poured warm water from the decanter into it, just delivered by the chamber maid. He straightened after washing his face. Every time he peered in the mirror, rage filled him.

The man had whipped him so hard, so violently, that the scars remained. Raised, knotty and hard on his face, his neck, across his head, they served as reminders of the agonies he had endured for his woman. He could scarcely see the scars without reliving the pain that had accompanied the attack. It was the worst pain he'd ever endured. It had caused him a fever and illness that had incapacitated him for several days. He was forced to trespass into another empty home and recover there. He never knew who the man was that attacked him and stole his Iselle. But he knew he was being sought for what they thought to be a crime. He fled the place as soon as he was sufficiently recovered to do so, and he bided his time, waiting for the inevitable wash of fear that would draw him out again.

He boarded the Willogen after a heavy breakfast. High tide came in the middle hours of the morning, and the last passengers boarded only moments before the gangplank was detached and the Willogen retreated from the harbor and turned its prow towards the choppy sea.

The ocean weather was bitterly cold. The snow and rain never stopped, and the wind was howling and relentless, and the sails snapped and rippled loudly day and night. Passengers did not emerge from the bowels of the ship. The crew endured against the elements, bravely driving it forward to cut its way through the briny, stormy seas, towards Baranith.

At last, thought Prentiss, *I will bring my Iselle home.* We will ride the tailwinds back to Mirithria, to Neddham, to the stylish, luxurious house he had prepared for her. *And then I will finally be happy as I have always deserved.* He was determined this time to prevail—to overcome the people who stood as obstacles between him and his wedded bliss. He would not let anyone stop him. He would destroy anyone who dared to try. Thrilling as her abject fear had been over the years, it was time to end this chase.

He came out of the ship the moment the din of the open ocean faded into quietude, when the sails dropped, and the ship took anchor off the shore of Baranith waiting to ride the tide in. He stood at the rail, looking at the deep green, thickly forested hills before him, grading layer by receding layer, into pale—into the mists. The plane of the quiet, reflective water of the bay stood between him and the tableau of hills before him.

"I am here, my beloved, dear Iselle," he whispered to himself. "I will find you."

CHAPTER 25

"I have no idea, Mr. Outvallen. What could we do with this information if it is real? How would I find the phantom of Miss Metrelees?" Iselle frowned. "I'm certain she could explain things, could she not?"

"I wonder, if we were to go to the temples..." he speculated, not completing his thought. It was mid-morning, and the snow was falling, the flakes swaying with the gusts of dry, frigid wind as they dropped, and accumulated into a smooth blanket over the gardens of Chestnut Hill House. Iselle was sitting on a cushioned window seat in the morning room, looking out upon this serene picture with a distant look in her eyes.

They heard the bell ring, and to her surprise, Dorya was announced and then ushered freshly relieved of her hooded cloak and muff. She was just in time to join them for a hot cup of tea after a bracing ride from the school. Iselle rose and greeted her, taking her hands and smiling at her. "I am so happy to see you," she said sweetly.

Dorya, in her customary effusive way, grinned and exclaimed the like, before accepting the cup of tea offered by Forrest. He went to the sideboard to furnish himself with a teacup.

"You are so very missed. Meddin is about to burst with curiosity, and even Ryle has been asking after you, Iselle." Dorya sank down into the chair by the window, holding the saucer in both hands. She looked rather fetching in a wool day gown of burgundy, cream, and gold plaid. There were still little blobs of snow on the toes of her boots.

Ryle is a pathetic fool. Iselle's eye twitched and she shifted in her seat.

"Why would he do such a thing after his disastrous confession?" Forrest asked. "He's rather a dolt, seems to me," he mumbled sourly. He went back to reading with his teacup on the small table by the arm of his chair.

"Forrest will be returning to campus tomorrow," Iselle informed Dorya.

"Oh, who cares about the meat-pile of pessimism that is Forrest? It's *you* who is deeply missed," Dorya blurted frankly, eliciting a small nod of agreement from Forrest, accompanied with an expression of ironic acceptance.

"I miss it too. I've become so accustomed to living in academic institutions, I feel out of place in such a house," Iselle admitted. "I cannot lie, however. It's something I could easily grow accustomed to again."

Dorya, unsure what Iselle was saying, tilted her head. "You don't go home to your family at all?"

Iselle let the question pass without an answer.

"What is your plan once you graduate? I would hope that perhaps we could go and set up our lives someplace near to one another. Where do you live, Iselle? When you are not in school?"

Iselle realized that Dorya knew extraordinarily little about her. She had confided it all to Forrest, but Dorya knew nothing about her struggles; the dangers she'd faced; her injuries, her hurt, her fear. None of those things. Iselle had always kept it to herself. Even with Redlan. Because she did not want to create a friendship that would entail unnecessary sympathy and commiseration. She wanted what she did not have; warmth, comfort, pleasantries and all the things she had to fight to feel for herself. She wanted normality from Dorya. And that meant keeping her private matters from her.

She glanced at Forrest, ensconced in his leather chair, in his tan trousers, and a sapphire waistcoat made of a plain matte silk. He had no frockcoat on and remained in his shirtsleeves even when Dorya entered. His cravat was a bit limp, and his collar was loosened because of it. He had one hand on his cheek, his elbow that supported it rested it on the arm of the chair, the other clutched the page of his book. His legs were crossed. With his plain black leather slippers, and heavy-lidded eyes, he looked relaxed and content.

She sipped her tea, and examined his strong, aquiline features. The straight slope of his prominent nose, the angles of his face, the passivity of his eyes as they danced over the script of his book, his black lashes fluttering with movement. His hair was tousled and unkempt, falling forward rather wildly onto his forehead. He was breathtakingly handsome to Iselle. To others, he might look hard and unbending, unapproachable and severe in his looks. But to her, she saw a vulnerability that she somehow shared with him. And he was always so attentive of her, without demand or expectation. He was simply happy to be beside her. Because he liked *her.* He understood her.

She then let her eyes return to Dorya's pretty face, as she rattled on about this or that, gossiping extensively about the goings-on in school, and who was doing what.

"When are you coming back?" she asked. "You're going to fall behind on your classes if you're not careful."

"I've been reading to keep up. Forrest was kind enough to bring some of my books, and secured some summaries from the teachers," Iselle explained. She quietly wondered as she spoke how long Dorya expected to stay. It was an hour's coach from the school. Iselle loved Dorya very much, but she was not disposed to visitation on this particular day. She wanted quiet. And as her friend prattled on, she grew increasingly weary of it.

"Why are you here, you never told me," Dorya asked. Iselle didn't want to answer.

"Dorya, I…" Iselle began.

"Miss Moon has been feeling unwell since the day of the picnic as you might recall. My mother invited her to take respite and convalesce here. She is not quite recovered. She will return when she has."

Iselle was glad of his rescue.

As usual, Forrest understood what Iselle was feeling, and he chimed in again after a bit. "Well, I'm sorry to interrupt this social event, but Miss Moon and I are to go to visit the physician. This is why I stayed today and have not returned to school. And we must leave upon the hour. I would ask you to shoo, and next time, to write before you come so we can be sure we do not have any other engagements." He got up, rang the bell for Dorya's coat and coach, and walked out, ostensibly to fetch his frock coat and make himself presentable for the fictitious visit to the physician.

"That man is such an insufferable, rude bully," Dorya blurted. "Could he be more impolite?"

"Yes," Iselle retorted. "Yes, he can."

Dorya laughed through her nose, and rose, and Iselle did the like. They met in the center of the rug, just outside the perimeter of the little seating area around the bay window and the window seat.

Iselle hesitated and glanced at the rug under their feet for an instant. Her easy air stiffened a little as she ruminated briefly upon something.

"I suppose I'll be off, then. I had hoped to stay the afternoon with you. But you also will have to change clothes and such before you set off yourself. It was lovely to see you, Iselle," she said kindly. "You look a little pallid, and distant," she observed.

"I'm not quite well yet. But I hopefully will be soon," Iselle replied. As Dorya turned to take her leave, Iselle reached out and grasped her arm, pulling her to face her again. She stood a spell, taking the girl's fingers gently into her hands.

"Dorya... I know this might sound strange and out of sorts; but if you..." she paused again, and then with a resolved expression, continued. "If you happen to come face to face with a stranger, one with possibly some kind of mark across his face, as tall as Forrest, but of Mirithrian features, rather rangy and lean, with ghostly eyes, I beg you, do not speak to him, and don't let him speak to you. If you see him, promise me you will turn and walk calmly away. When he can no longer see you, run away as fast as you can. Find some place of safety."

The small young woman gaped up at Iselle with bewilderment.

"I don't understand," she muttered.

"I can't explain," Iselle exhaled impatiently. "Promise me, if it happens, that you will do exactly as I ask."

Dorya studied the expression on Iselle's face, taking in the barely veiled fear and desperation.

"Very well," she replied. "But I will hold it against you always, for not explaining why." There was disappointment in Dorya's eyes that cut a fissure in her heart.

Iselle's eyes dropped.

The door opened and the chambermaid entered carrying Dorya's winter coverings. She helped her into them. Dorya was silent as she fastened the frogs at the front of her cloak and put the hood over her head. The school's coach awaited at the front of the house.

Iselle stepped forward and put her arms 'round Dorya's shoulders. "I'm sorry," she whispered. "I'll see you soon."

Dorya set forth into the snow back to Whitewater.

Forrest reappeared when she rolled away and flopped back into his chair, taking up his book again.

Iselle, still standing in the middle of the room, peered at him. He too, had an air of wretchedness that he had scarcely managed to suppress, since the visit with the old man. Iselle dwelled upon that, shifting her mind away from Dorya and her displeasure, and to Forrest's state of mind. It had been a curiosity she had not been prepared to broach with him. But she decided it was time.

What was it that made him become even more despondent than usual? She moved to the chair beside him, and sat down, looking at him squarely while he stared, unblinking at his book.

She thought back to their visit with the old man. To that moment that rested on her mind since then. To the transient second where Forrest had reacted ever so subtly to the bizarre interchange—when the old man mentioned a murderer. She stared at him, trying to figure out the best way to query him about his reaction to the word.

He could sense her curiosity. Her reticence. He shifted, his eyes sliding towards her.

"Forrest... The old man talked about figments. And a murderer. Do you have any idea what that was about? Were those simply senile blatherings?" She peered at him expectantly.

He gazed upon her, his expression thoughtful. He studied her face and then turned his eyes to the fire.

"I'm not sure about the first bit about figments, but the other thing, *that* struck a chord." Forrest snapped his book closed and took a deep breath, watching the flames as he spoke. "It is difficult to hear that word thrown about. No matter how many times I am assured otherwise by my immediate family, I cannot help but feel it is a word that describes me." He then turned his gaze back to her, and peered at Iselle for a long, thoughtful moment. "My aunt, she might agree with the description. She struggles with it."

He took a deep lingering breath and exhaled shakily.

"Since you entrusted me with your secrets, I will trust you with mine," he murmured.

The fire snapped and popped, and the quiet of the snowy day wrapped around them. The clock rang the quarter hour in the foyer, and they gazed at one another.

He looked at her for a moment more, and his eyes dropped onto the front of the book balanced on his knee. He rubbed his chin. His fingers made a rasping sound as his afternoon shadow was growing in. His hand dropped to his book again. There was a pall of silence.

"I killed my father," he said, looking up again with a matter-of-fact expression, his words blunt. Iselle gave him the courtesy of silence and listened.

"I murdered him using his own powers. I wormed my way into his rage and his hate and his self-loathing and his sense of inadequacy, and I mirrored it with my own hatred for him; all the similar feelings he created in me as a boy, and I consumed him with our feelings, our emotions combined. They twisted him into a madness so great, he set himself ablaze and threw himself from the roof of our home." It was a missive heavy with darkness. Iselle was expecting something, but nothing quite this vivid.

Iselle stared at him blankly, her brain processing what he had said.

"You asked me why I helped you. And I told you the truth. I've lived with this alone. The burden of my crime, the memories of my father's black heart inside my own head, feeling all of the things he felt; the odium, the misery, the self-hate. All of it. I recognized your lonesomeness, because it is what I have lived with for most of my life. Because of him. And even more so since the incident of four years ago."

The fire danced in the hearth, and snowflakes ticked on the glass of the windows. It was just her, him, and Pip, who had idly followed him into the room upon his return and taken his place by the fire. Talia called the folded blanket placed by the fender, his roastery.

Iselle recalled what he had said to her that first day they met, word for word, which had deflated her anger with him so suddenly. *Because when I saw you, I thought you looked like you were in desperate need of peace, security and solitude in spite of your being irrevocably alone, and nobody understands that need more than I do.'*

She stared at him. She thought about his remoteness. His reputation as such an angry soul, that everyone feared. He pushed everyone away with his aloof and sometimes outright cruel nature. He let nobody except her, and sometimes Meddin in, and she suspected Meddin knew nothing about this. She heard of his confrontations and his brutal, injurious brawling with other boys. How many times he was brought before the Chancellor for disciplinary reasons. She knew he practiced his fighting skills every morning when he was at school. He had calmed in his final year, from what she had gleaned from the gossip brought by Dorya and a few others.

He was lost, in many ways, as she was. But she knew he was not evil. He would not do anything like that without good reason.

"Your sister called him a monster. Was he truly a monster?" she asked.

Forrest's eyes rose up with a haunting, loathing gaze, and he met hers, his face set in a mask of darkness she'd never seen before. "My father was the worst of monsters. Little Talia, she does not remember what he did to us. But *I* do. I am the keeper of those memories. She was too little. But I remember. I suffered by his hand until I went away. We three have scars, Iselle. We three have signatures of the etched in us by the beast that hurt us. I have seen some of yours. Mine are like festering tumors inside of me. Talia's are encapsulated in a place where she cannot see them. She was little," he repeated. "So innocent." His voice broke.

"She doesn't remember yet, and I will ensure she *never* does." He revealed these horrors without speaking them explicitly, and with a grimness that made Iselle's skin rise up in goosebumps.

"She did not see what happened to him either. I waited until she visited my aunt with my mother. I had been planning it for some time. Waiting for the right moment. I was in my eleventh year of school then; just shy of seventeen years of age. I sneaked out of the school; it's only about half an hour on foot from here. Nobody saw anything. He was only found as he was. I was back at school before morning. My family knows it was me because they know what he was. They do not speak of it, but they know it had to be done. For all of us, but mostly for Talia." His voice was terse and grave. His brow hardened and his jaw rippled.

"My aunt, she knows too. She adored her brother and denied he could be capable of the things he'd done to Talia and me when we were small. She called me a liar when I told her when I was thirteen. I tried to tell her what violence I endured in my efforts to stop him from hurting Talia. She overlooked the wounds and bruises and burns and cuts..." he paused.

"My mother was in no better state than us. Cowed and terrified. He ruled the house with his fists. I succeeded in protecting Talia from further harm for the three years before I had resolved to kill him.

"And kill him, I did. Aunt Niria has never forgiven me. Aunt Niria fears me. I can feel it in her every time I see her. She is civil, but wary. I can feel her denial of the truth. She knows. But she hates and fears me, nonetheless—even seeing the damage her brother had wrought. My mother does not hate me. Talia does not fear me." He paused again and took another shaky breath. His hand rose and he massaged the back of his neck. When he dropped his hand again, he continued.

"I destroyed my father with his own vileness. I made him feel it all and it was so terrible, he set himself on fire and jumped from the roof. Now I carry that memory of vileness too. It is the price, for it all to end."

Iselle found herself filled with not horror or shock at his actions, but with a profound, unmistakable wash of envy. *To dispatch my nemesis, my monster in such a way*. She glanced up at the portrait, and let her eyes linger on the face of a man who had done so much harm. She understood that the family held onto it and displayed it for propriety's sake. Their family was prominent in the local society. They could not reveal the horrors they had suffered at his hand. They had to look at this every day in spite of the memories it contained.

She turned her eyes back onto Forrest, whose gaze had never left her face. His aggrieved and almost violent expression had softened, and he looked trepidatious now—if not a bit worried. He was trying to detect her feelings without trespassing upon them.

"You *were* just in what you did, Forrest, to protect Talia, and others," Iselle articulated with care and purpose, making rare eye-contact with him, to demonstrate her earnestness. "Would that I could do the same," she added.

CHAPTER 26

Whitewater was the finest school Iselle had ever attended. It was a broad campus, with fetching buildings of red brick with sandstone corners, windows, and trim; all matched and scattered across countless acres of park. There were osteal, leafless trees that surely shaded the parks well in summer, and gardens were meticulously kept and looked orderly and tidy underneath the layer of snow that blanketed the ground and the webs of brick walkways cutting through from one place to another.

He liked it here. She certainly must like it here too, he imagined. It was bustling, like the last place he had sought her, where he had dispatched with those two obstructions. This was a large school with many students.

He stood out in his plain clothes amongst the throngs of uniformed bodies, also draped in cloaks and redingotes and graceful garricks swaying, some people with hats and bonnets, and ladies with hands dug into muffs of rabbit, fox, and weasel fur. He imagined her amongst them, her sullen little face, and her frigid air, cutting through the groups like a shark through a school of fish. They would make a wide berth around her. It made him laugh a little, how she had that effect on people. So attractive to the eye, yet so cool and untouchable. She suited him so well. He wondered in passing what she chose to study here—and mused about what books he ought to buy for her that would match her interests. Reading about her attractions would keep her fulfilled when she was safe at home. *She will have no need to seek employment. She would have been an old-fashioned girl, if she had not been forced to flee and hide in all these schools.*

He walked with leisure past some buildings, taking in a snowy-edged sign here and there. Beshrim Hall, Main Library, Forsham Hall, Magical Sciences, Hornesley Dormitory, Refectory & Commons. So many buildings, so many people.

And then they disappeared. A bell rang and the students flowed into buildings and the campus was quiet again. He would not find her like this. He needed to find the dormitories. He would find her room first. She was certainly studying, hearing lectures or such. Prentiss felt a frisson of excitement as he always did when he was near her. When he was about to set his eyes upon the prize he knew was his, and his alone.

He lingered.

He purposefully wore dark clothing so as to not stand out too much. A black frock coat, a grey waistcoat, and black breeches. Over all of that, he wore a black greatcoat made of the finest wool. He made sure they were stylish, as he wanted to look handsome for Iselle.

He had not taken the time to do so last time they had seen one another. Perhaps it had contributed to her reaction; her struggle against him. He had seen her face when she looked up to find him in front of her, and that was why he was forced to enchant an *animatus custodia* upon her and make her into his marionette. She would have run. *No*, he admitted. He had planned to enchant her the moment he could put his hand upon her.

But he wanted to look nice for her. She was *always* his primary consideration.

Enchanting parts of the body had always been his special skill. And he had practiced carefully on people over the years as he grew up, in his own schools, on weaker boys. Objects were easy enough; but he discovered his ability to do his works upon the internal parts of a human being wholly by accident, when he willed someone who mocked him to still their tongue. When the spell abated, the bully never looked at Prentiss again.

His first practical magic instructor, Professor Midlane, a strange, remote, and awkward man, had been shocked by this ability. It was something he'd never seen before. There were spiritual mage who could coerce the mind of others to enact their will—but to enchant a brain; a part of the body, hands, feet, legs, it was unprecedented for mage who were often regarded as little more than artists and performers. He was fascinated—and he helped Prentiss to hone his skill, to test it. They studied anatomy and Prentiss learned about all the bits and parts he could manipulate. They would, however unethical in nature, practice on the unsuspecting students milling about the halls of the school.

He had learned to visualize the places in the body he would enchant, to see what effects his spells would have upon them. The Professor slipped him into the gross anatomy classes; huddled in with the students of medicine to observe dissections.

Through his experiments with living people, he learned a great deal about the parts of the brain and what they controlled. He did not know everything, but he knew more than enough to manipulate people, at will. With the touch of his hand.

Paralyzing Iselle had been a matter of course. He did not want to do it or like to do it. He preferred if she simply had walked beside him as he wished. He felt compelled to do so. The spells on the grey and white matter never lasted exceedingly long. Some spells lasted longer than others. He could still not fully understand why some of his spells persisted while others did not.

The fear spell had a pleasantly and unexpectedly long duration, although he did refresh it of his power whenever he did have the chance to be in her presence. His old friend Professor Midlane had supposed that it was the fact that it was in the amygdala, in the core of the brain, where they had hypothesized to be the source of emotional processes, that it had such staying power. Almost all of his spells cast into that sacred part of the brain were lasting and powerful. Because emotions, no matter if the person had magical ability or not, were unique sources of power if one could tap into them or make use of them.

Prentiss could not control emotions or derive power from them as much as others could. He could only absorb them, feel them, and only if he could get close enough to extend his powers into the mind of his victims to enchant the organ that contained all this delicious feeling. He could only truly drink in the fear. Joy, sadness, disappointment, all those other emotions were more difficult to grasp. Fear was a clear, resonating vibration that could travel for a thousand miles with the right magic to carry it to him. To fill him. To summon him.

He strolled about the lively campus. He lurked. He watched. When he found the ladies' dorm, he found a space to observe the comings and goings of the young women. So long did he remain, that the sky began to release more of its wintry snow, and it gathered on the top and brim of his hat, and on his shoulders. He did not feel the cold. He watched, in the lee of an evergreen rhododendron, so large and looming, that he almost disappeared in its silhouette.

Dorya was remarkable to him because she was so tiny. A little thing marching through the snow, her train leaving a clean wake of exposed brick behind her. *As small as Iselle when I first set eyes upon her.* She moved towards the building, and was intercepted by a tall, dark figure before she went inside. It was Iselle's name that drew the whole of his attention.

"Oh! Hello Lord Forrest of Outvallen! What brings you here?" The young lady greeted him with an affected, exaggerated curtsy. She was bright and cheerful. The looming, sullen character merely stopped before her and bowed his head a shade. He did not seem to appreciate her good humor.

Undeterred by his seeming impatience, the girl went on. "When is Iselle returning? I miss her so very much. Teena is not exactly the equal to her company," she asked cheerfully.

"I came to tell you that it isn't definite at this juncture," he replied. "There are extenuating circumstances that will keep her from school. I was wondering if you could go to her classes tomorrow and see if there are any assignments she might miss or has missed. I have a treatise I must present this evening to the Master's Union, so I cannot do it."

"Fine," the tiny girl exclaimed in an explosion of breath. The cloud it made floated away and dissipated. "I suppose I'll go and see. Should I visit and bring it to her at endweek?"

"Best not for now," Forrest murmured dismissively "Find me after classes tomorrow, and I will bring it home to her. My mother has been strict about visitations, as her constitution is not fully recovered. Even your last visit fatigued her greatly. Best go inside, Sage said there's to be a great deal of snow tonight." He then pivoted and stalked away.

Prentiss curled his fingers, closed his eyes, and drew the waxy leaves around himself until there were only his eyes peering out from the rhododendron.

His pale eyes fixed upon the young man. *Who is this Forrest?* He assessed the figure with a deathly stare, shrinking back into the rhododendron like a shadow as the man's gaze passed unnoticing over him.

Draped in the robes of a final year, Forrest looked like a scarecrow—a sapling, with a dour, doleful air about him. His lank hair fell almost into his hateful eyes. Who was *he* to curate the needs of Prentiss' Iselle? *Who was this upstart? Another skulking mongrel sniffing about Iselle.*

Prentiss' glare grew black with hatred as he watched the man's lean shape recede into the snowfall. His eyes then shifted to the door of the dormitory into which the small woman had vanished. Divided, he hesitated. Follow the scarecrow, or the imp?

Forrest clenched his teeth, and bit back his immediate instinct to react. But he felt it. Like a searing poker drilling into his brain. The hatred. Pure, unfettered, unrestrained loathing focused into him as sunlight through a lens. He could not source it, but it was nearby. And clearly it was within view of him. But he subtly took a sweeping glance around as he turned away from Dorya and began to walk back towards the Masters' Union. The source did not follow. Its rage faded as he moved away. Once he was sure he was out of line of sight, he dipped back onto the westerly path and circled back.

Hatred was like clay, so thick and malleable it could be. The deeper it was felt, the easier it could be manipulated. There was a little smile curling on the corners of Forrest's mouth. He reached up and unbuttoned the front of his robes and drew them off his shoulders as he walked. The draping fabric always hung from his frame and concealed its strength and musculature. His years' worth of practice of the art of combat, tested and sharpened upon the bodies of other students who locked horns with him. Fine-tuned each morning in the light of the high windows on the grass mats of the sporting atrium. It was easy to underestimate the man upon first sight. His wrath, and his resentments, his guilt and his shame took form in his body—shaped it. An opportunity to quell those feelings, to direct them into an appropriate vessel would not be ignored. And an opportunity it was.

He was sure *this* was the monster who deprived Iselle of freedom and happiness. He could feel the seething jealousy intermixed with the shadowy hatred. There were wisps of her in these expressions. The attachment. The obsession. The desire to have and to control. All these trivial things fueled his anger—and his desire to do right by Iselle.

He could free her. He could free Iselle of this predator. He dropped his robe on a stone bench he passed, and now in his shirt sleeves and wool waistcoat, he loosened his cravat and his cuffs, rolling them up to his elbows. As he approached the dormitory, the wash of the man's feelings returned, stronger and blacker and oilier with each step.

He stepped off the path when he reached the back of the dormitory, where Iselle had taken his hand that night, weeping with relief for the return of her spider-stone. His jaw rippled at the thought of her being in danger. He bit back his own rage. He saved it. He would need it. He knelt, and pressed his fingers into the snow, into the hard earth. He closed his eyes and opened himself back up to the flow of the monster's feelings. He would use them to create the mold of the beast. And then funnel all his ire into it. He needed to get him away from Dorya. From the school.

He needed to kill him.

CHAPTER 27

Iselle ignored the soreness in her thigh from clutching it onto the fixed head of her sidesaddle, and the growing rawness on her coccyx from the cantle. She resolved to ride more, to reacquire her tolerance for the saddle. She'd refrained for so long that it hurt her body, and despite gloved hands, her fingers were tender from the leather of her reins.

The little mare she'd been given to ride by Mrs. Outvallen was a plucky, energetic little thing, all a-fluff in her winter coat, the deep wine-tinted brown of her looking like a thick, piled rug. Her raven mane was long and shiny against her neck, a graceful forelock fell upon her dainty face and tousled in the cold breeze. Not a dot of white interrupted the purity of her coat, and her legs looked like she'd stood in a vat of black dye for a spell. She snorted pleasantly and battered the ground with one hoof communicating her desire to continue moving. Clods of snow went flying.

Despite her mare's impatience, Iselle chose to stare out at the pastoral scene before her. She needed air. Openness. Quiet. Room to think. She swept her gaze over the open scenery. Wheatfields, now blanketed in snow spread out as far as the eye could see, interrupted by the occasional lines of poplars, the white face and slate roof of a farmhouse, with windows reflecting the rosy morning sky behind her. The few trees besides the poplars were flocked in snow, and as she sat, the clouds were gathering to cover the splendid watercolor of a sky in the grey of a looming snow shower.

Her breath boiled out of her mouth in billows of vapor, and steam blew from the nostrils of her horse. Around her, on the Outvallen's hunting reserve, at the edge of which she stood, winter's chill had encased the branches of the skeletal trees in ice, giving them the appearance of lace.

The knocking sound, in the stilled wintry silence, echoed around her. She followed it, and her eyes fell upon the bright red head of a woodpecker, who was diligently tapping away at a tree.

"Lovely isn't it? I adore winter. I always have," a voice said.

Iselle jumped at the suddenness of it, and twisted to look at her side, and saw none other than Miss Amma Metrelees, sitting on her own horse— a white one, with a shimmering summer coat that made it almost look silver. It was lithe and uncanny in its appearance.

Iselle said nothing, she simply stared, there were no tracks behind the animal. Miss Metrelees was stylishly appointed in a similar riding habit to hers, made of wool and fur, with a fur hat like Iselle was wearing; borrowed from Mrs. Outvallen's wardrobe. Only hers was all white.

"Oh, come now, you have nothing to say?" Amma asked. She smiled precociously. "You have figured me out. Well… Almost," she admitted.

"What are you then?" Iselle asked. Miss Metrelees's horse shifted and tossed its head. Iselle's horse made no indication it saw any of this. Only her ears rotated here and there when Iselle spoke.

"What would you imagine me to be?"

"Oh, I beg you, stop with the games. I don't want to play riddles with you," Iselle snapped. "Why must there be such subterfuge and mystery? It's aimless and stupid."

"We," Amma began, "were never creators of the aspects that define us. You are all so mistaken there. We do not create love, or wisdom or justice. We merely seek it because we too, are like you. A person who desires justice becomes a judge. A person who desires knowledge becomes a scholar. A person who desires love, seeks and fosters love just as you do. We are not creating these things, we are living these things, just as you do every day. The only difference is that we do so with power that most people do not possess.

"Long ago, we led, not always as corporeal beings—and because we were endowed with powers, you obeyed us. We set examples for your people to follow. But we never created the things for which we are known. We merely exemplified them for people who had yet to better understand the world. That is all." Miss Metrelees sighed.

"You aren't a Fury. You are Obraya." Iselle realized this almost as she spoke it. "You are a god." Her eyes grew wet with tears as she looked upon this illusion of a creature.

Amma seemed to ignore Iselle's exclamation and instead inhaled and exhaled with a thoughtful smile. "Old man Desh is the only living soul remaining in this region, who has had any dealings with the old guard. His life was greatly lengthened for it. You would think he would treat me with gratitude and even a little deference," the figment said ruefully. "So uncivil. I suppose I shouldn't expect thoughtfulness from your kind. You're rather selfish creatures. I think we *all* became a little disaffected by it all, in all honesty. Your qualities, and our boredom drove us into dormancy, really.

We consumed a great deal of magic before our retreat, and then there was not enough left to emerge again." She said this introspectively.

She paused and then in a non-sequitur, she chuckled. "I *knew* you would go to the old man."

"I feel as if you knew what I was doing all the while," Iselle replied. Amma's head swiveled towards the girl, and they gazed at one another.

"I've been with you all along, my dear. Since the moment you stepped into the temple of the trinity. You were everything a goddess of revenge could want; consumed by a desire for vengeance and nearly bursting with all that swallowed accumulated rage. You kept it so fast inside you, to feel it when you came to me, it was like elixir. Add to that, all the magic I needed to free myself from the prison of my own making was right there, bundled up in that little bauble resting against your breast.

"Clever little object, ingenious little spell; clearly cast by a skilled, and ancient sorceress; long-lived like your little old man Desh." She reached up and pushed away a tendril of her hair. Her freckles seemed so innocent and charming.

"I chose to meet you there in order to awaken you because it's time. I have come to disabuse you of your misunderstanding of who and what I was. Although it is amusing to create a mystery than simply spill it all out, the situation requires spillage." She laughed a little, and then sighed, her shoulders sagging a bit. "Ah, well. It's out on the table now. Most of it. There's some you must learn for yourself."

She continued. "The modern mage are lacking, and they could not discover exactly what is inside that, scarred little body of yours. The fear-eater's spell, well, as puzzles go, is rather mundane. It is skilled magic for a mere enchanter—rather distinct; to enchant what others could or would not. But he uses unusual methods to achieve his ends. I would be impressed by his innovation, if I were not insulted by the very principle of his existence." Her face twisted into a look of hate.

"The other mages you sought out, they would not recognize the presence of what's inside you besides your—what did she call it? Ah, yes, the *entanglement*, yes? They *would* recognize the presence of something old inside you. Something from a time when magic was beautiful, and fathomless. Not the miserable facsimile it is today," she interjected with a sardonic smirk. "So sad and useless, really. Except maybe *his* family's kind…" She paused.

"Using emotion and empathy, *these* are key to strong skills. Your Forrest masters it. The fear-eater, he has reckoned it in a roundabout way, not wholistically, but more by accident. He doesn't fully understand what he's done, but he's done it, nonetheless. The father-killer, he knows what he is doing. You, so powerless, found someone who is with great power—only to end up not needing his skills at all." She laughed easily.

Iselle sat rigid. She let the creature ramble. The goddess—or whatever she claimed to be.

"It was you, talking in my head," Iselle grumbled. "The nastiness made me shudder."

Miss Metrelees only laughed, eyes twinkling.

"Forrest was right. You indeed freed me. And now, *we* are going to free *you*."

"Why would you want to help free me?" Iselle asked. "And how?"

"Oh, don't mistake my actions for altruism, my dear. Our kind rarely acts in kindness. We make no apologies for investing in things that ultimately benefit us. Your benefit is only happenstance," she replied. "As for the how; that is something you must come about on your own. For it to be effective, it must come from you. Not me. But there is no shortage of what you need inside you, to make it happen."

She turned her horse next to Iselle's, guiding it to face the opposite direction. She came up abreast to her, so close, her knee brushed up against Iselle's. She leaned in and stretched out her arm. Her delicate gloved hand pressed against Iselle's chest. The black widow, as if her layers of clothing were nothing more than glamours, passed through them and out into the cold, hard air. The figment snatched it in her fist, and then opened it in front of Iselle, the token resting on the flat of her palm.

She blew on it and spread her fingers. The chain and the wire cage that held the stone disintegrated and all the metal bits showered Iselle's skirts and sprinkled to the ground. All that was left was the stone spider.

"You don't need this, Iselle," she said with both admonishment and assurance, garnished with a whimsical smile. She gazed benevolently upon the astonished girl. And then Iselle watched as the stone grew so hot, it began to glow like a coal, and the heat and orange embers quickly consumed it, and it grew black and sooty. The goddess, or figment, whatever she was, leaned forward and blew another breath upon it, and the shape dissolved into nothing but ash.

"I'm leaving you now, in earnest. Your fate is in your hands, but fear not, my dearest child. You are not alone. You will never be alone again."

Iselle swallowed, her face wan and her eyes wide.

"Oh, don't fret, my girl," she said with exaggerated compassion.

She picked up her reins and made to leave—then drew the horse to a halt, looking over her shoulder, contemplating for a moment, her fair face and pretty eyes so strangely juxtaposed against her haughty air.

"Oh, and to answer the questions you have sought to answer so ardently, and studied so hard to understand—the answer is no. We did not imbue anyone with power. We are not such creatures. The only difference between us and you is that we are born with greater power. We can manifest familiars to suit our ends. Nothing more.

"We possess only greater, deeper understanding of the magical aspects of our world. We are... *Hm*... think of us as higher people. We are not and have never been *gods*. Simple-minded people decided to call us such. We are people who long ago evolved to become one with the magic of the world. We consumed the greater part of it when we did. Hence the reason *most* of the mage of your world only have fragments of it for themselves. Sadly, I could never empower you with the magic you seek, dear Miss Moon. But I *can* bestow upon you the only thing I *am able to* give, and that is to make you mine—nay... ours. And when you walked into my temple, I knew you were my child. And so now you belong to us."

She smiled broadly and gave Iselle a gaze overflowing with such benevolence and pride.

"Make your new mother proud, Iselle. Free us all."

And with that, she rode away, leaving nary a mark in the snow.

Iselle turned her horse back towards the Chestnut Hill House, the glory of a morning ride now lost to something murky and strange. She mulled it all over as her horse retraced its path through the snow. As she did, the now grey sky began to shed more of its cold and ice upon the world.

She was terrified and felt wholly vulnerable without the weight of the widow about her neck. She fought back the burn of tears as the stable boy helped her down from her saddle and walked up the steps into the house.

She could no longer stay. She would have to go. He knew where she was, and here, there were people she cared about. She would not endanger them. She could not suffer the grief like that for Redlan again. It would be too much. She would not be able to go on. If suffering was her fate, then she would take it with her and face it alone. She shed her hat and her gloves and made her way up to her room to pack her bag. She had no other choice.

CHAPTER 28

Dorya's cry was immediately silenced by the wave of a hand. *Silence the tongue. A useful spell.* "Now, look at you, you precious little thing—you are remarkably pretty," he intoned. Lacklow straightened over her inert form which was propped up against the side of her bed, and he towered over her. "But you are not even remotely equal to Iselle. Her beauty is not of this world." He inspected his fingertips and then shook them off, as if there had been dust or soot on them.

"I can see by your expression that Iselle is familiar to you. Of course, I heard you speak of her with that sullen, gangly fellow. Forrest, I think. Who is he to her?" He sank down into a squat again, looking down at her face expectantly, and then he barked out in laughter and shook his head. "Oh, of course, I've silenced you. Silly me. I can't have all these hordes of other girls hear you shrieking and howling and the like, can I?"

"You will take me to her. At once. Or I will kill you and every girl in this building." He reached out and touched her temple. "Apologies, I dare say it is ungentlemanly to touch a woman that is not mine, but the situation requires it, I'm afraid," he murmured. "Now up." Rising, he reached for her arm and pulled her to her feet. "We will follow your eyes. Look where we should go."

He opened the door to Dorya's room, and was about to usher his marionette out, and instead found himself face-to-face with Forrest.

Forrest could feel Dorya's distress and her terror. It flooded his mind. He pushed it away, and at the same moment, drew back his shoulder, and then spun forward, his opposite leg rising up, heel first. He cut it down as it circled, and it connected with Prentiss' head and sent him hurtling to the floor.

"Vile interloper," Prentiss hissed through his teeth. His cheekbone was scraped raw by the rasp of Forrest's boot heel, and the ridge of the whip-scar on this side of his face had tiny lacerations that had beads of blood forming upon them. "You think you can best me?" He staggered to his feet, rubbing his injuries with his hand. He laughed. "Fool!"

A wave of his hand, and the floor rose and fell like a ripple of water, and Forrest was unbalanced. But he did not fall; he threw himself forward and used his body to fling him to the floor. Dorya was suddenly freed from her invisible restraints, and she stumbled out of the room, still silent, but fast upon her escape, as Iselle had instructed her to do.

They wrestled, Forrest trying to grip his throat, and hold him down with his knees. His rationality was lost, his fury for this monster's existence consumed him. He hurt Iselle. He wanted to hurt her more. That disgusting collection of feelings invaded Forrest's brain and overwhelmed him. He could only see red. He was resorting to physicality. To brutal strength. To the fighting that shaped him. But he had to remember where his true strength resided.

He had to center himself and set aside his rage. *Don't let the anger control you. Set your mind inside his Forrest.* He felt something wrap around his neck, and his hands reached up to grip it. It was a piece of wood plank, bending like a serpent. It tightened around his throat, forcing him to sit up. The enchanter, Prentiss rolled away from underneath Forrest, laughing. "One oughtn't tangle with a Mage, boy," he chuckled. Forrest wheezed as the plank tightened around his neck.

Concentrate. What is he feeling?

Focus was nearly impossible as he struggled for breath, but he dove into the rage that the man was exuding. Black and roiling, flavored with betrayal even he knew was unfounded. He *knew* he was wrong. He *knew* he was a monster.

Forrest gasped for air, and clenched his eyes closed. And he found something amid the boil of emotion Prentiss felt in this moment. Feelings of injustice for being interrupted in his chase. A pang of vulnerability. *A fear… of what? Of losing. Of losing her. Of being alone.* He followed this thread of feeling, which wended its way from its source inside the man's psyche.

Forrest wrapped his power around this and like a fist, he punched it into the man's head. The plank slackened, and Prentiss gripped his temples and stumbled a few steps. It gave Forrest enough time to get to his feet. He could *fight.* Or he could **fight.** He picked up the plank and smashed it over the back of Pretniss's head. He kicked him down again and as that happened the window shattered and the glass speared at him, embedding into his left side and arm, and part of his chest.

His mind probed into Prentiss's like fingers, in spite of the pain of his wounds. He sought the depths of what fueled this man's madness. A chair, he swung at the mage, who was still partly stunned by the first blow, but not so much that he could not wield his powers over objects to fight back.

The chair broke apart, and the parts turned back at Forrest. He could not win a physical match.

He could feel something trying to take hold in his mind. It took only a sharp jab of his emotions to knock it out. The man was trying to do something inside Forrest's head. He could not allow that to happen. He ventured forth, between kicks, and ducks as the man flung objects at him.

There was so much to feel in what the man was experiencing. So much to sense in his emotional release. Forrest was, however, keenly skilled at finding the things that could weaken someone. It was how he had destroyed his own father. He'd dug so deeply; he'd evoked such feelings founded upon the memories that shaped the monster that his father had become.

A demon who could beat a boy to near death and put his hands on but a tiny girl and do unspeakable things. Things Forrest had to suppress inside his little sister's mind to make her life bearable. To make her joyful when she ought to be anything but. To make her not remember. To cover over the dark memories with happiness.

Forrest's rage fueled him as much as that of his opponent. He swam against the flow of it, feeling the washes of this man's ego, the very core of his madness. And through it, he found the buried feelings that he needed. Aside from the hate, aside from the rage, the loneliness, and the longing, he found it. The vulnerability of a wounded child. Just like his father. Just like him. Just like his sister. But there was so much more. There was lonely, miserable, unwanted.... *Unwanted. Unneeded. Abandoned. Disliked. Unworthy. Pathetic. Ashamed. Humiliated. Unloved. Wanting. Needing. Emptiness. Desire. Failure. Rejection.* All were wrapped up by the deluge of the rage and anger they bred—they were the roots of all of his madness. All so seemingly slight and frail, like the child he had been, now dressed in a costume of lunacy. Forrest amplified these little slips, tangled in Prentiss' obsessive self-absorbed anger. He flooded him with his own feelings too; the fuel of his memories, the guilt for killing his father. And inside the mold of this person's head, they swelled and expanded and cut through his hatred and ire with their power.

Prentiss howled in agony, and recoiled from the skirmish, his face twisting into anguish and his hands clutching his head again. His eyes, black with rage, now grew glossy with tears, and he staggered back, falling into a corner holding his head. "No!" he cried.

He fought back against the emotions. He struggled against it with everything in his power, just as Forrest's father had. The years of avoidance, justification, twisting of reality did not unravel easily. Something large crashed into Forrest's back, and struck his head, but he held on. The room shuddered and the objects in it acted as avatars for the man who was now immobilized by his own emotions.

Forrest intensified and distilled the feelings of hopelessness; the need to end this onslaught of emotional ruin, he found these in Prentiss and pulled them forth, in front of his want for Iselle, over his desire to harm everyone who he felt harmed him; he used it to slaughter the feelings of happiness and wellbeing he longed for in his imaginings of a life with Iselle. He was going to make this madman take his own life.

"*NO!*" Prentiss screamed, "She's MINE!"

Weeping, snotty, bleeding, he threw back his hands and emitted a bellow that was an amalgamation of all the injustice he felt had been cast upon him, the rejection, the cruelty, the misery. It was raw and primal, and it came with tears, and spittle. The room exploded around them. Forrest was thrown back out of the door, the wood splinters following.

It was then that all went black.

Prentiss, hardly able to see or to make sense of anything, tripped over Forrest's legs as he hurtled himself out of this confounded room, which was now wholly destroyed. He fell onto his knees, and then managed to get back up, his hand finding purchase upon the wall of the corridor. Around him, there was only chaos. There were screams, and girls fleeing, pushing past him in shrieks. A candle had surely caught fire to something in the madness, for there was smoke.

He stumbled down the stairs, tumbling down the last landing to the bottom floor. Amidst the herd of girls in flight, he escaped the dreaded place. Across the campus he limped, his mind still crushed in the grip of his emotions, unable to restrain the power of them, to master them. He wept as he moved, wretched, emitting great wracking sobs. He could not bear being faced with who he truly was; all the inadequacy and atrocity he had existed with; that he embodied. He struggled to hold onto who he preferred to be; to feel what he needed to feel. Justified. Righteous.

Worthy of her love.

He leaned on a tree and looked back. The dormitory was ablaze. Another destroyed house, he managed to think between the surges of his self-loathing. He reassured himself; he was almost there. He had shattered the obstacle. Now he would finally have her. And she would make him feel better. She would eradicate all this misery. He could take solace in her love.

And he would find her. He could sense her fear, powerful and alluring. He could feel her calling.

CHAPTER 29

Iselle folded the last of her summer gowns and pressed the delicate, wispy garment into the opening of her fraying tapestry bag. She then drew the drawstring of the inner lining and closed the button at the top. Talia was weeping on the bed. "Please don't go!" she blubbered through her tears.

"I'm sorry, Talia. It's for your own safety, and that of your mother that I must depart." Iselle was heartbroken by her obligation to flee. She should have fled the moment she'd lost the bauble at the picnic. She'd gambled enough, and now, she was in their home, and she represented a significant danger to all of them. Especially now that the widow was gone for good.

Why had that mad figment done that? Why had she so cruelly exposed me?

Forrest was the most endangered. Her heart tightened into a fist at the thought of Forrest. She could not compare him to Redlan, it was impossible. They both represented such distinct types of affection. Forrest was unique. He was the first man she had ever liked in *that* way. She could admit it now, because she could scarcely contain her sorrow at the idea of parting from him, let alone from his sister and his mother. She had come to adore them all so very much. But him, the most.

If she had sought normalcy from Dorya—then what she needed Forrest for, was to heal—for stability—protection and trust. He was all those things, and more.

She bit back her tears, and a sob that was strangling her. Her voice wavered when she spoke to Talia. "Let me embrace you, you terror," she said. She swallowed a sob.

Talia slid off the bed and threw her arms around Iselle, her slight body wracking with tears. "Don't go..." she cried. "I want a sister so, so badly. And you are the sister I want!"

The days before, without Forrest looming about in his spectral way, Talia had been her shadow. Iselle was yet unaccustomed to direct, constant attention, and she had taken her ride that morning to take a much-needed break from it. Before that, she had played cards with her, completed puzzles, sorted through, and tried on old-fashioned gowns and perilously tall wigs from Talia's great-grandmother's old trunks, played hide and seek, and read from a romantic novel in the library together.

These were frivolous things, but for Iselle, they were downright magical. To understand the idle nonsense pursuits of two sisters with nothing better to do; she felt like she had missed so much growing up alone. She did not want to leave it all behind. But she had no other recourse. The notion made a knot in her throat. Her eyes burned.

Why must you be so wretched and stupid all the time?

She pushed away from Talia and tried not to let the image of the girl, wiping her eyes with the heels of her hands, break her heart even further. Add to it all, Mrs. Outvallen was now at the door, having finally heard of Iselle's imminent departure. She pushed through the obstacles of tears and questions, and padded down the stairs, bag in hand. Mrs. Outvallen ran around her and blocked her path, her face red and her eyes washed with tears.

"Don't abandon him, Miss Moon, I *beg* you. He appears so strong and impenetrable, but he is so fragile. It will tear his heart in two…" Mrs. Outvallen begged so plaintively. "I've never seen him love someone like this before. Please don't leave him." Her voice was ragged and raw with desperation for her son. Iselle felt like she could die from the sound of it.

Iselle's tears won at those words, and she clamped her hand over her mouth to stop herself from losing control of her feelings. She sobbed under her fingers and could barely see where she was going for the blurring of her eyes from the tears. She hurried past them. She clattered down the steps.

She turned and looked back at them, both standing at the top of the stairs, gazing down at her in confusion, faces red and tear streaked. How could they need her so dearly in so short a time? How could she need them so much? She pivoted back to the door and opened it.

And there he was.

Prentiss.

Why did he always appear like this—at moments where people she loved would fall into his sphere?

Her heart and belly turned to ice. She stumbled back, and he sauntered in. There was something crazed in his expression. Something blacker and madder than she'd ever seen. His eyes searched her, there was a bizarre half-smile upon his face, and tears were pouring out of his eyes.

His face was scored with marks from the whip, and there were bruises and cuts that were fresher. Glistening globules of blood were drying on the wounds. He reached up and wiped his cheeks and eyes dry and composed himself. He peered around, taking stock of the world, as if he hadn't been quite part of it until this moment. With his hands behind his back, he let his eyes wander up to the girl and her mother standing at the railing looking down upon him in surprise and bewilderment.

"So, you hide in *this* place this time," he murmured. He stalked around the entry hall, inspecting the space. His eyes, narrowed and menacing, turned back onto Iselle, and he frowned. "It's *his* house. Covetous bastard. Are these his family?" he asked, gesturing idly towards them with his sooty fingers and dirty cuff.

Iselle had fallen deathly still. Her eyes were glistening with a layer of moisture and her face grew wan.

"Leave them alone," she said in a wavering whisper.

"Oh, I won't do that," he laughed easily, waving his hand dismissively. "I've had enough, frankly. I've suffered enough. I will exercise no consideration nor kindness for you anymore. I will take them all away from you. Everyone. Your uncle, your governess. The whole lot of them," he told her, stopping to face her.

"I first slaughtered that frail little fop you were seeing, and I will take the life of any other man who dares to even look at you. You will have nobody to love, but me." He gazed impassively upon her, but she could see the simmering madness underneath his façade. He was beyond the lunacy she'd known. He'd gone over an edge she could tell there was no coming back from.

"The *boy* that I imagine belongs to this house... ah, yes... Forrest. He's burnt up like so much ash. He went down with the dormitory. I don't know what happened to the wee girl that is your friend," he said with strange detachment, "but I'll find her too."

What an odd thing, thought Iselle, how the sound in the room seemed to change when he uttered those words.

Like the natural reverberation had been sucked out with the air, and the words fell into a barren vacuum with no dimension or shape to receive or reflect them. The world fell away. What was left was just she, and he, and an emptiness she'd never felt before.

She half-heard Prentiss say: "Where did you go? Why can't I feel your fear?"

She sensed herself falling back. Not her body but her essence—her awareness. Present but now looking in from the outside; from this strange, hollow place she'd entered. All she could see was Prentiss, standing in front of her, peering at her with the strangest expression in his eyes.

Where were her feelings?

Where was her fear?

It made no sense.

But then, she felt it, snaking up from beneath her like tentacles.

The rage.

It had taken a moment, perhaps; what felt like a minute, two minutes, was merely a flash; a second. It was the words; they had only just been said. He'd only just finished speaking. Or had he finished speaking?

You've had enough? He's had enough! A part of her laughed scornfully. The voice she thought was Miss Metrelees, still resided inside of her.

Redlan

Mrs. Hallwell

Forrest.

Dorya.

Talia. Mrs. Outvallen.

What existence is worth this?

I cannot fear him anymore when all I want to do is die.

He has taken everything.

The pain was suffocating. It felt like a fist was clutched around her heart, and her chest felt like there was a fire growing within it. For a moment, her detached body, her remote senses seized. She could not suck in a breath of air, and her head swam.

Whatever it was, it bound her—constricted her, until she could scarcely wheeze—until she began to see flashes of lights behind her vision. Until there were pulses of darkness which grew longer and larger with each flash. And when she could no longer sustain it, and she was about to succumb to the mysterious force that crushed her in its grip, it abruptly shattered like so much glass, fragile, yet deadly-sharp.

The weight of it collapsed, fractured, and erupted as if it had been contained under great pressure. She saw herself, from her strange, remote perspective, consumed by a cloud of black. So black, there was no dimension. So black, it looked like a hole in the world. It whorled and roiled as if it were coils of steam at the edges, but smoky, empty tendrils of sooty steam that expanded out of her body and enveloped her entirely.

And it felt like something. Like distilled wrath. Like slick rage.

Like blind fury.

It was all of the fury she had swallowed. The years of it. Behind her wariness and her vulnerability. It had become viscous and thick, her anger, years of accumulation, ages of swallowing it down into a lump which grew larger and larger, darker, denser, until it could no longer be contained.

Forrest.

He killed Forrest.

The feelings consumed her as if they were a conflagration, lapping around her being and burning with heat and hatred.

The roiling wrapping of black that expanded from her being, suddenly retracted, but not into her; but coalesced around her. It retreated into a new shape that cocooned her body. It wrapped itself like a costume around her delicate form. It took a horrifying shape; a monstrous beast, with leathery wings, and spikes bristling from the head, shoulders and down its spine.

She recognized her own shape.

She knew what she was now.

She'd seen it painted upon the walls of the temple.

She opened her mouth to cry out, and a sound like no other split the air, and sucked reality back into the room; and everything was as it had been, except for her. Iselle was a beast. One with an absence of color, a bristle of spikes, wings spread with sharp claws upon taloned wings of leathery bottomless membrane—an impossible creature of lore.

She was the Fury. *She* was Rage embodied. *She* was Revenge.

The unearthly roar was shrill and deafening and sent Talia and Mrs. Outvallen to the floor with their hands upon their ears.

Oddly, Prentiss looked unphased by what had transpired before his eyes. He stood there before her motionless, watching her delicate form withdraw into itself, and then with a jerk of her body, the explosion of blackness flowing from the core of her body, an animated form, which cloaked her inside the shape of a fathomless beast. He watched her feet lift off the floor and her legs bend. He saw her body furl into itself as the wash of black surrounded her.

His eyes were wide with madness, a peculiar look of fascination upon his face, and a strange smile upon his lips.

"Yes," he whispered.

Iselle, or whatever she was now, reached out her beastly claw, and almost tenderly gripped Prentiss by the neck. Her rage burned so hot through her, his skin sizzled underneath the grip of her preternatural claw.

She desired him to suffer.

She longed for him to writhe in agony.

She wished nothing more than to exact as much pain, fear, and terror he had exacted upon *her* and the ones she loved all these years. Cumulatively, it was a mountainous sum of agony. She did not wish to spread it out over the years she'd suffered. No.

Killing him would be too easy. She wanted to revel in his undoing. She wanted not a shred of his remaining sanity to linger when she was done with him—*if* she was ever to be done with him. The thought of it made a wicked smile curl upon the lips of the creature that enshrouded her. The roiling beast of black. This was who the voice was. Her rage.

She lifted him by his neck and hurled him. He sailed across the room and landed with a crack against the door of the day room. The door split from the force of it. She dropped her front claws to the floor, and the body of her avatar settled into its natural animalistic shape. Its wings folded gracefully against its sides.

Iselle was withdrawn within its large trunk of a body; curled up in the murk like a newborn baby, floating as if in soft, soothing water. Secure and warm—the whole of her own being at peace while all around her, the dark skin of her new outer shell, her manifested rage, moved with the liquid grace of a predator—its tail, tapered and supple and edged in blade-like spikes, undulated with serpentine elegance back and forth, its end curling like a delicate scroll upon parchment.

It walked, idly, curiously, towards his form. Prentiss groaned and then broke into a tortured laugh. He stared at the inky thing looming over him, watching it near him, his amusement melted into an expression of terror as it came within reach.

The Fury reached out its right claw once again, and turned, dragging him flailing, slowly from the house. Prentiss screamed and choked, kicked, and howled.

He was struggling at last, thought Iselle, smiling from inside her little sanctuary of darkness. She emitted a peaceful sigh, basking in the strangled, unintelligible words he shrieked as he was pulled along the smooth marbled floor.

She dragged him as if he were nothing more than a doll made of rags, through the open door. Maybe like that doll he sent her, animated with his magic. He did not sing a little ballad declaring his love. He screamed, cried, and begged.

Behind her, Talia and Mrs. Outvallen watched, their tear-streaked faces pale and horrified. She pulled the man down the steps to the house, his head hitting each stair, his cries interrupted into staccato by each bump. The nails of her clawed feet clicked loudly on the stone.

Am I earthly or an apparition? Maybe I am both.

How absurd it must appear, for others. This beast, so foreign, against the normality of this day, she thought, turning the head of her monster to the pale blue sky peppered with whisps of clouds. She could see more than that through its gaze. She could see little flits of unseen things. Little creatures nobody else could see. *What are those?* She stared at them in fascination for a moment. Then she was reminded of her burden gripped in her hand as it squirmed.

What should I do to him first? The thought intruded upon her mind. *Much to ponder,* she contemplated, *much to decide.*

As her terrifying form stood in the light of day and alighted its black talons into the white of the snow-covered, oystershell driveway, Iselle was shocked to hear footfalls crunching in front of her, and as her beastly gaze dropped from the sky, she discovered none other than Forrest standing before the shroud around her, looming and black, the stain in the light of day.

Forrest was hurt, his face covered in dry blood and soot. There was blood caked on his hands and his fingers. There were red welts and purple bruises on his neck and his arms. She wanted to cry.

He peered upon the inky beast-shaped hole in the world, and it gazed down impassively upon him. She could see him. Through its eyes. Through its skin.

What is he thinking? Why is he not terrified at the sight of me?

"Iselle…" he muttered. "My Iselle…"

How does he know? Iselle wondered. *How does he know it's me?*

You're alive, she said. But no words came out of the creature's mouth. She wanted to say it; she wanted him to hear her. *Forrest, you're alive!*

Relief washed through her at first, and a shudder of emotion and burning hot tears pressed against the eyes of her real body. She twisted within, wanting to throw herself into his arms; his bruised, battered arms. But the sight of his injuries only served to further enrage her, and her monster pulsed with more strength as she added to the wrath she felt.

But she felt him. Forrest's mind, reaching into the core of her monster, the seed floating unseen within its horrifying form. Her eyes opened, inside the black. Her natural sight saw only inky nothingness. It gripped her still, and it gripped Prentiss still, who struggled fruitlessly against the talons' crushing grasp on his leg.

Forrest's gaze fell to the man, squirming and struggling, laughing, and crying out. His eyes were impassive and without feeling for him. "Finish this, Iselle," he said quietly.

The beast tilted its shapeless face, peering at Forrest with empty eyes. They stood there examining one another; the wounded and battered young man, and blackness itself in the shape of some unimaginable monster.

No. Not yet, thought Iselle. *Not yet.*

She felt Forrest in her head; he was absorbing the feelings that roiled through her. She could feel him there, inside the kernel of this monster with her. That was how he knew her.

He is with me, in here. The idea of it filled her with warmth. And her heart swelled when he simply gave a small nod and stepped away.

The monster dropped Prentiss. He immediately tried to wriggle away to no avail. The creature stepped back and gripped the scrabbling figure with its foot. Talons like a raptor's clutched him around his thigh, and the great wings unfurled, and spread with preternatural grace. They flapped once, twice, the air ballooning in the inky membranes, lifting her up, and up. The beast rose into the sky, with Prentiss wailing, fighting, and shrieking all the while.

Forrest's sister and mother had come from the house and lifted their hands up to shield their eyes from the light, so they could watch Iselle fly away.

CHAPTER 30

The screams echoed. Which seemed surprising.

Should they echo here?

In this place?

She dug her talon into the hole she'd slowly punctured in his shoulder and tilted her head as Prentiss's shrieks of agony resonated out into the still air.

Yes. It's echoing. Why would it echo? It's not such a vast space, Iselle thought. *Thick forests don't echo.*

She dropped her claw and sat back on her haunches. *How strange.*

A small swarm of black creatures flitted by and disappeared into the trees with nary a rustle. They reminded her of Goblin.

She lowered herself onto her forelegs, and padded away distractedly, looking about the dense growth that enclosed this remote space. She couldn't quite recall how she even got here. How she knew it was here.

The only sounds now were the whimpers of the man suspended from his ankle from the thick branch of an ancient beech tree with strange rope that looked much like a length of fresh gut. From where it was gleaned was a mystery to both. Her feet thrashed through the leaf-fall, noisy as she moved. There was the sound of the branch creaking as his body swung. His occasional sob. *But those things won't echo.*

As she pondered this, the monster melted away, and Iselle alighted gracefully onto her natural feet. The leaves crunched as the weight of her body rested upon them. It felt good to be herself for a moment, even if it was in this otherworldly place. She felt oddly at peace.

"My precious Iselle," the other monster blubbered. "*There* you are."

She turned languidly and peered up at the man. His face was red from being suspended upside down. His other leg bent at the knee, away from him, as he swung lazily from the tree. Blood flowed from the fresh hole she'd punctured into his shoulder, and the two others she'd made in his thigh. There was that sound too… the blood droplets landing with gentle *tss* sounds into the leaves.

"Here I am," she said quietly, tilting her head again. "Your *precious* Iselle."

"You must escape that thing… it will return. It will destroy us both," he bawled.

"Mr. Lacklow… are you feigning ignorance? I *am* that thing," she muttered. "You *made* me into that thing. Your presence in my life invited it into my body. I was forced to become it, to escape you."

"Where are we?" he asked, his voice ragged and petrified.

"I don't know, really. Someplace between here and there, I suppose," Iselle answered distractedly, turning away again. She moved to where the leaves were spattered with blood and stared down at the bright pop of color in what was a rather colorless forest. The whole place was painted in a wash of yellowy brown light, muting the greens, turning them into values of olive, and the shadows looked muddy and strange. Little black creatures rustled about in the brush now and again. The blood, however, was ruby red. Shining and thick, *drip, drip, drip.*

"That man… F… Forrest… He's a remorseless animal. You must run from him. Or destroy him. He got inside my head, he's done something, I can barely think. He…"

"Your powers don't work here," Iselle interrupted with her realization. Prentiss fell silent. "They don't work at all," she surmised with a whimsical smile. "You can't dig your fingers into my head and turn my feelings into a beacon. That is what Niria said you did. She called it an 'entanglement.'

"You can't enchant the tree to help you get down or whip me with its limbs. Tell me… is it difficult, to be deprived of those powers when you have used them so liberally for so long?" she asked. "How dependent you magic bearers must become upon your gifts. How much you must take them for granted. It must be fearsome for you, to suddenly be rendered powerless like the rest of us," she mused.

"I…" he began.

"I've long resented anyone with the gift of magic, simply for having it. I hated them bitterly and harbored such jealousy. I despised people I did not know. Just because of you. You asserted your power onto me, to your ends, without regard to my wants—my desires. I had none to defend myself with.

"Tell me… did you even see me as a person? Have you *ever* seen me as a person? Or anyone else, for that matter. Redlan. Even that other obsessed excuse of a man. You took the lives of others in your selfish pursuit of possessing me. But *I* never really mattered, did I? It was only *you* that ever did."

Iselle ruminated on this anger for a spell, turning her thoughts and rage around in her mind.

"How *dare* you vilify Forrest. Forrest is no animal. On that matter, you are terribly mistaken. Forrest possesses the most honest magical gift of them all." She said this decisively. An expression of curiosity crossed her delicate brow, her perfect face peering up at Prentiss. "Do you know what he did to his father?" she laughed softly. "He did nothing *to* him. He merely *encouraged* his father to peer at his reflection in a mirror, of sorts. He turned him to stand squarely in front of it, and forced his face forward so he could not look away. He made the monster see himself, in earnest—to look directly into the eyes of the person he had swallowed, and suppressed, in order to continue to justify the person that he was.

"And that is what my dear, sweet Forrest did to *you*, I suspect. He winnowed his way into your head like you did into mine, and turned your regrets, your unworthiness—worthlessness, your self-loathing against you. You did not like what you saw. That is lamentable," she waved her hand dismissively, "but you did it all to yourself. What you're feeling, that was all *already* lurking inside of you. You couldn't simply run away from yourself forever. Just like I couldn't run away from *you* forever. And now *I* am the coldblooded monster, and you are here powerless like I've always been. You are at *my* mercy now," she ended with a whisper and a half-smile.

"What a conundrum. We have exchanged roles. The question, Mr. Lacklow, is have I become as cruel and callous as you? Will I make you suffer as long as you have, me? Will I inflict as much harm and pain upon you as you have me? Those are the questions, are they not? And if I choose this route of revenge, will you bear it with as much strength and dignity as I have? This I very much doubt."

"Then kill me and be done with it!" he barked. "Find that monster of a person you call your dear, *sweet* Forrest, and be free to throw your life away on him!"

His words seemed to help her comprehend something. Her eyes widened. He had elucidated her of the choices she'd been deprived of for over half a decade. It lit her up and infused her with joy.

Iselle's laughter was like music in this strange in-between place. *It echoed.*

Her eyes twinkled, and her normally sullen face broke into a smile so radiant; it almost emitted its own ethereal light. This was something few had ever seen her do. She was divine. Glorious. Beautiful. It was the first time she believed that she *was* those things. Her heart swelled. She twirled as she laughed, her arms spreading out from her sides.

"I shall learn to dance," she declared, and a voice brightened with delight. "I will learn the Rains of Spring—Randall's Revel… oh! and the Lady's Emerald Eyes, I cannot forget that one. Redlan liked that one very well. We whirled and skipped along to the music once right through the center of the square at Arrowood," she exclaimed, her swell of elation melting away into sadness as the memory returned to her.

She stared at the ground for another long moment, her bright eyes glazing over with tears. When she looked up again, there was a darkness in her eyes. A black furious hatred.

"My mind is made up, Mr. Lacklow. I have decided your fate. I will dedicate every shriek, every scream, every plea for mercy to the memory of Redlan. You wronged him so greatly, and for that, he will watch from the underworld and see justice for what you made him suffer."

Somewhere, beyond the scrim of growth and trees, in the still air of this strange place, sudden bouts of raucous, delighted laughter echoed.

Iselle's face transformed into a smiling mask again. She threw back her head with an expression of ecstasy, with tears falling onto her smooth,, flawless cheeks. As she did, tendrils of inky smoke emitted from her forehead, and swirled around her, billowing around her slight frame, and enrobing her whole being until she was obscured by black. She was lifted as if cradled in the arms of some unknown being and disappeared inside the smoke; and as she did, the shape of the beast appeared. It alighted on its forelimbs and shook itself like a dog.

Prentiss watched as it stood again on its hind legs and reached out its claw. It gripped his leg, and tore him down from the tree, leaving his ankle and foot behind, swinging on a bit of gore.

CHAPTER 31

"It was truly pleasing to witness for ourselves, some of the old traditions coming back," Mrs. Outvallen declared over tea. She put down her cup and peered out the window of the morning room. "What a lovely excursion with new friends!"

It was a splendid day. The snow was newly capped with a cover of fresh white, smooth and sparkling on this crisp late winter morning. A bird had left little footprints in the pillow of snow on the outer sill.

In spite of the fresh snowfall, there was that magical hint of spring in the air. The hard cold of winter seemed to give way to just a whisper of warmth to come; the quality of the light was different, and down below the window, one of many of Mrs. Outvallen's long stone planters was filled chockablock with myriad bulbs of jonquils, crocus, tulips and hyacinth—all of which already showed little spikes of vibrant green poking through the snowy cover.

In a nearby room, there was the sound of a planer sliding over the surface of hardwood. Mrs. Outvallen had chosen white oak this time. She was never too keen on the hints of pink in the red oak the former door had been made of. She decided to replace all the doors on the lower floor. The carpenters were fitting them as she spoke.

She loved the scent of the wood; and had two curls of oak shavings on the table beside her, which she'd taken from the basket by the fire. She picked one up and twirled it in her fingers under her nose. The chambermaid had been sweeping them up and collecting them in the kindling baskets almost as quickly as the carpenter made them.

"Indeed, I did enjoy our little expedition yesterday," the masculine voice of Uncle Ude replied. His teacup alighted into its saucer, and he lifted his leg over the other, balancing the cup and saucer on his knee. His eyes followed Mrs. Outvallen's gaze out over the park. "Where are the children? I was certain I heard they would be joining us for tea."

Mrs. Outvallen found the timber of the Judge's voice most appealing. Such a handsome man. Her eyes slid over to the other gentleman in his company, the Lord Thrait, who was too, exceptionally handsome. She could scarcely recall the last time she'd had such company. She thought how few social engagements she'd partaken in since the death of the former Earl. The attentions of these gentlemen rekindled feelings of her girlhood; the blush of cheeks, the flutter of her heart as they complimented or flattered her. She flushed.

"They went out for a ride oh, two hours ago? Forrest had Noan harness the silver drafts to the sleigh. We haven't used it since he and Talia were wee little things. And now it's been used twice in so many days! I forgot how diverting such an excursion could be, I am so grateful for the opportunity presented by my guests.

"As your sweet girl had not experienced riding in one yet, he took the whole party out in it. It's spacious for all of them, and with the drafts paired up, well…" she waved her hand to demonstrate the negligible effort for the horses.

The adults had visited the Orlen temple the evening before. It was closer than the Torem temple complex, and it was a temple dedicated to the old gods. There were nooks dedicated to individual gods between the columns. There was little indication remaining as to which god belonged to which space.

It wasn't an ornate temple, it had few carvings, or statuary remaining. What was left was mostly the structure. It had been mostly lost to the forest, smothered in wild growth, and choked with tangles of vines made barren by the wintry weather.

But it had been cleared lately, by the people. In the past two months, the tops of the old empty plinths were now filled with small effigies and statuettes, candles, and small offerings, like sweet buns, and bowls of dried fruit. Dedications and godly names were written on the rough stone walls in chalk wash, or charcoal. It was a lovely effect, with light glowing from between each column of the inner temple as one walked through to the main altar.

At the altar was Emridus, the emissary of all the gods. He was so worn from exposure to the elements that his face was no longer recognizable, and the stone was stained green from algae. Some areas had blossoms of lichens creeping over them, in deep golds and olive greens. Its feet were festooned with decorative offerings as well; bundles of silken flowers, gold and silver coins, bottles of wine and spirits. The air was scented with the blend of libations poured onto the ground before it.

The people had taken a renewed interest as the mage sensed the tinglings of the old world in their magic again. Signs of renewal, stronger magic, a connection renewed between the world they knew, and the veil that connected it to the unfamiliar world of gods and spirits. The elder mage were replenished with new strength, new life. Something was nourishing the wasted spirits of that mysterious world. Something was swelling them with life and infusing them with strength again. Something.

Above the statue, ropes of woven hair, one color blending into another, swagged across the span of the knave, studded with skulls, and pendants of bone. It was a ghoulish garland, but it was the practice as it had been so many centuries before. The people had taken no time to rekindle these old traditions. Especially with the signs of the gods of the old world returning to the land.

Mrs. Outvallen and her group of guests walked reverently into the temple and admired its transformation. Its revived state.

"The hair is shorn from new temple dedicants," Mrs. Hallwell had muttered. "The bones of their ancestors strung to summon their spirits," she had explained.

This kind of primitive worship was an oddity in this new world. It soon would no longer be.

"I hope they don't take too long. The chocolate will get cold." Forrest's mother murmured. She sighed. She was eager for them to return.

"Oh, they will be along. Have patience, Mrs. Outvallen," Dame Arwey said over her spiced wine. She was huddled in a warm, intricately woven goats' wool shawl by the fire, with her tiny black dog curled up on her lap, snoring quite loudly for a creature of its size. Pip was in the opposite chair sitting next to Mrs. Hallwell, balled up on her thick plaid wool shawl, getting white hairs stuck all over the deep green and black check. Mrs. Hallwell's arms were bare to the elbow, and small, pale figures riddled her skin. Her eyes recovered, her sight sharp and enhanced by a magic that now infused the whole of her being.

As the Dame spoke, Goblin lifted his little head and barked, and Pip leapt to his feet and did the same. The elders could hear the sound of lively voices, laughter and bootheels clacking upon the hard floors. "Ah… Speak of the little imps," the hostess chuckled. The elders turned to the door in expectation.

The door abruptly burst open, and a horde of lively young people spilled into the room. They brought with them a gust of air scented with fresh outdoors, and wood shavings. They were all smiles and red cheeks, with a small squadron of the house staff in their wake, collecting the scarves and redingotes, the greatcoats, hats, and gloves.

Talia led the small multitude, her face all happiness. Mrs. Outvallen was filled with warmth at the sight of her daughter's delight. Clutched in the loop of her right arm, and one pace behind was Iselle, who was grinning guilelessly as the child tugged her along. Forrest was beside her, his cheeks red, and his face, although not overtly cheerful, was warm and content. Hidden behind him, barely to be seen, save for the edge of her bonnet, was Miss Dorya, the young man named Meddin, and the other young lady, oh, what was her name again?

Ah yes, Teena. Another young man wearing spectacles whose name completely escaped her, who'd only lately arrived, took up the rear. Mrs. Outvallen stood to welcome them.

The young people, fresh from their outing crammed in the large sleigh swathed in woolen blankets, were eager for a steaming cup of chocolate or tea, and they served themselves from the urn on the sideboard, or the pot under the quilted cozy, and assembled by the fire with the elders when they had their steaming cups, and then they descended upon the tiered platters of fixings on the tea table in the center of the seating area. Small sandwiches, scones, cakes, savory filled vol au-vents, and stuffed mushrooms were cheerfully devoured over laughter and conversation, which was delightfully lively and mirthful.

Mrs. Outvallen could hardly contain her joy at the experience of it. All this happiness and delight around her; Talia imbibing the attention of the young people closer to her age, reveled in it, her sweet face peering at one of her seniors, and then another; so incredibly pleased to be allowed to be part of their group. Forrest glowed. He was accepted with warmth and friendship, his eyes so fixedly locked upon the face of his beloved Iselle. The happiness was artfully contained in his seemingly withdrawn expression, but his mother knew it was there. Iselle, with her unrelenting beauty and grace, had her hand gently resting on Forrest's.

Mrs. Outvallen's heart swelled, as come morning, the two would be married. She could scarcely contain her glee.

It had not taken more than a few hours for her to work through what she and Talia had witnessed that day when the blaggard had so brazenly defiled their home with his presence. A woman who had already accepted the killing of her husband at the hands of her son, she was not fragile to extraordinary, frightful things. Neither the mother nor daughter were. She was well-apprised of the terror that the man had inflicted upon poor Miss Moon. She knew the monster deserved everything the elegant Fury inflicted upon him. That dark swirl of a beast was a product of what *he* had done to her. It existed by no fault of Miss Moon.

Miss Moon was still Miss Moon. The Iselle she had come to adore. The Iselle her precious, protective, good son, loved. For her and her daughter, there was nothing to lament or fear from what occurred. They understood the burden the young woman now carried. Iselle only needed the support and love of all of those she cherished. There was no other way about it. She needed acceptance, for whatever she was, *and the Outvallens are disposed to give it to her. Full stop,* thought Mrs. Outvallen.

For Iselle, in her new, larger family, there was only love.

Lo, and she brought with her such a horde of lovely guests, one, Iselle's uncle, another, her rescuer. Her governess, a dowager, a swarm of chocolate-drinking youths. Soon, her own sister and her husband and Forrest's two cousins and their wives would arrive to add to this merry party. Even Niria was to join them. She could scarcely wait for dinner when the whole group would be together.

Could there be no greater happiness?

Mrs. Outvallen was wholly certain there could not.

Iselle's perfect side-curls bounced with each bump in the road, the lacy inner brim of her bonnet framed her beautiful, glowing countenance. The shining black of her hair looked even more striking against the white lace. Her pale blue eyes rested with adoration on the face of her soon-to-be husband. In her light blue gloved hands, she clutched a bouquet that was simply an explosion of tiny forget-me-not flowers, from afar, it looked like a spray of sky-colored mist rising from a blue ball.

On her body, over the simple muslin round-gown of snowy white, and tatted lace edging, she wore a taffeta walking gown of ivory, embroidered with a riot of spring blossoms down the front and the hem, around the cuffs and across the yoke of the spencer. Tulips and jonquils, lilies of the valley, hyacinth, all sprouting from a weave of pale green stems, with leaves peppered throughout.

Forrest was equally well appointed; dressed as an Earl would for his wedding; a polished silk frock coat of sapphire blue, with pale blue waistcoats with pinstripes of ivory, ivory breeches, pale blue stockings, and patent slippers with a shining buckle on each foot.

The temple was festooned with bright spring flora, swags of greenery interwoven with blossoms. The family and friends gathered at the front of the temple, waiting for the coach to halt, and the pair to disembark and join them inside. When they did, there was delighted applause and a round of hoorahs as the entered the broad, newly hewn temple door.

Inside the temple along the sides and rear of the space, standing against the wall and columns, some sitting on the stone pews that had only lately been installed, more of the townsfolk had come to see the marriage of their young Earl. The troublesome young man seemed much less unpleasant of late, and he looked handsome in his fine attire with his transcendently beautiful betrothed by his side.

The couple traversed the aisle between the myriad witnesses, and came to a stop at the dais, where a cleric of the Emridian Temple awaited in voluminous red silk robes that draped down over her feet, and puddled dramatically onto the floor. Her jingling ceremonial headdress radiated like sunlight in golden rays from her head, dripping in red beads and shimmering coins. She gazed down upon the pair before her.

Iselle twisted and glanced at Dorya who looked remarkably pretty in her spring-green gown and garnet bonnet with gold ribbons. Behind her, the retinue from the school beamed at her.

Forrest and Iselle had discussed the practicality of a quick marriage. A fastening of their hands. Although Iselle now continued her matriculation with the goal of graduating, together they had decided that marriage would not hinder her desire to accomplish this objective. She had removed herself from the Multi-Interdisciplinary Magic track, and from law altogether. She chose instead to pursue History and World Studies. She hoped one day to perhaps teach these things herself to classrooms of students and perhaps write some of her own books on the subjects.

For Iselle, the choice to marry a man she had yet to kiss, had come with some trepidation. She feared Forrest would be impatient with her. That he would grow to regret his marriage to her, if she were not as overt, or effusive with her affection as other girls would be. She was worried that her scars would disgust him, even though he had already seen them. These were doubts that niggled at her mind, but he reassured her, as he always had.

"Iselle, I hope you know," said he, "that I will only do what you want me to do. I will always shield you from the things that cause you distress. I will wrap my arms around you, and I will keep you safe until it passes, and I will not venture to demand anything more of you that you are not wholly willing to give. I can wait. We are still so young. As long as we are together, those things don't matter," he said to her.

Their bond, rooted in their pain; their loss, their hurt, had budded into something strong, beautiful, and intertwined. The understanding of the other was of a depth few could know. They were one without giving up a mote of who they were.

For Forrest, there was acceptance and love for every part of his being, his flaws, and his choices alike. He had a sanctuary of her embrace, wherein he could retreat, where he could set aside the thoughts and memories that plagued him.

In Forrest's arms, Iselle had the luxury of fragility and vulnerability. She was given all the time she needed to heal and feel loved regardless.

Outside of his purview, Iselle was anything but fragile, or vulnerable. Outside of Forrest's embrace, Iselle was still a horrifying monster, a force of nature capable of terrifying things. She was the embodiment of her lingering fury—the scars, beyond those that engraved her skin, would likely never go away, her rage, and the very shape of the wrath of those who were wronged and left powerless to defend themselves, bound her to her alter-ego—to the blackness that enveloped her and that desired agony and suffering for those who inflicted such things unjustly upon others.

Simmering inside the core of the elegant, graceful, sweet bride, gripping her spray of forget-me-nots, was a swirling being. A skin, an armor, an avatar hewn by the gods, and by all the ire swallowed and bitten back, pressed down, distilled into black hatred, year after year, as her freedom, and her sanctity, her autonomy was stolen. And it was fetid, pitch-black, and bottomless.

But that was all separate from her now. She still carried the scars, the trauma, the sadness, the loss. But all the rage resided inside the beast now. It kept those things contained; to use in moments when a Fury was needed. And for that, Iselle could live freely. She could plan a future. She could love openly. She could breathe.

The cleric raised her arm and presented the flat of her hand to the guests. On her palm, the sigil of the Emridian God was branded into the skin. It glowed faintly like the embers of a stuttering wood fire.

"I am the channel through which the light of the otherworld burns. It is lit by the power of the gods; a light that has been nearly extinguished for unknown eons. This light has returned. Burning steadily, a beacon to guide the people, it nourishes our magic, and protects our wellbeing," she said.

As she said it, the sigil flared up and grew as bright as a lantern. The congregants gasped. The cleric's shock and surprise, unconcealed. She was filled with sudden emotion, a burgeoning joy that took form in glassy tears and a swell of her chest. She turned her palm and looked at it for a moment, squinting her eyes against the brightness, and then turned it back onto the temple to light the faces of the wedding guests.

"The gods are with us, they are near!" the cleric's voice raised. "They surely have come to bless this sacred union of the named Earl Forrest Outvallen and his bride, Miss Iselle Moon," she declared.

The guests broke into applause again.

As the cleric began the ceremony of invocations and blessings, Iselle, eyes misty, clutching tightly to Forrest's hand, glanced over her shoulder. Iselle felt something. Heard something. A rustle, or a whisper.

There, standing in the doorway, were three figures. She recognized Obraya, the figment of Amma, standing between the other two. And there, Iselle saw the two sisters, Raseet and Tanaju, elegant and stylishly dressed in the latest fashions, in spite of being invisible to nearly everyone in the temple.

Goblin growled from Dame Arwey's arms. Iselle could see his blackness pulsing in tendrils. Dame Arwey shifted as well, looking back at the door.

You set us free, child. The least we can do in return is to properly attend your wedding, Obraya's voice filled Iselle's mind. There was irony in it. As if it was all a great joke.

Obraya had escaped her dormancy thanks to Iselle and her talisman. The suffering and pain of Iselle's first act of vengeance as a Fury was the spark that brought all the goddesses back. The torment exacted upon a man, whose magic was drained and consumed like lifeblood for their world, enlivened the sleeping power of the underworld. His agonizing, prolonged death brought color to the underworld. It awoke the creatures that resided within it. How many, Iselle could not be sure. His physical body, when she was finally finished with it, and was sated, had been consumed by myriad dark little creatures, scrabbling through the leaves.

But it seemed like every time she was called upon by the powers to become the beast, and cross into their realm with a subject for vengeance, there was more life in that strange, empty world. It grew more vibrant and alive with every new scrap of agony and pain, of vengeance and retribution Iselle served upon her victims. It surged when it was a wielder of magic. Every injustice avenged brought life and vibrancy into the god realm—and it brought life and vibrancy to Iselle.

"I now pronounce, by witness of the temple and the gods, that you are now wed," the cleric declared. "You may now seal your union with a kiss."

Forrest bent gently down, his eyes fast upon hers, questioning. Hers peered back, assenting. His hand rose up and he softly pushed her chin upwards.

His lips alighted upon hers, stiff at first, both, and then yielding gently. Iselle's vision washed with white light, and her body relaxed into the grasp of his other arm as it laced around her back. A welling of joy swelled up from inside her body.

This is what it's like, she thought. *This is what all the fuss is about.*

A tear fell from her eye and rolled down her cheek. Forrest gingerly drew away, and if she could have, she would have floated up to follow his lips. His eyes were brimming with emotion that he offered only to her.

"I love you Duchess Outvallen," he whispered.

"I love you, not yet Earl of Outvallen," she replied, yearning for just one more of those kisses.

The so-called gods were coming back to life, yes.

But finally, Iselle would be able to live her own.

OTHER TITLES BY MIRANDA MAYER

The Trilogy of Tinna:

Tinna's Promise

Tinna's Might

Tinna's Reign

Red Slipper series:

The Wizard King

A Problem of Ghosts

The Beast with Silver Eyes

The Red Witch of Tirdonne

The Seed of Winden

The Belletrist

Blackroot

With author Shéa MacLeod

Wolffe & Bane – Book 1: The Talisman Killer

ABOUT THE AUTHOR

Miranda Mayer lives in the Mount Hood territory of Oregon. A polyglot, artist, avid historic costumer, and lifelong equestrian; her interests are broad, and edge on geekery most of the time. She is married with one child.

Miranda's stories range from Science Fiction to Urban Fantasy to Fantasy. She writes from her heart, imbues her writing with her quirky humor, and tries extremely hard to make her characters as real and three-dimensional as possible. Her unpredictable and rather Attention-Deficit-Disordered nature guarantees that her stories will take readers to unexpected places.